D0846315

THE BURNING

Tor books by Graham Masterton

The Burning
Charnel House
Condor
Death Dream
Death Trance
The Devils of D-Day
Ikon
Mirror
Night Plague
Night Warriors
The Pariah
Picture of Evil
Sacrifice
Scare Care (editor)
Solitaire
The Sphinx
Walkers
The Wells of Hell

THE MANITOU

The Manitou
Revenge of the Manitou
The Djinn

THE BURNING

Graham Masterton

A Tom Doherty Associates Book
New York

This is a work of fiction. All the characters and events portrayed in this book are fictitious, and any resemblance to real people or events is purely coincidental.

THE BURNING

A TOR Book
Published by Tom Doherty Associates, Inc.
49 West 24th Street
New York, N.Y. 10010

Library of Congress Cataloging-in-Publication Data

Masterton, Graham.
The burning / Graham Masterton.
p. cm.
"A Tom Doherty Associates Book."
ISBN 0-312-85121-9
I. Title.
PR6063.A834B8 1991
823′.914—dc20

90-48773
CIP

Printed in the United States of America

First edition: April 1991

0 9 8 7 6 5 4 3 2 1

The San Diego Opera Company
in association with Mander Promotions
extends a personal invitation to

---

to attend a Gala Evening of
Operatic Tributes to Richard Wagner

San Diego Civic Theater, Second Avenue at A Street
June 21, at 9 P.M.

Dress Formal

THE BURNING

1

If Bob Tuggey had thought for an instant that the girl in the red checkered cowboy shirt was carrying that bright red gasoline can across the parking lot with the intention of burning herself alive, he would immediately have thrown down his spatula and vaulted the counter and run out of the restaurant as fast as his light-heavyweight build could have taken him.

From where he was standing in the kitchen, he was probably the first person in the Rosecrans Street McDonald's to catch sight of her. And—ironically—he was probably the only person who had the experience to realize what was wrong about the way she was walking, even though she was smiling and swinging her gasoline can like a basket full of summer flowers.

In another time, in another life, Bob Tuggey had been a junior clerk for Deputy Chief of Mission William Trueheart in South Vietnam; and one evening late in June 1963, when he was driving back to the embassy after buying himself a half-dozen new sport shirts from his Chinese tailor in Cholon, a Buddhist monk had walked across the road in front of him in just the same way, swinging a gasoline can. *A-tisket, a-tasket.*

Bob's Valiant had been brought to a halt a little farther up the road by a long military convoy grinding past, and while he had sat smoking and listening to Peter, Paul, and Mary, the monk had eased himself down on the sidewalk less than seventy feet away, splashed sparkling gasoline all over his head, and set himself alight.

"The answer, my friend, is blowin' in the wind . . ."

Bob had never forgotten the soft flaring noise of burning gasoline; the whirl of ashes from burning robes; the stoical agony on the monk's gradually blackening face. There had been shouting, arguing, bicycle bells ringing, but nobody had screamed. Bob had heaved himself out of the car, dragging his picnic blanket after him with the intention of smothering the flames, but three more monks had pushed him away, persistently, with the heels of their bony hands, until their brother had fallen stiffly sideways, still burning, beyond the ministrations of anybody but Buddha.

Bob had doubled up by the side of the road, under that bronze smoky sky, and vomited churned-up chicken and tomatoes. Even today, "Blowin' in the Wind" made his stomach tighten.

Maybe the smallest of small bells tinkled in Bob's memory as the girl came into view. But of course there was nothing about her that would have put him instantly in mind of a protesting Buddhist monk. She was petite and blond, with bouncy brushed-back hair that reminded him of Doris Day. Her cowboy shirt was matched with a wide tan-leather belt, cinched tight, and well-fitting 501s.

"Four Quarter-pounders down," called Sally, the ginger-haired manager. Bob peeled off the greaseproof paper and pressed the burgers onto the grill. Outside the window, the girl was already halfway across the parking lot, still swinging her can, her shrunken shadow dancing after her. The sunlight flashed for an instant off the red enamel paint.

Bob was balding and overweight and by far the oldest employee at McDonald's Rosecrans Street. When his left eye looked west, his right eye looked nor-nor-west. But all of the kids liked him, and called him Unca Tug. He was fifty-one next week, a birthday he would have to celebrate on his own. After William Trueheart had left Saigon, Bob had drifted through one menial government clerkship after another, black coffee, brown offices. He had started to drink, a bottle of Ricard a day, often more. Days of milk-white clouds and aniseed. In France one rainy afternoon, in his small apartment in the Domaine de la Ronce, he had tried to commit suicide by gassing himself. What was the point of living, with no prospects, no money, and no companions but a brindled boxer with slobbery jowls that kept chewing the furniture?

All that had saved him was the stink of gas, which (with a stomachful of Ricard) had made him feel unbearably dizzy and sick. He had gone out for a breath of fresh air. Absurd, in the middle of killing himself, but he hadn't wanted to die nauseous. While he was out, the gas had blown up his kitchen, and deafened his dog. The concierge had been furious, and had followed him around for an hour, shouting at him.

"Idiot! You think it's a good joke, to blow up your apartment?"

"What?" he had repeated, again and again. He, too, had been deafened, but only temporarily.

The girl kept walking toward the far side of the parking lot. The hot shuddering air made it look as if she were walking through a crystal-clear lake. It was ninety-five degrees outside, which in San Diego was exceptional. She was walking toward the far side of the parking lot with what was obviously a full can of gasoline, by the slow way it swung. Yet where was she taking it? There were no cars parked on that side of the lot, none at all; and no vehicles in sight on the road.

Bob turned the Quarter-pounders over, and took two special orders for cheeseburgers. "Sally—filets up!" called Gino, next to him, all Adam's apple and razored black sideburns. And the girl outside stepped with her can over the scrubby row of bushes that separated one section of the parking lot from the next.

"Unca Tug, where's those Quarter-pounders?" Sally demanded. Bob glanced down. They were almost ready. "Three chicken sandwiches down," Marianna called. "Big Macs up!" said Gino. "Two cheeseburgers down!" said Doyle.

Bob looked up again and the girl was still walking. She was probably five hundred feet away from the restaurant now. He didn't know why he kept watching her, but she was so far away from any parked vehicles now, with that can of gasoline, and she was slowing down, and looking around her, as if she were lost, or as if she had decided that *this* was the spot.

The sizzle of Quarter-pounders distracted Bob for a second, and he scooped them off the grill and shoveled them into their buns. "Four Macs down!" called Sally.

Bob lifted the metal tray of Quarter-pounders onto the counter, and as he did so he saw the girl lowering herself cross-legged onto the concrete. He frowned, trying hard to focus. His eyes weren't so good at this kind of distance. He always wore his glasses when he went to the movies, or to Jack Murphy Stadium to watch the Padres. But when the girl turned herself slightly to twist open the gasoline can he instantly interpreted the meaning of her gesture and it was *then* in a thrill of total horror that he connected the buoyant determined walk to nowhere in particular, *a-tisket, a-tasket,* with the red can swinging, and the dignified cross-legged posture, and the terrible composure with which she reached out to turn the screw top.

His ears heard the spitting of cheeseburgers and the chattering of Girl Scouts. But his eyes saw a burning Buddhist monk.

"Oh Christ," he said.

"Unca Tug?" frowned Gino.

"Two filets down!" called Sally.

He dropped his spatula. It rang on the grill, bounced to the floor. "Hey, Unca *Tug—*" Sally began.

But Bob was already shouldering his way past Gino and David, jarring his thigh on the edge of the counter. They were shouting at him but their voices sounded like nothing but a deep blur. *"Unnncccaaa Ttttuuggggg . . ."* He hoisted the bright-red fire extinguisher off the wall. For Fat Fires Only—Jesus! Then his shoulder had collided with the emergency exit at the back of the kitchen and he was out in the heat, in his McDonald's hat and his flapping apron, carrying the fire extinguisher like a quarterback heading for a touchdown.

He circled the restaurant, awkwardly hop-hurdling the low chain-link fence at the side. *Oh please God don't let her, oh please God don't let her.*

His sneakers slapped loudly on the hot tarmac. His vision jumbled. *Hunh!* he panted. Overweight, unfit. *Hunh! hunh! hunh!* He heard a soft explosion, scarcely audible, *poooffff!* and a woman scream. He saw orange flame wagging in the breeze like a burning flag. His heart was bursting; the hot air scorched his lungs. But then he was crashing his way through the crackling-dry bushes into the next section of the parking lot and there she was, sitting right in front of him, on fire.

She was still cross-legged, but sitting rigidly upright. Her back was arched, her hands stiffly clenching her thighs. Her eyes were tightly shut; nobody had the willpower to burn with open eyes. Her blond hair was already blackened, a thousand ends glowing orange like a burning broom. Flames poured out of her face. She must have poured most of the gasoline down her front, because her lap was a roaring nest of fire.

"Hold on!" Bob screamed at her, although he didn't know why. He banged the fire extinguisher against the concrete, and

it started to spurt out foam. He directed a jet of foam straight at her face, then at her legs, and kept on squirting foam at her until the last flame had been smothered. There was foam, steam, and oily smoke, and an overwhelming smell of burned flesh.

Five or six people were running from the shopping mall toward him. Some children were crying, and a woman was screaming, "Oh, God! Oh, God!"

"Call an ambulance!" Bob roared, almost hysterical. Spit flew from his mouth. "Call a fucking ambulance!"

He turned back, off-balance, gasping, to look at the girl. She was still sitting upright, although all of her hair had burned off, and her face was corked black like a minstrel's. She was shuddering with pain and shock. The skin on the back of her hands had burned through, and the bare bones were exposed.

"It's all right," Bob told her. He knew better than to touch her. "Just stay still; try not to move. The ambulance is coming."

She opened her shriveled eyelids, and stared at him with milked-over eyes.

"You bastard," she whispered. *"You bastard. Why didn't you let me burn?"*

"It's all right," he reassured her. "You're going to be fine. Do you want to lie down?"

A curious and shuffling crowd was already gathering around them. Bob heard a teenage kid say, "Shit, man, just look at her."

"Would you go away, please?" Bob demanded, with a stiff sweep of his arm. There were tears in his eyes. "This woman's hurt. Would you please just go away?"

Nobody moved. Somebody even knelt down and started taking photographs. But when Bob looked back at the girl, she had stretched her cracked scarlet lips across her teeth. She was staring at him as if she could have damned him to hell.

"Bastard," she repeated. Then she coughed, and coughed again, and suddenly vomited up a bibful of blood and blackened lung and unburnt gasoline. She fell sideways, trembling, and then she lay still. Bob would never forget the sound of her hairless skull, knocking against the concrete.

With an odd genuflection, he laid down his fire extinguisher. *By the rivers of Babylon, I laid my fire extinguisher down.* In the distance, he could hear the yelping of a siren. He didn't know what to do. He didn't know what made him feel worse: the fact that he had tried to save her, and failed; or the fact that he had tried to save her at all. Nobody had ever looked at him with such hostility before; nobody. If looks could kill, he would have been lying beside her, burned to death, just like she was—and *his* soul, too, would have been blowing in the wind, like smoke.

2

"Did you ever cook grunion, Mr. Denman?" asked Waldo.

Lloyd swallowed wine and looked up from his cluttered roll-top desk. "Grunion? No, I never even *thought* about cooking them. Why?"

"Oh, nothing. It's just that the grunion season finishes August 30. I was wondering whether I ought to take the kids grunion-catching. Trouble is, I don't know what you're supposed to do with grunion once you've caught them."

"Did you ask Louis?"

"Louis said he didn't have a clue."

Lloyd eased himself back in his captain's chair. "Well . . . you remember Charles Kuerbis? The Realtor? He was always the first one down on the beach when the grunion started running. I asked him once how he cooked them. He said he didn't know; he gave them to his wife. Whatever it was she did to them, they were always excellent. So I asked his wife, and *she* said she fed them to the cat, and went out and bought some decent fish."

"Maybe I'll take them to Sea World instead," Waldo suggested defeatedly.

"Didn't you take them to Sea World last time?"

"Sure, and the time before that, and the time before that. I can't remember a custody visit in three years when I haven't come back soaking wet. The kids always like to sit at the front. Did you ever smell a killer whale's *breath*, Mr. Denman?"

"Sure," joked Lloyd. "Halibutosis." He shuffled a heap of

bills together and jammed them onto a spike. "You're enough to put a guy off getting married, you know that?"

Waldo shook his head. "Don't take no notice of me, Mr. Denman. There's only one woman in the world as bad as my Tusha, and that's my Tusha. Celia's perfect for you, and you know it. Celia's bright, she's pretty, she's classy. She knows all about music. Not like Tusha. Tusha thinks that Pavarotti is some kind of cheese, you know, like ricotta. Besides, you never met her; she's hideous."

"Why on earth did you marry her in the first place, if you think she's hideous?"

"Oh, no, don't get me wrong. On the outside, she looks great. Great eyes, great smile. Great gazongas. It's just on the inside she's hideous. A really hideous inside."

Lloyd stood up, and carried his empty glass out of the office and through to the bar. He took a bottle of San Pasqual Chenin Blanc out of the refrigerator and poured himself a generous measure. He allowed himself only two glasses of wine during the afternoon: otherwise things would start getting a little unreal by the time the restaurant opened for the evening.

He checked his watch, the Corum Gold Coin watch that Celia had given him for his birthday last April. Waldo the maître d' always came early, because he really had no place else to go. They talked usually, or shared a bottle of wine, or played checkers. The rest of the staff would be arriving in ones and twos within a half-hour, ready for their opening at six-thirty.

Lloyd walked through the twenty-six-table restaurant, checking each place setting individually. Fresh orchids, gleaming Lauffer cutlery, shell-pink linen napkins folded like chrysanthemums. Quite a few restaurants let their wait staff leave for the afternoon without resetting the tables, but Lloyd insisted that when the staff returned for the evening shift, the place should look as entrancing to them as it did to their customers.

It was still magical for Lloyd. After eleven years as an insurance assessor for San Diego Marine Trust, working out how much rich men's boats were worth, this restaurant was everything he had always wanted. Freedom; independence; profitable hard work; fun. Denman's Original Fish Depot, an informal but stylish seafood restaurant with Victorian-tiled walls and an oak parquet floor and mahogany ceiling fans, and a balcony outside overlooking La Jolla Cove.

San Diego magazine had already complimented Lloyd on his

Northwest salmon steaks broiled over alder wood, his glazed mahi-mahi, and his trademark dish, the Denman's Original Fish Depot Delight, which was lobster chunks, shrimp, clams, crab legs and mushrooms, served with poured-over chowder in a hot French-style brioche.

He walked across to the sliding glass doors that led out to the balcony, and opened them. A warm briny wind was blowing off the water, and gulls were sloping and crying around the steep sandy-colored cliffs. He leaned against the wooden rail and breathed in the evening air. This was it. This was the dream. It was all so ridiculously idyllic that sometimes it made him grin to himself in shameless self-satisfaction.

He had it all—or most of it, anyway. His own restaurant in a posh and profitable location; a talented and startlingly pretty girlfriend who loved him like crazy and wanted to marry him; a white 5-Series BMW with the personalized license FISHEE; and a $568,000 house close to UCSD with a hot tub and an olive tree and what his realtors had called "a tantalizing peek" of the North Shore. A full peek would have cost him $30,000 more, and so far an actual view was financially out of the question.

But think of it: his father had been a mail carrier, his mother had taken in sewing, and here he was.

Lloyd didn't really look the part of a *restaurateur*. He was very lean and tall, with a mop of gray-streaked hair and a prominent bony nose, which had led his mother to describe him as "proud-looking" and his father to call him "the human can opener." But now that his fortieth birthday was approaching, and he was lightly suntanned and psychologically well-balanced and everything was well with the world, he had an air about him that was both distinguished and lighthearted. Celia always said that if Basil Rathbone had been both Californian and funny, then he would have been Lloyd Denman instead.

He turned around and watched Waldo setting up his reservations book on the oak lectern beside the front doors. Waldo had smoothed-back hair, a clipped Oliver Hardy mustache, and a wide, dark green cummerbund that made him look like a ribbon-wrapped Easter egg. He spoke to the customers with an amazingly over-the-top French accent, "*Zees way, sair, see voo play—pardonnay mwuh, madarm,*" but in fact his name was Waldo Slonimsky and he was Lithuanian, the only survivor of his entire family. Sometimes Lloyd could look at his face and clearly see the plump, lonely seven-year-old boy who had been brought over to America just before the war. Waldo had married, had kids, divorced, dated a few women the same shape as him. But Lloyd thought, *When you've lost forever the people you love the most, how can you ever stop being lonely?*

"Waldo," he called. "Come on out here."

Waldo stepped out to the balcony, tugging his cummerbund straight. "You want something, Mr. Denman?"

Lloyd nodded. "Yes, I do. I want you to drop everything for just a couple of minutes and come out here and take a look at the cove."

Waldo kept his eyes on Lloyd; obviously tense, obviously thinking anxiously about everything he had to do. Check the menus, update the wine lists, call for two replacement waitresses because Angie and Kay had both phoned in sick. *Sick, my ass—excuse my Lithuanian—surfing, probably.*

Lloyd said encouragingly, "Relax; look around. What do you think of the cove this evening?"

Waldo glanced at it quickly. "This evening, it's a nice cove."

"Is that all? Just *nice?*"

Waldo contrived to look around some more. "This evening, it's a *heck* of a nice cove."

Lloyd laughed and clamped his arm around Waldo's shoulders. "You know what your trouble is, Waldo?"

"What?" asked Waldo, uneasily. "What's my trouble?"

"You never stop to think how lucky you are."

Waldo plainly didn't understand what Lloyd was trying to say to him. He shrugged, twisted the napkin that he always used for polishing fingerprints from knives and forks. "I do what I can, Mr. Denman. You know that."

"Sure, Waldo, I know that. But just close your eyes and take a breath of this good Pacific air and let your muscles loose. You may have had your troubles with Tusha, but you've got yourself two beautiful children, and your own apartment, and a car that actually runs; and a whole lot of people who like you."

"Well, that's nice, Mr. Denman. Thank you very much."

"Waldo . . ." Lloyd began, squeezing Waldo's arm. But he knew that it was no use pushing Waldo any further. He would simply embarrass him.

Waldo went to the rail and looked out over the ocean. Now that the sun was setting, La Jolla and all its jostling restaurants and souvenir shops and color-washed apartment buildings were thickly coated in a glutinous shellac of amber light. The gulls continued to wheel and scream, and Waldo lifted his double chin and watched them.

"My family used to live in Palanga, you know, on the Baltic," he said. "It seems very far from here now, very long ago. My grandfather used to take me for walks along the shore. It's funny, don't you think, Mr. Denman? I can see him as clear now as I did then. He always used to wear a long gray wool coat, and an old-fashioned black felt hat."

"That's not so funny," smiled Lloyd. "I can almost see him myself."

Waldo slowly shook his head. "Grandfather used to say to me that when we die, our souls become seagulls. They fly, they swoop. That is why seagulls always sound so sad. They are always looking for the people they left behind."

Lloyd said, "That's a cute little story."

Waldo wiped his eyes with his fingers. "I used to believe it. I think I *still* believe it. Maybe in the Baltic my grandfather still flies and swoops along the shoreline, looking for that boy that he once used to take for walks."

He shrugged, and then he said, "I'd better get back in now. There's a whole lot to do."

As Waldo went in, however, Lloyd saw two men in budget-priced suits push their way in through the restaurant's oak-paneled front door, and stand uncertainly among the potted plants. They certainly didn't look like the Fish Depot's usual type of customer, but then they didn't look like health inspectors, either. One of them was cavernous-cheeked and unshaven, with glittering eyes. The other was pudgy and rumpled, with a surprised-looking face, and an uncontrollable tuft of fraying brown hair. Jackie Gleason meets Jim Belushi.

The unshaven one came up to Waldo and spoke to him. Waldo nodded, then shook his head. The unshaven man said something else, then turned and pointed toward the deck. The two men weaved their way between the tables with their hands in their pockets, and emerged out on the deck.

"Mr. Lloyd Denman?" the unshaven one asked him, with a slight catch in his throat.

"That's right. How can I help you?"

The man produced a gold badge. "I'm Sergeant David Houk, sir, San Diego Police Department. This is Detective Ned Gable."

"This doesn't concern unpaid parking tickets, does it?" said

Lloyd, mock-defensively. "There's a whole bunch still in my glove compartment. You know how it is. Busy, busy, busy."

"Well, no, sir. We just wanted to ask you a couple of questions, sir."

Lloyd could sense their disquiet. "What is it?" he demanded. "What's happened?"

Sergeant Houk cleared his throat, and then he said, "There's been an accident, Mr. Denman, on Rosecrans Street, downtown."

"An accident? What kind of an accident?"

"Woman got fatally burned, sir. Right in front of McDonald's restaurant."

"Well, that's terrible."

"Yes, sir."

Lloyd waited. He didn't know what else to say. "So, a woman got burned. What does that have to do with me?"

"Do you know Ms. Celia Williams, sir?" asked Detective Gable.

Lloyd was baffled. "Sure I know Ms. Celia Williams. She's my fiancée. But she's in San Francisco right now, giving a series of music lectures."

"She's in San Francisco?" asked Houk, glancing at Gable with unconcealed surprise.

"Sure. She left this weekend. I don't expect her back until Saturday afternoon. She called me last night . . . I don't know—it must have been twelve, half after twelve."

Sergeant Houk massaged his bony, unshaven jowls. "Mr. Denman . . . I don't know how to start saying this, sir. But as far as we can tell, Ms. Celia Williams was the woman who burned to death in front of McDonald's today."

Lloyd stared at him and then laughed. The idea that Celia had been outside McDonald's today, only six or seven miles away from La Jolla on Rosecrans Street, was so patently absurd that he wasn't even upset. "Sergeant, that's impossible. That's totally impossible. Celia's in San Francisco. She was giving a lecture this afternoon at the Performing Arts Center."

"Did you speak to her today?" asked Detective Gable, sniffing, and wiping his nose with the back of his hand.

"No, not yet. She usually calls me around midnight, when the restaurant's emptying out."

"And you're expecting her to call tonight?"

"Of course I'm expecting her to call tonight. She's my fiancée. We're going to be married come September."

Sergeant Houk reached into the pocket of his creased Sears suit and produced a transparent plastic envelope. He held it up, so that Lloyd could see what was in it. A white credit-card wallet, badly charred at one end, and a gold charm bracelet.

"Mr. Denman, do you recognize either of these two items?"

Lloyd stared at him. "She's in San Francisco. If you doubt my word, you can try calling her. She's staying at the Miyako. Listen—do you want the number?"

A small spasm of panic. The wallet's clasp was curved and gold, in the shape of the Chinese symbol for yin and yang, just like the clasp of Celia's wallet. And although he hadn't looked closely at the charms, the charm bracelet looked startlingly like the one that he had given Celia when she had first moved in . . . and to which he had added a new charm each month. A treble clef, for the day she had graduated as a doctor of music; a house, for the day they had moved into 3337 North Torrey; a heart, for the day he had proposed to her.

"Mr. Denman," Sergeant Houk told him, with heartbreaking professional gentleness, "do you want to sit down and take a look at these things? The wallet contains a social security card and credit cards belonging to Celia Jane Williams, as well as business cards from this restaurant, and two photographs of a man who I now recognize to be you."

Lloyd looked mechanically around, and then dragged over a rattan chair, and sat down. Sergeant Houk handed him the wallet, and then the charm bracelet. Detective Gable coughed uncomfortably and sniffed.

This can't be real, thought Lloyd. *Something's slipped; something's gone haywire. This is not me, this is somebody else. Or maybe I'm still asleep, and this is nothing but a dream. But I can feel the wind. I can hear the gulls crying. And there's Waldo, staring at me pale-faced through the tinted glass window, and Waldo wouldn't stare at me like that, so apprehensive and so sorrowful, if this weren't real.*

He opened the wallet. He stared inside. The embossed label said F. David, Del Mar. He knew it was hers. He had been with her at the Flower Hill Shopping Center when she had bought it. He didn't have to look at the credit cards, but he did. Sears, Exxon, American Express. *Don't leave home without it.*

"Where were these found?" he managed to say, his lips woolly and numb.

"They were found on the body of a white Caucasian female

aged about twenty-nine, in the parking lot outside McDonald's Restaurant, Rosecrans Street, at eleven-thirty this morning," said Houk.

"She was blond," added Gable, trying to be helpful, trying hard to be sympathetic. "She was pretty, by all accounts, with blue eyes. She wore a red checkered shirt and blue 501s."

Lloyd didn't look up, but rubbed his thumb across the white leather wallet again and again, as if he were expecting a secret message to appear. "Red checkered shirt?" he asked.

"That's right, sir. Red checkered shirt and 501s."

"Outside McDonald's on Rosecrans?"

"That's correct, sir."

"I don't understand," said Lloyd, and he didn't. He was so sure that Celia was in San Francisco that he was prepared to call her now, at the Performing Arts Center, even though he knew she was right in the middle of a lecture on reading operatic scores. Just to call her and say, "You're there, aren't you, in San Francisco?" And to hear her say "Yes! Of course I am!"

"And what did you say? *Fatally* burned? Dead?"

Sergeant Houk sucked in his cheeks even more cavernously. "I'm sorry, Mr. Denman, but it sure looks like it. I mean, there's still a possibility it *isn't* Ms. Williams. Somebody could've stole your fiancée's wallet. But I wouldn't count on it."

"What the hell are you talking about?" Lloyd protested. "She flew out of here Sunday afternoon! I put her on the flight myself! She was giving five lectures on Wagner and operatic technique, and then she was coming directly back home! There's no conceivable reason why she should have come back to San Diego before Saturday; none at all. And I can't believe she wouldn't have called me."

"Well, there must have been some motive," Sergeant Houk said, gently. "The only trouble is, we don't yet know what it was."

Detective Gable said, "She wasn't under any kind of a strain, was she? Worried about this lecture series, anything like that? Some people crack up without any warning whatsoever, just crack up, and the next thing you know they've left their family and their friends behind and they're riding lettuce trains all over the country."

Lloyd slowly shook his head. *Lettuce trains?* He couldn't make any sense of what they were telling him. It was totally unbelievable that Celia was dead. On Sunday morning they had lain side by side in bed together with fresh coffee and the Sunday paper and the sun striping the sheets. She had leaned on her elbow, one hand thrust into her tangled blond hair, and said to him, "We're going to have babies, aren't we?"

He had finished reading *Calvin & Hobbes* and then leaned forward and kissed her forehead. "Sure we're going to have babies. A boy like me and a girl like you."

She had smiled a distant smile. "One baby will do, thanks."

"Just one? I want a dynasty!"

"One's enough. If you have a baby, you know, you live forever."

But she hadn't had a baby, hadn't even had the *chance* to have a baby. Now she was dead, impossibly and unimaginably dead. No life everlasting, nothing.

The tears dripped down Lloyd's cheeks and he didn't even know that he was crying.

"When did this happen?" he asked, trying to remember if he had experienced any unusual feelings during the day. Any feeling of coldness, any sudden sense of loss. But lunchtime had been chaotically busy, and for most of the afternoon he had been writing up his accounts. He couldn't recall anything but frantic hard work and wondering how to keep laundry costs down. Ah Kim's had just put up their prices two cents a napkin.

Houk said, "It seems like she poured gasoline over herself. Kind of a ritual suicide. One of the cooks from McDonald's managed to reach her with a fire extinguisher, but it was too late."

"She *killed* herself?"

"I'm sorry, Mr. Denman; it sure looks that way."

"I don't even know what she was *doing* there," Lloyd protested. "I mean—what in God's name was she *doing* there? She wasn't depressed; she wasn't upset."

"I'm sorry, Mr. Denman, we really don't know. We don't even know how she got there. There were no private vehicles anywhere in the vicinity left unaccounted for, and nobody saw a woman riding a bus with a gasoline can."

Lloyd dragged out his handkerchief and wiped his eyes. "God, what a waste. God, what a terrible waste. I can't tell you how—" He stopped. His throat was too tight, and his mouth didn't seem to work. She had killed herself, burned herself to death, and she hadn't even tried to tell him what was wrong. That was what hurt. She hadn't even asked him for help.

Sergeant Houk waited for a long moment. Two of Lloyd's waitresses had arrived, and Lloyd could see them anxiously talking to Waldo, and glancing out at the deck now and again. He gave them a hesitant wave, but they probably didn't understand what he was doing, or else they were too upset; because they didn't wave back.

Sergeant Houk glanced around at them, and then carefully took back the wallet and the charm bracelet. "You'll have these back as soon as possible, Mr. Denman. Meanwhile there's one thing I'm going to have to ask you to do. It won't be easy; but we do need somebody to come downtown to the morgue tomorrow morning to identify Ms. Williams's remains."

Remains, thought Lloyd. *What a forlorn, contradictory word. When your soul has left your body, nothing remains. Only memories, only a scattering of objects. Clothes, photographs, a voice that speaks over and over again on video recordings, an endlessly repeated smile.*

"We'll have to ask you a few more questions," Sergeant Houk told him. "We're going to have to piece together everything that happened."

Lloyd nodded. "All right, I understand."

Detective Gable laid his hand consolingly on Lloyd's shoulder. "You okay, sir? You want a ride home or anything?"

"No . . . no thanks," Lloyd replied. "I have a restaurant to run."

The two policemen left him out on the deck, and went to have a word with Waldo. Essentially, it was "Keep an eye on him; he's already in shock." Then they left. Lloyd sat alone for a long time, unaware that the restaurant wasn't filling up; that no customers were coming in. Waldo had put up a hastily chalked sign outside saying CLOSED: FAMILY BEREAVEMENT and Suzie was calling up all the customers who had made reservations, apologetically canceling them all, and offering them free Fish Depot cocktails the next time they came.

Lloyd stood up and leaned against the deck rail. The ocean lay below him like molten solder, with a gradually wrinkling skin. The seagulls turned and cried. Lloyd wondered if one of them were already Celia, circling around La Jolla Cove, looking for him.

Waldo came out and stood a little way behind him. "You all right, Mr. Denman?" he asked, at length. "You want a drink, maybe?"

Lloyd shook his head. "No thanks."

"You want that I should drive you home?"

"I don't know. I don't feel real. I feel like I'm here, but at the same time I'm not here at all. Can you understand that?"

Waldo came up and clasped Lloyd's shoulder. "It's a beautiful evening, Mr. Denman. The cove is beautiful. Do you know what they say in Lithuania, when somebody dies on a day like this? They say that God loved them so much that he lit all the lamps of heaven to guide them on their way."

3

A little after eight o'clock, Lloyd drove himself back to North Torrey. He switched on the car radio but KFSD was playing "Un bel di vedremo" from *Madama Butterfly* and he couldn't bear it: it had always been Celia's favorite. He drove the rest of the way home with tears leaking down his cheeks.

As he turned into the driveway, a lantern was lit on the front veranda, and the living-room lights were shining, but only because they had been tripped by automatic timers. There was nobody waiting for him; and now there never would be.

He parked his white BMW in the driveway and killed the engine. He stayed behind the wheel for three or four minutes, trying to decide if he really wanted to go inside. She was dead, but all of her clothes would still be there; her towel would still be hanging in the bathroom. Her photograph would still be smiling at him from his night table. Most painful of all, he would still be able to *smell* her. Red, by Giorgio of Beverly Hills.

He had opened the BMW's glove compartment to find the remote control for opening the front gates, and her sunglasses and her lipstick had been lying inside, just where she had last tossed them. He had opened the lipstick case. Cantata Red.

The evening was growing shadowy. The air was thick and warm, and there was a strong smell of eucalyptus and pine. Up above him, it looked as if God had stirred boysenberry jelly into the sky, the way Lloyd's mother used to stir boysenberry jelly into his milk, when he was a kid. *I prefer the boysenberry more than any ordinary jam,* somebody sang in the back of his brain.

At last Lloyd climbed out of the car, slammed the door, and walked up to the single-level *L*-shaped house with the terrible reluctance of true grief. The ocean gleamed knowingly through the ferns—that peek of the North Shore for which they had paid so much, and about which they had teased themselves so often. They had even considered renaming the house *Peek House.*

He opened the front door and went inside. The house seemed so pillow-silent that he was almost tempted to call out, "Hello? Celia?"

His shoes barked across the hallway, which was floored in bleached and polished oak; but then he walked in silence across the living room floor, which was thickly covered in cream-colored carpeting. He walked right into the middle of the living room and looked around, as if he hadn't been there for years. There was a strong smell of oak and new rugs. *I prefer the boysenberry more than any—*

The living room was painted plain pottery white and furnished with tasteful sparseness. Celia had always preferred simple furniture, open spaces. If only Lloyd had known how complicated her mind was. There were two couches, upholstered in pink-and-blue glazed cotton; two French-style armchairs; and a coffee table with a driftwood sculpture on it, as well as a neatly marshaled stack of *Opera News* and *Musical America.*

On the walls hung vivid oil paintings by local artists. A view of the Presidio, domed, white-walled, in shimmering sunlight. Next to it, a portrait of a Mexican woman, standing by an open adobe, selling lemons from a basket. The portrait was entitled, *Who'll Buy My Lemons?*

But the center of visual and emotional gravity in the living room—in fact the center of visual and emotional gravity in the whole house—was Celia's ice-white Yamaha grand piano, which Lloyd had given her when they first moved in. That piano had meant commitment and permanence. A house of their own; a relationship that was going to last. "After all," Lloyd had told her, "you can storm out of the door with an overnight bag; but you can't storm out of the door with a grand piano."

Fatally burned.

Lloyd went over to the piano and picked out two or three plaintive notes. All those years that Celia had practiced. All those years that she had dedicated to Wagner and Verdi and Puccini. Fingers flying across the keys. Eyes closed, voice uplifted. *Fatally burned*. He played the first three bars of "Evergreen" because he could never play opera: "Love, soft as an easy chair . . ." then stopped, and closed the lid over the keyboard, and turned the key. From now on, it was going to stay silent, unplayed. Nobody else was going to touch it.

On top of the piano, meticulously arranged, was Celia's collection of scrimshaw from Nantucket and Salem and the Barbary Coast. Some of them dated as far back as 1720, but her favorite had always been the fragment of twenty-thousand-year-old fossilized mammoth tusk, exquisitely carved by Bonnie Schulte, one of the most accomplished scrimshanders in the country.

Lloyd had promised Celia another Bonnie Schulte piece for her birthday. But the only carving she needed now was her headstone.

It was so difficult for Lloyd to believe that their life together was all over, when it had scarcely started. Even worse, there was nobody that he could call. Celia's parents were both dead, and although she had mentioned an older sister in Denver, Lloyd had no idea of where her sister lived, or what her married name was, or how to get in touch with her.

He poured himself a glassful of Wild Turkey from the heavy crystal decanter on the black-enameled Spanish linen chest that they had brought back from Baja. His hand was shaking, and the decanter clattered against the rim of the glass. He walked through to the bedroom with his drink in his hand and stared at the big oak bed. On the wall behind the headboard was a stylized painting of two California quail, touching beaks, and Celia had said that it was a painting of them, kissing, in another incarnation.

"You want to come back as a quail?" he had asked her.

She had smiled. "Better to come back as a quail than not to come back at all."

On impulse, he called the Miyako Hotel in San Francisco.

"I want to speak to Ms. Williams, please."

A pause, and then politely, "No Ms. Williams registered here, sir."

"Maybe she checked out. Was she there yesterday, or the day before?"

"No, sir. Nobody by the name of Williams."

"How about Denman? Anybody by the name of Denman?"

"No, sir. Denbigh, but no Denman."

Lloyd hung up, frowning. Celia had told him on the phone last night that she was calling from the Miyako; he was quite sure of it. She had even mentioned the Japanese meal she had ordered from room service, the teriyaki shrimp. But unless she had registered under a different name altogether, she hadn't been there at all.

Plainly, she had been deceiving him. But why?

He swallowed whiskey and thought to himself, *Maybe the grand piano hadn't been enough to hold her back, after all. Maybe she had found herself a new lover.*

He paced around the living room, his mind helter-skeltering. A lover? It didn't make any sense. Celia had always told him the truth, even when it hurt. She wouldn't have fallen for another man without telling him. She couldn't. Besides, she had seemed to be deliriously happy. Come September, they were going to be married: they had even talked about how many children they wanted, and what they were going to call them. Joseph for a boy; Tershia for a girl.

And, if she had fallen in love with another man—really fallen in love—why had she set herself on fire?

He leafed through the telephone book, and found the number of Sylvia Cuddy, Celia's best friend from the San Diego Opera—designer glasses, sensual pink lips, wildly tangled hair. He jabbed the phone buttons with his middle finger, then tucked the receiver under his chin and waited for Sylvia to answer.

"Sylvia? It's Lloyd."

"Well, hello! This is a surprise! How can I help you?"

Lloyd found himself swallowing tightly. A throatful of burrs. "Sylvia . . . I'm afraid I have some really bad news."

He heard himself telling Sylvia in a clogged-up voice that Celia was dead. He heard Sylvia denying it. He heard himself say that it was true. He was desperately sorry, but it was true. He didn't even know whether he believed it himself. Maybe he was making some kind of surrealistic mistake, like one of those movies where you pick up the wrong suitcase and open it up and *voila!* no pajamas, no dirty rolled-up socks, no shaver, only four million dollars' worth of pure heroin in plastic bags.

"Sylvia . . . I've been trying to find out who might have seen Celia last . . . before she left San Francisco."

A hesitant pause. "San Francisco? What do you mean?"

"She was lecturing for the opera in San Francisco, wasn't she? A two-week engagement at the Performing Arts Center."

"Well, she may have been lecturing, Lloyd, but it wasn't for us. She never told *me* anything about it."

"When did you last talk to her?" asked Lloyd.

"Why, just yesterday morning. She told me she was calling from home."

"You mean from here? From La Jolla? What did she say to you?"

"I don't know . . ." Sylvia confessed. "Nothing much, really. She gave me her recipe for veal tarantino, the one I was always nagging her about. Then she said something about how excited she was, looking forward to the future. Then she hung up."

"She didn't say anything unusual? Anything that struck you as weird?"

Sylvia thought about it for a while. "I'm not sure. I suppose the whole phone call was weird, in a way—just suddenly calling me out of the blue to give me that recipe. And the way she said, at the end, 'Well, *good-bye*, Sylvia.' It was so *final*. I said, 'You sound as if you're going on a trip.' But she didn't answer."

Lloyd slowly replaced the receiver. The more he discovered about Celia's last moments, the more mysterious and unsettling they appeared to be. He had imagined that he and Celia had shared everything. Their friendship, their passion, their ambitions; their most inconsequential thoughts. Now he felt that a mask was slipping, and that a different Celia was coming into view, a Celia who had kept herself secret. A Celia who had told him lies, and lied to her best friend, too.

Through the open door to the bedroom, he could just see Celia's photograph laughing at him; the photograph he had taken in the courtyard at the Rancho Santa Fe. *What are you laughing at, my lady?* he thought. *What were you doing in that parking lot today, dousing yourself with gasoline, and setting yourself on fire?*

He walked through to the bedroom and picked up the photograph and stared at it closely, trying to see if her face gave anything away. *Most of all, Celia, why didn't you tell me what was worrying you? Why didn't you ask me to help?*

Maybe she had, he thought; but maybe he hadn't understood. The pain of that was almost more than he could bear, and he uttered a sob of grief that hurt his throat.

* * *

He drained the last of the Wild Turkey, holding the decanter upside-down until the last drop had fallen into his glass. *Plip*, the last drop. Then he struggled awkwardly out of his pants, and bundled the Danish duck-down quilt around himself, and huffed, and puffed, and made a determined effort to sleep.

She's dead, she's gone, but you have to sleep. If you don't sleep, you won't be able to cope with the restaurant; and Waldo; and everybody else who's depending on you.

Soon the quilt grew impossibly hot, so he untwisted himself, and lay spread-eagled across the bed, feeling drunker than he had ever felt in his life. The mattress tilted and swam as if it were adrift off Point Loma. His whole head seemed to be filled with potentially explosive whiskey fumes.

"Celia?" he said, knowing that she wasn't there, but drunk enough to defy reality. "Celia, I love you, for Chrissake! Don't you know that? Celia!"

Celia didn't answer; Celia was gone; burned in a parking lot on Rosecrans. Tomorrow he would see her body for himself, and then maybe he would be able to accept it. He slept, with his mouth hanging open, and dreamed that he was arguing with his realtors. *You said there was a conversation pit. This isn't a conversation pit, it's a grave.* Then he dreamed about the restaurant kitchens. Louis was stirring the fish stock, oblivious to the giant lobsters that crawled and heaved and clattered around the floor, blue-black and glistening, slowly waving their claws at him. The swinging doors swung. *Ee*-urk—*ee*—urk! There was somebody behind him, running away from him. He pushed his way into the corridor. The restaurant was blazing. All around him, naked women were running screaming in all directions, with their hair on fire. *Eeeeeeeeee!!*

He opened his eyes. He was still drunk, but he was conscious that he had heard a noise. He lay still, tense, listening. A creak, a rustle; a hollow-cheeked whisper like the draft of a door being opened, and then closed. He listened even more intently.

Something dropped with a thud, and rolled. Then a drumming, tumbling noise. Lloyd swung his legs out of bed, and made his way unsteadily out of the bedroom door, jarring his shoulder painfully on the door frame.

Shit, that hurts. He may have said it out loud. He stopped, swayed, almost lost his balance, listened.

The house was silent. But he was sure that he could *feel*

something, feel somebody moving. He was sure that he could sense somebody breathing. He was supposed to be alone, wasn't he, now that Celia had gone; and yet he was sure that he wasn't.

His next-door neighbor, Hal Pinkerton, had always nagged him about buying himself a gun. Now he wished very much that he had listened. He could imagine a six-foot, two-hundred-and-seventy-pound junkie with sweaty muscles and a Rambo knife waiting for him in the living room, next to the conversation pit that was more like a grave.

He patted the wall, searching for the light switch. He found it, and switched it on. He stood blinking at an empty living room. Nobody there. Only the painted face of the Mexican woman, with her unbought lemons. Only rugs and floors and furniture.

When he looked over toward the grand piano, however, he realized that something was different. All of the scrimshaw had disappeared. Twenty or thirty pieces of carved whale ivory, which Celia had carefully and artistically arranged on the piano lid. Now the top of the piano was completely bare.

Lloyd went up to the piano and laid his hands flat on the lid. Cool and shiny and white as death. The Chinese always said that death was white. He looked around, but nothing else seemed to be missing. Who the hell would risk breaking into a house for the sake of a couple of dozen pieces of scrimshaw?

He went through to the kitchen. The back door was wide open, and the cool night air was flowing in. He could smell the ocean. Cautiously, he edged open one of the kitchen drawers and took out his largest Sabatier butcher knife. He stepped out on the back porch, bricks on bare feet, and strained his eyes in the darkness.

He thought he glimpsed something, out by the avocado trees beyond the patio. Something that flickered quick and pale.

There was no logical reason for it, but he was suddenly gripped with a terrible sense of dread.

Don't be ridiculous. Whoever it was, they're gone. Some spaced-out kid, most likely, looking for crack money.

He called out, "Who's there?" But he didn't really expect a reply. What was a burglar going to say—"It's me; don't worry. Just been doing a bit of burgling"?

He thought he heard a faint rustling in the undergrowth by the back fence, but he couldn't be sure.

"You get this straight!" he shouted, harshly. "You'd better not try breaking into this house again! Not if you want your goddamn head to stay on your goddamn shoulders! I've got the biggest goddamn shotgun you ever saw, and I'm not afraid to use it!"

He waited for almost a minute, but there were no further noises; no indication that anybody was hiding behind the avocado trees or crouching in the bushes. *Be serious; they're probably halfway to Leucadia by now.*

He stepped back into the kitchen and closed the door. He was shivering a little, but not from the cold alone. It was then, turning around, that he realized the intruder had entered the house without forcing the door. There were no broken panes of glass, no screwdriver marks. He opened the door again, and there, still in the lock, was the spare key.

The spare key, which they always kept concealed deep in the soil of the Sicilian terra-cotta planter, on the opposite corner of the patio.

The spare key that only he and Celia had known about.

Christ, this is ridiculous. Somebody must have watched us putting it there. The Pinkertons' gardener, maybe. He was always up on his stepladder, pruning the creeper. The pool cleaner. Or anybody. Or maybe it was one of those hiding places that dumb innocent householders thought was totally unfindable, but which an expert thief could locate in a matter of minutes.

Celia was dead. Celia was never coming back. And in the morning, oh God, he would have to identify her body. He would have to confront her burned remains, and say, "Yes, this was the woman I loved." He had no idea what a burned body would look like, and he was terrified.

He closed the door and locked it, tugging at the handle to make doubly sure. Then he walked back into the living room, feeling parched and hung over and nauseous. He went across to the Spanish bureau and splashed out a huge glass of club soda, half of which he swallowed in three breathless gulps.

While he was drinking, he happened to glance down at the floor behind one of the sofas. To his surprise, all of Celia's scrimshaw was lying scattered on the carpet. It had been hidden from sight when he had first crossed the living room on his way to the kitchen. But here it was, all of it, twenty or thirty pieces. That must have been the tumbling noise he had heard. It looked exactly as if somebody had cleared the whole lot off the top of the piano with one impatient sweep of his arm.

Lloyd knelt down on the carpet and examined the pieces of ivory carefully, turning them over and over. Schooners, harbors, mermaids, storms at sea, all engraved in meticulous spidery detail. Why should anyone have wanted to throw all of this scrimshaw on the floor? It didn't make any kind of sense. Not unless the intruder had been totally crazy, or out of his brain on crack; or angry because he hadn't been able to find anything particularly valuable—or at least anything that could be fenced for the price of a score.

Lloyd stood up again. This was nuts. This was completely nuts. Then he caught sight of Celia's most valuable piece, her twenty-thousand-year-old piece of fossilized mammoth ivory, laid with obvious care on the seat of the couch.

He slowly picked it up. He couldn't understand this at all. What kind of housebreaker would have known that this one piece was worth twenty times the price of all the whale ivory arranged around it? How had he managed to pick it out from twenty or thirty others, in the dark? Even more to the point—if he had been able to pick it out, then he must have known what it was worth. *So why hadn't he slipped it into his pocket and taken it with him?*

Lloyd couldn't begin to think of a logical answer. He was too hung over, too shocked, and he really didn't want to think that the answer might not be logical at all.

He sipped the rest of his club soda. Then he switched off the lights and stood in the dark for what seemed like an hour. Exhausted, haunted, and hopeless. *Celia*, he thought, or whispered. Or both.

He heard the Italian clock in the hallway prissily chiming three. *Uno, duo, très.* He took a last reluctant look around him, and then he made his way back to bed. He fell backwards onto the quilt as if he had been shot. Celia had always hated the way he did that.

In his head he heard the words that Allen Ginsberg had written. *And you're out, Death let you out, Death had the Mercy, you're done with your century, done with God, done with the path thru it—Done with yourself at last—Pure—Back to the Babe dark before your Father, before us all—before the world—*

There, rest. No more suffering for you. I know where you've gone, it's good.

He thought that he wouldn't be able to sleep, but after a half-hour his eyes closed and his breathing grew deep and harsh, and he was slowly swallowed by the night.

He dreamed that there was a marble-gray face pressed close

to his bedroom window, watching him for almost an hour with the strangest expression of bereavement and greed. It might have been real; he might not have dreamed it at all. But whatever it was, it faded when the night faded, and by the time that morning broke, there was nobody in the garden at all.

4

They smelled burning on the wind from three or four miles away, long before the bus came into view. Then they began to run into occasional drifts of pale filthy smoke.

If they hadn't been so hungry, if they hadn't been so tired, they probably would have realized immediately that it was burning flesh.

But Ric wound down the patrol car window and sniffed two or three times, and gave a nod of approval. "Can you believe it?" he remarked. "Somebody's having a cookout."

"Oh, for sure," growled Sergeant Jim Griglak, without taking his King Edward cigar out of his mouth. "A hundred-fifteen in the shade, in the middle of the desert, at twenty after three in the afternoon, and somebody's having a cookout?"

"No, come on, smell it; that's a cookout," Ric assured him. "Baby back ribs, charred on the outside, tender on the inside. A nice frosty jug of margaritas. Egg and avocado and green-onion salad, with crispy tacos, salsa, and a little sprinkling of cilantro."

"Muñoz, my friend, you're hallucinating," retorted the sergeant. "If that's barbecued anything, that's barbecued Goodyear." He took the cigar out of his mouth and tapped the firm fedora-gray ash onto the floor mat. "Somebody's overheated, or blown out a tire. Now, you want to shut that frigging window before we dry-fry?"

Ric rolled up the window. "It sure *smells* like a cookout," he insisted.

Jim Griglak continued to drive at the same monotonous fifty-five, his mountainous shoulders hunched, his huge hands grasping the steering wheel as if he were driving a tiny fairground bumper car. All around them, the scrubby off-white hills of the Anza-Borrego Desert were blinded with heat, hill after undulating hill, with the highway running undeviatingly up and down them like the dusty sloughed-off skin of a huge desert snake.

Up they went, and the next valley came into view. Deserted and baking-hot, just like the valley before it, and the valley before that. The sky was so blue it didn't seem to fit together with the horizon properly, a badly printed jigsaw. Down they went, and the previous valley disappeared from sight.

"This whole barbecue thing is a closed book to me," Jim Griglak sniffed. "I can set fire to my food any time I feel like it, no trouble. All it takes is a can of unleaded and a match. Who needs mesquite wood at seven bucks a sack and a fifteen-dollar apron with a picture of a whore's underwear on it?"

"It's not just a question of heat and meat," Ric insisted. "It's all in the marinades. You should try chili and tomato with your chicken, teriyaki with your pork. Maybe some lime and yogurt with your lamb."

Jim Griglak shook his head, and sucked hard at his cigar, which had decided out of sheer cheapness to extinguish itself. "Muñoz," he said, "you watch too many of these faggy cookery shows. You should've come to Norm Fox's barbecue last year. Norm was up to his Bermudas in fancy marinades, but what did we get? Coalburgers, chicken à la coal, shrimp coaletti, coalfurters. Barbecue? That was a frigging cremation."

Ric didn't let Jim Griglak upset him. Jim was huge—six feet, three inches in his conspicuously self-darned socks and probably well over 270 pounds if his bathroom scale had been able to protest out loud. He was country-freckled and slow and wise, and just a little sad, but he was one of the best sergeants that Ric had ever worked with. Ric had seen him shoot an armed crack dealer between the eyes so quick that it was all over before Ric had even unholstered his .357, and another time he had seen him pursuing a fleeing wetback through a bean field with all the speed and majesty of a charging rhino. The Mexican himself had stopped running just to watch the spectacle of Jim Griglak thundering toward him, a whole lifetime of Pabst Blue Ribbons and bacon cheeseburgers in undulating motion.

Ric was well aware that—in return—Jim considered him to

be an irredeemable wimp—a law-enforcing yuppie. He was one of the new generation of well-groomed, career-conscious Highway Patrol officers who always wore Reynolds Engineering sunglasses and drank Carta Blanca beer and went to "Space in Time" at La Jolla to have their hair cut and their little Magnum mustaches trimmed. In spite of that, Ric and Jim maintained a cautious truce between them; a truce that occasionally flirted with genuine affection. There was, after all, no real contest between them. By the time Ric came up for senior promotion, Jim would have handed in his badge and hung up his gun, and retired to his two-bedroomed chalet in the Cuyamaca forest, just him and his shaggy crossbreed dog Akron and his pale moonlike belly and the real moon and miles of fragrant manzanita.

Ric said, "You know something, Sergeant? You should come round to my place. I'll show you how to barbecue. It's something in the blood, you know what I mean? No Yankee ever knew how to barbecue."

"This smoke's goddamn thick," Jim interrupted him. "Goddamn what d'you call it?" He flapped his hand, trying to think of the word. "*Pungent.*" He was a halting but devoted reader of *It Pays to Increase Your Word Power.*

"Well, that's the whole key to a successful barbecue," Ric told him. "You have to keep on spraying the mesquite with—"

He stopped as abruptly as a switched-off radio. They had topped another rise, and ahead of them lay just another valley, glaring and dusty. But two or three hundred feet north of the highway, among the thorn and the scrub and the prickly pear, smoked the blackened skeleton of a burned-out bus.

"Holy Cremona," Jim breathed. He didn't have to say "There's people in it," because they had both seen them the instant they crested the rise. Burned people, maybe a dozen of them, maybe more. And for the past three miles, they had been bantering about hamburgers and ribs and chicken kebabs. Because of the smell. Because of these people, burning.

"Oh, Mary, mother of God," whispered Ric. "Don't let this be."

As they descended the hill, they could see that the rib-cage structure of the bus was still blossoming with tiny orange flames, almost as if it had been decorated with marigolds, and that its tires were still thickly smoldering.

The hot afternoon wind was blowing from the southwest, and it was hanging out the ragged brown smoke all across the valley.

"Oh, Mary, mother of God," Ric repeated. "Don't let this be."

Jim picked up his transmitter and said matter-of-factly, as if he were ordering dinner at a Korean takeout, "One-four-six, this is one-four-six. Doris, this is Jim Griglak. I have a multiple traffic fatality here on Highway Seventy-eight, just about fifteen miles due east of Borrego Springs. I'm going to need choppers and fire trucks and ambulances, make that at least ten ambulances, repeat ten; we have a considerable number of casualties here; and backup. I'll get back to you, okay?"

"Don't let this be," Ric whispered, more to the Holy Virgin than to Jim, as the patrol car jounced off the highway and sped across the scrub toward the burned-out bus, a plume of dust rising high behind it.

"It *be,* all right," Jim assured him. He took a last suck on his extinguished cigar, and then tossed the butt out of the window. Fire department regulations forbade smoking at the scene of a blaze. "You can pray all you like, Muñoz, but it frigging well be."

They swerved to a halt about thirty feet away from the bus, and climbed out. Ric wrestled out the fire extinguisher, but Jim called across the roof of the car, "Forget it, Muñoz. They're all dead. Better to leave everything the way it is."

Ric nodded, and gave him an oddly clogged-up "Sure," and obediently replaced the fire extinguisher. He took off his sunglasses and followed Jim closer to the bus, glancing at it with hesitant up-and-down motions of his head, and swallowing, desperately wanting not to look, but knowing that he had to. He didn't know how Jim managed to stay so goddamn calm. Ric had been with the California Highway Patrol for six-and-a-half years, and like all patrolmen he had seen some shockers. Bloody and scarcely recognizable children, jet-propelled through car windshields because their parents hadn't bothered to buckle them up. Irrationally cheerful men, crushed flat as cardboard from the chest down, still joking and asking for a smoke. Women lying in the road screaming, unable to get up, because they had both of their arms torn off.

He had seen people trapped behind brown smoked-up windows, burning alive, pleading with him, screaming at him, "Save me! Save me!" but unreachable because of the heat. But he had never seen anything like this.

Maybe it was the silence that affected him so much. Usually there were sirens and traffic and people shouting. Out here in the desert there was nothing but the warm soft fluffing of the breeze and the *ping-tikk-pinging* of slowly cooling metal. Occasionally one of the tires flared up, but for the most part the fire was out now.

Maybe it was the dense charred-pork smell of burned human flesh. It saturated the air, so that every breath he took was greasy with it. *Oh Christ,* he thought to himself, *I'm breathing in dead people. I'm actually breathing them in.*

It looked like a regular bus, a ten-wheeler GMC. Most of its paint was burned off and what was left of its aluminum bodywork was darkly discolored, but Ric could make out the words *Balboa Hi-Way Bus Rental* in brownish-red letters on the side.

The blackened driver was still sitting in his seat; still grasping his carbonized steering wheel. A rough head-count came up with twelve more passengers, men and women. They were all dead, no doubt about it, although the fire had charred them unevenly. Those sitting on the left-hand side of the bus were burned into tiny crispy monkeys, their teeth grinning brown through their black flaking skin, their little fists raised in front of them as if they had all been drumming, but their drumsticks had been suddenly confiscated.

Those sitting on the right-hand side, particularly those at the back, had been less devastatingly charred, and one Hispanic woman about twenty-four years old looked almost untouched at first. It was only when Ric walked around the back of the bus that he saw that her black hair was all burned off down one side of her head, and her pretty floral-pink sundress had been incinerated from her left knee to her left shoulder. He could see her scorched white panties and it made him feel like a ghoul.

Ric and Jim met each other on the far side of the bus. Ric took out his handkerchief, folded it into a triangle, and pressed it against his nose and mouth.

"Some cookout, hunh?" asked Jim, although he was far from laughing.

"What the hell do you think *happened* here?" Ric asked him, unsteadily. "You think maybe the gas tank exploded, something like that?"

Jim grunted and hunkered down, and examined the underside of the bus. "No *signs* of explosion. Nothing's ripped apart, no distortion. Gas tank's intact; luggage is burned but not blown apart. This baby just caught fire and that was that."

He stood up, and wiped the perspiration from his forehead

with his fat gingery arm. "It can happen, I guess, especially with fuel injection. But you don't often see it with diesel."

He squinted at the tire tracks that the bus had left in the dust between here and the highway. "No signs of any other vehicle involved. The driver headed straight here, no swerving, no skids. It's hard to say for sure, but it doesn't look like he was panicking none."

"His whole goddamn bus was on fire and he wasn't panicking? It doesn't make sense."

Jim reached into his shirt pocket and took out a roll of wintergreen Lifesavers. He offered one to Ric but Ric shook his head. "*Nobody* was panicking," he observed, tucking a Lifesaver into his cheek. "Look at them; they're all sitting in their seats, no heaps of bodies next to the door, nobody anywhere near the emergency exits."

Ric walked back along the side of the bus and stared up at the girl in the floral pink sundress. The unburned side of her face was Spanish-looking and remarkably pretty, and her right eye was open and staring at him, or just past him, anyway. The extraordinary thing was that she looked like she was smiling. She looked *happy*.

You, young lady, you're a goddamn conundrum, you are, thought Ric. *How can you smile when your legs are on fire? I mean, Jesus—how much that must have* hurt.

Jim came up and stood beside him and stared at the girl, too.

"She's smiling," said Ric, with a nervous laugh.

"Naw," Jim's Lifesaver rattled between his teeth. "It's the heat, shrinks the facial muscles, same way a steak curls up. Saw a guy burning in a truck once, trapped, couldn't get out. Looked like he was laughing his head off. I felt like calling out, 'What's the frigging joke?' "

They walked back to the patrol car. Ric glanced back once or twice, and the girl was still staring at him with that single expressionless prune-brown eye.

Jim reached into the car and lifted out the transmitter. "Doris? Jim Griglak. Listen, tell the coroner we got thirteen of them. That's right, a baker's dozen. Yeah, that's right, baked pretty good, too."

There was nothing else for them to do but wait. They stood leaning against their patrol car in the wavering afternoon heat, watching the bus tires burn themselves down to criss-cross hoops of radial-ply steel, and the last few flames around the body framework gutter out. In the distance, from the west, they heard the echoing *flacker-flacker-flacker* of approaching helicopters.

"You know what we've got ourselves here, don't you, Ric?" asked Jim, lifting his bulk away from the car. Jim had never called him Ric before.

Ric shook his head, conscious that Jim was going to tell him something serious.

"We've got ourselves a massacre, that's what we got."

"You think this was *deliberate?*"

"Come on, Mũnoz, use your gray matter. This was no traffic accident, for Chrissake. You don't have to be Sherlock Holmes to see that. This is a massacre. A crack massacre, or a sect massacre, or maybe both. Santaria maybe. You know the kind of thing. Candles and beads and plaster madonnas and sacrificed chickens, and the kids with the Uzis will get you if the voodoo dolls don't. Whoever it was, they were seriously less-than-amiable."

He shook his head in exasperation. "What I can't understand is why they all look so frigging happy about it."

"It sure seems kind of unusual," Ric agreed.

"Unusual? I'd call it frigging unreal. I mean, think about it. A busload of people get themselves driven out to the desert. Very nice, very scenic. Then they get burned to death with happy smiles on their faces and without making the *slightest* attempt to escape. That, my friend, is what I personally define as a problem I could do without."

They were still waiting for the first helicopters to come into sight when Ric noticed something shifting at the top of the ridge, something tawny brown, maybe a dog or a coyote. He nodded to Jim Griglak and said, "Did you see that?"

Jim Griglak shaded his eyes with his hand.

"I can't see nothing."

"Top of the ridge—there, to the left."

They glimpsed what looked like a shoulder, then an arm. "Goddamn it, there's somebody up there!" Jim Griglak exclaimed; and then yelled out, "Hey! Hey up there! You come on down here! Do you hear me? You come right down here!"

A dark head bobbed just above the horizon, then ducked away.

"Goddamn it," Jim cursed. "Goddamn it to hell." He hitched up his gunbelt, and began to trundle around the burned-out bus and up the slope. Ric started after him, but without turning his head, Jim waved him away. "You stay there . . . guard the bus. I'll get this bastard."

Ric watched him as he scaled the dusty, heat-dazzled rocks. His arms pumped, his pants flapped, his saddlebags bounced with every stride, but he clambered up to the top of the ridge with awesome agility, and disappeared from view.

Ric turned his head. He could see the first helicopter now, its canopy reflecting a sharp star of sunlight as it came skimming low and fast over the desert hills.

Ric blinked and grimaced and looked around in deep uncertainty.

The helicopter was landing now, and lashing up smoke and dust and fragments of blackened fabric. The hair of the half-burned Hispanic girl flew up over her head like a fright wig. She seemed to be laughing. A blizzard of ash suddenly burst from the bus driver's face, and was swept away in the downdraft.

As the helicopter's rotors were whip-whistling to a standstill, Jim reappeared on the crest of the ridge. At first he looked as if he were alone, but when he moved aside, Ric saw that he was prodding in front of him an Indian boy of about twelve. The boy came down the slope crabwise, clutching at the rocks. He had long greasy black hair, circular granny Ray-Bans and a red bandana around his forehead. He was dressed in a grubby Elvis Presley T-shirt and yellow and purple Bermudas.

"Hey, Sergeant!" called Ric.

"Yeah, look what I found," Jim called back. He nudged the boy down the slope and around the wreck of the bus.

Two lean young Highway Patrol officers climbed out of the helicopter and came walking slowly across toward them, staring at the bus in disbelief.

"Jesus," said one of them, wiping the sweat from his face with his neckscarf. "What the hell happened here?"

"I was hoping Geronimo here might be able to tell us," Jim replied. "What's your name, son? Were you here when this bus went up?"

The boy said, "Sure, man, I was here." He kept nodding, and turning his head around as if he were high.

"Did you see what happened?"

"No way, man. Didn't see nothing."

"The bus was burning and you were here and you didn't see nothing?"

"That's what I said, man."

Jim said harshly, "Will you stop calling me 'man,' for Chrissake."

"Sorry, man."

"What's your name, son?"

"Tony." Again that odd distracted head-nodding.

"Tony who?"

"Tony Express."

"*Tony Express?* Who the hell are you trying to kid?"

"I'm not trying to kid nobody, man. That's what everybody calls me. I guess it's kind of a joke. My Indian name is Child-Who-Looked-at-the-Sun."

"Child-Who-Looked-at-the-Sun, hey?" asked Ric. "That's some kind of fancy name."

Jim said, "Where do you live, Tony? And what the hell are you doing out here in any case?"

"I live here, man," Tony told him. "Well, just back over the ridge a ways. My pa runs that Indian souvenir stand next to the Seventy-six gas station."

"And you were here when the bus burned?" asked one of the helicopter patrolmen, vigorously chewing sugar-free gum.

Tony nodded. "Sure. I was right on top of the ridge."

"So how come you didn't see nothing?" asked the patrolman.

Tony took off his Ray-Bans. Underneath, his eyes were milky and swiveling, and blind as marbles. "I was born this way, man," he explained. "Child-Who-Looked-at-the-Sun, get it?"

"Oh, shit," swore Jim Griglak. He stood with his fists on his hips and shook his head over and over as if he were never going to stop. "For Chrissake. The luck of the frigging Griglaks."

Ric said, "Tony, listen, even if you couldn't see anything, maybe you *heard* something? Voices, footsteps? Anything at all?"

"Come on, Mũnoz, what's the frigging use?" Jim demanded.

"Hey, come on," Ric told him. "Blind people are supposed to have this really acute sense of hearing. Like they can hear dog whistles and stuff."

"Man, I didn't hear no dog whistles, man," Tony replied. He replaced his Ray-Bans and stood scratching the dry skin on his elbows and staring at nothing at all.

"What did I tell you?" Jim complained. "The luck of the frigging Griglaks."

Two more helicopters were circling, and it was hard to hear what anybody was saying. But Tony suddenly said, "I heard the bus leaving the road, and coming this way. And I heard somebody talking, too."

"You heard somebody talking? What did they say?"

"I was way back in the rocks, there. I couldn't hear too good."

"Was it a man or a woman?" asked Ric.

"It was a guy. He sounded old, man, know what I mean? Kind of croaky. He was talking but I couldn't understand what he was saying."

"You didn't catch anything at all?" asked Ric, raising his voice above the flackering of helicopters.

Tony said, "Unh-unh. Only one thing, maybe. He kept saying 'You knew us.' Real loud. 'You knew us.' "

" 'You knew us'? Any idea what he meant?"

"I don't know, man. Some old guy stands in the desert saying 'You knew us,' how am I supposed to know what he means?"

"Was this before or after the bus burned?" asked the gum-chewing patrolman.

"It was before, and it was during, too. Like, while it was burning, he kept saying it. 'You knew us.' "

"How come he didn't see you, this old guy?" Jim wanted to know.

"I was in the rocks, man, way back there, over there. My pa wanted me to mind the store, see, but I didn't want to mind the store, so I came out to listen to my Walkman, man, and have a smoke. When I first heard the bus, I thought maybe I should come out. Sometimes the marks give you money to have your picture took."

"But you didn't come out?" Ric asked him.

Tony Express hesitated. Then he said, "No."

"Why?" Ric coaxed him. "Was it something you heard? Something somebody said?"

"I don't know, man. I just had this weird feeling that something weird was going down."

"Jesus, the frigging articulate youth of today," said Jim. Then, "Okay, Tony, that'll do it for now. Somebody'll want to talk to you later. You live right by the gas station, that it?"

"Indian Jack's Genuine Pechanga Souvenirs."

"Sure, made in Taiwan."

"You need any help getting back?" asked Ric.

Tony Express shook his head. "I may be blind, man, but I'm not stupid."

"I bet you fall ass over tit down the first arroyo you come to," Jim Griglak retaliated.

But they all knew that he wouldn't. They watched him climb without hesitation back up the ridge again, and disappear from sight. A weaving black silhouette; then nothing but ink-blue sky.

"Look at him go," said one of the patrolmen, impressed. "He's *blind*, and look at him go."

"They're all the same," Jim answered, aggressively. "The deaf and the dumb, the blind and the lame. They all think they're God's gift. If only they knew what a pain in the ass they really are."

The Highway Patrol officers exchanged a quick, encyclopedic glance. Everybody on the force knew that Jim Griglak was awkward and prejudiced and mean as a sackful of polecats. They also knew that it wasn't worth arguing with him; not unless you wanted months and months of aggression and sarcasm and practical jokes. He was a paradox, but maybe you had to be a paradox to be a really good policeman. Maybe a mild variety of fascism was one of the basic requirements for the job.

One of patrolmen turned around to the burned-out bus and said, "So what do you think went down here, Jim? You have to admit that it's pretty weird."

"How the hell should I know what happened?" Jim snapped at him. "But something sure stinks around here, and it ain't just these human hamburgers."

They shuffled their boots in the white uncompromising Anza-Borrego dust, and waited for the far-off scribbling of sirens.

5

At almost the same moment that the first Highway Patrol helicopter landed next to the burned-out bus, Lloyd stepped out of the morgue at San Diego police headquarters. He turned momentarily toward his BMW, parked alongside three blue and white patrol cars with To Serve and Protect emblazoned on their doors, but decided against it. He was too shaken to think about driving. He had to walk. Under a furnace-blue sky, he crossed the street, and started treading his way northward along the Embarcadero, his shirt sticking to his back, his eyes stung with sweat and tears.

He had never seen a dead body before. Not even a peaceful, unmarked, cosmetically prepared dead body. Celia's had been horrendous, blackened and reeking of gasoline, raw. Her tendons had been tightened by the heat of her immolation, and she had been crouched in her gray-green body bag like some terrible huge incinerated embryo. But he had known as soon as the zipper began to slide down that it was her. He had recognized her; he had recognized her. He had nodded desperately, swallowed, turned away, blinked back tears, while his mouth had suddenly filled up with hot orange juice, regurgitated from breakfast. Sergeant Houk had taken him by the elbow and steered him out into the corridor.

"I just want you to know that we're all real sorry about this, Mr. Denman."

Lloyd had been unable to speak. *Sorry?* How could a word like *sorry* apply to such a horrific invasion on his whole existence: his happiness, his sanity, everything that he had invested in the future? He felt as if all he could do was to walk and walk and walk under the grilling midmorning sun, until he finally collapsed from exhaustion and grief, and lay on the ground, where he wouldn't have to focus on anything larger than a few grains of dirt.

As usual on a summer's morning, the harborside was crowded with sightseers. Lloyd walked through them as if he were a half-drowned man walking up a beach. He jarred his shoulder against a fat woman in a pink T-shirt emblazoned with a cartoon drawing of three macho surfers and the legend San Diego—No Wimps. "Well, pardon *me,*" she snarled at him.

He passed the dark wooden hull of the *Star of India,* one of the historic old sailing ships moored along the Embarcadero. There was a strong aroma on the breeze of old timber and coconut Coppertone and cotton candy. He sidestepped a crowd of Japanese tourists who were clustered around the gangplank, endlessly taking each other's photographs. It was then that he heard somebody calling his name.

Lloyd! Lloyd! A voice as small as a hornet in a sealed glass jar. Tiny, desperate.

He looked around him, then up at the sides of the ship. Tourists filed around the upper decks, talking and pointing and staring around them in a way that suddenly struck Lloyd as particularly odd; as if they were expecting something momentous to appear. But what? A magnetic storm? A sea serpent? A flying saucer from outer space?

There was a strange tightness in the air. He couldn't understand it. Maybe it was just him. He was reminded of the atmosphere in those 1950s science-fiction movies, *Them* and *This Island Earth.*

He was about to start walking again along the Embarcadero when he glimpsed a girl high up on deck, close to the *Star of India*'s bow. She was wearing a yellow silk headscarf and dark upswept sunglasses, and a black raincoat with the collar turned up. Lloyd's attention wasn't only caught by the incongruity of the girl's clothing, on a hot day in June. There was something else, too. Something disturbingly familiar about her. Something in the way she turned her head that reminded him of Celia.

He hesitated. Of course it couldn't be Celia. He had just seen Celia lying raw-burned-dead in the San Diego police morgue. But at the same time he couldn't walk away without taking a closer look at her. Just to make absolutely sure.

Absolutely sure of what, Lloyd? That you're not hallucinat-

ing? That you're not going out of your mind? Or absolutely sure that things couldn't conceivably be different; that life couldn't possibly have different endings, different manifestations, different destinies?

He remembered his grandfather telling him after his grandmother's funeral, "It isn't the dead that haunt the world; it's the people they leave behind."

Apologetically shoving his way through the crowds, he made his way up the *Star of India*'s gangplank. He paid for a tour and waited impatiently while a simulated salt in a Popeye's-pappy hat gave him a ticket and told him to have a good day. "And don't forget to look at the whaling exhibition. Harpoons and scrimshaw."

Scrimshaw. That was it—scrimshaw! Why the hell hadn't he thought of it before? He hurried forward, through light and shade, through the criss-cross pattern of rigging.

The foredeck was deserted, except for a family of father, mother, and daughter, all wearing mirror sunglasses. They turned away from the rail and stared at Lloyd as he approached them, and Lloyd saw himself cross to the other side of the deck six times over, in miniature, in their bright and meaningless lenses.

He returned to the shadows. A sandy-haired man passed him by, telling his wife, "It's no damn good, you know. It never was any damn good and it never will be any damn good."

Ahead of him, around the side of the *Star of India*'s wheelhouse, he thought he glimpsed the skirts of a white raincoat. He pushed his way more urgently along the crowded deck. The planking echoed under his white leather-soled Gucci loafers.

Lloyd, he heard her whisper. *Lloyd*. Or maybe it was nothing but the kerfuffle of wind in the rigging, or the slap of water on the hull of a passing motorboat, or a gull mewling as it turned its feathers to the morning sun.

He searched twice around the upper deck, but the girl in the yellow silk headscarf was gone. He hesitated for a while, looking this way and that, biting his lip. Then he went slowly down the companionway to the lower deck, where it was gloomier and cooler. In illuminated glass cabinets, charts and knots and compasses were neatly displayed, along with antique carvings and scrimshaw. The lower deck was almost as crowded as the upper, and Lloyd had to edge his way through the tourists with a repetitious litany of "Pardon me, thank you; pardon me, thank you," until he reached the souvenir counter.

There he stopped, and stretched himself up so that he could

see better, and meticulously scanned everybody around him. The girl behind the counter watched him for a while. She was freckled and blond, with a striped nautical-style T-shirt and a peaked cap with a gilt *Star of India* badge.

"May I help you, sir?" she asked him.

He turned around. "I was looking for a girl."

"Any special girl or will any girl do?"

Lloyd was too abstracted to understand. "She was wearing a white raincoat and a headscarf and dark glasses."

The girl behind the counter widened her eyes. "She was wearing a *raincoat?*"

Lloyd kept on looking around. "A white raincoat and a yellow headscarf."

The girl watched him for a little longer. "You sure you're okay?"

"I'm fine; I'm okay."

"Well, if you don't mind my saying so, you look pretty upset."

Lloyd frowned at her. He didn't quite know what to say. "Look," he said, reaching into his back pants pocket, and taking out his billfold, "here's my card . . . if you ever see a girl looking like that . . . if she buys anything here . . . maybe you could let me know. Maybe note down her name from her credit card." The girl shrugged, then nodded.

At that instant, however, Lloyd thought he saw that yellow headscarf; a flicker as bright and as fleeting as a gale-blown sunflower behind a yard fence. Immediately he pushed his way through the crowds around the souvenir counter, and made for the exit.

Damn it, there she is again! That scarf, that raincoat, halfway down the ramp!

He struggled past the huge hard unyielding belly of a black Marine; then found himself scrambling through a bespectacled and camera-jostling crowd of chattering Japanese. He had almost made the top of the gangplank when a frail old woman in a straw hat and a flowery dress stepped out in front of him, her sun-measled hand reaching for the rail and obstructing his pursuit as effectively as a three-car roadblock. He was powerless to do anything but follow behind her as she made her slow and painful progress down the gangplank, and the girl who had looked so much like Celia disappeared into the throng of tourists on the Embarcadero below.

He thought he had lost her completely. But then he glimpsed that sunflower scarf flashing through the crowd. She had reached the curb, and was just about to cross the road.

"Celia!" he yelled at her. "Celia!" Even though it *couldn't* be Celia; even though all of this running after her was total madness. It was nothing but exhaustion, and hysteria, and devastating grief.

But just before she crossed the street, she turned, and stared at him, and even though she was wearing those black upswept sunglasses he was *convinced* with a shiver that stopped him right where he was, unable to remember how to run, unable to remember how his ankles worked. He was convinced that she was Celia.

"Celia," he said, out loud. People bumped and jostled against him, laughing, as if they were all in on the joke and he wasn't. "*Celia!*" he shouted, so loudly that he stunned himself. Faces turned; somebody said, "What, is he crazy or something?" Then he was quarterbacking across the sidewalk, colliding, bumping; and all the time that flicker of yellow danced in front of him, just out of reach.

He started to cross the street, but stepped right in front of a Federal Express van, which bucked to a halt, both sliding doors slamming shut. Its black driver indignantly blared the horn at him.

"What the hell are you trying to do, asshole, meet your goddamn maker?"

Lloyd lifted both hands in apology. The van drove off; but by the time it had passed in front of him, there was no sign of that tantalizing glimpse of yellow. He searched quickly left and right, taking two steps hesitantly forward when he caught sight of a dancing lick of yellow amidst the crowds. But the dancing lick of yellow turned out to be a child's balloon, and the woman in the raincoat was gone.

He felt as if he could drop to his knees on the sidewalk, struck deaf and dumb by sheer illogicality. He was so sure that the woman in the raincoat had been Celia. But how could it be, when Celia was dead and burned in the San Diego police morgue?

He was still standing on the curb when a dusty saddle-brown Riviera drew up in front of him, and parked. Sergeant Houk climbed out, wearing a sweaty-looking drip-dry shirt and a narrow brown necktie.

"Mr. Denman? I was hoping I'd catch up with you. Don't forget that fancy automobile of yours. Our captain's been giving it the eye all morning. Reckons it's his kind of car."

Lloyd unhooked his sunglasses. "I'm sorry. I was going right back to pick it up. I just had to take a walk, that's all. Breath of fresh air."

"Sure, I understand," said Sergeant Houk, sniffing. "What you had to do today—well, I wouldn't ever try to pretend that there's anything easy about it."

Lloyd said, "You know something . . . Celia loved life so much. She enjoyed everything she did, from morning till night. She was so damned *happy*. I can't think of one single reason why she should have—"

Sergeant Houk sniffed again, and looked around him. "There's no grass here; no pollen. I'm seriously beginning to think that I must be allergic to tourists."

Lloyd said, "I called the Miyako. She never even checked in. So far as I can make out, the lecture series was all a lie."

"We know that," Sergeant Houk nodded. "What we don't yet know is when she came back to San Diego from San Francisco; and how; and why. She didn't use the return half of her airline ticket, we know that much."

He squinted at Lloyd against the sunshine. "You'll pardon me for asking—maybe it's a bad time—but she wouldn't have had any close men-friends? What I mean is, apart from you?"

Lloyd shook his head, and let out a funny blurting noise that was nearly a laugh. "No," he mouthed. "She didn't have any close men-friends. That's if you mean by close what I *think* you mean by close."

"How about you? Did you have any extracurricular friendships? Anything which might have upset her? You see, you'll forgive me for asking, but these self-immolations, they're almost invariably motivated either by wacky political grievances, like the U.S. invasion of Outer Weirdolia, or saving the purple-spotted parakeet; or else they're about personal relationships."

He paused, and cleared his throat, and then he said, "People who torch themselves . . . well, I've seen people on fire, and that ain't the way that *I* want to go. No, sir. But I was talking to our psychologist this morning and she was saying that they do it to kind of *purify* themselves. Almost like they're disinfecting themselves of all the infections they think the rest of us are crawling with."

"I'm not too sure I understand that," Lloyd admitted, although he was only half-listening.

"Well, I wanted you to think about it, Mr. Denman, because any kind of clue to your fiancée's state of mind could possibly be helpful."

"All right, I'll try to think of something."

Sergeant Houk gave him an unshaved, cavernous grin. "How about a ride back to headquarters? I just had my air-conditioning fixed. It's like sitting in a goddamn igloo."

Numbly, Lloyd accepted his invitation. Inside, Sergeant Houk's car smelled of pine air freshener and stale cigarettes, and there was a sticker on the dash that said No Farting Zone. The rubbery beige upholstery was penetrated with dozens of cigarette burns. A naked plastic doll with scarlet-painted nipples swung from the rearview mirror: a souvenir from Tijuana. Sergeant Houk thrust his arm out of the window and illegally U-turned on squittering tires.

He was right about the air-conditioning. The interior of the Riviera was penetratingly cold: cold as the morgue in which Celia's body had been rolled out in front of him. So cold that Lloyd began to tremble.

Sergeant Houk drove with his wrist draped casually on top of the steering wheel. "It's a funny thing, with suicides. Most of the time they leave a note. But even if they don't, the nearest and dearest almost always come up with the answer. Once that first shock has worn off, they start to think about their loved ones the way they really were, and they start to *analyze*. And suddenly, *bingo!* They understand what happened, and why. At the beginning, though, it's pretty hard to accept that somebody you were in love with didn't love you enough to want to stay around. I mean, not even in the *world*. Packing your bags and going home to Momma is one thing. Setting fire to yourself, well, that's something else altogether."

"Yes, it is," Lloyd agreed, dully.

They drove for a minute or two without talking. Then Sergeant Houk started to say, "In my view, you know—" when he was interrupted by his radio.

"Three-niner, three-niner."

He picked up his handset, which had been lying loose on the seat, under an untidy loose heap of newspapers and Snickers wrappers and folded-up warrants. "Three-niner, gotcha."

There was a crackle as somebody else was patched through.

Then, "Dave? Lieutenant Pratt. Listen, we just received an urgent bulletin from the state police out in the Anza-Borrego Desert State Park."

"Oh, yeah?" asked Sergeant Houk. "What are they squawking about now?"

"Two Highway Patrol officers located a burned-out bus, about a half-hour ago, fifteen miles east of Borrego Springs."

Sergeant Houk didn't reply, but turned to Lloyd, and said, "This is typical, you know? A burned-out bus in the middle of the desert, and they're telling *me*? You can bet your ass to a beef burrito this is going to turn out to be some chore so menial you wouldn't let your dog do it."

Almost as if he could hear him, Lieutenant Pratt said, "The state police have requested assistance in checking the bus rental company. Balboa Hi-Way Bus Rental, 2339 Mark Street."

"I know them," replied Sergeant Houk, dispassionately. "Run by a guy called Dan Browder. Just opposite the Playa Hotel."

"They're also asking for assistance in checking the identities of the casualties."

"Casualties? How many casualties?"

"Thirteen. No survivors."

"Thirteen? Jesus."

There was a long pause. They waited at a Ped Xing sign while a long crocodile of chattering Mexican children crossed in front of them. Sergeant Houk sniffed, then sneezed. "What did I tell you? Tourists! I'm allergic."

The voice on the radio said, "Sergeant? Are you still there?"

"Still here, Lieutenant."

"I want you to check out the bus rental; then I want you to drive out to Borrego Springs and liaise with the Highway Patrol and the state police and see what you can do to assist. Ask for a Sergeant Jim Griglak."

Sergeant Houk sniffed. "Can't you get Rollins to do it? I'm up to my duff."

Lieutenant Pratt ignored him. "Dave, I want us to keep in touch with this one. We haven't had the full details yet, but there are two possible explanations for what happened here, and both of them are potentially explosive. All the casualties were burned alive, and the first indications are that it wasn't an accident. Either this was a crack massacre, some kind of major revenge killing, Colombia comes to Southern California. But judging from the way the bodies were found, there's an even stronger possibility that it could have been a mass suicide."

"Hey, come on, Lieutenant," Sergeant Houk replied, shaking his head in disbelief. "A massacre I can swallow. But thirteen people torch themselves *deliberately?*"

"I'm not sure, Sergeant. As of now that's all we know. They were all burned to death and the circumstances seem to point to the probability that we're dealing with mass homicide or mass suicide. I'll give more information as and when."

"Okay, I'm coming in now anyway."

Sergeant Houk tossed the handset back onto the seat. "Jesus. How about a chorus of 'I Don't Want to Set the World on Fire?' "

He looked across at Lloyd and suddenly realized what he had said. "I'm sorry. That was very tasteless. I'm sorry. I apologize."

Lloyd's mouth was dry, and he was shaking with cold and tiredness. "Do you think there might be some connection?"

"What do you mean?"

"Do you think there might be some connection between Celia's death and these people on the bus?"

Sergeant Houk wiped his nose with a tiny screwed-up Kleenex. "I'll tell you something, Mr. Denman. From now on, every time you switch on your TV or every time you pick up a newspaper you're going to see a report about somebody burning themselves to death. It's happening all the time; it's just that you didn't notice it before. There's a certain type of suicide who feels that burning themselves to death is the way they have to do it. Who really knows why? There's no connection. It's happening all the time."

He turned into police headquarters and parked at an angle next to the steps. "About six weeks ago, I investigated a suicide that was exactly similar to your fiancée's, out in Florida Canyon. Red gasoline can, everything the same. The only difference was that nobody got to *that* suicide with a fire extinguisher. There was nothing left but ashes, believe me. It took us two weeks to identify the victim. A store assistant from Sears. No connection with your fiancée whatsoever, apart from mode of demise."

Lloyd climbed shakily out of the freezing-cold car into the grilling heat of the downtown sun.

"Take it easy," Sergeant Houk told him, leaning across the front seat. "Throw yourself into your work, maybe. A lot of people find that helps."

"Thanks for the tip," Lloyd replied, although Sergeant Houk didn't hear the sarcasm in his voice.

"And if anything occurs to you . . . any conceivable reason why Ms. Williams might have wanted to take her own life . . . even if it was nothing more than premenstrual tension, well, you'll call me, yes?"

"For sure," Lloyd told him.

He crossed the dazzling white parking lot. He was conscious that Sergeant Houk was watching him as he went. He unlocked his BMW and climbed in, and sat for a while with his eyes closed, and repeated the words of Allen Ginsberg's "Kaddish."

"There, rest. No more suffering for you. I know where you've gone, it's good."

He didn't see the girl in the black raincoat standing on the opposite side of Broadway, staring at him, unmoving, her yellow scarf flapping in the warm harbor wind, her upswept sunglasses reflecting two dazzling points of light.

6

When he arrived back at North Torrey, he was surprised and annoyed to find a metallic red Lincoln Continental parked in his driveway. He drew into the curb, climbed out of his BMW, and cautiously approached the Lincoln across the lawn, jingling his car keys in his hand.

As he came closer, he saw that a balding man of about sixty-five was sitting in the driver's seat; and next to him was sitting a white-rinsed woman in a purple and white blouse and more gold necklaces and bangles and brooches than Nefertiti. Lloyd tapped with his knuckle on the window, and both of them beamed at him.

"Hi there! You must be Otto," the white-haired man greeted him, letting down his window. He held out his hand, still beaming.

Lloyd said, "I'm sorry, sir. I think you have the wrong house. This is 3337 North Torrey."

The man frowned and unfolded a pair of heavy-rimmed glasses. He fished a well-folded letter out of his shirt pocket, and examined it closely. "That's right. That's the address I'm looking for, 3337 North Torrey."

"Well, I'm afraid there's no Otto here," Lloyd told him. "Never has been, to my knowledge."

"Oh, I'm sorry," the man answered. "We weren't actually looking for Otto. We were looking for Celia—Celia Williams?"

"You're friends of hers?" asked Lloyd.

The man laughed, and the woman joined in. "You could say

that. Do you happen to know where we might find her? We've driven all the way from San Clemente this morning, and we've been waiting here for almost an hour."

Lloyd rubbed the back of his neck. "I'm afraid I have some pretty bad news for you."

"Don't tell me she's gone off on one of her lecture tours?" said the woman. "Oh, *Wayne* . . . I told you to call first."

"What kind of surprise would it have been if I'd called first?" the man demanded.

"It would have saved us two hours on the freeway, for goodness' sake."

The woman gave Lloyd a fixed grin, and asked, "Do you happen to know if she's going to be away for very long?"

"Ma'am," said Lloyd, and he couldn't stop his throat from tightening, and the tears from prickling his eyes. "I'm sorry to tell you that Celia died yesterday."

The man and the woman stared at him with their mouths open. At last, the man managed to blurt out, "She *died?*"

"How could she *die?*" the woman asked.

Lloyd took out his handkerchief and wiped his eyes. "I'm sorry. There was an accident; she was burned. Nobody really knows what happened."

"Oh my God," said the woman. Her hair was white, her face was white. "Oh my God, tell me it's not true."

The man climbed out of the car and stood next to Lloyd. He was short and bulky-chested and large-headed, but still quite handsome for his age.

"Sir," he said, "I don't even know who you are. It seems like Celia hasn't been giving us the whole picture. I'm sorry."

Lloyd shook his hand. "Lloyd Denman. Celia and I were going to be married. This house here . . . well, we *were* joint owners."

"This is quite a shock," the man replied. "We didn't even know that Celia was seeing anybody, let alone planning to marry. I'm Wayne Williams . . . this is my wife, Vela."

"Do you want to come in?" Lloyd asked them. "I've just been down to the morgue. I could use a drink."

"Thank you," said Wayne. He walked around the car and opened the passenger door so that Vela could climb out. "Burned, you say? How did that happen? Was it an auto accident?"

"Come on inside, and I'll tell you," said Lloyd.

He led them into the house. The two of them jostled against

each other as they looked around the white-painted living room, as if they were out-of-town tourists in a smart La Jolla art gallery.

"The lemon picture," said Vela, suddenly. "That used to be mine, the lemon picture. *Who'll Buy My Lemons?*"

"Please, have a seat," Lloyd told them. "Do you want a drink? Or coffee maybe?"

"Do you have a diet soda of any kind?" asked Wayne.

"Nothing for me, thank you," said Vela.

"Please, sit down," Lloyd insisted, as he walked through to the kitchen, but still they wouldn't sit.

"We'd really like to know what happened," said Wayne.

Lloyd came back with a can of diet 7-Up, popped the top, filled a heavy-bottomed Boda glass, and handed it over to Wayne. Then he poured himself a large Wild Turkey.

"It seems that she took her own life," he said.

"*What?*" said Vela.

"It seems that she committed suicide."

"But *why?* She was so happy! I never knew her so happy! Her career at the opera was going so well . . . she had so many friends. And she was going to be married, which we didn't even know. Why in heaven's name should she commit suicide?"

Lloyd stared at the carpet. "I'm sorry. I don't have any idea."

"She didn't leave a note?" asked Wayne, his voice trembling.

"Nothing. No clues at all. The police have asked me to try and think of some reason why she might have done it, but I can't."

Vela was shaking her head and sobbing, her wrinkled red-fingernailed hands slowly clawing at each other in anguish.

"I can't believe it; I can't believe it. I just can't believe it."

Lloyd said, "Maybe you can think of some reason. You obviously knew her pretty well."

Wayne's crumpled-up expression unfolded like origami in reverse. "Pardon me? Of course we knew her pretty well. I thought you understood. We're her parents."

Lloyd stared at Wayne; then at Vela; and then back at Wayne. "You're her *parents?* Her real parents? She told me that both her parents were dead."

Wayne at last sat down, and laid his arm around Vela's shaking shoulders. "Lloyd," he said, "I don't know what the blazes has been going on here. But whatever it is, I think Vela could use a doctor right now. Her heart's not too good, and this is just about as much shock as she can take."

Lloyd nodded. "I'll call Dr. Meyer. He's one of the university doctors. He can probably come out right away."

"Oh, my darling, my little darling," Vela wept. "Oh, Wayne, what are we going to do?"

Dr. Meyer arrived in his Porsche sunglasses and his golfing shoes and gave Vela a light sedative. "I'll call by tomorrow morning, just to check she's okay," he assured Lloyd, climbing into his gleaming charcoal Seville. "If you want me this afternoon, I'm out at Whispering Palms, playing with Bill Manzo. Ball therapy." He showed his teeth.

Vela slept in the spare bedroom for most of the afternoon. Lloyd and Wayne stayed in the living room and talked.

Most of what Celia had told Lloyd about her life turned out to be true, but there were occasional inexplicable discrepancies, not the least of which was her almost fanatical interest in religion and life after death. She had never spoken to Lloyd about religion, and when he had asked her if she believed in God, she had laughed and answered, "Whose God? Not mine, my darling!"

Since Vela was far too shocked and distraught to be driven back to San Clemente that night, Wayne graduated from diet 7-Up to Four Roses. He lit a cigar, too, and took off his shoes. Usually, Lloyd found cigar smoke offensive, not to mention old men's sport socks, but that night he didn't object at all. At least he wouldn't have to spend the evening there in the house alone, with nobody for company but Celia's haunting, incommunicative photograph.

Wayne said, "Celia started getting serious about religion when her grandma died. That was when Celia was . . . oh, I don't know, fifteen or sixteen. Sixteen I think. She adored her grandma. They were so close, those two, such affection, such understanding. Peas in a pod. Vela used to be jealous sometimes, although there was never any need. But Celia was hit real hard when her grandma finally went. I don't think that she could believe it, you know? She used to say, 'Why couldn't grandma live forever?' She said that over and over, and she used to say, 'I'm going to live forever. I'm going to live forever and ever.' I used to tease her about it, she said it so often. But she always sounded totally serious, wouldn't be teased. I used to call her the Immortal Celia; or the Everlasting Girl. She used to smile and say nothing."

He paused, and lowered his head. Then he took a large swallow of whiskey, and mouthwashed it around his teeth. "That's why it's so hard to believe that she could have taken her own life."

Lloyd suggested, "I guess she could have come to believe that death is a way of living forever. You know . . . 'They shall grow not old, as we who are left grow old.' "

Wayne set down his empty glass. "I don't know. It doesn't make any kind of sense at all. Particularly the way she told you that she didn't have any parents. I mean—she was going to *marry* you and not invite us?"

"I don't know, Mr. Williams. I can't figure it out."

They sat in depressed silence for five or ten minutes, and then Lloyd asked, "You said that she was obsessed with religion. She never mentioned religion to me. Not that kind of religion. We discussed God. We talked about our faith—how we were going to bring our kids up, that kind of thing. But that was all. There wasn't anything unusual about it, nothing to raise your eyebrows about. Do you happen to know what *kind* of religion? She wasn't in with a cult or anything, was she? Like the Moonies, maybe? Or the Bhagwan?"

Wayne made a face. "I'm not sure. She started off at the Episcopalian church at San Clemente. She went to Bible meetings and church socials and all that kind of thing. Then about three months after they gave her a place with the San Diego Opera, she met this guy Otto—the guy I thought was you. She always talked about Otto like the sun shone out of his—well, like she thought a whole lot of him, you know? Otto had this group that was all into communicating with the world beyond, all that crap, if you'll excuse my French."

"Oh, sure." Lloyd got up and poured both of them another large drink. "You don't happen to know the name of this group? Where they hang out? What they're into?"

Wayne shook his head. "All Celia ever talked about was how much she enjoyed the group, the group was brilliant, and Otto was brilliant, she thought Otto was wonderful. God, practically."

"You never met Otto?"

"We only came down to see the opera once. Personally I can take it or leave it, opera. I don't know where Celia got her interest from. Especially that goddamn Wagner. After she met Otto, it was Wagner this and Wagner that, and when she came home weekends she played this real loud heavy stuff with screaming women. I used to take the dog for a walk. That Wagner music,

Jesus. It sounded like somebody dropping an A-bomb on an afternoon session of Weight Watchers."

Wayne paused, cleared his throat, and then said, "Barbershop, that's more my style. 'In the Good Old Summertime.' " There were tears in his eyes.

Lloyd sank back into the sofa and toyed with his glass. Wayne puffed at his cigar and blew smoke rings up to the ceiling. He was quite drunk now, which was probably just as well. The full impact of his daughter's death wouldn't hit him until he woke up tomorrow morning with a cement-truck hangover.

Twenty minutes later, Wayne's eyes drooped and he dozed off. Lloyd gave him a moment or two to fall more heavily asleep. Then he walked softly across and removed the half-burned cigar from Wayne's lifeless fingers.

He went through to the kitchen, picked up the telephone, and dialed Sylvia Cuddy's number. While he waited for Sylvia to answer, he switched on the portable television next to the spice rack and watched a Wrigley's Doublemint commercial with the sound turned down to gnat-in-a-jelly-jar level.

Sylvia answered. There was opera in the background, Verdi, played at devastating volume.

"Sylvia? This is Lloyd."

"Oh, Lloyd! I've been waiting for you to call! I was just about to go out."

"Don't let me keep you."

"Oh, not at all. Wait, just let me turn this down. I can't hear myself think. Leonard Katzmann's taking me to Mario's for dinner, as if I haven't had enough opera for one day. Or enough of Leonard, come to that. How are you, my dear? Was it terrible today?"

Terrible? He could he possibly put into words the sheer grisly horror of those gaping Lon Chaney nostrils, those stretched-back lips, that incinerated hair? That beautiful face that had been turned into a grinning blackened voodoo death mask?

"Well," he said, trying to sound matter-of-fact, "it was pretty difficult, to be honest with you. It was just about the worst thing I've ever had to do in the whole of my life."

"Lloyd, my love, I'm so sorry. You don't know badly everybody feels for you."

"Thanks, Sylvia. Listen . . . I'll talk to you tomorrow about the funeral and all that kind of thing. The medical examiner hasn't released the body to the morticians yet. Apparently it's a rule that they always have to carry out an autopsy after a suicide."

"Take your time, Lloyd. I'll stop by tomorrow, if you like."

"Sure, I'd like that. There's just one thing I wanted to ask you."

"Anything. Go ahead."

"Well . . . do you happen to know anybody at the opera called Otto?"

There was a pause. "Otto? Not that I know of. Do you happen to know his last name?"

"Otto, that's all I've got. Maybe he's not exactly a member of the opera company, but just knows some of the people there. He's involved with some kind of religious study group."

"I can't say that I've ever *heard* of any Otto. But I'll ask around, if you like. Maybe Don knows him."

She hesitated, and then she said, "Is it something you want for yourself? I know a marvelous priest you could talk to, Father Bernard."

"No, no, it's just . . . just somebody that Celia happened to mention. I guessed I ought to tell him what happened."

"Oh, sure. Well, I'll ask. You don't know anything else about him?"

"Just that Celia thought he was something between Jesus Christ and Robert Redford."

"Did she? Well, knowing how critical Celia was, he sounds like just the kind of man I'd like to get my hands on. I'll ask around, okay? Goodnight, Lloyd; and take care of yourself."

Lloyd recradled the receiver. As he did so, the seven o' clock news came on TV. Immediately, he saw the unsteady hand-held image of a blackened, burned-out bus, out in the desert. The same bus that Sergeant Houk had been sent to investigate. Lloyd pressed the remote control, and caught the reporter in mid-sentence.

". . . this morning by two Highway Patrol officers on a routine journey through the Anza-Borrego Desert State Park . . ."

Lloyd watched as the TV news cameras circled around the skeletal wreck of the bus. ". . . only known witness was a blind Indian boy who claims to have heard voices in the vicinity of the bus immediately prior to its burning, but . . ."

The camera pulled back to show three ambulances parked on the edge of the highway, and a row of body bags lying on the ground. The reporter said, "Only two of the victims have so far been positively identified. One was Mr. Ronald Korshaw, a carpet salesman from Escondido. The other was Ms. Marianna Gomes, a scenic designer for the San Diego Opera Company . . ."

Lloyd stared at the television with a tight feeling of fright and elation. *So there's no connection between the deaths of all of these people in a burned-out bus in the Anza-Borrego Desert State Park and Celia's suicide on Rosecrans Street, is there, Sergeant Houk? But what do you think the odds are that two women from the San Diego Opera Company should burn to death on successive days? A zillion to one?*

Lloyd had once met Marianna Gomes. He remembered a vivacious, dark-skinned girl in a flouncy red blouse. Red lips, black eyes, hips that swayed to a silent salsa. Hardly the suicidal type —no more than Celia had been.

He recalled Celia talking to him about Marianna, too. "She's so bright and so talented, and she has the craziest sense of humor." Several times, when Celia had returned home late, she had told him that she and Marianna had been "working on something" together, and that they had "lost track of time."

Was this what they had both been working on? Their mutual suicide by fire?

Lloyd swallowed the rest of his drink. His mind was clamorous with images, possibilities, snatches of remembered conversation.

"Marianna and I have been working on this idea together . . . I guess we just got carried away . . ."

He could picture her now, in her sheepskin jacket, turning around as she closed the front door.

"We were talking about what you could do if you had all the time in the world."

When had she said that? He could distinctly remember her saying it. "All the time in the world."

Maybe both Celia and Marianna had been attending religious discussions with this mysterious Otto character. Maybe they had been working out their self-immolation with him. Because—think about it—how had Celia managed to get to Rosecrans Street with that red gasoline can, if she hadn't had somebody to take her there? She hadn't been seen on the bus, no taxi driver had reported taking her, and there were no vehicles in the area that were unaccounted for.

Lloyd picked up the phone again and redialed Sylvia's number, but Sylvia must have left for her dinner at Mario's. He went back into the living room, collecting the Wild Turkey bottle from the table. He hadn't bothered to refill the decanter. Wayne was still dozing, his head thrown back and his mouth open, cackling like a cat.

Lloyd opened his desk drawer, and lifted out a thick yellow legal pad. Writing in firm italics, in dark purple ink, he set down the title *Celia Jane Williams* and then underneath he wrote June 14, the day of her death.

He had no real evidence; nothing to go on but speculation and fear. But he was sure now that Celia's decision to set herself on fire hadn't been done spontaneously or rashly, nor had she done it in a moment of irrationality. She had planned it, maybe for weeks, maybe for months.

Whether Otto and his religious study group had anything to do with it, he didn't yet know. But he was determined to find out.

Otto, he wrote on his pad; and then filled in the two *O*s with two eyes and a smile. *Have a nice day.*

He hadn't been brought up as a fighter; not in the physical sense, anyway. His father had always said that it was crazy people who demanded an eye for an eye. Survival was more dignified than trying to do unto others what they had done unto you. But now Lloyd found himself consumed with a feeling of revenge that was like nothing he had ever experienced in his life. It was almost like being on fire himself. He couldn't sit still; he could scarcely breathe. He was going to find out who had taken Celia away from him, no matter how long it took, no matter how much it cost, and he would get even.

7

La Jolla was masked in a pearl-gray Pacific fog the following morning when Lloyd drove down to Denman's Original Fish Depot. Waldo's light-blue Cutlass Supreme was already parked outside, and behind the Victorian-style frontage, with its parlor palms and its Art Nouveau window frames, Lloyd could see the lights inside the main restaurant. He unlocked the door and went straight in.

"Waldo?"

Waldo was sitting at one of the dining tables, writing menus. Outside the window, La Jolla Cove was invisible, as if the world ended just beyond the deck. "Mr. Denman, how are you? You didn't have to come in to the restaurant yet. Everything is fine. Everything is running smooth."

He stood up, and they embraced each other, a little awkwardly because of Waldo's intervening pot belly and his insistence on proper protocol. Lloyd would never be "Lloyd" to Waldo, not even if they were still running the Fish Depot together when they were nonagenarians. Waldo's first law of industrial relations was that if a man gave you a job, then you respected that man. If you couldn't respect him, you should find another job.

"You went to the morgue?" asked Waldo, gently. "You saw her?"

Lloyd nodded. "Yes. I've met her parents, too."

Waldo frowned at him. "Didn't you say she didn't have no parents?"

"Well, yes, that's what she said; but it turns out she does. They came down from San Clemente last night and stayed over. I saw them off about a half-hour ago. They're very broken up about it."

"Everybody is broke up, Mr. Denman. Everybody is broke up real bad."

Lloyd went through to the kitchens. A huge copper saucepan of fish stock was simmering on the stove. He lifted the lid and sniffed it. "Smells good. Louis is going to be giving Marcel Perrin a run for his money one of these days. Did he manage to buy any bluefish?"

"He's gone down to the dock to get some now. He wanted more abalone, too."

Lloyd looked around, and then he said, "I'm going to need some time off, Waldo. I want you to take charge of things for a while."

"Sure, Mr. Denman. You can count on me. How long do you think you're going to need?"

"I don't know, it could be a couple of days; it could be a week. There's a problem I have to take care of. I'll try to keep in touch; but if you get into any kind of trouble you can always call my lawyer, Dan Tabares. He's in the phone book, Tabares Oldenkamp Tabares."

Waldo watched Lloyd uneasily. "You want to tell me what's wrong, Mr. Denman? Maybe there's something that I can do."

Lloyd squeezed Waldo's hard, pudgy arm. "Not this time, *amigo*. This is one that I have to sort out on my own. I'll pay you two hundred dollars a week more, okay? And you'll have full authority to sign checks."

"Mr. Denman, it wasn't for the extra money that I offered to help."

"Of course you didn't. But you're going to have extra responsibilities now, and extra responsibilities means extra pay. Okay?"

"Well, okay, Mr. Denman, if that's what you want."

Lloyd went through to his office. He collected his Filofax, his spare set of keys, and the cassette from his answering machine. Then he went across to the small table where he kept his business checkbooks. Somebody had crowded the top of it with about a dozen of the old salt-and-pepper pots they used to use, before Lloyd had bought a complete new service from Villeroy & Boche. He unlocked the desk, and eased the lid up only a quarter of an inch so that he could retrieve a checkbook without dislodging any of the pots.

He had managed to grasp one checkbook between two fingers when the pots suddenly slid and scattered all over the floor.

"God damn it," he cursed.

"Everything okay, Mr. Denman?" asked Waldo, peering around the door.

"Oh, sure, fine—I just—"

He looked down at the scattered salt-and-pepper pots and they suddenly reminded him of something: *Celia's scrimshaw, scattered across the carpet.* And why had the scrimshaw scattered like that? Not because somebody had swept it all off the top of the piano with his arm. If somebody had done that, the scrimshaw would have been sprayed over a much wider area. No—it had all slid off the piano top together, in the same tumbled cluster as these pots. Because somebody had done what he had just done with this desk. Lifted the lid, to retrieve something that was inside.

He gave Waldo a last quick list of instructions, and then he left the Original Fish Depot and stepped quickly out into the cool, moist fog. He wanted to go home and see what it was that his late-night visitor had been looking for.

The house seemed even quieter and emptier during the day than it did at night. He carried all his office papers inside, and left them on the kitchen counter. Then he went into the living room, and across to the piano.

He listened. Nothing but the sound of insects in the yard, and the whispering of lawn sprinklers. Nothing but the measured dripping of a bathroom faucet.

It was like a life, dripping away. *Drip, drip, drip,* down the drain.

Carefully, he took all of the pieces of scrimshaw off the piano lid, and laid them out on the cushions of one of the sofas. He was conscious as he did so that the photograph of Celia was watching him from the open bedroom door. *Come, my Celia, let us prove . . . while we can, the sports of love.*

The telephone rang and made his skin tingle with shock. He took off the last two pieces of scrimshaw and went to answer it.

"Lloyd? It's Sylvia."

"Oh hi, Sylvia. I guess you heard about Marianna."

"Wasn't that terrible? I was devastated. And the day after Celia, too."

"She was a really terrific girl."

Sylvia said, "I came back from Mario's and saw it on the late-night news. I was just devastated. You don't think there's any connection, do you?"

"That's what I asked the police, but they really didn't know. I think there's a pretty strong chance that there *is* a connection. It seems like far too much of a coincidence, two women from the same opera company dying by burning two days apart."

"I don't know, Lloyd. It's not as if Marianna killed herself on her own. You know, not as if she was following Celia's example. She had twelve other people with her, and none of *them* had anything to do with the San Diego Opera."

"Well, I guess the police will come up with something," Lloyd told her, guardedly.

"I guess so," Sylvia agreed. "It's such a terrible waste of life."

"I really have to go now," Lloyd told her, eyeing the bare white lid of the piano. "Did you say you were coming around today?"

"For sure . . . that's if you still want me to."

"Why don't we go out for drinks? I could use somebody to talk to. I'll pick you up at six-thirty."

"I'd like that."

Lloyd put down the phone and returned to the piano. Gently, he eased up the lid, and peered into the shadowy interior. Pianos always smelled the same inside; of wax and resin and felt dampers—almost like church. He lifted the lid right up, and propped it open.

At first glance, there didn't appear to be anything inside it. The trouble was, he didn't know what he was supposed to be looking for. A key, maybe? A wad of dollar bills? A message? A chamois-leather bag, crammed with diamonds?

Nor did he know if his nocturnal visitor had managed to find what he was looking for. It was quite possible that he had already taken it—in which case, Lloyd would *never* find out what it was.

And there was still the question of who had hidden it, and why, and how come a burglar had known what to look for and where it was?

As he peered around inside the piano, he came up with all kinds of random, half-developed, kaleidoscopic theories. Maybe some drug dealer had been using the piano store as a front for selling crack, and had stashed some of it inside the piano he least expected to sell. Maybe the piano frame had been cast out of solid gold by the Brink's-Mat gang, as a way of smuggling it out of Europe. Maybe some spy had been using the piano as a drop for information stolen from the U.S. Navy.

Maybe—

He inclined his head sideways and caught sight of a pale-brown manila envelope Scotch-taped to the inside of the piano. He carefully picked off the tape and lifted the envelope out, making sure that he held it right by the very corner. After all, it might have some Russian agent's fingerprints all over it, and what would the FBI say if he smudged them? He had seen enough episodes of *Mission Impossible* to know the correct procedure. *This message will self-destruct in ten seconds.*

He laid the envelope on his writing desk and opened it. Inside, there was a sheaf of yellowed papers. He slid them out onto his blotter, and carefully fanned them out. He wouldn't have known what they were before he had met Celia, but he recognized them immediately as an operatic libretto. It must have been a pretty major opera, too, since the pages were numbered from 125 through 137.

There were also some pages of music manuscript, written with a spidery, splotchy pen, and heavily crossed-out and corrected. On the very last page there was a pencil note: "Wagner 'Junius,' January 1883."

Lloyd sat back in his chair and stared at all these discolored sheets of paper in perplexity. They looked as if they could be Wagner's original score—although Lloyd had no idea what Wagner's writing had been like. If they were, they were probably quite valuable. But why had Celia hidden them inside her piano? Why hadn't she locked them up at the bank? And who had known, apart from Celia, that they were hidden there?

He leafed through the libretto again and again. He couldn't understand it, because it was all in German, and written in a handwriting that he could scarcely decipher anyway.

Maybe he should show it to the police. Celia had never mentioned it to him. Maybe her big secret was that she had stolen it. He knew what a nut she had always been for Wagner memorabilia. Maybe its rightful owner had killed her out of revenge. Despite what several eyewitnesses had said on the local news, Lloyd still found it difficult to believe that Celia had actually poured gasoline all over herself and set herself on fire. Maybe somebody had forced her to do it—at gunpoint, perhaps. Somebody who had been standing sufficiently far away not to be noticed when the gasoline went up.

Wagner "Junius," January 1883. He left his desk and went across to the bookshelf, taking out *Richard Wagner* by Hans von Kiel. Licking his finger, he leafed through it until he reached the index of Wagner's operas. *Die Feen; The Flying Dutchman; Tannhäuser; The Twilight of the Gods; Lohengrin;* and, lastly, *Parsifal,* which had been written in 1882, the year before Wagner died of a heart attack. No mention of an opera called *Junius.*

Lloyd looked through the list of overtures and pieces for chorus and orchestra. The *Siegfried Idyll,* the *Faust Overture,* but no *Junius.* He closed the book and sat with his mouth covering his hand, deep in thought.

Was it possible that Celia had *faked* this opera—either as a wicked joke or as a way of making herself some extra money, and that somebody who resented that kind of fraud had found her out? She had been brilliant at improvising Wagneresque music. At parties, she had been able to sing great bursts of pretense verses from *The Ring.* She had even invented a Wagnerian operatic character of her own, Bulkhilde, and she had once discussed Bulkhilde with the San Diego Opera's artistic director Tito Caporosso for over twenty minutes before he realized he was being leg-pulled.

He had heard of homicides in the art world, after forgers had tried to con dealers and auctioneers out of millions of dollars. But was there a music Mafia, too? People who would burn you alive because you sold them a fake opera? It didn't seem particularly likely. In fact it seemed almost laughable.

Lloyd found a spare plastic record sleeve, and slipped the pages of music manuscript into it. His first step would be to take them to Sylvia's tonight. Sylvia was an expert when it came to long-lost music manuscripts; and her knowledge of Wagner was almost as encyclopedic as Celia's had been. In 1972 Sylvia had found nine previously undiscovered piano suites written by Debussy after his visit to the Bayreuth Festival in 1889—compositions that were strongly influenced by Wagner.

If anybody would know about *Junius,* it would be Sylvia.

Lloyd was beginning to feel hungry. He hadn't been able to eat well since he had first heard about Celia, and despite the horror of having to identify her body, or even because of it, his stomach had started to growl. He decided to go down to Michelangelo's Italian restaurant on Rosecrans and treat himself to a plate of their *spaghettini alla vongole.*

There was another reason why he wanted to go to Rosecrans: he wanted to see for himself the place where Celia had died.

He called Waldo to check how the Original Fish Depot was faring. "You don't worry about nothing, Mr. Denman. All booked up this lunchtime, all booked up tonight. No problems."

Lloyd was still talking to Waldo when he thought he glimpsed a shadow moving silently across the kitchen floor. He paused in his conversation for a second, keeping his eyes on the open kitchen doorway. Then he said, "Okay, Waldo, thanks a lot. I'll check in later, okay?"

"You got it, Mr. Denman."

Lloyd gently replaced the telephone receiver, and waited. He thought he heard the back door handle eased on its spring. Somebody trying to turn it. Somebody with infinite patience, trying to open the back door without him hearing. This time, however, they wouldn't have any luck. He had not only locked the door, he had shot the bolts, too, top and bottom. Nobody would be able to break into the kitchen without kicking the door out of its frame.

He softly crossed the living room until he reached the kitchen door. He hesitated for a moment, his chest tight with anticipation.

Supposing somebody's standing outside the back door, trying to force their way in? Even worse, supposing it's—

He let out a long, controlled breath. *Don't be so goddamn ridiculous. Celia's dead. You saw her body; you saw it for yourself. They gave you back her charm bracelet, and they gave you back her purse.*

He stepped into the kitchen, and turned immediately toward the back door. For a fraction of a second, he thought he glimpsed a black-coated figure, ducking down. He heard footsteps brush quickly on the brickwork outside.

"Come here!" he shouted. "If you run, I'm going to call the cops!"

Furiously, he twisted the key in the back door, and cursed as he forced back the bolts. He hardly ever used them, and they were so stiff that he chipped the heel of his hand on the edge of the metal. He hurled open the door, knowing how foolish it was, knowing that it was madness, but he was convinced that he had glimpsed a fleeting triangle of bright yellow, and a fawn blur that could easily have been a raincoat.

He rushed out to his backyard, alarming a brace of California quail. There was nobody there. No yellow scarf, no raincoat. What was more, the sprinkler was glittering in the middle of the lawn, and if anybody had run away through the garden, they would have had to pass directly through the spray.

There were no tracks across the silvery moisture-beaded grass; no sign that anybody had run that way. But sidling toward the fence was a cloud of slowly fragmenting smoke, like a ghost that was coming apart at the seams. Eventually, it rose in the breeze and was abruptly whirled away. No—not smoke, but *steam*, as if somebody had run through the sprinkler whirling a red-hot poker around his head.

8

His appetite wasn't as hearty as he had imagined it would be, and he left most of the pasta pushed to the side of his plate. Gino was hurt, and came out of the kitchen and stared at him with cowlike eyes.

"There's something wrong? Maybe I should cook you some of my *rognoncini di agnello saltati con cipolla.*"

"You've got to be joking," Lloyd responded. "Gino, that was brilliant. *Spaghettini* like they make in heaven. But I guess my eyes were bigger than my stomach."

"Aren't you the man who said to me, 'To waste food is to waste life itself?" Gino demanded.

"Sure, but I'm also the man who said, 'Never eat anything you can't lift.' "

Gino sat down at the table with him and snapped his fingers for the waiter to bring them two glasses of Verdicchio. "You tease me, Lloyd, you make fun," he said, laying a hand on Lloyd's arm. "But you must miss her so much. Such a lady. Such elegance."

"Yes, well," said Lloyd, and lowered his eyes. He was trying very hard not to think about the Celia that he could remember, but to concentrate on the Celia that he had obviously never known. The secret Celia, the Celia who had pretended that she had no parents. The Celia who had believed so obsessively in living forever. The Celia who had gone to Otto's religious study group, and who had burned herself alive not five blocks from where he was sitting now.

"What are you going to do?" Gino asked him. "Maybe you should take some time off?"

Lloyd nodded. "Two or three days, maybe. But I can't keep away from the job too long. You know what it's like. You take too much time off, you lose your edge."

"Hey . . . if you get bored, come back down here, and I will show you how to make *insalatina tenera con la panceteta.*"

"What the hell is that? It sounds like a street direction to the Vatican."

Gino swallowed wine and shook his head. "Lettuce, fried. It's wonderful. But I can't explain how to do it; I have to show you."

Just then, Gino was called back to the kitchen to whip up some *coste di biete saltate*, and Lloyd was left to finish his wine on his own. He was glad of the chance to be silent. He was summoning up all of the courage he possibly could, so that he would have the strength to visit the place where Celia had died. He had to go. It was not just an investigation; it was a pilgrimage. He had to know exactly where it was before he could begin to visualize it, and then to understand. He couldn't imagine what pain had been suffered by wives in wartime, to learn that their husbands had been killed, but never to know exactly *where*. It seemed to him then that the place where somebody dies is even more important than where they were born.

He stood in the parking lot opposite McDonald's with his hands by his sides, staring at the smoke-stained curb. Some of the bushes had been scorched, too, so Lloyd could judge how fierce the fire must have been. He wished he had brought some flowers. Lilies had always been Celia's favorite.

What a place to die. Barren and public, noisy with traffic. He couldn't imagine why she had chosen such a dreary location.

He tried to say a prayer. He hoped that her soul was at rest. He hoped she hadn't suffered. He hoped that she would forgive him, for not understanding that she was suffering so much that she wanted to die.

"And one day we'll meet again, for sure. Amen."

He was walking back to his car when one of the cooks came out of the side entrance of McDonald's and began to walk hurriedly toward him. A bulky man, with a startling wide-apart cast in his eyes.

"Pardon me!" he called. "Sir!"

Lloyd waited for him to reach him. He was in his fifties, gray-haired and sweating. He smelled strongly of hamburgers.

"I'm sorry to bother you, sir," he said, wiping the palms of his hands on his apron. "But I couldn't help noticing you standing over there."

Lloyd said, "I'm not one of your sensation-seekers, if that's what you think. The woman who was burned . . . well, she was my fiancée."

"I figured something like that. Well, I saw the BMW. Your average ghoul doesn't usually turn up to gawk in a BMW."

He held out his hand. "Bob Tuggey. Most people call me Unca Tug."

"Lloyd Denman."

Bob said, "I was here when it happened. I tried to stop her. It was terrible."

"You were the one with the fire extinguisher?"

Bob lowered his eyes, and nodded. "I tried, believe me, but I just wasn't fast enough. Fifteen seconds sooner, and I could have saved her."

Lloyd looked back toward the burned bushes. "I appreciate what you did."

"I saw her walking across the lot, swinging this red can. I should have guessed right away what she was planning on doing."

Lloyd shook his head. "I don't think anybody could have guessed what she was planning on doing."

"I was in Saigon," Bob told him. "I saw one of those monks setting himself on fire. Your young lady sat right down, cross-legged, exactly the same way that monk did, and then I knew for sure what she was going to do. I just wasn't fast enough."

"Well, thanks anyway," Lloyd told him.

"Hey, listen—" said Bob, reaching into the breast pocket of his shirt. "I found something afterwards, in the bushes. I was going to take it to the police yesterday but I didn't have the time. It must've been hers; so I guess the best person to give it to is you."

Between finger and thumb, he held up a small gold charm, discolored by heat. Its link was broken, as if it had been tugged from a chain or a bracelet. But Lloyd had never noticed it on Celia's bracelet. All of Celia's charms had been soldered on by the jeweler; it was not likely that they'd fall off. Certainly he hadn't given this one to her, and she had never mentioned buying it.

"I don't recognize it," he frowned, holding it flat on the palm of his hand. "It must be somebody else's."

The charm was a circle, and inside the circle was a lizard, with its head bent sideways and its legs and its tail bent sideways, too.

"You're sure?" asked Bob. "I found it right where it happened, the same afternoon. I kept meaning to take it in."

"I could show it to her mother, see if *she* recognizes it."

"Okay," Bob agreed.

"Do you want a receipt for it?" asked Lloyd.

Bob gave him a smile. "Don't worry about it. You're not going to get very far in a white BMW with a license plate that says FISHEE."

"I guess not. Listen, Mr. Tuggey—I run Denman's Original Fish Depot, at La Jolla Cove. Here—here's my card. Why don't you come by sometime, and have a drink on the house?"

"Thanks. I might just take you up on that."

They shook hands. Bob returned to McDonald's, and Lloyd walked back to his car, holding the charm tightly in his fist, as if he were afraid it might jump out of his hand. He unlocked his car, but as he was about to climb into it, he noticed a red neon sign on the opposite side of Rosecrans announcing Copie Shoppe: Xerox, Printing, & Fax. He picked up the sheets of libretto from the passenger seat, relocked his car, and crossed the road.

As Bob reappeared in the kitchen, Sally the manager called out to him, "Unca Tug? You just missed a phone call."

"Oh, yeah, who was it? Not the president again, asking for advice on the Middle East? I wish he'd formulate his own policies, for God's sake, and leave me alone."

"It was a girl. She sounded sexy, too."

Bob looked up from the grill. "A girl?"

"Sure. Real hoarse and provocative, know what I mean?"

"For me?"

"Well not *specifically* for you. She wanted to know if anybody had handed in a gold charm. Apparently she lost it in the parking lot."

Bob put down his spatula in exasperation. "Would you believe it? I just gave that charm to that guy out there. Well, he *was* out there. He's gone now."

"What did you do that for?"

"He said that girl who burned herself was his fiancée. I was sure the charm must have been hers."

"This girl sure didn't sound dead."

"Well, the guy didn't recognize the charm, either; so I guess it couldn't have belonged to his fiancée, after all. Damn it."

"Do you know who he is?" asked Sally.

"Oh, sure. He owns a fish restaurant at La Jolla. Guess I'll just have to call him and get it back."

"I told the girl on the phone you had it," said Sally. "She said she'd come by later to get it."

"She described it?"

"Sure, kind of a lizard, in a ring, that's what she said."

Bob nodded. He left the kitchen and went through to the corridor, and picked up the pay phone. He punched out the number of Denman's Original Fish Depot, and waited while it rang.

Waldo answered. Bob explained what had happened, but Waldo told him that "Monsieur Denman weel not veezeet ze restaurant *aujourd'hui*. Pairhaps tomorrow."

"Just tell him the gold charm didn't belong to his fiancée, please, and maybe he could call me."

"*Avec plaisir, monsieur.*"

Bob put down the phone, and went back to the Big Macs and the Filet o' Fishes and the Quarter-pounders. The afternoon passed quickly: his shift was due to end at seven-thirty. Tonight he was planning on bowling with his friend Stan Kostolowicz, another marooned pen-pusher from the Far Eastern embassies of the 1960s.

As it gradually grew dark, however, he failed to notice the large silver-gray Mercedes sedan with darkly tinted windows, which drew up outside the restaurant and which remained parked there, even though none of its doors opened. Whoever was inside it had obviously decided to remain inside it, waiting.

Lloyd arrived outside Sylvia Cuddy's downtown apartment building a little more than ten minutes early, and Sylvia wasn't yet ready. He walked up the tile-flagged steps to the second floor, and Sylvia let him in.

"Excuse the chaos," she said, kissing his cheek.

Like the living accommodations of many people he knew, even successful musicians and restaurateurs and interior designers, Sylvia's apartment was tiny. Real-estate prices in San Diego had risen stunningly, and even a cramped two-room apartment was beyond the reach of all but the most affluent.

Only one drawer had to be left open, or one newspaper dropped on the floor, and the whole placed looked untidy.

Sylvia's "chaos" amounted to nothing more than a coffee cup left in the kitchen area, and an open file of drawings for the San Diego Opera's forthcoming production of *Mefistofele*.

"Have a seat," she said. "There's wine in the fridge. Or Perrier. Or fresh-squeezed pineapple. There's even some stuffed olives. Or some strawberry Jell-O."

Lloyd poured himself a glassful of cold Cakebread chardonnay, and stepped out onto Sylvia's tiny redwood balcony. The balcony had been built up to chest-height to give her extra privacy, and to mask the view of water towers and warehouses and tract housing rooftops. If you didn't peer over the edge, all you could see was Banker's Hill and the Coronado Bay, glittering gold in the distance.

"You've worked miracles with this place," he told her, turning around with his back to the parapet. "I love this dark green wallpaper, and all these drapes."

"I have to have drapes because I don't have room for closets," she called back. "I'm so tired of living in Lilliput, you know? It's so damned small here I can do swan dives off the ironing board, straight down the toilet."

She stepped out onto the balcony beside him. She was short, only a little over five-three, with a wild tangle of backbrushed Titian hair, an owlish pair of Paloma Picasso glasses, lips as plump as pink silk cushions, and huge rounded breasts that were wrapped up like well-ripened cantaloupes in a crimson and green floral blouse by André Laug.

"You know what Celia used to say about this blouse?" asked Sylvia. "She said it was like somebody shouting in the jungle. Wasn't that just *typical*?"

"I went to see the place today," said Lloyd. "The place where she died."

Sylvia didn't answer, but waited to hear what Lloyd would say next.

"It's a parking lot, that's all," he told her. "A concrete parking lot. What a goddamn awful place to die."

"Any place is a goddamn awful place to die," Sylvia told him, taking his hand and squeezing it. "Come on, let's go find ourselves a real drink."

They left the apartment and Lloyd drove them out to Harbor Island Drive, to Tom Ham's Lighthouse. Apart from being a bar and a restaurant, Tom Ham's was a genuine certified Coast Guard lighthouse, with a spectacular view of the harbor. It was dark now, except for a last diagonal streak of grainy orange light across the horizon. They sat at a window table, looking out over the dipping lights and the reflections of downtown San Diego. Sylvia ordered a Kahlúa on the rocks, but Lloyd stuck to whiskey. There were times when only whiskey was any use.

"You said you thought there might be some connection between Celia and Marianna," said Sylvia.

"I don't know. I don't have any proof. It seems too much of a coincidence, that's all."

"Coincidences do happen."

"Well, sure . . . but I've got a weird kind of feeling about it. That's one of the reasons I wanted to talk to this Otto character."

"I'm afraid I haven't had any luck finding out about him. Don hasn't heard of him; but I'm sure that Joe North sometimes used to go along to see him, with Celia and Marianna. He's back at the theater the day after tomorrow. I'll ask him then."

"Thanks," said Lloyd. Then, "Do you happen to know what was the last opera that Wagner ever wrote?"

"That's a peculiar question."

"Some pretty peculiar things have been happening."

Sylvia frowned at him. "Listen, you've had a terrible shock. Are you sure you're okay?"

"I'm not too sure of anything, to tell you the truth. But tell me what was Wagner's last opera."

"Well," she said, "the last opera that Wagner wrote was *Parsifal*, 1882. In 1883 he went to Venice and died of a heart attack."

"He didn't write an opera in 1883?"

Sylvia took off her glasses. Her eyes were unfocused and a little bulbous; but they were richest shade of Belgian-chocolate brown. "Lloyd, I could talk about Wagner till the cows come home. However, the question is, is this relevant to anything at all?"

"I don't know. But inside Celia's piano, I found this manuscript." He reached under the table and produced the plastic envelope. "It's probably a fake, or a mistake. I'm not sure what. But it looks like part of a Wagner libretto, for an opera called *Junius*. It's dated 1883."

"Let me see that," said Sylvia. She took the envelope, eased out one of the pages of manuscript, and peered at it closely. Lloyd watched her, feeling uneasy, as if he were the fall guy for some elaborate practical joke.

"What do you think?" he asked her, at last.

"This isn't a put-on?" she asked him, suddenly suspicious.

But she realized from the expression on his face that he was serious; and why would he joke, at a time like this? She examined the pages carefully, turning them over one by one and laying them face down on the table.

"If this is genuine," she said, "then it's incredible. Do you have any idea where Celia might have found it?"

"I have no idea. She never mentioned it to me. It was Scotch-taped inside the piano."

Sylvia said, "Of course you won't be able to tell if it's genuine until you have the paper and the ink properly analyzed. But if it *is* genuine, you're going to be rich—especially if you can locate the rest of the opera, too."

She peered at one of the pages closely. "It certainly *looks* like Wagner's handwriting."

"And if it is?"

"Come on, Lloyd, think about it! If that's an original score for an unknown opera written by Richard Wagner in the last year of his life, and you can show that you own it, then you're made for life. You can retire. I can think of at least four musical publishing companies who would pay you millions for it."

Lloyd said, "To tell you the truth, I wasn't so much interested in the money. I'm more interested in how Celia got hold of it, and why she hid it, and whether anybody else knows about it. Obviously she never talked about it to you . . . but somebody broke into the house the night she died and I think this was what they were looking for. If it's worth millions, then that could have been a motive for somebody killing her."

"You didn't tell me that somebody broke in! That's terrible! What did the police say?"

"They didn't say anything," Lloyd admitted. "I didn't tell them, either."

"Any particular reason?" asked Sylvia.

"I don't know . . . just a feeling, I guess."

"But if you think she might have been killed . . ."

"Oh, I don't think that. I mean, I guess I'm satisfied that she actually took her own life. But I want to know is, *why?*—and whether anybody put her into a suicidal frame of mind."

"Are you sure that's something you really want to find out?" Sylvia asked him. There was no doubting Sylvia's kindness or wisdom.

Lloyd nodded. "I know what you're suggesting. There could have been another man involved. But, believe me, Sylvia, not knowing is worse than knowing."

Their waitress came up and asked them if they wanted another cocktail.

"No, no," said Sylvia. "Two's my limit. Otherwise I start singing 'Loike Old Times in Kilkenny, Begorra' and dancing on the tables."

"We'll just have the check," said Lloyd. But as he did so, he caught sight of a woman on the far side of the bar, in the corner of one of the booths, and she looked so much like Celia that he shivered as if somebody had unexpectedly laid a cold hand on the small of his back. She was deep in the shadows, and she wore dark glasses, and a black scarf that covered her head like a turban. But there was sufficient light from the small crimson-glass lantern on the table in front of her to illuminate her face, and if she wasn't Celia then she was certainly Celia's *doppelgänger*. He couldn't take his eyes away from her, but her glasses were so dark that it was impossible to tell if she had noticed him.

Sylvia touched his hand. Then—when she failed to attract his attention—she turned around to see what he was staring at. "Am I missing something?" she asked. "I'm terrible like that. I was out with Don the other night and Robin Williams came into the restaurant and I didn't even see him."

"That woman opposite . . . in the corner booth."

"Excuse me, I must put my specs on. Which woman?"

"That woman in the scarf and the dark glasses. There—right in the corner."

But as he was trying to explain to Sylvia which woman he meant, a crowd of six or seven laughing businessmen came into the bar and stood between them. Lloyd leaned from right to left, desperate not to lose sight of the woman, but then the businessmen were joined by their wives, and for two or three minutes he couldn't see the booth at all.

"Lloyd—what on earth's the matter?" Sylvia asked him.

He grasped her hand. "It sounds totally crazy, but I keep seeing Celia. Or women who look like Celia. I saw one just after I left the morgue. I tried to follow her, but she disappeared in the crowds."

"And now there's another woman over there who looks like Celia?"

"Exactly. It's uncanny. She's wearing dark glasses but she's so much like her."

Sylvia gave Lloyd's hand a gentle squeeze. "Lloyd—Lloyd, sweetheart."

He looked at her quickly, then went back to searching for the woman in the booth.

"Lloyd, you're only torturing yourself. Celia's dead."

"But the resemblance is totally uncanny."

"Lloyd, she's *dead.* Dead people don't come back and sit opposite you in cocktail bars. You're just projecting your grief onto a woman who looks a little bit like Celia. It's like an afterimage. I did it myself when my father died. I spent four thousand dollars on two shrinks, to sort myself out."

At last, the crowd of businessmen moved away, still laughing noisily. "*There*—" said Lloyd. But as the last man walked with infuriating slowness out of his sightline, he saw that the booth was empty and that the woman was gone.

Sylvia looked at Lloyd with sorrow. "Oh, Lloyd. I know how much you must be hurting."

Lloyd stood up, and searched around the bar for any sign of the woman. The front door was slowly closing, as if somebody had just walked through it; and through the brown-tinted glass he thought he saw a slim dark figure, and the back of a woman's calf, but then there was nothing but darkness, and the reflection of a man lighting a cigarette.

He drove Sylvia back to her apartment and helped her out of the car. A cool wind was blowing from the harbor, and Sylvia shivered.

"Don't bother to come up," she told him. "Get yourself safely home and take a couple of Nytol. You'll feel better when you get some sleep."

Lloyd kissed her, and hugged her. "Thanks, Sylvia. You're a genuine authenticated angel."

"Listen . . ." said Sylvia. "Do you mind if I keep that score? Oliver Drexler's coming in for rehearsals tomorrow; I could show it to him. I know that he'd love to see it."

"For sure," Lloyd told her, and reached into his car for the plastic envelope. "Take good care of it, though. It could be evidence."

"Oh, I'll take care of it, all right. I'll guard it with my life!"

She watched Lloyd U-turn across the street, then waved as he headed off northward, back to La Jolla. She let herself in through the heavy bleached-oak door of her apartment building, and climbed the tiled stairs.

As she climbed, she softly trilled "Pace, pace, mio Dio" from Verdi's *La forza del destino*. She felt worried about Lloyd. It was obvious that he hadn't even begun to face up to the reality of Celia's suicide. It was understandable, of course. Suddenly to lose the love of his life in such a grisly and baffling way must have been enough to drive him half-crazy. By concentrating with such ferocity on finding out *why* she had killed herself, his mind was still protecting itself from the shock.

His hallucinations of Celia were probably a symptom of the same self-protective mechanism.

Sylvia opened the door of her apartment and stepped inside. She wished there were something she could do to help Lloyd get over Celia. But Celia had been so pretty and so talented and so full of life that nobody could ever take her place. Sylvia missed her, too. Until today, she hadn't realized how badly. She had heard from Don that Exxon was going to put up the money for a major production of *The Marriage of Figaro*. She had actually started to say, "Wait till Celia hears about this," until it had struck her with almost physical pain that she would never see Celia again.

She went to the fridge and took out a bottle of white wine. She didn't usually drink as much as she had today, but she felt like something to help her sleep. She shucked off her shoes and walked out of the kitchen into the tiny living room, carrying a glass of wine in one hand and the libretto in the other. She sat down in her favorite spoonback armchair, and put up her feet on the coffee table.

Provided they were authentic, the pages of this libretto were one of the greatest musical finds of the century. Even if Lloyd couldn't find the rest of the opera, they were still worth a fortune. She didn't read German very well—particularly Wagner's spidery script—but she managed to work out some of the meaning.

Junius I confess that I listened
To His sweet and tempting words
And that I gave myself willingly
Body and soul.

And,

Many hundred thousand goodnights,
Dearly beloved Veronica
Innocent have I come into prison
Innocent have I been tortured
Innocent must I die.

She leafed through to the pages of music, and hummed a few bars to herself. The score was unusually monotonous for Wagner, although it had all of the Teutonic sinew of the *Valkyries* and *Rhinegold*. Sylvia slapped the arm of her chair with her hand to the beat. The music sounded almost like a barbarian war chant, the kind of song that would have been sung by Goths and Visigoths on their way to battle.

She was still humming and slapping when she began to have the feeling that she was being watched. She used to feel it quite often, before she had built the high balustrade around her balcony, and it was a feeling that particularly disturbed her. She had imagined that somebody in one of the tract houses was spying on her with binoculars. Her then-headshrinker had told her that she suffered from a mild form of paranoia.

But this evening, the feeling was different. She didn't feel that she was being watched from a long way off, but from very near. Almost as if somebody were standing right behind her, and breathing on her shoulder.

She stopped humming, stopped slapping, and glanced quickly and furtively around. There was nobody else in the room. But the building did seem unusually quiet. There were no televisions mumbling in other apartments; no music playing; no feet chip-chipping up the tiled steps outside.

A jet took off from Lindbergh Field, its engines thundering. The sliding door to the balcony rattled and vibrated. For a moment, as the airliner circled out over the ocean, Sylvia's whole world was engulfed by shattering noise. She looked toward the balcony and there, to her intense fright, a dark figure was standing, with its back to her. A woman, in a black raincoat, her head wound around in a black turbanlike scarf.

Carefully, her heart still caught on the hook of her fright, Sylvia set down her wineglass and the pages of Wagner's libretto, swung her feet off the coffee table, and stood up. She looked around for something to protect herself with, and decided that the swan's-head umbrella beside her writing desk would do. This was only a woman, after all, and not an especially big or powerful-looking woman; and by the way she was standing on the balcony with her back to the living room, it certainly didn't appear to Sylvia that she had the intention of doing anything violent or sudden.

All the same, the very presence of a stranger outside her living room, treating her balcony as if it were her own, was more threatening than Sylvia could have believed possible.

Sylvia gripped the umbrella in her left hand, took a deep breath to steady herself, and then slid back the balcony door.

"Hello," she said, her mouth dried out. "Do you mind telling me what the hell you think you're doing on my balcony?"

For a long time, the dark woman said nothing, but continued to stare out over the sparkling lights of downtown San Diego and Coronado. On the horizon, lightning flickered like vipers' tongues.

"This is a private apartment," Sylvia insisted. "If you don't leave immediately, I'm going to call the super, and the super will call a cop."

At last, the woman turned around. She wore glasses with lenses so perfectly black that she looked as if she had no eyes, just two circular holes in her head. Her skin was very pale, with almost a grayish pallor, but very smooth.

"Hello, Sylvia," the woman replied, with the faintest of smiles. "I believe that you've got something of mine."

Sylvia recognized the voice at once. A thrill of fright ran down her arms, like ice-cold centipedes racing each other to reach her wrists. It was Celia. It had to be Celia. Yet Celia was dead, burned. There had even been photographs in the San Diego newspapers of Celia burning, although Sylvia hadn't been able to do more than glance at them quickly. She had glimpsed flames, a bowed black head, knees that protruded through the fire like kindling-sticks.

Sylvia opened and closed her mouth. Celia stayed where she was, her hands in her raincoat pockets, watching Sylvia with just the faintest touch of a smile on her lips; her eyes masked by those two black circles, black as the Bible-paper that the pirates in *Treasure Island* had cut out to make the Black Spot.

"*Fine* way to welcome your best friend," she said, and her tone was quite vinegary. "Now, you have something of mine. Something I need. I'd appreciate it a whole lot if I could have it back."

"You're dead," Sylvia hissed at her. *"I'm imagining this. You're dead."*

Her feet and ankles felt as if they had sprouted cold, clinging tentacles, which had wound around the balcony and left her powerless to move. Celia stepped closer, and her brain said *run,* but she couldn't even step back. *Run, she's dead! Run!*

"I followed you out to the lighthouse," said Celia. She didn't take off her dark glasses, didn't smile. She was so much like Celia, yet there was something about her that was unnervingly unfamiliar. "Then I followed you back here. Of course I've still got that key you gave me."

She paused, and then she added, "Lloyd gave you my music, didn't he?"

"You're dead," gasped Sylvia, breathlessly. Her voice sounded as if she had somehow spoken into her own ear: intimate, secretive, but utterly hopeless. She had never felt so frightened in her entire life. She couldn't bring herself to move a single inch, couldn't even raise her swan's-head umbrella. Celia approached so close that Sylvia could have lifted her mouth and kissed Celia's smooth gray cheek, but still her muscles refused to work. She wondered in dumb lungless panic if she would ever be able to move again.

"I was waiting for you to go to bed," said Celia. "I was hoping so much that you wouldn't see me."

Sylvia at last managed to take one stiff step away from her, then another. "You're . . . *dead,"* she repeated. She couldn't think of anything else to say.

Celia moved past her into the living room—moved strangely and silently, her raincoat rustling. Sylvia caught a distinctive smell as she passed her by. A smell of *heat,* like a burned ironing-board cover.

She turned around and watched in fascination and horror as Celia bent over the Wagner libretto. With one black-gloved hand, Celia sorted quickly through the pages, obviously making sure that none of them was missing.

"It was very wrong of Lloyd to give you this," she remarked, without looking up.

"I'm sorry, I was only borrowing it, out of interest," Sylvia replied. Then, "You're not dead, then? Are you all right? Were you really burned? Or wasn't it you at all?"

Celia gathered up the pages and stood up straight. "Do I *look* dead? I'm more alive than ever."

"I don't understand. You don't seem like yourself at all."

Celia almost smiled. "On the contrary, my dearest. I've blossomed at last."

"You're going to tell Lloyd that you're okay? He's so upset he's almost crazy."

"I can't," Celia told her, dismissively. "Not yet. But I will, as soon as I can. Believe me. I miss him as much as he misses me."

Sylvia came back into the living room and managed to sit unsteadily down on the arm of her sofa. "Celia . . . you must tell me! What's happened to you? Where have you been? If *you* weren't burned, then who was? Whose body was it that Lloyd had to go to identify? And if you weren't burned, why have you put everybody through so much *anguish?*"

Celia stared at her for a long time with those smoke-black glasses, saying nothing.

Sylvia said, "We love you, Celia. We care about you. If something's wrong—"

Celia hesitated a moment longer, and then she said, "The truth is, Sylvia, that I was given the chance of a lifetime; and I took it; and there was no other way."

"A chance? What chance?"

"Look," said Celia, "I'm very sorry for all the pain that I've caused you, and everybody else. But I had no choice. It had to be done secretly. It had to be done without anybody knowing in advance. And until it's truly finished, it has to remain secret."

"But what's the secret?" Sylvia demanded.

"Life, Sylvia. That's the secret. Life."

"I don't understand."

Celia said, as if she were quoting, "There is one sure way to everlasting life; and that is the baptism of fire."

"Celia," Sylvia persisted. She was still afraid, but she was becoming irritated, too. She had seen the distress that Lloyd had suffered, because of her apparent death. She had experienced that same distress herself. She didn't consider it at all funny that Celia should now reappear, without regret, without apology, and behaving in the oddest, most arrogant way imaginable.

On the other hand (and here's where she had to be careful) it was possible that Celia had gone through some kind of mental breakdown. She had always been a brilliant musician, effervescent but high-strung, and she could have been suffering a nervous crisis without anyone realizing that anything was wrong. Sometimes it happened that way. She remembered Giorgi Boutone disappearing, the night before he was due to play Truffaldino in Prokofiev's *Love for Three Oranges.* The musical director had found him by accident three days later, on a child's swing set in Balboa Park, unshaved and filthy, singing "Muh-nuh-muh-nuh" from *The Muppet Show.*

"Celia . . ." said Sylvia. "Maybe I should drive you back home. You owe it to Lloyd, if nobody else."

Celia shook her head. "It isn't time yet. We have to wait until the solstice."

"The *solstice?* What's the solstice got to do with anything? How do you think he's going to *feel?*"

"How do I think he's going to feel about what?" Dead words, deadly spoken.

"About your being alive, of course!"

Celia said, almost with regret, "I was hoping very much that you wouldn't tell him."

"How could I *not* tell him?"

"Even if I begged you not to?"

"Celia, Lloyd's been through *hell,* thinking you killed yourself. I couldn't let him suffer a moment longer."

Celia turned away. Sylvia said, "Celia? Celia?" But Celia was plainly thinking very deeply about something, and didn't even appear to hear her.

"Celia, I *have* to tell Lloyd. I simply have to."

Celia looked back at her. When she spoke, her voice was measured and quiet and chillingly matter-of-fact. "You know something, Sylvia, fire has two properties. The ability to destroy, and the ability to recreate. Do you know why the Germans burned the bodies of all the innocent people they slaughtered?"

Sylvia was perplexed. "I don't know what you're talking about."

"The guards at the concentration camps didn't know why they had to do it," said Celia. "Nor did the SS officers. But higher up it was policy. When inferior races are exterminated, they must be burned."

"Celia—" Sylvia protested. "What on earth does this have to do with—"

"Everything!" Celia retorted, and her voice came out in a soft, threatening roar. "If your body is burned, your soul will be damned. The Germans were determined to torture the Jews and the Poles and the Russians and the Lithuanians, the homosexuals and the crippled and the insane, not only in this world, but the next, forever and ever, for time everlasting."

"Celia, you're sick," said Sylvia. "Why don't you let me call Lloyd, or maybe your doctor?"

"*No!*" roared Celia. "Don't you understand what I'm telling you? Fire can condemn you to hell, but it can save you, too! If the proper rites are observed when your body is burned; and if the proper sacrifices are made at the next changing of the year; your soul won't be damned, but saved. Saved! And not for a month, or a year, or ten years, or even one human lifetime. Your soul will be saved forever!"

Sylvia was trembling. "Are you trying to tell me you *did* burn yourself?"

Celia nodded, triumphantly.

"And are you trying to tell me that what I'm seeing here . . . this is just your *soul?*"

"I'm a Salamander, Sylvia. A life everlasting, made of fire and smoke and human soul. A creature of perfect purity. Superior in mind, indestructible in body. The perfect race that humankind was always meant to become."

"A Salamander?"

"That's what we call them. That's what we are."

"Who's *we?* Is Marianna one of these . . . Salamanders, too?"

Celia circled the room, until she was standing quite close. "Marianna and many others."

"So that bus—?"

"That's right! Burned on purpose. Burned happily. The time has almost arrived!"

Sylvia glanced up at her nervously. "Celia . . . this is *very* hard for me to believe."

"It was hard for me, too, when I first heard about it," said Celia. "In fact, I dismissed it. But then I met Otto and Helmwige and then I understood."

"What are you going to do next?" Sylvia asked her. "Where are you staying?"

"With Otto and Helmwige," Celia replied.

"And you won't talk to Lloyd?"

"Not yet. Not until the solstice. He mustn't see me yet. I'm not . . . well, I'm not stable. Physically, I mean. Not mentally."

Sylvia said, "Do you want a drink? I could use one myself."

"A glass of water would be good."

"Is that all? Just water?"

Sylvia stood up, and circled around Celia, and went to the corner table where she kept her drinks. She poured herself a Kahlúa, and then said to Celia, "Just going to the kitchen . . . get your water for you. And ice, too."

Celia was standing with her back to her, leafing through Wagner's libretto. She gave the smallest nod of acknowledgment.

"You know something . . . I was saying to Lloyd, that libretto must be worth a fortune," called Sylvia, opening up her refrigerator and rattling the ice tray. "Darn it, this ice is all stuck! I'll have to put it under the hot water faucet!"

Celia said, "We were lucky to find it. In fact, we've found almost all of it now. All the pieces that matter."

"You mean there's a whole opera?" Sylvia dropped the ice tray noisily into the sink and turned on the cold water faucet at full volume. Then she quickly stepped across to the other side of the kitchen and unhooked the telephone. Holding her breath, she punched out Lloyd's home number and prayed and prayed that he had managed to get back by now. *Please, Lloyd, please don't decide to visit the restaurant, I don't know the restaurant's number. Please just be home.*

Celia said, "Wagner wrote it in 1883. He still hadn't quite finished it when he died. He took it with him to Venice, and after his heart attack it disappeared. Not many people knew about it. His widow Cosima mentioned it in one of her diaries, but not by name."

"Oh, really?" said Sylvia. "Damn this ice! I think there's something wrong with my thermostat or something."

Lloyd's phone was ringing now. *Please be there, Lloyd. For God's sake, please be there.*

"In fact Otto was the first person to make any kind of serious search for it," Celia went on. "That was back in 1938, when Hitler was in power. Otto had Hitler's personal approval to look for *Junius*, and as much Nazi party finance as he needed. And of course, Mussolini was only too eager to help."

Lloyd picked up the phone, and said, "Lloyd Denman here."

"Lloyd," breathed Sylvia, with her hand cupped closely over the receiver. "Lloyd—it's Sylvia."

"I'm sorry, I can't hear you," Lloyd replied. "I just got in—the door's open. Can you hold on for a moment?"

"Lloyd, for God's sake, it's Sylvia!"

Celia was saying, "Otto was given a team of five musical

historians. They searched the whole of Venice . . . following every possible clue. It took them three years, until 1941. But they found it in the end. It had been hidden by the Roman Catholic priest who had taken Wagner's confession on his deathbed."

"Lloyd!" begged Sylvia.

She could hear Lloyd closing the front door. She could hear his footsteps crossing the hallway. He picked up the receiver with a squeaking, jostling noise, and said, "I'm sorry about that. I just couldn't—"

Sylvia slowly lowered her phone. She wanted to shout to Lloyd, "Celia's here! Celia's alive!" but her lungs were empty and she couldn't breathe. Celia was standing in the kitchen doorway, staring at her with those black, black glasses. Without a word, she came over to Sylvia and lifted the phone out of her hand, and laid it down. Lloyd's tiny voice said, "Hello? Hello? Is anybody there? Hello?"

Celia asked, "Is that Lloyd?"

Sylvia nodded dumbly. She didn't know why she was so frightened. Perhaps it was Celia's black glasses. Perhaps it was the thought that she might take them off.

"Celia, he has to know. You can't—"

Celia raised one black-gloved finger to her lips. "You promised me, Sylvia. You promised you wouldn't tell."

"Celia, this is crazy. I don't know what nonsense this Otto has been cramming into your head, but I really think this has all gone much too far—"

"Sylvia! You promised!"

On an impulse, Sylvia reached up and snatched off Celia's glasses. She was prepared for almost anything—bruises, burns, blindness. But when she saw Celia's eyes she screamed and screamed and screamed and couldn't stop. They were as black and empty as her dark glasses, holes in the gray featureless skin of her face. They gave her an expression of utter deadness, like a thing that walked but shouldn't walk; a death mask.

Celia seized Sylvia's wrist and pried the glasses out of her fingers. "Stop screaming!" she commanded her. "Stop screaming!"

"Ah! Ah! Ah!" Sylvia gasped, shuddering with terror.

"Stop it!" Celia shouted at her. "Stop it! Shut up!"

"Oh God you're not real; oh God you're not real!" Sylvia shrieked at her. "I'm having a nightmare! Go away! Go away!"

Celia seized the lapels of Sylvia's blouse and shook her so

hard that one of her earrings flew off. "Shut up, shut up, shut up! Shut up! You're hysterical!"

But Sylvia screamed and gibbered and dropped to her knees. Her brain felt as if it had fused, and she couldn't stop herself. Seeing Celia alive when she thought she was dead had been frightening enough. But seeing her dead when she was obviously alive was more than her mind could accept.

Celia hesitated, turned, then turned back again. She could hear footsteps outside the apartment, then the doorbell jangled. "Ms. Cuddy?" called a man's voice. "Ms. Cuddy, you okay in there?"

Celia lifted her right glove and unbuttoned it, tossing it aside. Then her left glove. Her hands were as pale and as smooth and as grayish as her face. Deftly, she unbuttoned her raincoat, all the way down, and slid out of it. Underneath the raincoat she was completely nude, except for her tightly wrapped black turban, her black high-heeled shoes, and a wide black leather belt, cinched tightly around her waist. The skin of her naked body was the same pearly gray—a gray that gleamed in the shadows of Sylvia's kitchen like softly polished aluminum, or the skin of a baby, three days dead.

She took hold of Sylvia's hands, both of them. "Come on, Sylvia," she coaxed her, "Come on, Sylvia, up."

Sylvia stared up at her, wide-eyed. "You're naked. You're dead. Go away."

"Come on, Sylvia, up you get."

"Ms. Cuddy!" the man's voice repeated. "This is Ramone the super. Ms. Cuddy? Is everything okay?"

"Everything's fine, thank you, Ramone!" Celia called, in a fair imitation of Sylvia's Boston accent.

Sylvia was standing with her knees slightly bent, as if she couldn't find the strength to stand up straight. "What are you going to do to me?" she asked, in a voice as scattered as a burst-open bag of dolly-mixtures. "What are you going to do to me? Please! I won't tell! I promise you, Celia! I promise you!"

Celia held Sylvia close, wrapping her arms around, pressing Sylvia's cheek close to her breast.

Slowly, almost sensually, she began to stroke Sylvia's hair.

"You feel hot," Sylvia muttered. "I thought dead people were supposed to be cold."

"Ah, but I'm not dead," Celia told her, still stroking her hair, over and over. "I'm very much alive. I'm so much alive that I shall never die."

"Celia, you're so hot. Don't hold me so close. I can't stand it."

Pale gray fingers stroked her hair, over and over. A first wisp of smoke, from the top of her scalp. A first smell of burning.

"Celia, please! You're hurting me! You feel so *hot!*"

But Celia's eyelids closed over those empty eye sockets as if she simply didn't choose to hear, and she kept on stroking Sylvia's hair, her fingers running deeply and sensually into her curls. Another wisp of smoke; a small sharp crackle of burning ends.

"I shall never die, Sylvia, my darling; and nor shall Marianna, nor David, nor Leonard, nor Carmen, nor Julie, or any of us. We're all pure now, every one of us. Salamanders! And we shall find more to purify, thousands more."

Her fingers stroked and stroked. Sylvia tried to struggle free, but Celia held her even more tightly. Celia's arms were so hot now that Sylvia's silk blouse began to scorch, and the flowery fabric started to shrivel up. Smoke was pouring from Sylvia's hair, and filling the kitchen with an acrid, eye-watering stench—except for those who had no eyes. Suddenly, her hair burst into flame, and she shouted in pain. Celia instantly clamped her hand over her mouth, and her fingers were so hot that Sylvia's lips sizzled and seared, like raw steak pressed against a red-hot skillet.

Sylvia twisted and writhed and thrashed, but she couldn't get free. Celia's body temperature had risen so high that Sylvia's blouse and skirt had scorched through, and her first layer of skin had actually fused to Celia's, breast and hip and thigh, so that for all practical purposes the two women were actually welded together.

Sylvia breathed in superheated air, and it burned the hairs in her nostrils and dropped into her lungs like blazing gasoline. She had burned herself badly only once before in her life, six or seven years ago, when she had dropped a panful of scalding water on her foot, and she had thought that what she had suffered then was agony. But she understood now that what she had suffered then was simply pain, and that true agony was so intense that it was beyond physical description. It was a spiritual experience, so unbearable that it was beautiful, so devastating in its effect on her central nervous system that she felt as if she had discovered at last the full implication of what it was to be a human being.

In Celia's incandescent arms, she understood that God had created His children with the ability to be able to suffer to such a degree that death would seem like blessed relief. That was the horrible beauty of it.

She was incapable of screaming out loud. But inside her mind she was screaming and screaming until she couldn't even think any more.

Celia held her tighter, caressing her shoulders, caressing her back. Celia's hands left wrinkled, blistering tracks wherever they touched her. Blistering scarf-skin dropped from her back, until she looked as if she wearing a ballet-skirt of curled-up crackling.

Sylvia lifted her puckering blistered face to Celia; and Celia opened her black empty eyes; and even though Sylvia couldn't speak, she communicated with every shriveling nerve in her body: *Kill me, kill me, please. Don't make me suffer any more.*

Celia stared at her with terrible black blindness, and then closed her eyes again. It was at that instant that Sylvia exploded into flame. Her lungs swelled, and then burst apart, and blood and flesh geysered out of her mouth. Chunks of burning muscle flew from her shoulders; her legs collapsed like charred chair legs; her intestines fell through her cracked-apart pelvis in a roar of fatty flame; her skull detonated.

The whole kitchen was strewn with burning ashes and lumps of shriveling flesh.

Sylvia's remains blazed on the kitchen floor with ever-intensifying glare and heat. Celia stood watching, naked, unmoved, even when the ceramic floor tiles began to break, one by one, with a gritty popcorn crackle.

Smoke filled the entire apartment, although it was slowly beginning to drift out through the open balcony door. Celia paced slowly around, as if she were reluctant to leave, tense, anxious, almost *angry*. She kept returning to the kitchen to look at the last guttering flames. It was extraordinary how it took nothing more than heat to reduce a living, talking human being to a small heap of oily ashes, in which flames fitfully burned.

Celia wondered if she felt sad, or regretful. She wasn't sure. She felt sorry that Sylvia was gone; yet Sylvia had brought it on herself; and Otto had always said that we must all accept the consequences for what we do, no matter how painful those consequences might happen to be. In a way, she felt that she had saved Sylvia from something far worse; although she knew that Sylvia's soul would suffer and suffer for all eternity.

She approached the antique mirror next to the front door, and stared at herself. She knew how much she had changed. She looked the same, but she wasn't the same at all. She was purified; utterly purified. She could never again be swayed by lies or deceit or broken promises. She would never again succumb to any kind of weakness. She was one of the chosen, one of the truly eternal.

Her empty eyes, which had horrified Sylvia so much, were the symbol of everything she had now become. "The eyes are the windows to the soul," somebody had once said. She needed no windows. She was *all* spirit, *all* soul, made flesh by the smoke of her own sacrifice. She had no need of eyes.

She cupped her hands over her small bare breasts. Her skin was cool now; the burning had passed. She thought of Lloyd and her nipples stiffened between her fingers. She knew how much pain she had caused him. She had known from the very beginning that he would have to suffer. But when the time came, they would be back together again, whole, perfect, and their passion would last forever.

"My dear, you will never die," Otto had told her, with a thin smile, clasping both of her hands between both of his.

She reached down and twined between her finger and thumb the fine curly hair that grew between her legs. She watched herself in the mirror. She had always been highly sexed. She hadn't realized how much she would miss Lloyd's lovemaking, even though they had been apart now for only three days. It would be wonderful, after the solstice, when she could take him back into her arms.

It was then that the phone rang. She hesitated for a moment or two, then she walked back into the smoke-filled kitchen and picked it up.

A voice said, "Sylvia? Sylvia? Is that you?"

Lloyd, she thought, closing her eyes. She was almost tempted to answer, although she knew that she mustn't.

"Sylvia . . . I had a call about five minutes ago. I thought it was maybe from you."

She didn't answer, but she placed the receiver against her lips, and kissed it, slowly and lingeringly.

"Sylvia?" she heard him say.

She pressed the earpiece against her breasts, touching her nipples against the tiny holes from which his voice was emerging.

"Lloyd . . ." she murmured.

"Sylvia . . . can you hear me? Are you able to talk? Should I call you back? Can you hear me okay?"

Now she massaged the receiver against her stomach, and

between her legs. She rubbed it slowly around and around against her vulva, until the plastic was slippery and shiny.

"Who's there?" asked Lloyd, right against her shiny flesh.

"Your lover," she replied, and then laughed. But all the time the tears were running out of her empty eyes.

Then, in the silence of Sylvia's smoke-filled apartment, she heard the telephone click, and whine, as Lloyd hung up.

She clutched the receiver in her left hand, and screamed at it in fury. Blue smoke began to pour from between her fingers, and the receiver started to soften and twist. She screamed and she screamed, a scream of fear and frustration and dark black anger, and the telephone burst into flame, and molten plastic dripped and crawled down her wrist, and dropped flaring onto the tiled floor. Smoke burst from her mouth and her ears; and for a moment she thought that she had gone too far, and that she herself would explode into flame.

At last, she threw it away, a smoldering knot of polystyrene on the end of a twisted telephone cord, and she knelt on the floor, shaking with emotion.

She had understood right from the very beginning that she would have to suffer. She had understood that she would be one of the first—different, and dangerous, and difficult for her friends and her lovers to understand.

But she hadn't been prepared for the strangeness of it, nor for the huge surges of anger that she would feel. She was immortal. She had inherited the whole world, forever. But what had she lost? *What had she lost?*

She stood up, picked up her raincoat, and hung it over her shoulders. Then she carefully replaced her smoke-black glasses. She would have given anything to see Lloyd that evening; but she knew that she couldn't trust him to keep her secret, and most of all she couldn't trust herself.

She collected the Wagner libretto, let herself out, and closed the door behind her.

9

"That's me for tonight, folks!"

Bob Tuggey tossed his apron into the linen basket, balled up his paper hat, and gratefully unhooked his old tan leather jacket from the peg. He reached into the pocket and took out a crumpled pack of Lucky Strike Lights, and tucked one into the corner of his mouth. He was just about to light it when Sally bustled past and said, "Unh-unh, Unca Tug. No smoking in the kitchen, corridor, washrooms, or staff recreation areas. Besides, the Surgeon General has determined that smoking cigarettes is bad for your self-image."

"You're a goddamn Tartar," he retorted. "Besides, I don't have a self-image. I sold my self-image in Paris, about twenty years ago, for a plateful of calves' kidneys and a bottle of Rully and twenty *Disque Bleu*."

"That was pretty cheap, for a self-image."

Unca Tug put his arm around Sally's shoulders and gave her freckled cheek an affectionate smackeroo. "In those days, my darling, we were more interested in peace and love and wondering what the hell we were fighting for."

"I know, I know. 'Come on Baby Light my Fire,' all that stuff."

"See you tomorrow, Tartar," Bob grinned, and left the building. He took two or three steps into the parking lot, and then paused to light his cigarette. He hoped Stan Kostolowicz wouldn't have any trouble getting out tonight. His daughter-in-law could be something of a pain in the ass. She didn't like Stan drinking, that was the trouble. When he drank, he always got up in the middle of the night and flushed the toilet and made himself Polish sausage sandwiches and drank milk out of the carton and messed up her perfect kitchen.

Bob reckoned that there was quite a lot to be said for living on your own. You could come in when you chose; go out when you chose. You could smoke in the john. You could eat chips in bed and nobody complained about the crumbs. You could fart whenever you pleased, and nobody wrinkled their nose up or started spraying lavender air freshener around the place.

He tugged up his collar and began walking across the parking lot. His pale-blue '69 Pontiac Grand Prix with the tattered vinyl roof was parked close to the exit. He had been meaning to repair the roof for nearly four years now. He still liked the car. It was old, but it had plenty of muscle, and as he was fond of pointing out to anybody who would listen, it had the longest hood in GM production history.

He didn't even glance at the Mercedes with the darkened windows. The soft crunch of car doors being closed behind him didn't register. Even when he heard footsteps close behind him he didn't turn around.

But when a woman's voice called, "You're Bob Tuggey, yes?" Bob stopped, and slowly turned, one eye closed against the smoke of his dangling cigarette, and said, "Who wants to know?"

Who wanted to know was an overpoweringly tall, heavily built woman in a short black sleeveless leather dress. Her eyes were the color of green seedless grapes. Her white-blond hair was scraped mercilessly back from her broad pale forehead, and braided into a ropelike Teutonic crown. Her nose was straight and short, her jaw could have cracked walnuts. She wore fine black fishnet pantyhose, and short black high-heeled boots. Altogether she looked like a dominatrix out of a masochist's favorite nightmare.

Not far away with his hands in his pockets stood a painfully thin man in a loose gray business suit and a wide-brimmed hat. He was taller than the woman; but where she was robust and well-fleshed and stocky, he was sere and fragile, and looked as if one healthy smack on the back would crumble him up like ashes.

His face was long and oval, with a generously bulbous nose, but collapsed cheeks, criss-crossed with dry wrinkles, and eyes that swam around in his face as if he couldn't make up his mind what to look at or what to feel. His shoes were as bulbous as his nose: old-fashioned oxfords, with toecaps, from a generation of shoemakers long gone.

"You're Bob Tuggey, yes?" the woman repeated, without answering Bob's question. She sounded as if she had an accent of some kind, Swedish or German, something like that. Bob could talk Vietnamese like a native, and French like a Belgian, but he couldn't speak any of those hurdy-gurdy Nordic languages.

The woman came closer. She was at least six-foot-two, and her breasts were gigantic. Yet she walked with the ease of total fitness. Close up, she smelled of leather and cigar smoke and Chanel No. 5.

"You have something that belongs to us," she told Bob.

Bob meticulously took the cigarette out of his mouth, and blew smoke sideways. "I have something that belongs to you? How do you work that out? I don't even have anything that belongs to myself."

The thin man in the gray business suit raised his hat, revealing a soft mat of white crewcut hair. "Otto Mander, at your service, good sir. And this is Helmwige von Koettlitz. We have no desire to alarm you. But of course we must insist that you return our property."

"What property?" Bob demanded. "I don't have anything that belongs to you."

"I think, a small charm. An amulet," Otto told him.

Bob glanced at the woman called Helmwige. "Are you the lady who called the restaurant today?"

She didn't smile."How do you think I knew your name?"

"Well . . . I'm real sorry," Bob told her. "But I picked that little charm up thinking it belonged to the woman who was burned here a couple of days ago. Did you hear about that?"

"Yes," said Otto, "we heard about that. The question is, what did you do with the charm?"

"I'm real sorry. It was a genuine mistake. I gave it to that woman's fee-ants."

"What?" Helmwige demanded, sternly.

"I told you, it was a genuine mistake. The guy didn't know whether it was hers or not. He'd never seen it before. But he took it anyway in case it was."

"I see," said Otto, as if he hadn't really been listening. A moth flickered past, caught in the floodlights that illuminated the parking lot. Without appearing to look at it, he snatched it out of the air. Then he opened his hand, and inspected it.

"Pretty quick reflexes," Bob smiled at him.

Otto stared at him as blankly as if he had said something in Czech. Then he pushed the still-fluttering moth between his lips, sucked it in, chewed it for a moment, and swallowed it.

Bob found this distinctly unsettling. "Bit of a damned nuisance, right, moths?" he joked. "Good thing they're full of protein." He let out a short, abrupt laugh; then stepped away. "Listen, I'm calling the guy tomorrow. I'll get your charm back for you, even if I have to drive up to La Jolla myself."

"That's all right," Otto told him, raising one hand. "That won't be necessary. We'll drive up to see him ourselves."

"Well, if you want to go to all that trouble . . ."

"Believe me, Bob," Helmwige told him, in a deep, operatic voice, "it will be no trouble."

Bob waited for a moment. Neither Otto nor Helmwige appeared to have anything to say, so he shrugged and said, "Good night, then. Unless there was anything else."

"Wait!" said Otto. "Before you leave . . . may I make an impertinent demand on you?"

"I don't know," Bob replied, cautiously. "Depends what it is."

"You will say nothing about us, to anybody."

Bob drew slowly and suspiciously on his cigarette. "Why should I? I don't care whose charm it is, so long as the real owner gets it back."

"But, you will say nothing?"

"Listen, mister," Bob told him, "it's a free world. If I want to talk about it, I'll talk about it. If I don't, I won't."

"Helmwige?" Otto suggested.

Helmwige smiled. "There was no charm. That would be easy to accept, *nicht wahr?* That there *was* no charm?"

Something told Bob that this confrontation had just gone beyond the parameters of acceptable everyday wackiness. He sensed danger; the same way that he had sensed danger in Saigon. "Avoid the wacky like the plague," William Trueheart had once told him. "They can go from hilarious to homicidal as quick as a blink."

"Sure," he nodded, taking his cigarette out of his mouth. "Sure, that would be easy to accept."

Otto approached him. The breeze blew from Otto's direction,

and smelled like milky Dutch cigars and lavender and death. Otto licked his middle finger and picked a tiny spider from Bob's shirt collar, and bit it between his teeth. "Arachnid caviar," he remarked. "Their little black bodies . . . they make the same sharp *pop!* when you bite them."

"Listen," said Bob, uneasily. "I don't know what the fuck this is all about."

"You don't have to," Helmwige insisted. "All you have to do is to say nothing. Is it so difficult to forget?"

"What's so damn significant about this charm that I have to forget it anyway? If I'm going to forget it, I'd sure as hell like to know what I'm supposed to be forgetting it *for.*"

"Bob . . ." replied Otto, with great middle-European courtesy. "This affair is really nothing which should concern you. You are better off accepting that there are things which happen in this world which are not for the likes of you. Go about your business. Say nothing. You are an ant, that is all."

Bob was already tired and irritable from a long shift cooking hamburgers. "Wait up here," he snapped. "Who are you calling an ant?"

"You're so sensitive, about the lowly reality of your existence? You are an ant. That is not an opinion. That is a fact."

"At least I'm not a fucking stick-insect."

Helmwige came around and stood in front of him. She gave him a quick little shake of her head. "You are not to speak to Herr Mander in that way."

"Pardon me, lady, but I can speak to him any way I please. And if you think I'm going to keep my mouth shut about this lucky charm, or you, or this little charade we're playing out here, you've got another think coming. Special delivery."

He lifted the two fingers in which he was holding his cigarette, and gave Otto a disrespectful salute.

"Well, be seeing you," said Otto, with a smile as thin as the edge of a sheet of paper.

"Not if I see you first," Bob replied.

He stepped around Helmwige and carried on walking toward his car. *Jesus Christ,* he thought to himself, wackos *isn't the word for those two. Those two come from the Planet Bananas.*

He was halfway to his car when he suddenly began to realize that the soles of his feet felt hot. Not just tired-and-sweaty-from-cooking-all-afternoon hot, but *really* hot, like walking barefoot across the beach on a midsummer day.

He half-hopped, and walked more quickly. It had been warm today, for sure, but not warm enough to heat the parking lot up to *this* kind of temperature. His feet almost felt as if they were *burning*.

He glanced behind him. Otto and Helmwige were still standing where he had left them, except that Otto was shading his eyes with his bony hands.

Suddenly Bob's feet hurt so much that he shouted out loud, and danced from one foot to the other. "Jesus! I'm on fire!" he yelled. "Jesus! What have you done to me?"

He dropped to the ground, and yanked at the laces of his worn-out Keds. Smoke was dribbling out of the lace-holes, and out of the ventilation holes at the sides. His feet were actually on fire!

Panting with effort and pain, he dragged off his sneakers and tossed them smoking across the parking lot. God almighty, that Helmwige woman must have given him a double hotfoot! Even his socks were scorched! But he was just about to stand up when both feet actually burst into flame, flaring and spitting like candle wax.

He screamed, and tried to beat at the flames with his hands. But then his hands caught fire, too, and started to blaze just as fiercely.

"Help me!" Bob screamed. *"I'm burning! Help me!"*

But neither Otto nor Helmwige moved a muscle. Otto remained with his hands shading his eyes, as if he were thinking very intently about something inconsequential, like his nephew's birthday present, or what he was going to have for lunch. Helmwige simply watched, with her arms folded under her breasts—not pitiless, but not particularly interested, as if she saw men burning every day.

Bob struggled to his knees, his hands melting in front of his eyes. At first, the pain in his blazing fingers and blazing toes had been excruciating, but then they became numb, and the pain encircled his wrists and his ankles instead. He didn't realize that the fire had burned away his nerve-endings, and that his hands and feet were approaching sixth-degree burns, which meant their complete destruction.

They're not going to help me, he thought, with an overwhelming dullness. *They're just going to stand there and watch me burn.*

He shuffled forward on his knees. The flames from his feet

licked up his back, and abruptly his trousers and the back of his tan leather jacket caught fire. *My ass, for God's sake, my ass is on fire.*

He could see his Pontiac parked only twenty feet away. The dull handpainted fenders; the shredded vinyl roof. There was a fire extinguisher under the passenger seat, if only he could—

Blazing, he stumbled on his knees toward his car. A fiery penitent; a man lurching in flames toward his God. He suddenly thought that he had been doomed to die this way, ever since he had first seen that monk burning himself in Saigon. It was one of those bizarre twists of destiny in which he had become inextricably entangled, the moment he had stepped out of his car on the Cholon road and tried to prevent that monk from doing what he believed he had to.

Cars and buses whished past, this way and that, on Rosecrans Street, only thirty or forty feet away from him. What their occupants thought when they caught sight of a man burning in the parking lot, he couldn't even guess, but none of them stopped. "Oh, look, Morton, there's somebody on fire." "That's all right, dear; it's nobody we know."

Bob's back was burning furiously now, and tongues of flame licked up between his legs. He staggered forward on his knees. It didn't seem to hurt any more, he couldn't think why. It was like kneeling in a very hot wind, that was all. It was almost funny.

He reached his car, and managed to heave himself up with his elbow beside the passenger door. *Extinguisher, extinguisher —then I can put it out, and everything's going to be fine.* He grasped the door handle with his blackened hand. Thank God the locks are broken; I could never turn a key. He pulled, and the door opened, but with a crackling, agonizing wrench, his hand broke off, too, as if his fingers were sticks of charcoal.

He lifted the blazing stump of his wrist in pain and amazement. He understood then that he was dead, that he was beyond healing, beyond any kind of help. In a way, it came as a huge relief, because it took away the burdensome lifelong responsibility of having to take care of his body, of having to survive. No more worries about driving safely and drinking sensibly and giving up smoking.

Bob Tuggey tried to yell, a sort of a rebel yell, to show Otto and Helmwige that he didn't give a damn, that he was going out defiant. But he breathed in nothing but flame, he choked on a throatful of fire, and fell forward into the passenger seat of his Grand Prix without another sound. His body shuddered wildly as it burned, but the movements were probably caused by shriveling muscles.

The vinyl seats caught fire almost at once. Fanned by the warm ocean wind, the interior of the car was soon blazing furiously. All that anybody could have seen of Bob Tuggey were his legs, protruding from the open passenger door.

Now that a vehicle was burning, somebody called the fire department, and sirens began to honk and wail and warble in the distance. Just as the first fire truck turned into the parking lot, Bob's coveted Grand Prix exploded, sending up a huge rolling ball of dazzling white flame that was far brighter and far fiercer than nine gallons of gasoline could have produced.

Burning chunks of car tumbled across the parking lot. Even the engine block rolled over and over, like a monstrous blazing die. Fragments of blazing fabric were caught in what felt like a sudden strong gust, and whirled around and around.

In the eye of this fiery storm stood Otto, slowly lowering his hands from his eyes; and Helmwige, who was looking the other way now, obviously bored.

"Are we going to go to La Jolla tonight?" Helmwige asked, glancing at her fingernails.

"Oh . . . the morning will do," Otto replied. "If Celia's *liebling* believes that the amulet is hers, he will keep it quite safe."

"Bist du müde, meine kleine Taube?" Helmwige cooed, her pink lips shining in the light of Bob Tuggey's burning car. Are you tired, my little dove?

Otto didn't answer, but remained where he was, staring at the glittering embers of steel and rubber and upholstery, his face intermittently lit crimson by the flashing lights of the fire trucks. A moth flickered past in the darkness, attracted by the brightness of the fire. Without hesitation, Otto snatched it out of the air, and pressed it with two fingers flat on his protruding tongue. Then he slowly sucked it against the roof of his mouth.

For no particular reason, he thought of Gretchen.

Gretchen still haunted him, in a way which nobody else that he had killed could ever haunt him. It was her sadness; her sweet gullibility. Young Gretchen, who had trusted him so much, who had believed his every word.

Gretchen's death had been nothing to do with fire. Gretchen's death had been coldness and darkness and tightly twisted wire. But all that had been a long time ago, before the war, before Helmwige, before America.

Helmwige sighed restlessly, and began to pace up and down. Unlike Otto, she found death completely uninteresting. How could anybody be interested in death, when they knew that they were going to live forever?

10

After his shower, Lloyd wrapped himself in a thick white Turkish bathrobe, and sat down in the living room with a large glass of Wild Turkey and all the San Diego newspapers for the past three days. He hadn't looked at them until now. He had known that some of them had carried horrific photographs of Celia sitting burned and smoking, on the point of death, and he hadn't been able to face the idea of seeing her last seconds alive, when there was no possible way that he could turn back the clock and save her.

He was afraid, too, that he would see how much she had suffered.

However, his fear had at last been overcome by his curiosity about the charm that Bob Tuggey had found. He wanted to see if this particular charm were visible in the newspaper pictures.

He turned it over and over, frowning at it. It was discolored by fire, so it must have been *near* her, at least. And its link was broken, as if it had accidentally been twisted and snapped off. But why had she been wearing it at all, on a bracelet that was supposed to symbolize all the important things that had happened in her life?

Maybe it *was* important, but Lloyd certainly didn't know why. A lizard in a circle? What had happened recently that had anything remotely to do with lizards?

His CD was playing Bellini's *La sonnambula*. He remembered Celia singing along with it once, waving a glass of champagne from side to side as she sang, so that champagne flew all over the carpet.

"Celia," he said, although he knew that she could never answer him now. God damn it, why hadn't she told him what was wrong? Why hadn't she even left him a letter?

He picked up the *San Diego Tribune,* and slowly unfolded it. Woman's Fiery Death in Rosecrans St. Parking Lot. Horror-struck McDonald's Diners Witness Apparent Suicide. He stared at the photographs with a feeling of growing numbness. The *Times* picture was quite blurred, but Lloyd could still recognize Celia's face. Her hands were resting in her lap, and it was difficult to make out any detail, but there was a thin white line around her right wrist that was almost certainly her charm bracelet. Unfortunately none of the charms was visible.

He examined the picture on the front of the *San Diego County Post.* This must have been taken a few seconds later, because Celia had collapsed to the ground, but it did show more distinctly that she was wearing her bracelet. Reaching across for his magnifying glass, Lloyd scrutinized the photograph intently. He thought he could distinguish the gold treble clef that he had given her, but there was no obvious sign of the lizard charm.

He went through all the photographs again and again, but none of them was clear enough for him to be able to tell whether she had been wearing that particular charm or not. Maybe somebody at her religious study group had given it to her—and that's why she had kept it a secret from him. He decided to visit Civic Theater tomorrow to see what he could find out about this mysterious Otto and his mysterious get-togethers.

On the front page of yesterday's *Tribune* there was a photograph of the burned-out bus in Anza-Borrego, too; but there was nothing in the report next to it that told him anything he didn't already know.

La sonnambula came to a finish, and Lloyd dropped the newspapers on the table and stood up to put on another disc. He hated the house being completely silent. He kept imagining that he could hear Celia in the kitchen, or in the bathroom, and at night he didn't dare look into her dressing-table mirror, in case he should glimpse her sitting there, making up her eyes, on fire.

He put on *La traviata* and returned to the sofa. Standing up, he could see the newspaper photographs side by side; and it was then that something odd struck him. He frowned first at one newspaper and then at another. He took out his magnifying glass. It was crazy, but the evidence was indisputable. And it was far too much of a coincidence to have happened by chance.

In the background of the photograph of Celia stood twenty or thirty people, most of them children. But two tall figures stood out. A man in what appeared to be a business suit, and a soft wide-brimmed hat; and a blond-haired woman, who had her hand clamped over her mouth.

Then, in the photograph of the burned-out bus, the same two people appeared. They were standing quite a long way from the bus, next to a car that looked like a large Mercedes sedan. There were several other bystanders there. Three men who were probably truckers, and a woman holding a dog on a leash. But there was no question about those two. The man with the soft wide-brimmed hat, and the woman with the bright blond hair.

As far as Lloyd was concerned, that was indisputable proof that Celia's death had been connected with the bus burning—and indisputable proof that these two people knew what the connection was. Damn it, they probably even knew *why* Celia had committed suicide.

He picked up the telephone and dialed Sylvia's number. He had already phoned her two or three times during the evening because he had received two peculiar calls: one from a woman who had *sounded* a little like Sylvia, but who had refused to do anything but whisper; and the other from somebody who had made only kissing noises. Each time he had called Sylvia, however, he had heard a busy signal. He knew that she must be all right—after all, he had seen her go into her apartment building—but he would have liked to have been able to tell her about these extraordinary bystanders, whose fascination with death by burning seemed to go way beyond even the worst excesses of human prurience.

Again, Sylvia's number was out of service. He replaced the receiver, and punched out Sergeant Houk's number instead.

"Sergeant Houk?"

"Houk's out on a call right now. This is Detective Gable. What can I do for you?"

"Oh . . . this is Lloyd Denman. From Denman's Original Fish Depot, remember? My fiancée was the one who—"

"Sure, Mr. Denman. I remember you. Is there anything that I can do?"

"Will Sergeant Houk be very long?"

"Naw . . . shouldn't think so. Thirty minutes tops. Do you want him to call you?"

"Please . . . yes, I'd appreciate it."

He put down the phone and sat back with his fingers laced behind his head. Sergeant Houk had been assigned to assist the state police in their investigation of the burned-bus fatalities, and so it was possible that he already had information that could help Lloyd find these two bystanders. Perhaps they'd been there when the bus was actually burning, in which case the police would have taken their names and addresses.

He wondered what he ought to do if he found out who they were.

He wondered what he ought to do if he found out that they were somehow responsible for Celia's death.

Should he report them to Sergeant Houk, or should he take the law into his own hands? At least if he took the law into his own hands, their punishment would be sure and certain and absolutely final.

He was still drinking and thinking when the telephone rang. He scooped it up and said, "Denman."

"Mr. Denman? Sergeant Houk. I understand you called me."

"That's right, Sergeant, I did."

"You heard the news, then?"

"News? What news?"

"The news about your fiancée's friend Ms. Cuddy."

"Sylvia? I was out with Sylvia earlier this evening. She's all right, I hope? I was trying to call her number, but it's out of service."

"You didn't hear the news, then."

"Well, don't you think you'd better tell me?" asked Lloyd.

There was a pause. It sounded as if Sergeant Houk had put his hand over the receiver and was answering a question from somebody in his office, because he finished up by saying, "Sure, and take it right down to the ME."

Then he said, "Sorry, Mr. Denman, we're a little busy here this evening. I'm afraid that the news is bad. There was a serious fire at Ms. Cuddy's apartment about two hours ago, and she was very regrettably unable to escape."

Lloyd licked his lips. They felt as dry as insects' wing cases. "You're trying to tell me she's *dead?*"

"I'm sorry, Mr. Denman. Really, truly, sorry."

"God almighty. First Celia, then all of those people on the bus. Now Sylvia."

"There's still no suggestion that there's any connection," Sergeant Houk told him, with a noise like swallowing hot coffee. "Since you were one of the last people to see Ms. Cuddy alive, however, I'd like to come around and ask you some routine questions. You know how it is."

"Sergeant—" Lloyd began, and for a moment he was tempted to tell him about the bystanders. But something told him not to, to keep it to himself, at least for a while. He had the feeling that there was an extra double knot in what had happened that logical detective work would never be able to unravel.

"Sure, Sergeant," he finished. "I'd be glad to help." He took a breath, and then he asked, "This fire at Sylvia's apartment . . . does anyone know how it started?"

"Hard to tell. She was literally burned to ashes. The fire department investigators were even talking about spontaneous combustion."

"I thought spontaneous combustion was a myth," said Lloyd. His voice shook.

"You haven't seen Ms. Cuddy's apartment yet. All that got burned was her, and her telephone. Nothing else at all. We've got engineers from Pacific Bell working on it, too. Somebody came up with the theory that she might have been struck by a freak bolt of lightning down the telephone cable. There were a few electric storms around that time."

Lloyd asked cautiously, "Were there any witnesses?"

"None," said Sergeant Houk. "The super said he heard noises, laughing or screaming, but when they stopped, he thought she was having a bit of a private party, if you know what I mean. Nobody saw nobody enter the building, apart from Ms. Cuddy, and nobody saw nobody leave the building, neither. And the door sure wasn't forced in any way, although the security chain was off."

"Is there anything else I can do?" said Lloyd.

"Just sit tight, Mr. Denman, that's all. Sit tight and stay in touch."

"Very well, then," Lloyd agreed, and put down the receiver.

Sylvia, burned to death! My God! He swallowed a mouthful of Wild Turkey and sat on the sofa hunched up and shivering. This was like a forest fire, sweeping through his life, incinerating everybody he knew and loved. How could Sylvia have possibly burned to death? Ashes, Sergeant Houk had told him. Nothing but ashes.

After a while, he went back to the newspapers, spreading them out yet again and reading every story with exaggerated care. Three eyewitnesses had been interviewed for the report on Celia's death. One was Bob Tuggey, whom Lloyd already knew. The others were a twenty-five-year-old gas station attendant (who was unlikely to be dressed in a business suit and a soft felt hat), a thirty-two-year-old babysitter called Maria Salazar (who was unlikely to be blond), and an sixty-six-year-old gardener with the improbable name of Dan Kan.

Lloyd turned to the report of the burned-out bus, to see if any of the names of the eyewitnesses matched those of Celia's burning. The story stated that

. . . the only witness to the burning of the bus was a 12-year-old Pechanga Indian boy, nicknamed "Tony Express" who has been blind since birth. "Tony" told Highway Patrol officers that he had heard a man's voice shouting words that sounded like "You knew us!" in the vicinity of the bus while it was ablaze.

Apart from a guess that the man was elderly, however, he was unable to identify any marked accent or linguistic peculiarity which might have given detectives a pointer.

Lloyd looked back at the photograph of the man and the woman watching Celia die. The man's face was in shadow, because of the wide brim of his hat, but his stance and the stoop of his shoulders suggested to Lloyd that he was about sixty, sixty-five —maybe even older.

But "You knew us"? What did that mean? Maybe he had torched the bus because the people in it could identify him. "You knew us"? "You *knew* us"?

With that extraordinary power of which the human mind is sometimes capable—the power to add two and two together and come up with seven-and-a-half—Lloyd found his eyes drawn across the coffee table, past the spread-out newspapers, to the photocopies that he had made of Wagner's libretto. The name was written in pencil, almost as an afterthought. Junius. *Junius*. Pronounced, in German, not with a *J*, but a *Y*. As in, "You knew us."

He sat staring at the libretto, feeling chilled and excited but not knowing what to do next, in case he broke the spell. It fitted too damn well to be true, like a crossword answer that seems to fit all of the spaces and all of the known letters but turns out to be *banished* instead of *boneyard.*

Could it really be possible that some elderly man had been standing watching that bus burn, with thirteen people inside it, shouting out, "Junius!"? The same opera that somebody had broken into his house to look for? The same opera that—

He closed his eyes in painful realization: *the same opera that Sylvia Cuddy had had in her possession when she was incinerated in her apartment.*

He poured himself another large whiskey and paced up and down the living room, his head churning with ideas. He could tell Sergeant Houk everything that he had guessed. But what did it really amount to? Would Sergeant Houk follow it up? And if he didn't follow it up, would he take active steps to prevent Lloyd from following it up? Lloyd knew how much police detectives disliked amateurs . . . even certified PIs.

In any case, what did his discoveries really amount to? The coincidental appearance of the same bystanders in two news photographs . . . the coincidental death-by-burning of three members of the San Diego Opera in as many days . . . and the phonetic similarity between "you knew us" and "Junius."

Not exactly what any hardnosed detective would call clues.

But Lloyd was so hurt and shocked by what had happened—inside of him, such a rage had built up against whoever was responsible for Celia's burning—that he was prepared to pursue any fragments of evidence, no matter how circumstantial, no matter how coincidental—so long as he found out eventually who had done it, and why, and so long as he made them suffer as deeply and as savagely as he had; and Celia had; and Marianna had; and now Sylvia, too, whose death had agonized him so much that he could scarcely cry.

Tomorrow he would find this Otto character, if only to eliminate him from his investigation. Then he would drive out to the desert and find the Indian boy called Tony Express. He was determined to try anything and everything. He had far more time to spare than Sergeant Houk, and a far fiercer motivation for finding out what had happened.

He went into the kitchen, spooned out heaps of arabica coffee, and switched on the percolator. He wanted to stay sober from now on. No more self-pity, no more tears. Nothing but revenge.

The coffee had begun to *ploop-plip* noisily when the telephone rang.

"Mr. Denman? Waldo. We've taken the last orders; I thought you would like to know that everything is very well."

"Thanks, Waldo, I appreciate it."

"The new-recipe *bouillabaisse* was not such a success. Louis thinks it has to have a different presentation somehow. The dish is too messy to serve somebody who is all dressed up for a special dinner. Too much shell, too many bones."

"All right," said Lloyd, not really listening. "Tell him to work on it."

"Oh . . . one thing. A man called to tell you that the charm did not belong to Ms. Williams. He said his name was—wait a minute, please, I have it here. Uncle Tug. You know this Uncle Tug?"

"Sure, I know him," said Lloyd, with a frown.

"He said the charm did not belong to Ms. Williams, and to call him."

"Okay, then, I will. Thanks, Waldo. Anything else?"

"Everything's smooth, Mr. Denman. Don't worry about nothing."

Lloyd went through to the living room and found the San Diego telephone directory. He leafed through it until he located the Rosecrans Street McDonald's, and punched out the number. It took a long time for anyone to answer, and when a girl's voice eventually said, "McDonald's, how can I help you?" she sounded flustered and distinctly unhappy. Lloyd was sure he could hear sirens in the background.

"I'm trying to get in touch with one of your cooks," said Lloyd. "A guy who calls himself Unca Tug?"

The girl seemed to find it a struggle to reply. Lloyd heard more sirens, and somebody shouting.

"Hey, is everything all right?" he asked. "It sounds like you've got yourselves some kind of panic down there."

"It's Unca Tug," the girl wept. "His car caught fire."

"*What?*" Lloyd demanded. "His car caught fire? He's not hurt, is he?" Understanding at once from the way the girl was sobbing that he *must* have been hurt; that he must have been worse than hurt; that he was dead.

The girl couldn't speak. Lloyd didn't know that it was Sally, Bob's manager, but he could tell that she was somebody who had cared for Unca Tug very deeply.

A young man's voice came on the phone. "I'm sorry, mister. Things are pretty crazy down here at the moment. A car blew up and one of our cooks got himself killed. I'm sorry. Maybe you could call back later."

There was nothing that Lloyd could do except to hang up the phone and sit back on his sofa and wonder what the hell was going on. *Another* fire? *Another* death by burning? This was beginning to look like very much more than a series of coincidental accidents. This was beginning to look like somebody had opened up the oven-gates to hell, and was pitchforking people in there like Old Nick himself.

La traviata came to its climactic ending, and suddenly there was silence. Lloyd felt very alone, and frightened, too. Frightened of his own imagination, frightened of fire, and frightened that people and things that were well beyond his comprehension might be walking the earth—even tonight, in ordinary familiar north San Diego County, while the insects sang and the breeze quietly blew from the ocean, and the moon rose from behind the mountains like a bleached shriek.

Joe North met him at the science museum in Balboa Park. It was one of those hot glaring afternoons when every tree and building seemed to have been drained of its color; and even the sky was white. Lloyd paid the museum admission for both of them, and then they wandered into the main hall.

For a while, they stood side by side watching a small plump boy pedaling a fixed bicycle until he was red in the face, trying to generate enough electricity to turn on the headlights of a sawed-off Ford Fairlane.

"Nice going, kid," said Joe, slapping the boy on the back. "How'd you like a job lighting up Civic Theater?"

The boy stared at Joe as if he were crazy. His black friend across the hall called, "Look out, man. Gays!"

Joe stared at Lloyd and then inspected his own clothes. He was an assistant scenery designer at the San Diego Opera, and he looked it: thin and *nouveau* hippie, dressed in off-white chinos and a red splattery shirt. His nose was noticeably pointed and he wore a natty little clipped mustache under his nostrils.

"Hey, do you think we look like gays?" he asked Lloyd.

Lloyd shrugged. "Even if we were, I wouldn't go for that ugly kid."

They climbed up to the mezzanine, and sat on either side of a vertical Plexiglas screen, face to face. If Lloyd twisted the knobs on his side of the screen, he could gradually impose his own reflection on Joe North's features, until Joe North turned into him. On his side of the screen, Joe North could do the same.

"Tell me about Otto," said Lloyd.

"Well, Otto . . ." Joe replied. "What can I say? Very strange guy. Very charismatic, no doubt about it. One of those people you can't take your eyes off of."

"What did he look like?" asked Lloyd.

"Sixtyish . . . no, probably older. Real dried-up looking, you know? Like you leave a bell pepper out in the sun."

"But where did he come from? How come he got himself attached to the opera?"

Joe cleared his throat with a high, hammering cough. "I thought you would have known him already. Like Celia obviously knew him so well. It was Celia who introduced him to the opera company. She brought him around when we were rehearsing that Opera Gala Night—what was that, April last year? She said he was starting up kind of a born-again study group . . . couple of times a week."

Lloyd twisted the knobs underneath his screen, and gradually his face melted into Joe North's face. The effect was unnerving, as if his whole personality had disappeared. Just like looking into a mirror, and seeing somebody else altogether.

Joe said, "Otto gathered us all around him on the stage. He had this woman with him. . . . Jeez, you never saw such a woman. The *Valkyries* in the flesh. She didn't say too much, but she gave me the feeling that if you couldn't arm-wrestle her in three seconds flat, she'd treat you like dog meat for the rest of your life."

Lloyd sat back. "What was her name? Did you ever find out?"

Joe shook his head. "I heard it, you know? But it was like German, I couldn't remember it. Something like Helmet, I don't know. Helmet, Earwig, I don't know."

"What did Otto say?" asked Lloyd.

On the Plexiglas screen, Joe's face began to recede, and Lloyd's face appeared in its place. Joe's voice came out of Lloyd's unmoving lips.

"He said that we'd all been suffering all of our lives from like a total misconception of what living was all about, you know? He said that we pretended to believe we had souls, and that our souls were going to live forever, but they weren't—not so long as we stayed in these rotting bodies."

Joe hesitated, and then he said, vehemently, "He really got through to us, man. Do you know that? He made us understand that right from the very *second* we were born, our bodies had already started to die. We're so incredibly vulnerable, you know? We can drown, we can fall off of a building. Some terrorist head-case can blow up our plane. Some asshole cab driver can run us down in the street. You know the woman who wrote *Gone with the Wind*, some cab driver knocked her down in the street? Otto really made you feel, where's the logic in that? Where's the sense? What's the point of being born if all you're going to do at the end of it all is die?

"A *germ* can kill you, for Chrissake, that's what Otto said. Something you can't even see. You can be the kindest, most philanthropic person in the whole entire universe; you can be a genius; you can be Einstein. But it only takes one germ, and all of that genius is wiped out forever. All of that kindness, all of that talent, *snap!* and it's gone."

Lloyd stood up, and walked across to the mezzanine railing, and looked out over the main hall of the science museum. Joe got up, too, and stood beside him.

Lloyd said, "Some people say that if it wasn't for death, life wouldn't be worth living."

Joe nodded. "In the end, yes, that's what *I* said. Otto was too goddamn what's-it's-name. Fanatical, I guess. Totalitarian. I never liked anybody telling me what to do. Not even my mom. But for a while there, right at the very beginning . . . well, I guess he made me believe that I could live forever. And a whole lot of the others went *on* believing it.

"How many joined the group?" Lloyd asked him.

"From the opera? I don't know. Maybe five, maybe six, maybe more. I went to the first couple of get-togethers myself, but like I said, Otto was too totalitarian for me. Those weren't discussion groups. Those were Otto-telling-you-how-it-was groups. He said that the pagans of Northern Europe had discovered the secret of eternal life centuries before Christ, you know? But apparently the secret was lost when they were conquered by the Romans and interbred with other, inferior races.

"He was incredibly racist. I mean it was like listening to Adolf Hitler. But he always held out this promise that everybody in the group was going to live forever, and a whole lot of the group really seemed to believe him.

"He said that a new master race was going to be born, a real master race; brilliant and pure and totally dominant. They would rule the whole world because they had no need for fear, or violence, any of that stuff. And the reason for that was, they were going to be immortal. They couldn't die."

Joe took out a pack of banana-flavored Hubba Bubba and unwrapped a piece. "That was when I bowed out. I can make some pretty wild leaps of the old imagination, you know, especially when I've been freebasing, but no wrinkled old guy in a business suit can make me believe that I'm going to live forever."

Lloyd said, "Did Otto explain to you *how* you were all going to live forever?"

"Unh-unh, not to me. I didn't stay around long enough to hear that bit. But there was a whole lot of mumbo-jumbo about secret hymns and special rituals and something they called Salamanders."

"Salamanders; what were they?"

"Search me. I never found out."

"But Marianna stayed on, didn't she?" asked Lloyd. "Didn't *she* ever talk about what they were doing?"

"Not a syllable, I'll tell you. All the people who carried on the study group kept totally silent about it. It was all some terrific secret. I used to ask Marianna about it, but all she said was 'Wait and see.' I said, 'Wait and see what?' but all she said was 'Wait and see.'

"Did it change her at all, going to Otto's group?"

Joe nodded. "It changed everybody who went there. Not for the worse. I mean they didn't get depressed or unhappy or anything like that. Marianna was really light and bright, always singing, always happy."

"But?" asked Lloyd.

Joe glanced at him quickly. "Who said anything about 'but'?"

"You did. I heard it in your voice."

"Well, for sure. There was a 'but'. And the 'but' was like Marianna never really *related* anymore. You see that Plexiglas screen back there? After she started going to that religious study group, I always felt like Marianna was talking through Plexiglas. No contact."

Lloyd said, "Where did the group meet?"

Joe nodded. "Otto rents this house on Paseo Delicias, out by Rancho Santa Fe. Well, I assume he rents it. Way back off the road, really secluded. Not one of your really expensive Rancho Santa Fe properties, though. It's pretty run-down. We used to meet in this kind of converted garage. The whole driveway was always jam-packed with Mercedes—four or five of them, one of them like Rommel's staff car, something like that. Sometimes the group met in different places, from what Marianna told me; but most of the time they met there."

Lloyd slowly rubbed his forehead with his fingertips, around and around. Then he said, "Do you have any idea what this Otto guy was really into? I mean, he was obviously peddling the idea of the life everlasting. All this talk about the body decaying with the soul trapped inside it. But what was he *into?* Did he charge for these meetings? Was it money he wanted? Or what?"

Joe slowly shook his head. "Beats me. He never asked any of us for a penny."

"And he was really offering immortality?"

"That's what he said. But I guess that message is nothing new. When you think about it, what does every TV ministry peddle? What does every spiritual healer promise you? Everlasting life, that's what it's all about."

Joe looked at Lloyd with narrowed eyes, and lifted one finger. "He made one promise, you know, that day he talked to us on the stage. He said, 'Any one of you who chooses to follow me, that one is going to live forever and a day, I promise.' And he didn't just say 'I promise,' like he was selling brushes or something. He said 'I promise' like it was a cast-iron guarantee."

"And Marianna believed him? Just like Celia must have done?"

"I guess. She kept on going to the meetings."

Lloyd said, "I'm just amazed that Celia never mentioned anything about it. Not one word."

"Maybe she thought you wouldn't like the idea."

"Too damn right. But you didn't like the idea, either, did you, and that didn't stop Marianna?"

"Come on, Lloyd, Marianna wasn't my wife-to-be. We were just good friends, who occasionally made it together. Blow hot, blow cold, you know the kind of deal. I wasn't in any kind of position to tell her anything."

Lloyd said, "It's the group, no doubt about it. It's Otto. They joined that group and Otto screwed their minds up. Like the Bhagwan, like the Moonies, like any one of those nutty religions. He promised them life everlasting and they believed him. How could anybody have acted so damn stupid?"

A museum orderly was eyeing them suspiciously. Joe said, "Come on, let's get out of here."

They left the science museum and were walking across the

heat-dried grass of Balboa Park. Joe said, "There was something else . . . something that's been bugging me."

They reached Lloyd's car. Lloyd unlocked it, but waited for Joe to tell him what was on his mind before opening the door.

"I don't know whether it's relevant or not," said Joe. "But about two or three weeks before Otto appeared on the scene, we were spending the weekend together at Dream Inn in Santa Cruz. Marianna had never seen the boardwalk before. Anyway, she was checking her breasts in the bathroom and she suddenly said that she could feel some kind of a lump."

"It wasn't cancer, was it?"

"I never found out. I told her to go to the doctor, and she went to the doctor. But then she didn't say anything more about it. I kept asking her what she was going to do about it, and all she said was she'd been talking to Celia and Celia was going to sort it out."

Lloyd wiped sweat from his forehead with the back of his hand. "Celia was always talking about Marianna, but she certainly didn't mention anything about Marianna having a lump in her breast."

"Well . . . no particular reason why she should, I guess," said Joe. "Girl talk, if you know what I mean."

"Come on, Joe. Celia and I talked about *everything*. And one of your best friends finding a lump in her breast isn't exactly unimportant, is it? Especially since *she* was supposed to be sorting it out. And in any case—how the hell *could* she sort it out?"

"Search me, pal," Joe replied. "But after Otto appeared on the scene she never mentioned it again, and when I asked her about it, she said, 'It's fine; it's all fixed.' "

He paused, and then he added, "And with all due respect, Lloyd, Celia couldn't have told you *everything*, could she? There was a whole lot she was keeping to herself."

Lloyd nodded, and opened the car door. "You want a ride back to the theater?"

Joe shook his head. "I want to walk for a while."

"Okay," Lloyd told him. "I understand. I've been doing a lot of walking myself. Walking, and thinking."

He drove away from the science museum and headed north. Joe watched him go, and then made his way slowly across the grass toward the shade of the trees.

Across the street, a woman was standing watching him. In spite of the heat, she wore a long white raincoat, and her head was tightly tied with a white silk scarf. Her eyes were concealed behind circular sunglasses with dead black lenses.

Joe glanced at her once, but her image was rippling in the heat from the concrete sidewalk and he didn't recognize her. After a while she began to follow him, keeping at least a hundred and fifty feet behind him, but never allowing him out of her sight.

11

Lloyd reached the house on Paseo Delicias a few minutes after twelve. His mouth was dry, and he would have done anything for a glass of cold beer, but finding Otto was more important than quenching his thirst.

Joe had told him that the house was on the second-to-last curve before the road entered the town of Rancho Santa Fe itself. It hadn't been difficult to find. He had driven up the winding road through lemon groves and bursts of flowering bushes; and located the house on a steep left-hand bend, behind a dusty-looking thicket of prickly pear. He had driven right past it, and then parked about three hundred feet further up the road, under the shade of some sadly trailing eucalyptus trees.

He climbed out of the car and put on his sunglasses. It was very hot and quiet, up here in the hills. He had driven up here for lunch on days when the coast had been thick with fog, and it had always been clear. A lizard scuttered out of sight into the undergrowth. There was a strong aroma of evaporating eucalyptus in the air.

His shoes crunched on the dusty blacktop.

Now, how am I going to play this? What if I ring the bell at the front door, and he's actually there, and he answers it? What the hell am I going to say to him? Supposing he really did *have something to do with Celia's death? And Marianna's, too? And Sylvia's? And poor Bob Tuggey's?*

He reached the driveway. It sloped at a sharp angle in front of the house and there were three large Mercedes-Benzes parked in it: an old-fashioned open-topped tourer, in a dull shade of German field gray; a large bulbous black 1950s limousine; and a 1960s 350SL sports car, in white. All three cars were grimy with dust and tree pollen and spattered with fruit-colored bird droppings.

The house itself was equally neglected. It had once been a very elegant adobe, painted white, with a long front veranda and a curved Mexican-style porch. Now its single-story roof was heaped with a thick toupee of dried-up creepers, the paint was flaking, and two of the steps leading up to the porch had rotted and collapsed.

Lloyd could see the garage that had been converted into a "study center." It was a flat-roofed side building built out of whitewashed cinder blocks, with sun-bleached wooden doors. He found it difficult to imagine that Celia had willingly come to a place like this. She had always been so fastidious about everything: her clothes, her hair, the slightest mark on the living-room rug.

What he found even harder to believe was that she could have fallen for Otto and his bullshit about master races and immortality. She had been nervy, yes, like a good many brilliant musicians. But she had never been gullible, nor superstitious, and she had certainly never been racist.

He stood in the entrance to the driveway for nearly five minutes, trying to make up his mind whether he ought to go in or not.

In the end, his mind was made up for him by a security patrol car cruising past, and the driver slowing down on the bend, and staring at him suspiciously through orange-lensed sunglasses. He gave the driver a nod and a smile, and tried to march into the driveway as if he belonged there. Behind the prickly pear, he heard the security car hesitate and then drive on.

Lloyd climbed over the broken steps and approached the front door. It looked as if it hadn't been painted in twenty years. It had probably once been bottle-green, but now it was blistered and faded. The only fixture that looked new was a large brass doorknocker in the shape of a fat, snarling lizard, and even that was discolored by the sun and had never been cleaned.

He listened for a few moments, then he picked up the knocker and tapped it twice. It sounded flat, no echo at all, like striking a coffin with a walking stick. He waited and waited but there was no reply; no sound at all. He knocked again, much louder this time. Again that curious flatness, as if the knocker could only be heard *outside* the house.

He stepped back a little way, and called out, "Anybody home? Mr. Otto? Anybody else?" The sweat was running down the back of his prune-colored Bijan polo shirt. He tried the knocker a third time, and shouted some more, but it was pretty obvious that there was nobody home, or if there *were* anybody home, they were quite determined not to come to the door.

He took off his sunglasses and peered in at one of the dusty windows. Now that it was early afternoon, the sun was sloping into the back of the house, and he could just make out the silhouette of a bulky rounded armchair, and a side table, and a 1930s-style sunray mirror gleaming on the wall. There was something about the decor of the room that disturbed him. It was obviously decorated in 1930s style. But he couldn't believe that anybody would have gone to such trouble and expense to recreate a 1930s room that looked so formidably dull.

It was almost as if the room had been left this way, untouched, for over fifty years.

Treading quietly on the boarded veranda, Lloyd crept along to the next window. Another sitting room, rather smaller, with a dark oak desk facing the back wall. Again the furniture was all pure 1930s . . . a bent plywood chair, a bent plywood table, and a plastic *Volksempfanger* radio, of the type cheaply produced by the German government in the 1930s to spread their propaganda message as widely as possible. On the wall above the desk was a large framed drawing of the same symbol that appeared on the charm that Bob Tuggey had given him: a lizard with its head crooked to one side, and its tail bent the opposite way.

Lloyd rubbed the grimy glass with the side of his hand, but he couldn't distinguish very much more. The rooms were furnished very oppressively, but in an age when fifteen-year-old kids were roaming the streets with loaded Uzis, it was hardly a federal offense to have oppressive rooms.

He walked around the end of the house, tugging aside a mass of creeper that had partially collapsed from the roof, bringing down two or three dozen shingles along with it. The only window he could reach was a small sash window next to the chimney; and he could only just manage to peek into it if he stood up on tiptoe.

He saw a third room, much larger than the other two, and filled with sunlight. Against the left-hand wall stood a black Bechstein upright piano, its top covered in a dark red velour piano-drape. The top of the piano was clustered with framed black and white photographs, although Lloyd couldn't make out who they were. In this room, there were several large bulbous armchairs, covered in anchovy-brown cotton, with "modern" patterns of red Art Deco rectangles. Beside one of the chairs stood a tall chrome ashtray, on which a dead, half-burned cigar butt was perched.

When Lloyd craned his neck around to have a look at the other side of the room, however, he felt a thrill of surprise and alarm. Kneeling on the carpet, with his head bowed, was a young blond man. Very muscular, deep-chested, and narrow-hipped, and from what Lloyd could see of him, very good-looking, if you went for slab-sided profiles and straight noses and deep-set eyes. A jock. More than a jock, a body-builder. The type that Celia would have half-mockingly called an ODYS: an Over-Developed Young Siegfried.

Lloyd stared at the man in fascination, trying to keep as still as possible, so that he wouldn't attract his attention. The man was completely naked, and his wrists and ankles were manacled behind him with shiny steel bands, at least an inch and a half wide, and those manacles in turn were chained to a ring in the floor.

Lloyd had been concerned at first that the man would look up and see him, but the man kept his head unremittingly bowed, as if he were staring at the fireplace and trying to make the hours pass by sheer force of will.

What the hell is this guy doing, chained up to the floor? Maybe he's been kidnaped. Maybe Otto's holding him hostage. Or maybe he chained himself up. You get to hear of stranger perversions than that.

He was certainly in peak physical shape, so he couldn't spend all of his time chained up here. His hair was cropped as flat as a flight deck, too, so he must have been to a hairdresser recently. His pubic hair was as blond as the hair on his head, and he had a huge heavy penis that hung halfway down his thighs, not circumcised, but with the foreskin rolled back to expose the glans.

Lloyd stood on tiptoe staring at him for as long as he could, until his calf muscles began to shudder with the effort. Then he carefully left the window, and retraced his steps along the veranda. He considered knocking at the door again, and even raised the lizard in his hand; but he let it down again, with nothing but the faintest tap. What was the use, when the only occupant that he had seen was incapable of moving more than a couple of inches?

He left the driveway, and walked back to his car. He was strongly tempted now to call Sergeant Houk. After all, Otto must be committing some kind of offense, just by having that young man chained up. If he was guilty of *that,* then surely he could be guilty of almost anything. Didn't the Lindbergh Law say that kidnapers were liable to be sent to the gas chamber? Or was that something he had read in that Joseph Wambaugh book *The Onion Field* and gotten mixed up?

He drove back home, playing *La Bohème* on his car stereo. He finally decided not to get in touch with Sergeant Houk, not yet. First of all he wanted to talk to Otto in person, face-to-face, and ask him some searching questions about Celia. If he contacted Sergeant Houk, he would never get the chance. He wanted to ask Otto how the hell a beautiful intelligent girl like Celia could have been bewitched by all the squalid claptrap of racial purity and dominant human species and immortality.

Then he wanted to ask him what had given him the right to intrude on their love and their happiness—whether he was directly responsible for Celia's death or not.

And then he wanted to ask him what kind of a creature he really was.

He called Waldo on his car phone. It took Waldo a while to answer. It was the middle of lunch, and the Original Fish Depot was hectically busy. When he came to the phone, he sounded flustered but cheerful.

"It's going good, Mr. Denman, believe me. Already this lunchtime fifteen lobsters and ten specials."

"That's great. I'll look in later. Meanwhile I'm off to the desert."

"You're going to the desert? Why for?"

"A little research, that's all. Any messages? Any calls?"

Waldo coughed. "Two people called by to see you. They said you were expecting them."

"I wasn't expecting anybody."

"Well . . . you didn't say that you would come to the restaurant today, so I guessed that you weren't."

"Who were they? Did they leave their names?"

"An old man, and a woman. Some kind of a woman, too. Too big for me."

An old man, and a woman. Lloyd felt a cold pain of anxiety and suspicion that was almost like neuralgia. "They didn't leave their names?" he repeated.

"They said not to worry. They said they'd find you, whatever."

Lloyd said, "This old guy . . . was he wearing a hat, and a suit?"

"That's right, hat and a suit. And the woman was wearing all black leather. Looked like a biker, you know? Or maybe a hooker. Biker or hooker, one of the two. Or maybe she was a restaurant critic." Waldo thought this was funny and laughed until he coughed.

Lloyd laid down the phone. This was a new and distinctly disturbing development. He was looking for Otto, but at the same time it seemed like Otto was looking for *him*. The only reason that Otto had been out when he had called at the house on Paseo Delicias was because Otto had been calling at the Original Fish Depot.

So what did Otto want?

There was only one possibility. The charm with the lizard on it. The same lizard that Lloyd had seen on the wall of Otto's house. Unca Tug had called him to say that the charm hadn't belonged to Celia, and the only way that Unca Tug could have found *that* out is if somebody had come looking for it.

Somebody had come looking for the lizard charm and Unca Tug had died by fire. Somebody had come looking for the Wagner libretto, too, and Sylvia had died by fire.

Lloyd was beginning to feel sure that all this burning was down to Otto, and that Otto was not simply some religious and racist wacko, but gravely dangerous. A homicidal madman with a taste for random violence was frightening enough; but a homicidal madman with his own rationale for changing the world was even more terrifying.

He stopped at a gas station at Escondido, and a little tubby lady in a back-to-front baseball cap filled up his BMW.

"Nice car," she commented.

"I like it," said Lloyd.

"My old man, he wouldn't have a German car for all the world," she remarked.

"Oh?"

She wiped a dab of grease from the end of her nose. "He was in the 4th Armored Division during the war. Liberated some of the concentration camps."

Lloyd gave her his credit card. "In that case, I guess he's got a reason."

"Won't even drink Milwaukee-brewed beer, for fear that it's made by Germans."

It was a long and pleasant and calming drive, out to the Anza-Borrego Desert. The road wound up through trees and mountains, and the quiet communities of Ramona and Santa Ysabel. Lloyd stopped at Julian for a cheeseburger and a beer, and then drove onward, into the dusty scrubby outskirts of the desert itself.

On the car stereo, he played a tape he had found of plangent rock 'n' roll from the Woodstock days: Country Joe and the Fish, the Doors, Captain Beefheart and his Magic Band. It brought back memories of business college, furry sideburns and flared jeans and girlfriends with miniskirts and chains around their hips and long shining hair. His first car (a Beetle, with a peace symbol painted on the door). His first joint (pukish). Sitting cross-legged all night in a friend's poster-plastered apartment, drinking Thunderbird Red and talking about Meaning and Being Yourself, Man, and how they were all going to go to London and find out where it was At.

He had stopped looking for Meaning a long time ago. Once he had started work, he hadn't had the time. As for Being Yourself, he had discovered how incredibly easy that was, once he had stopped trying to Be like Somebody Else (Paul Newman, for example, in *Cool Hand Luke;* or George Peppard in *The Carpetbaggers*). He had never made it to London, but he guessed that since the Swinging Era had long since passed away, London probably wouldn't be much different from anyplace else, all Burger Kings and bumper-to-bumper traffic—no more where it was At than Indianapolis or Pittsburgh or San Francisco.

He thought of the first time he had seen Celia, at that charity dinner at the Rancho Bernardo Inn. She had stepped out of the doorway of El Bizcocho restaurant, and the sun had dropped into her hair like a sign from the angels above. *This is the one for you, Lloyd, here she is; we'll even light her up for you, so there won't be any mistake.*

His throat tightened, and he sniffed. He missed her; by God, how much he missed her. He found a tissue in the glove compartment and loudly blew his nose.

He had been worried that it would be difficult to find the place where the bus had burned, but he came to the crest of a rise in the road, and there it was, about a couple of hundred feet off to his left, a blackened skeleton, more like a charcoal sketch of a bus than a real bus.

Movingly, the skeleton had been decorated with scores of white ribbons, tied in fluttering bows—tributes from relatives and passing motorists to all the people who had died in it. A single car was parked beside it now, a red open-topped Camaro.

Lloyd turned off the blacktop and drove slowly across the scrub. He parked not far away from the Camaro and climbed out. White dust blew away from his tires; the wind whistled softly past his car antenna. He walked toward the bus and stood staring at it, the saddest memorial that he had ever seen.

As he stood there, a young woman came walking around the side of the wreck. She was dark-haired, tall, and she was wearing a short black dress. She came up to him and said, "Hello, there. Are you a relative?"

Lloyd shook his head. "Just a friend."

"It was such a tragedy," the young woman said. She was wearing wraparound sunglasses, so that it was difficult for Lloyd to tell what she looked like. But she had high cheekbones and a strong jawline, that well-bred look that distinguishes many of the children of good-looking California parents. She was large-breasted but very narrow-waisted, and she had what a political friend of Lloyd's had once called Congressional Committee legs—in other words, they went on and on and you thought they were never going to come to an end.

She said abstractedly, "I didn't think I wanted to see it. But in the end I had to. It was like seeing Mike. I didn't think that I could bear it. But I did; and at least I won't have nightmares about it, trying to imagine what he looked like, and never knowing."

"Mike?" asked Lloyd.

"My husband. Mike Kerwin. I'm Kathleen Kerwin."

Lloyd shook hands. "Lloyd Denman. I hope you'll accept my condolences. It must have been a terrible shock."

She shrugged, to show her feeling of helplessness. "I was working in my shop and two state troopers came in and said that he was dead. I couldn't understand it. He wasn't even supposed to be here."

"He wasn't?" asked Lloyd. "I had a friend on this bus—well, a friend of my fiancée's . . . well, a friend of my *late* fiancée's. She worked with the San Diego Opera Company. Nobody knew what the hell *she* was doing out here, either."

Kathleen said, "They kept saying things on TV, like it's a suspected Colombian drug massacre. Or it's a mass suicide pact. But Mike wasn't into drugs; he was a manager for San Diego Federal. And he was so happy. . . ."

Lloyd said, "Do you mind if we talk about this? I've been trying to do a little detective work on my own, trying to find out what happened. Maybe you can help me."

"Well, certainly," said Kathleen. "Are you a private detective or something?"

"Not me. I run a fish restaurant."

She almost managed to smile. "Do you want to talk now, or later? It's very hot out here."

"As a matter of fact, I came out here looking for an Indian kid," said Lloyd. "The newspapers said that he was the only witness to the burning. I was wondering if there was any chance that he could give me some kind of clue who did it."

Kathleen looked around, as if she expected to see the Indian boy standing not far away. "Didn't the police talk to him?"

"Oh, sure the police talked to him. But I'm not too sure that the police would have asked him the right questions. It seems to me that there's more going on here than meets the eye. I mean, this whole thing has some very weird aspects to it. Like your husband, for instance. You know he wasn't a crack dealer or a potential suicide. Neither was Marianna, the girl from the opera, not a chance of it. So what were they both doing here, out in the desert, on a bus, getting themselves burned to death?"

Kathleen said, in a flat voice, "The police told me that none of them tried to escape."

"Well, that's right, they didn't. They just sat here and burned."

They were silent for a moment. It was eerie out here, on the face of this baking-hot desert, with the wind sighing through the black-charred wreckage of the bus, and fluttering the white ribbons.

"I thought I'd drive up the road a way and see if I can track down that Indian kid," said Lloyd. "Why don't you come along, too? He can't live too far away; he's blind."

Kathleen looked at Lloyd in surprise. "But if he's blind—?"

"He didn't see anything, but he *heard* something. He may have heard more, if he could only remember it. Whatever, it's worth a try."

"All right, then," Kathleen agreed. "But there's something I have to do. It won't take a minute."

"Sure thing," Lloyd told her.

While Lloyd waited, she went to her car, opened the trunk, and took out a wreath of white silk ribbons and white silk flowers. Across the center were written the words Michael Kerwin, My Beloved Husband, Now You'll Never Die. She walked across to the bus, and tied it on the front. Then she lowered her head for a moment in a silent farewell.

They drove less than a mile and a half farther before they reached a sharp left-hand turnoff. A sun-faded sign pointed northwest for Gas, Food, Indian R-T-Fax. Lloyd turned, and Kathleen, in her Camaro, followed him.

They followed a range of low sprawling hills, occasionally dipping deep down into the shadows of an arroyo, and then rising up into the sunshine again. After about two more miles, they saw a 76 gas station in the distance, with a small barnlike building standing next to it, and a ramshackle collection of trailers and pickup trucks in back, and a sign saying Trailers 4 Rent. Three windpumps circled overhead, and stray dogs roamed the perimeter.

As they came closer, they passed a large handpainted signboard, which announced Indian Jack's Genuine Pechanga Souvenirs. Beer Hot Dogs Blankets Beads. Turkwise Jewelre. Video Rental.

They pulled up outside the barnlike building, the double doors of which were opened wide and hung around like a roadside shrine with feathered headdresses and saddles and brightly colored blankets and peace pipes and rope and chaps and all kinds of Indian souvenir junk. A rusted Coca-Cola machine shuddered noisily at the side of the doorway, and a little farther away, at the end of a long chain, as if to prevent it from hopping off, stood an old-fashioned one-legged bubble-gum machine half-filled with sun-bleached gumballs.

A preteenage boy with dark glasses and black shoulder-length hair was sitting on a rocker in the doorway, smoking a cigarette and listening to Prince on a Sony Walkman. To him, the volume of "When Doves Cry" must have been earachingly loud, because Lloyd could hear what the music was while he was still ten feet away.

"I'm looking for a kid called Tony Express," said Lloyd.

The boy made a face, without taking off his earphones.

Kathleen suggested, "I don't think he heard you."

Lloyd stepped forward, lifted up the boy's left earphone, and yelled into his ear, "I'm looking for a kid called Tony Express!"

The boy lifted off his headset and resentfully rubbed his ear. "Shit, man, I may be blind but I sure as hell ain't deaf."

"I'm sorry," Lloyd told him. "You must be Tony Express."

"What's it to you if I am?"

"I've been looking for you, that's what."

"Well, now you've found me, man. What do you want?"

"A little help, that's all."

"Sure thing. How about some really neat moccasins, all handmade? Or maybe a pipe-tamper made of genuine bone, or a cradleboard? These cradleboards look great, you know, you can fill them with arrangements of dried flowers, and hang them on your kitchen wall. I've sold a whole bunch of them to Cannell & Chaffin."

"Cannell & Chaffin, the interior designers?" Lloyd looked at Kathleen in amazement. "Can you believe this kid?" he asked her. "A young upwardly mobile Pechanga."

"You got to move with the mood, man," Tony Express replied. "How about a sun-dance doll?"

He groped to one side of his chair and lifted up a long stick decorated with skin and fur and squirrel tails and beads. On the top of it, a small cross face had been painted.

"What's that for?" asked Kathleen.

"It grants you revenge, if you ask it nicely."

"Who said anything about revenge?" said Lloyd.

Tony Express let out a high, cracking laugh. "Nobody said nothing about revenge, man. You didn't have to. You didn't come here to buy nothing, did you, or else you'd've been asking me by now how much my blankets were, or did I take VISA, or coming out with stuff like 'look at that wonderful weather-dance shirt, darling; I could wear it to play golf.' "

"You've got a pretty jaundiced view of the world, don't you?" Lloyd asked him, immediately regretting the use of the word *view*.

"What's 'jaundiced'?"

"Sour, cynical," Lloyd told him.

Tony Express smiled. "That's because I can't see it, man. I can't see its colors and I can't see its false bright faces. I can't even imagine what a color *is*."

"So what's all this about revenge?"

"That's what *you* should be telling *me*, man. You're the one who came here looking for it. You don't want to buy, so you must want to talk; and who comes all the way out here to Nothing Junction in a fancy foreign car, just to talk to some blind Indian kid about the weather, or how you can't get good help anymore?

"Come on, man, get serious. You came here to talk about the only thing that's happened here in twenty years, man, that bus burning out, and all those people getting themselves killed."

"I could be a cop," Lloyd suggested.

"Unh-unh," said Tony Express. "You're not a cop because cops don't drive fancy foreign cars and they don't wear Geoffrey Beene aftershave, either. So you must be an insurance investigator or a relative of somebody who died. And since you didn't introduce yourself as soon as you arrived, 'Listen, my name's Dick Head and I represent the Never-Pay Insurance Company Inc.,' I guess you're a relative. And when somebody gets killed, what do relatives want more than anything else, especially in a Judeo-Christian society? They want revenge. Have a sun-dance doll, thirty-six bucks plus tax."

Lloyd shook his head, and said to Kathleen, "This guy's so sharp he's going to cut himself. How come you know 'Judeo-Christian' but you don't know 'jaundiced'?"

Tony Express tapped his nose with his finger. " 'Judeo-Christian' was on television, man. This brave always listens heap good, you understand? And when you listen—when you *really* listen—you can always tell exactly what's going down. Nobody can ever pull the wool over your eyes, man, because you ain't got no eyes to have the wool pulled over. I heard your car engine, man, and that's a six-cylinder import with overhead cams, and if you'd left it running a little longer I would have told you what it says on your bumper stickers. In fact I can tell you now; it says Save the Whales."

"Actually it says I Don't Brake for Smartass Blind Kids," Lloyd retorted.

Tony Express gave him a lopsided grin. "All right, man, I'm sorry. I've been running off at the mouth again. I do it sometimes. Either I'm silent and moody and don't talk to nobody for weeks, or else I get this verbal diarrhea. I spend too much time alone, that's the problem. I guess I'm overeducated, too. I listen to the radio all day and the TV for most of the night. What else is there to do? My teacher says I'm brilliant but wayward."

"Are you really twelve years old?" Lloyd asked him.

Tony Express nodded. "Twelve, going on thirteen."

"In that case you're too young to smoke. Does your father let you smoke?"

"My father's away on business. Avoiding the cops in other words. My grandfer's taking care of me, John Dull Knife. He lives in that old Airstream trailer way in the back, by the fence."

Lloyd said, "Do you mind if I ask you a couple of questions about the day the bus burned?"

"No problem; what's it worth?"

"A ten?"

"No problem."

Kathleen had already perched herself on the hitching-rail at the front of the store. Lloyd dragged over a cracker barrel and sat on that.

"It says in the paper you heard somebody talking while the bus was on fire."

"That's right," Tony Express agreed. "He kept on saying 'You knew us, you knew us.' "

"Could it have been that he wasn't saying 'You knew us,' but 'Junius'?"

Tony Express angled his head slightly. "Say that again, man."

"Junius. *Junius*, like somebody's name."

"Again, man."

Lloyd repeated it six or seven times. At last Tony Express lifted his small nailbitten hand as an indication that he should stop.

"Well?" asked Lloyd.

"You're right," said Tony Express. "It was 'Junius.' I said 'You knew us' because I never heard the name Junius before."

"You're certain about that?" Lloyd asked him.

"Absolutely. I'd swear it on the Bible."

"Now . . . this could be more difficult," said Lloyd. "Can you remember if he said anything else? Anything less distinct? Did he sing, maybe? Did he say anything in a foreign language?"

Tony Express thought about that, and then slowly shook his head. "I don't think so, man. There was so much noise going on when that bus was burning. Crackling, popping. Like sticking your head in a bowl of Rice Krispies."

Lloyd sat back in disappointment. "So there was nothing at all?"

"Well . . . one thing. But I couldn't be sure, man. I wouldn't swear to it."

"Tell me anyway."

"After the bus had been burning for quite a while, I thought I heard a sound like a trumpet or something. It was probably the bus, you know, the driver falling onto the horn, or maybe the alarm circuits melting. But that was all."

"One thing more," Lloyd asked him. "If you heard this man's voice again, the one who said 'Junius,' do you think you could identify it? Do you think you could pick it out and say, 'Yes, that's the guy.' "

Tony Express didn't hesitate. "Any time. Any time at all."

"You seem very confident about that," put in Kathleen.

"I've got a phonographic memory," Tony Express told her. "I can remember voices and sounds exactly. My teacher says it's uncanny. I don't know what's supposed to be so uncanny about it, especially since I can't see. I have this terrific nose for smells, too. You had garlic last night."

"What?" said Lloyd.

"Just kidding around, man. But if you can find this dude, I can pick him out."

"Good," Lloyd told him. "That's excellent. Here's your ten bucks, and here's another ten, in case it gets lonesome. Do you think I could call you, if I ever manage to find this guy, and ask you to identify his voice?"

"Sure thing. Do you think it was him who torched the bus?"

"I can't tell for certain, but it's beginning to look that way. Here—here's my card. It's a restaurant in La Jolla. I won't be there most of the time, but if you ask for Waldo, he'll help you out."

"Waldo, hunh?" asked Tony Express, with obvious skepticism. "Like in Mr. Magoo?"

"That's right, like in Mr. Magoo."

"You know what Mr. Magoo's problem was, don't you, man?" asked Tony Express. "He looked and he looked, and he *still* couldn't see."

12

Joe North arrived back at his apartment above the Smiling Sashimi restaurant on West Washington Street shortly after seven o'clock. To reach his front door, he had to elbow his way through the chattering, unhelpful line of would-be diners who were already out in the street waiting for tables. The Smiling Sashimi was one of the cheapest and most popular Japanese restaurants around Hillcrest, although after a month-long binge of eating there almost every evening after it had first opened, Joe hardly patronized it at all.

Marianna had always made corny jokes about it. "You're too tempura-mental," she used to tease him.

He closed the street door behind him (red-painted, to match the restaurant) and climbed the narrow staircase to the second floor. The lights didn't work, and he had to feel his way up in darkness, carrying a heavy sack of groceries in the crook of his arm.

He wasn't surprised that the lights were out. Joe had sent the name of Mr. Puls the landlord to the *Guinness Book of World Records* as the Meanest Bastard on God's Earth. Mr. Puls believed that if it didn't specifically state in the rental agreement that the tenant had the right to see where he was going, then he had no legal obligation to supply light bulbs.

"If you're shortsighted, do I have to buy you eyeglasses?" he always shouted.

Joe groped his way blindly along the landing until he found

his front door. He had to set his shopping bag down on his feet while he struggled to find his key and jab it into the lock.

He sniffed. He thought there was an odd *burned* smell on the stairs. He was used to the smell of sukiyaki and chicken teriyaki, and once the whole kitchen downstairs had caught fire. From Joe's apartment, it had sounded like the sinking of the *Musashi* at Leyte Gulf, screaming and yelling and doors slamming, and afterwards the building had smelled like scorched bean curd for weeks.

But this burned smell was different. This smell was like overheated radiators; or saunas. A dry smell. Not oily, not smoky. He couldn't place it. It was like nothing he had ever smelled before.

He opened his front door and switched on the light. He kicked the door shut behind him. He had lived over the Smiling Sashimi ever since it had been the Siete Mares Mexican restaurant, and *he* had been deputy assistant scenery painter at Civic Theater. He kept telling himself that he ought to move somewhere classier, somewhere up the coast; but somehow there never seemed to be time. Or money. Even for one studio room, a shower, and a kitchen so small that you had to step into the hallway to open the oven door, he was paying what his mother was paying in Minnesota for a whole three-bedroom house.

He backed into the kitchen and set his groceries down on the counter. A frozen lasagne, a large bag of cheese nacho chips, a dozen Washington Red apples, some cinnamon-flavored dental floss, a *TV Guide*, and a bottle of Chianti. Now was that Living, or was that a Loneliness Set in a brown paper bag?

He tore open the lasagne box and slid the lasagne into the microwave oven to defrost. He could still smell that strange overheated smell. Maybe the cooks downstairs had accidentally left one of their woks over a hot flame for too long. Maybe it was diesel oil wafting over from the Naval Station, or airplane fuel from the airport.

Rattling open his kitchen drawer, he scrabbled through shoals of ill-assorted cutlery until he found a waiter's friend. He opened up the bottle of Chianti, and poured himself a large glass with his right hand while he adjusted the microwave with his left. He hummed the "Humming Song" from *Madama Butterfly*.

He was still humming it when he went through to the studio room, and switched on the lamps in there.

He dropped his glass of wine on the rug. He heard it fall, a dull ringing noise, but he didn't make any attempt to catch it, didn't look down.

Sitting on the end of his bed, quite upright, her hands held loosely in her lap, was Marianna. Against the jazzy red and yellow gaiety of the Mexican blanket that covered his bed, she looked monochromatic and severe. Her hair was tucked up into a black beret. She wore black sunglasses and a black belted raincoat and black stockings. Her face was as gray as clay.

"Jesus," said Joe. "I'm seeing things. Jesus, I'm seeing things."

He turned around, and went directly back to the kitchen, and stared at the top half of his face in the mirror that was propped on top of his 1991 Smiling Sashimi calendar. The top half of his face stared back at him like a Venetian carnival mask. Blank, festive, and cruelly uncommunicative.

He told his eyes, "I saw Marianna sitting on the bed." His eyes stared back at him and didn't blink.

"Marianna's dead and I just went into the other room and there she was sitting on the end of the bed, wearing these shades and staring at me."

He was trembling. He hadn't trembled as wildly as this since he had caught the Asian flu, his second year at the San Diego Opera, and almost died.

"She was there!" he yelled at the mirror, pounding his fist on the kitchen counter so hard that his box of dental floss jumped onto the floor. "I walked into the studio and she was there!"

He covered his face with his hands. Marianna's death had shocked him, disoriented him badly. Even though he and Marianna hadn't always gotten along too well, he had always known that she was *there*, that he could call her, that he could surprise her, even if she told him to take a hike. It was only when she had completely disappeared from the world that he had been able to assess the size of his affection for her, the same way that you don't know how much you're going to miss a tooth until the dentist pulls it and you're left with this huge gaping Grand Canyon cavity in your mouth and you can't eat pizza for a month.

A soft voice said, "You weren't dreaming, Joe."

"See, now I'm hearing things," Joe told himself, lowering his hands. "It's the shock, right? I've been suppressing the shock. But now that I've talked to Lloyd about it, the dam's broken. I'm not shocked anymore. Just seeing things, and hearing things."

"*Joe,*" said the voice, amused.

He turned his neck stiffly sideways. Marianna was standing in the doorway, in that tilted black beret and those impenetrable black sunglasses, her hands thrust into her raincoat pockets.

"You're real," he told her.

She smiled, and stepped into the kitchen. He smelled heat again; that dry metallic heat. "Of course I'm real, Joe. I'm more real now than I was before."

"Well—*hanh*—good! What's that supposed to mean? *More* real?"

"Didn't you ever love me?" asked Marianna. "Don't you remember those times we went to Mexico? Dancing at Tijuana Tilly's? Eating ourselves sick on mixiote? Laughing, getting drunk? Remember that night at Popotla?"

"You died on that bus," Joe told her.

She turned her head away. "I was burned, Joe, but I didn't die."

"Everybody died on that bus, Marianna. You included. I'm experiencing some kind of hallucination here, caused by delayed shock. You hear that, Joe? You're hallucinating."

"No, Joe," Marianna told him. "I'm here; I'm here for real, and I'm here forever."

He stared at her. In spite of his natural skepticism, he was beginning to believe that *no,* she wasn't dead; and that *yes,* she was real. He slowly reached out his hand and touched her arm.

"I can feel you," he said; but more to himself than to her.

"Yes, you can feel me. I'm real."

"And forever?"

"Yes."

"So Otto was telling us the truth all along?"

"Yes, Joe. Otto was telling us the truth all along."

Joe covered his mouth with his hand, and leaned against the kitchen counter as if he couldn't think of anything to say.

"Did you tell Lloyd about Otto?" asked Marianna. He could still feel her heat. *Heat, heat, heat.* It was like standing next to an electric fire.

"I don't believe this," Joe protested. "You can't be real. It isn't possible."

"Joe, it was easy; once I'd made that leap. Once I had that faith. I'm pure now, Joe; purified. Nothing but smoke and soul."

Joe said, "I'm going crazy. Listen—I'm going to leave now. Okay? I'm going to walk out of this apartment for a while and if you're real you'll still be here when I get back. But if you're not

. . . well, I don't know. I'm going to have to think about that. Kirsty McLaren said that her shrink was pretty good."

"Joe," said Marianna, "I'm real."

"Sure you are. Sure you're real. Just like Daffy Duck's real and Batman's real and Roadrunner's real. They must be real; you can see them on TV."

"Joe—" Marianna began, stepping forward.

Joe bunched up his fists and roared at her like an angry two-year-old. "Damn it, Marianna! I'm scared! You scare me! You're dead, but here you are!"

"Joe, shush, it's okay. Everything's fine. I'm smoke and I'm soul and I'm absolutely fine."

"I'm going to call Lloyd."

"No, Joe, don't call Lloyd."

"Jesus, Marianna, this is insane. I'm going to *have* to call Lloyd."

"Did you tell Lloyd about Otto?"

"Of course I told Lloyd about Otto. What do you think?"

The smell of heat grew even stronger. Joe was so hot that he was sweating, and the sweat stung his eyes. All the time he was backing away from Marianna but Marianna kept circling around and edging nearer, circling and edging, until Joe began to feel that he would never get away from her.

Marianna said, "When you left the group, Joe, Otto made you promise that you would never tell. Don't you remember? You took an oath."

"That wasn't any oath."

"You laid your hand on the Book of Salamander and you swore not to tell."

Joe let out a half-broken laugh. "Hey, come on. The Book of Salamander isn't exactly the Holy Bible."

"No, it isn't. It's greater than the Holy Bible. It doesn't just tell you that life has its miracles; it tells you what the miracles are; and how they can be achieved."

"It's bullshit."

Marianna shook her head. "Don't blaspheme, Joe. You've already broken your solemn oath. Don't blaspheme, too."

"It may be blasphemy to you, but it's bullshit to me."

He reached out for the telephone, but Marianna seized his wrist to stop him. There was a sharp sizzle of burned hair and seared skin, and Joe let out a bellow of pain. "*Aaaahhh! Christ! Aaaahhh!*" He wrenched his arm away and held it up. Marianna's fingers had burned five scarlet stripes around his wrist, and his skin was already bubbling up into a mass of blisters.

Shocked, he stalked stiffly into the kitchen, and turned the cold faucet on full. He held his wrist under the running water until the agonizing burning was reduced to a thick, numb ache. Marianna came and stood beside him, watching him. Her gray face was impassive. There was no telling if she was pleased or sorry.

"You can get the fuck out of here," Joe told her, his voice shaking.

"You have to keep your oath, Joe. You can't tell anyone. Otherwise we're all at risk."

"Risk? What risk? Christ, how did you burn me like that?"

Marianna reached out for him again, but he backed away. "Just keep off, okay? Just stay away."

But Marianna continued to edge closer, and now she slowly twisted open the top button of her raincoat. Joe retreated to the opposite side of the kitchen, keeping his eyes on her all the time. He felt behind him for the counter, then for the drawer handle. As Marianna released the second button of her raincoat, and then the third, he tugged open the drawer and rooted around inside it for his carving knife.

"Joe . . . so long as you swear to keep your oath . . . everything's going to be fine. But you have to swear."

She unbuttoned the last button, and with a twist of her shoulders, the raincoat dropped to the kitchen floor. Underneath, she was naked, her skin shining pearly gray. Her small dark-nippled breasts were just the same as Joe remembered; her rounded stomach; her heavy thighs. But she had a dull subcutaneous glow that reminded him of nothing but death. As a boy, Joe had seen a drowned man dragged out of the Cahokia Canal in East St. Louis, and his skin had glowed with the same dim putrescence.

Around her waist, Marianna wore a wide black belt that was buckled so tight that it made her flesh bulge out, top and bottom. The belt's clasp was in the shape of a lizard inside a circle.

"Joe, don't you want to kiss me, Joe, the way we used to? Don't you want to hold me?"

"You just keep your fucking distance," Joe warned her. His fingers closed around the blade of his sharpest vegetable knife; and he felt it slice through flesh. He turned the knife around, and picked it up, and brandished it in front of Marianna's face. Blood was running down his fingers and dripping from his burned wrist.

"Don't you want to make love to me, Joe?" Marianna coaxed him, coming closer. She reached her hand down between her legs, and started rubbing herself sensually, and purring. "Remember those nights in Tijuana, Joe? Not a wink of sleep. Make love to me, Joe, come on; make love to me."

Joe stared in horrified fascination as she plunged her hand deeper and deeper between her legs. She opened the lips of her vagina with one hand and slid the index finger of her other hand right inside, right up to the knuckle, and stirred it around and around. She closed her eyes, and threw back her head, and cooed, "Come on, Joe, I need you so much . . . come on, Joe, I love you."

Joe hesitated for only a second. Then he dodged to the right, colliding with the edge of the refrigerator, and threw himself out the kitchen door, into the hallway.

Marianna's reaction was instantaneous. She clawed for his shoulder as he hit the refrigerator, then jumped on his back as he made his way to the front door. Immediately, Joe felt as if his back had been doused in blazing gasoline. He screamed in pain, and staggered sideways under the weight. His shirt scorched, then burst into flames. He twisted and grunted, and tried to swing Marianna against the wall, but she was clinging on too tightly, and her legs were burning into his sides, into his jeans, into his skin, into his flesh, and her arms were branding his shoulders like meat.

Reaching behind him, he stabbed at her frantically with his vegetable knife. But there didn't seem to be anything there to stab. In spite of her heat, in spite of her weight, she appeared to be completely insubstantial. Like smoke. Like someone's soul. Like nothing at all.

"*Marianna!*" he roared, with his clothes on fire and his hair shriveling.

But Marianna shrieked, "It's a game! It's a game! You have to guess who I am!"

"*Oh God!*" cried Joe, dropping to his knees. "*Oh God, Marianna, you're burning me!*"

"It's a game, Joe! Who am I? Who am I?" and she clapped her hands over his eyes, so that he wouldn't be able to see her.

Smoke poured out from between Marianna's fingers as she burned her way through Joe's upper cheeks and eyelids, and then fried his eyes. Through all of that pain, Joe felt his eyeballs burst, and heard the sharp sizzle of optic jelly. He was beyond screaming.

The pain was too much. The horror of being blinded was more than his brain could accept. All his brain was interested in right now was survival.

He stabbed at her wildly, stabbed again. But she forced him down and rolled him over onto his back and forced him flat onto the floor.

All he could think of was pain. It flooded over him, as if he had been washed over by a tidal wave of concentrated hydrochloric acid. He shuddered and shuddered and windmilled wildly at her with his fists, but she pressed down on him more and more heavily, and there came a moment when he understood that it was futile, that he was going to die.

It was at that moment that he felt no pain at all. His brain had plainly decided that he didn't need any further warnings that his body was under attack. He had accepted death; pain was no longer necessary.

He lay still, not dead yet, but remarkably calm; as calm as the dead; as calm as anyone for whom there are no alternatives left.

He didn't even flinch when Marianna reached down and opened his jeans with fingers that scorched the denim.

"You broke your oath, Joe," she sang. "You broke your oath."

With burning-hot hands she pried his penis out of his jeans, and stretched it upwards. The skin shriveled and blistered. The spongy tissue crackled, and smoke poured out of the meatus. All around it, Joe's pubic hairs burned like scores of tiny fuses. Then Marianna was holding what looked like a flaring candle, the last fiery moments of Joe's manhood.

Sometime after that, Joe thought he heard someone singing. It was "*Bei Mir Bist Du Schön.*" "Please let me explain, *bei mir bist du schön*, means that you're grand . . . again I'll explain . . . it means you're the fairest in the land . . ."

Marianna took off her dark glasses and stared down at him with empty eyes. Then she kissed him, and his mouth caught fire, and he died.

13

Kathleen lived in Escondido. On the night of her husband's death, her older sister Lucy had flown in from Tucson to stay with her. But Lloyd persuaded her to come back with him to La Jolla that evening, and to have dinner with him at the Original Fish Depot.

"You can't say that we don't have something in common," Lloyd told her.

"But I don't have anything to wear."

He smiled, shook his head. "The Fish Depot isn't formal. Not unless you want it to be. And, besides, you look great as you are."

Waldo was delighted to see Lloyd, and shook his hand up and down as if he were priming a reluctant pump. "You want dinner, Mr. Denman? Yes, of course! Look how busy we are! Full up to bursting! And every night this week!"

"Maybe I should stay away more often," Lloyd suggested, as Waldo fussily piloted them over to the special guest table by the window, overlooking the cove, and lit the candles.

"Mr. Denman, we miss you," Waldo told him. "We work hard, we fill up the restaurant. But the restaurant is yours. Your dream, yes? Your inspiration. You know what my grandfather always used to say, when we walked on the beach? You can take everything away from a man. His family, his money, his clothes, his dignification. But you can never take away his ideas." His voice dropped grimly. "Not unless you are prepared to kill him."

Lloyd clapped Waldo on the back. "After Plato, this man is

the world's greatest philosopher," he told Kathleen. "He's also the world's worst flatterer. Beware! That's how he gets whatever he wants."

They sat facing each other over the dipping candlelight. Kathleen looked tired but very pretty. She had strong cheekbones, wide brown eyes. A mixture of determination and vulnerability that Lloyd found very appealing. The kind of woman who would cry when things went wrong, but who would wipe away the tears and promise herself that nothing would ever upset her so badly again.

Nil illegitimae carborundum. Don't let the bastards grind you down.

"When you've been married for so long, you forget what it's like, being alone," Kathleen told him.

Lloyd nodded. "Celia and I weren't officially married, but I guess you could say that we were married in the eyes of God. I never expected to spend my life with anyone else."

"Tom misses him so much," said Kathleen.

"Tom?"

"Our son. Our one and only."

"I'm real sorry," said Lloyd. "Look—here's the starter."

They began with coquilles St. Jacques with a light mornay glaze. While they were eating, Louis came out from the kitchen and asked them how they liked it. He was a thin, diminutive Frenchman from Marseilles, by way of New Orleans, with a concave chest and a pale waxy face and a limited grasp of English. But he could cook with verve and delicacy, and flavor his creations as precisely as a pianist hitting the right note; and he was a living denial of Paul Prudhomme's notion that any chef lighter than three hundred pounds can't cook shit.

"Louis, this is brilliant," said Lloyd.

Louis modestly shook his head. "Not brilliant, *monsieur*. But just as it should be."

After he had returned to the kitchen, Lloyd shook his head and smiled. "Did you hear that? 'It is how it should be.' That man is so uncompromising. I've seen him throw away lobsters because he didn't like the color of their shells."

Kathleen said, "You surprise me, you know. You don't seem like the kind of guy who would want to open a restaurant."

Lloyd shrugged. "I fell into it, I guess. I was tired of insurance, I wanted to be free. I thought of starting my own outboard motor company . . . in fact, I was better qualified to start an outboard motor company than anything else. I can strip an Evinrude blindfolded. But I thought to myself, where's the class, where's the image? Where's the fun?"

"But a restaurant must be such hard work."

"Are you kidding? This isn't work. This is complete and utter self-imposed slavery, from morning till night. And still the customers complain."

Their mutual bereavement sustained them through the *hors d'oeuvres*. But when they got into the crabbed halibut they began to realize that they had very much more in common than the sudden death of somebody that they had loved. They both liked theater, they both liked music, they both liked water sports. They both liked Maria Callas and Robbie Robertson and Woody Allen.

"You've been marvelous," Kathleen told him, as they left the Original Fish Depot and walked out into the warm night air. "It's pretty hard to have fun after something like this, but I've had fun."

"I guess the world keeps on turning, no matter what," Lloyd told her. "Now, how about a ride home? You could leave your car in the parking lot here, and I could have one of the waiters bring it out to you tomorrow."

"All the way to Escondido? Come on, Lloyd, you're tired. I could take a cab."

"Well . . . if it doesn't sound too forward, maybe you could come back to my place for a nightcap, and then make up your mind what you want to do."

She took hold of his arm. "That doesn't seem too forward at all. In fact it sounds very inviting." He was breathing the smell of her perfume, Ombre Rose, and her hair was very fine-filamented and shiny in the streetlight. Somehow her plain black dress made her even more alluring. It was no good pretending: he liked her a lot.

They climbed into his BMW and Lloyd backed out of his parking space.

"I just love your license plate," Kathleen told him.

"What, FISHEE? I don't know. The joke's kind of worn off."

They drove down the long swooping curves of the road that would take them to North Torrey. It was slightly foggy, a late-night ocean fog, and the lights all around them were blurred and star-whiskered.

Kathleen said, "Do you know what Mike always used to tell me?"

Lloyd glanced at her quickly. "Go on. What did Mike always tell you?"

"Mike always used to tell me that when his grandfather died, he took off north, all the way to Eureka, even further. He said it was the greatest spiritual experience of his life. He stood on the seashore way up north, in winter, and he heard his grandfather speak to him clear as a bell. He said his grandfather told him that nobody dies until they're completely forgotten; until everybody that ever knew them dies, too."

"I guess that's right," Lloyd told her. "I guess it makes it a little easier."

"Well, maybe," Kathleen replied. "But I think I'd feel better if I thought that Mike had gone for good. Vanished, you know? Just like he never existed. My God, Lloyd, he was alive a week ago. He held me in his arms. Now there's nothing. Nothing! I find that pretty damn hard to accept."

Lloyd said, "Did Mike belong to any kind of religious study group?"

Kathleen stared at him. "Mike? You're kidding! He wasn't into religion at all! What made you ask me something like that?"

"I don't know, just asking," Lloyd said guardedly. He didn't want to tell her too much about Otto, not yet.

"He used to go bowling a couple of nights a week," Kathleen volunteered.

"Do you know where?"

She stared at him. "No, I don't know where. He went with a gang from the office. You're making it sound like it's something really important."

"It could be, yes."

"Then what are you trying to say? Was he doing something wrong? Was he mixed up in something illegal or something? Come on, Lloyd, you can't just let it go."

Lloyd turned toward North Torrey. His face was lit up by the passing streetlights—lit, then shadowed, then lit, then shadowed. "It seems like Celia and Marianna were both attending regular religious study groups run by a character called Otto. Otto, apparently, was offering them everlasting life."

Kathleen frowned at him. "Everlasting life? Are you serious?"

"My feelings exactly," Lloyd told her. "But it seems like a whole lot of people believed it. Enough people to make up a busload, anyway."

"What are you trying to say?" Kathleen demanded. "Mike

was always so positive. He couldn't have been interested in everlasting life, or anything like that. He wasn't even superstitious. He didn't mind spilling salt or breaking mirrors from time to time, or black cats crossing his path."

"He wasn't into drugs?"

Kathleen shook her head very firmly. "He hated drugs. He didn't smoke and he didn't drink. He had a physique like Sylvester Stallone. He ran three miles every morning before breakfast and he voted Democrat."

Lloyd turned into the driveway of his house, and killed the BMW's engine. "I'm sorry, Kathleen; I guess I shouldn't try to play detective. All I manage to do is upset people."

Kathleen laid her hand on his arm. "You've been great. Really. That's not just flattery. I was beginning to wonder if there was any kind of future after Mike; whether life was worth living. I admire what you're trying to do, you know that? Even if you find that Celia took her own life because of depression, or PMT, or who knows what. At least you're not giving in. You're looking for answers. You're fighting back. That makes life worth living, doesn't it? That alone."

They got out of the car, and Lloyd ushered Kathleen toward the house.

Kathleen said, "Do you smell burning? Do you smell smoke?"

Lloyd sniffed. The sourness of burning was unmistakable; and as they approached the house he saw a bluish curtain of smoke hanging over the backyard. *Dear God,* he thought, *they've burned my house down.* He unlocked the front door and turned to Kathleen and said, "Stay back!"

"It's still burning!" called Kathleen, frantically pointing toward the bedroom windows at the back. Reflected flames danced in the window of the house next door. Lloyd hesitated for a moment. If he opened up the front door, he might feed the fire with a huge surge of oxygen. On the other hand, he had to get inside to put it out. No matter how fast the fire department made it to North Torrey, his precious house would be ashes before they could connect up their first hose.

"Call the fire department!" he yelled at Kathleen.

"What?"

"Call the fire department! Call them now! Use the car phone!"

Kathleen shouted at him, "You're not going inside? You can't!"

"Just call the fire department, will you?"

He hesitated for only a second. Then he unlocked the front door, shouldered it open, and rolled head over heels across the hallway. He heard the fire bellow like a wild animal and felt the side of his face scorched. Crouched by the foot of the stairs, his hands clasped protectively over his head, he waited until the flames had subsided; then he stood up and quickly looked around him.

The living room had been ransacked. All the drawers were hanging open, and all of the display cabinets had been smashed. Celia's scrimshaw was scattered all across the carpet. The air was thick with smoke, and Lloyd coughed and spat to clear it out of his lungs. Then he ducked toward the kitchen.

In the kitchen, the story was the same. There was so much cutlery on the floor that it looked as if a fisherman had emptied his basket of sardines there. Every jar was broken open. Coffee, rice, cookies, salt. Even the burners had been pried out of the stove.

They were looking for their lizard charm, thought Lloyd. *They wanted it so much that they lost sight of the fact that it doesn't mean anything to me. Not yet, anyway. But it will.*

He hop-jumped across the living room. The bedroom door was wide open, and the bedroom itself was a mass of fire. He could see his bedside table burning, and the photograph of Celia twisting and curling up. He could see flames licking out from under his bed. It was so hot that he couldn't approach closer than six or seven feet, holding his hand up to protect his eyes. He didn't have a fire extinguisher in the house; but he guessed that a few bowlfuls of water might douse it down. He hurried back to the kitchen, flicked on the faucet, and waited impatiently while the red plastic dishpan noisily filled up with water.

Then he hurried back again, balancing the bowl, slopping water, but as he approached the fiery entrance to the bedroom, he realized that what he was attempting was completely futile. The bed was blazing, with huge flames roaring up to the ceiling; and fabric burning in a blackened blizzard. The heat was huge; it dried the moisture on his eyeballs as soon as he approached; and when he tossed the bowlful of water, it did nothing more than sizzle momentarily, and vanish into the smallest puff of steam. He might just as well have tried spitting.

He threw the plastic bowl aside, and hurried across to his

desk, where he kept his accounts, and his diaries, and the photograph albums that his mother had given him. If he could save nothing else, he could save those.

He fumbled for his keys, slotted them into the keyhole, and it was only then that he realized that the desk wasn't locked. Somebody had been here before him. Somebody with a key. He opened the desk and saw that everything had been searched and shuffled aside: diaries, photographs, files, papers, passports, checkbooks.

Still, he didn't have time to worry about that. He stuffed the most important papers into two large envelopes, and hunched his way across the living room with his arms full. The bedroom was burning so ferociously now that long tongues of fire were roaring out of it, and the bureau beside the door was already sprouting flames. It would be only a matter of minutes before the whole house was ablaze.

Lloyd had almost reached the hallway when he heard somebody calling him.

"Lloyd! Wait! Lloyd!"

At first he thought it was Kathleen, and he yelled out, "Kathleen! I'm okay! I'm coming out!"

But then he suddenly realized that the voice was coming from his left. He stopped, disoriented, and dropped some of his photograph albums.

"Lloyd! Wait! Please, Lloyd, wait!"

He shielded his eyes against the heat. The living room was filling up with smoke and he could scarcely breathe. He coughed, and coughed, and coughed again. At first, he couldn't see anything. But then he began to distinguish a shadowy figure in the bedroom doorway. He smeared his eyes with his fingers, trying to focus. The figure wavered in the flames, but didn't attempt to move—as if the flames meant nothing, as if the flames were no more than confetti, or flowers, or bright running water.

"Lloyd, wait."

Lloyd thought, *It can't be.* But he knew with a terrible certainty that it was. You don't have to see somebody's face close up to know for certain who they are. A shape, a suggestion, that's all you need. And this figure standing in the flames was the same figure that he had seen running away from him on the *Star of India;* the same figure that he had seen sitting opposite him at Tom Ham's Lighthouse.

Celia, no question about it. Celia, self-cremated but immortal.

For a second, she emerged from the flames. They ran up her gray naked body, ran up her face; and her hair stood on end in torrential fire. She stared at Lloyd with black, impenetrable eyes.

"Lloyd, I need that charm. If I don't have that charm, Lloyd, I'll die."

He stared at her in horror. Flames licked at her breasts, but didn't consume them. Flames licked at her face. What fascinated and frightened Lloyd more than anything else was the way in which flames licked *into* her eye sockets.

"I have to have that charm, Lloyd! I have to! Each of us has one charm only. It's so precious, Lloyd, you don't understand how precious! They made it from the bowl that Pilate washed his hands in! Did you know that? The very same bowl! Please, Lloyd!"

Lloyd hesitated for one more second, mesmerized by Celia's appearance; but then he heard the whooping of fire sirens approaching the house, and the moment of hesitation was broken. He ducked out of the living room, along the hallway, and out into the night.

Kathleen was waiting for him on the sidewalk, just as a shining fire truck came around the corner with its lights flashing and its horn bellowing.

"Lloyd, are you okay?" she asked him. She was trembling.

"Sure, yes, sure. I tried to put it out, but it had too much of a hold."

"I moved your car back, just in case."

"Thanks."

A fire fighter came stalking up to Lloyd, adjusting the straps of his helmet. "This your property, sir?"

Lloyd nodded.

"Is there anybody in there?"

Lloyd thought of Celia, standing in the doorway, empty-eyed, on fire.

"No, officer. There's nobody in there."

"No domestic animals?"

"No, none."

"How did the fire start?" the fire fighter asked him. Already the first hose was connected to the hydrant across the street, and two more fire fighters were approaching the house behind a wide high-pressure spray.

"I have no idea. We just came back from having dinner. It looked as if it had started in the bedroom, but God knows how."

"Chief!" called one of the fire fighters. "The back roof is coming down!"

"Okay," the officer called back. Then, to Lloyd, "I'll talk to you later, sir. Let's get this little bonfire under control first."

Lloyd and Kathleen stood and watched as the fire fighters axed their way into the back of the house and sprayed gallons of water into the kitchen. Lloyd felt shocked and detached. It was hard for him to believe that what he was witnessing was real. First he had lost Celia to fire, now his house. He felt like packing up and leaving everything behind him. Maybe traveling north to Eureka, the way Kathleen's late husband had done.

Most of the neighbors had come out of their houses to watch the fire. Rog Kazowski from next door came across and asked Lloyd if he wanted to come in for a drink.

"It's okay, Rog. I think I'll just stand here and watch it burn."

"I sure hope you got good insurance," said Rog, the fire-light dancing on his shiny bald head. "If you have any problems, let me know."

Lloyd looked around, and as he did so, he saw two unfamiliar figures standing among the main knot of neighbors. It was difficult to make them out clearly in the swiveling light from the fire and the flashing lights from the fire trucks, but the more intently he peered at them, the more convinced he became that he had found the man and woman he was hunting for. With a cold tingle of excitement and alarm, he recognized Otto and his tall German *fraülein*. Helmet, or Earwig, or whatever.

He couldn't be certain, but it looked very much as if they were watching him, too.

"Kathleen," he suggested, "I think it would be a good idea if we got away from here."

"I'm sorry?"

"I'm not really too keen on watching my house burn to the ground, you know?"

Kathleen took hold of his hand. "Well, of course, sure. Do you want to come to my place?"

"That'd be great."

He edged his way back through the onlookers, making sure that the fire chief didn't see them leaving. A police car had just arrived, too, and the last thing he wanted was to have to answer a whole lot of routine police-type questions. He glanced back across the street at Otto and his companion, and as he did so he saw a figure in dark glasses and a black turban skirting around the back of the crowd. Celia, no question about it. Or the gray-skinned, empty-eye-socketed creature who had taken Celia's shape.

He gripped Kathleen's hand more tightly, and hurried her over to his car.

Kathleen said, "Hold on! You're hurting me!"

"Quick, get in," he told her. "They've seen us."

"Who's seen us? What are you talking about?"

Otto had detached himself from the main crowd and was walking toward them, straight and purposeful. The tall German woman followed him, although Celia remained where she was.

Kathleen said, "I wish you'd tell me what's going on."

"No time," Lloyd told her, slamming the car door and starting the engine. As he did so, Otto abruptly stopped where he was, fifty or sixty feet away, and raised his hands to his forehead. He looked as if he were protecting his eyes from the glare. Lloyd released the parking brake and swerved the BMW across the road in reverse.

"Lloyd!" Kathleen exclaimed.

Lloyd slammed the T-shift into second, and the car skidded forward again. As they approached Otto, however, Lloyd felt the leather-covered steering wheel heating up in the palms of his hands. Otto made no attempt to move aside as they slewed past him, and as they did so, the steering wheel burst into flames.

"*Aaahhh!*" Lloyd yelled, trying to keep control of the swaying car with his fingertips. The leather steering wheel cover was blazing furiously, and strips of fiery black hide kept dropping onto his unprotected thighs. His palms were branded, his fingers blistered, but in spite of the pain and the panic he managed to keep his hands dancing around the wheel, and to keep the car under some sort of control.

"Here!" said Kathleen, and dragged off her knitted shawl so that Lloyd could use it to smother the flames. He wound it around the top of the steering wheel, and managed to damp down the worst of them.

They skidded onto the main highway next to the university entrance. Lloyd's teeth were clenched with pain, and his eyes were filled with tears.

"Under my seat," he managed to tell her. "Fire extinguisher."

"For God's sake, can't you *stop?*"

Lloyd glanced in his rearview mirror. Already a large silver Mercedes sedan was swerving out of North Torrey, in obvious pursuit. It pulled right in front of a van, and Lloyd heard a horn blaring in indignation.

Kathleen unclipped the fire extinguisher and blew five or six squirts of foam on to the last guttering flames on the steering wheel.

"That's fine," Lloyd told her, "that's fine."

"Why can't you stop?" Kathleen demanded, frantically. "Who was that man? How on earth did your steering wheel catch fire? Would you *please* mind telling me now what's going on?"

Lloyd checked his mirror again. "You see that Mercedes? It's following us."

Kathleen turned around in her seat. "Are you sure? Why?"

"It's that man you saw in the road back there. As far as I can make out, that's Otto. The leader of that religious study group I was telling you about."

"But what does he want?"

"This, I think," said Lloyd, and reached into his coat pocket and took out the lizard charm. "I don't know, it's some kind of symbol. He has the same symbol on the wall in his house." He couldn't think how to tell her that he'd seen Celia, or what she'd said about the charm. *Each of us has one charm only. I's so precious, Lloyd, you don't understand how precious! They made it from the bowl Pilate washed his hands in.*

Kathleen turned the charm one way, and then the other. "Why does he want it so badly?"

"I wish I knew. But it was found in the parking lot where Celia burned herself. If you look at the newspaper photographs, Otto was there, too, standing in the background. And Otto was *also* standing in the background in the newspaper photographs of that burned bus. What's more, anybody who has shown even the slightest interest in Otto and these burnings seems to have gotten themselves burned to death."

Kathleen looked around again. "They're gaining on us. Your poor hands. Are you going to be okay?"

Lloyd grimaced, and nodded. The sharp burning in his fingers had become a silently roaring fire, and he was doing his best not to think about it. *Pain? What pain? That pain doesn't belong to me.*

Kathleen said, "I don't understand it. How did your steering wheel catch fire like that?"

"I don't understand it, either. But I think Otto did it. Maybe he can make things catch fire just by thinking about it. Did you ever see that movie about a little girl who could make things catch fire just by thinking about them? Maybe it's the same kind of thing. It's like using your mind as a magnifying glass—concentrating all your energy on just one spot. The spot heats up, then *whoof!* it catches fire."

The Mercedes was driving with its high beams on, less than three car lengths behind, and Lloyd had to deflect his mirror so that he wouldn't be dazzled. "There's something else," he told Kathleen, as they negotiated the long left-hand downhill curve toward the ocean. He couldn't keep it to himself any longer, whether Kathleen believed him or not. "I saw Celia in the house tonight."

"You did what?"

"Believe me, Kathleen, I know it sounds crazy, but she was there. Or her ghost was there. Or some kind of apparition. She was standing in the bedroom and the bedroom was blazing and she wasn't even *touched*, wasn't even *singed*."

"Lloyd . . ." said Kathleen, gently. "You don't think maybe that Celia's death has upset you more than you realize?"

Lloyd shook his head. "It wasn't my imagination, Kathleen, I swear to God. And if I'm really going screwy, how come this steering wheel caught fire? It's all part of the same damn thing. This charm has something to do with it—something important. Celia said it was made out of the metal bowl that Pontius Pilate washed his hands in. She said they had only one charm each."

"She said that tonight, when she was on fire?"

"That's right. You can call me crazy if you want to. I don't blame you if you do. But they're all connected—the charm, Celia's death, the bus burning, Mike's death, too."

"But I told you . . . Mike didn't belong to any religious groups."

"You mean that he didn't *tell* you that he did. But Celia didn't tell me, either. Celia, the love of my life, the woman who was going to share everything. She didn't even tell me that her best friend had cancer."

"Her best friend had cancer?"

"That's right. Marianna, the one who was burned on the bus, along with Mike."

They sped northward on the coast road. In the darkness, the Pacific foamed lonely and cold, and even the seagulls—the souls of the dead, the spirits of the lost—had found shelter for the night.

"You know something," said Kathleen. "Mike went for a

check-up about three months ago, and when he got the results he was really quiet for a couple of weeks."

"Did he tell you what was wrong?"

"Unh-unh. He kept insisting that everything was fine. But I could tell that he was worried. In the end he said that he had problems at work, that was all."

Lloyd quickly looked around. The Mercedes was still close behind, but it was keeping its distance. It seemed to be intent on following them, more than trying to overtake them. On the other hand, they were driving through Del Mar now, a well-lit, built-up stretch of the road, with rows of beach houses and bars and hotels and Chinese restaurants and bookstores, and if Otto tried anything too catastrophic, there would be scores of witnesses.

Kathleen said, "Look . . . there's a late-night drugstore. Let's get you something for your hands."

Lloyd gave another quick glance behind. "Okay . . . they'll probably keep away from us here."

He drew up to the curb beside Del Mar 24HR Drugs. It was a calculated risk, with Otto so close behind them, especially since Otto seemed to be capable of setting things on fire from such a long way off. If he could burn Lloyd's steering wheel, there was no reason why he couldn't burn Lloyd, too. But Lloyd's hands were raging with pain, and both he and Kathleen needed a few moments to get their breath back.

They went into the drugstore just as the Mercedes drew up about sixty feet behind them, and remained at the curb with its windows darkened and its motor running. Lloyd paused at the brightly lit drugstore door and gave the Mercedes a long, intent stare, but there was no way of telling what effect he was having on the Mercedes' occupants. The car was as blind-looking as Celia had been, if that burning figure in the bedroom doorway truly *had* been Celia.

He was beginning to realize that he no longer knew the difference between the living and the dead.

14

With a fatherly care that brought Lloyd closer to the brink of tears than the pain itself, the pharmacist at Del Mar 24HR Drugs covered his hands with antiseptic cream and then bandaged them up.

"You're pretty lucky; these are only very superficial," he said, taking off his heavy tortoiseshell eyeglasses, and massaging the deep indentations in the side of his nose. "Trouble is, it's always the superficial burns that give you the most pain. My mother always used to put on chicken fat. It healed the burns okay, but I used to have half the cats in the neighborhood following me around for days. Take two Tylenol now, and another two before you go to bed tonight, and don't drive."

They were about to go to the checkout counter when the drugstore door opened, and a thin elderly man in a wide hat and a gray business suit stepped in, followed by a tall woman with tight blond braids and a floor-length black leather coat. The coat was unbuttoned, and underneath she was wearing what looked like a skintight black leather swimsuit. The two of them waited by the magazine rack, leafing through copies of *Sunset* and *Barbecue Recipes* until Lloyd and Kathleen began to make their way toward the door. Then the woman stepped forward to bar their way.

"Mr. Denman," the woman said, in a strong German accent. "You have something that belongs to me."

Lloyd hesitated, his heart beating fast.

"I don't see how that can be," he replied. "I don't even know you."

The man slipped his magazine back into the rack, and stepped forward with a grin that looked like a pig's caul stretched across a wire coat hanger. "Allow me to introduce myself. Otto Mander, my dear sir. And this is Helmwige von Koettlitz."

Helmet, or Earwig, something like that. Helmwige.

"Well, good to have met you," said Lloyd. "But if this is some kind of touch, then you're out of luck."

Otto gave a dry, restricted cough. "This is no touch, Mr. Denman, as well you know. You have been looking for me as intently as I have been looking for you. Now, you have something that belongs to us, not to you, and I would appreciate your returning it without the necessity for any unpleasant confrontation."

Lloyd said, "Is Celia in the car?"

"I don't understand, Mr. Denman. I was under the impression that your fiancée was dead."

"The hell you say. I saw her tonight."

Kathleen said, "Lloyd . . . I think I want to go."

"All right," Lloyd agreed. "If this gentleman will agree to answer some questions."

"Of course," Otto nodded. His eyes roamed independently around the drugstore, as if he were constantly scanning the air, constantly searching for something. "I am not a secretive man, Mr. Denman, and I have done nothing of which I need to feel ashamed. I will answer any question that you care to put to me, as fully and as openly as I can. First, however, I want the charm."

Lloyd shook his head. "Questions first, charm later."

"I must insist that you give me the charm, Mr. Denman, and that you give it to me now."

"Even supposing I've got it, what's so darned important about it?"

Helmwige stepped forward and stood so close to Lloyd that her breast pressed against his arm and he could feel her breath on his cheek. "Mr. Denman, that charm is of no earthly use to you, yet it is critical to us."

"You mean critical to Celia?"

"Your fiancée, regrettably, is dead. You identified her body yourself."

Kathleen, anxious, begged, "*Please*, Lloyd, let's just leave."

But Lloyd said, "I saw her tonight. You can't convince me that I didn't. She's alive, in some way. She's been following me."

Otto pursed his lips. "An hallucination, my good sir. The living are living and the dead are very dead. There is no conceivable state of in-between."

"That's not what you teach at your study groups."

Otto's eyes momentarily concentrated on Lloyd's face as if he could have quite happily set fire to his forehead. But his eyes said one thing and his mouth said another. "You are a gentleman, Mr. Denman. A man of honor. You must understand that the charm does not belong to you. It is very important that we have it."

"Is Celia alive?" Lloyd asked him.

Otto didn't answer, but continued to stare at him with that same incendiary stare. Helmwige said, "You have the wrong ideas, Mr. Denman. We are students and worshipers, not witchcraft workers."

"I saw her with my own eyes, Miss von—"

"Koettlitz," said Helmwige. "But of course this was impossible. Your fiancée, we are afraid, is quite gone."

"She's alive," Lloyd repeated.

Otto gave that stretched-caul grin. "Perhaps you are then a fan of Goethe? *Und so lang du das nicht hast dieses: Stirb und werde! Bist du nur ein trüber Gast auf der dunkeln Erde.*"

He kept on grinning and said, "It means, 'So long as you fail to understand the notion that death transforms you, you will only be a miserable guest on this gloomy planet.' "

"I believe that Celia is still alive," Lloyd repeated. "I don't know how, I don't know why. Maybe I've totally flipped. But I believe that she's still alive, and I also believe that you know how, and why."

"Well! well! We are all entitled to our fantasies and our aberrations!" Otto replied. His laugh could have desiccated a coconut. "But I insist on the charm."

"Or what?" Lloyd challenged him.

Kathleen said, "Lloyd, please let's go. I don't like any of this."

"Or what?" Otto demanded. "You want to know, 'Or what?' Well, let me tell you this: if you refuse to give me the charm, if you *absolutely* refuse to give me the charm, then you must burn and burn until I can pick the charm from out of your ashes."

Lloyd was shaking with pain and anger. He never would have counted himself as brave, but with his hands bandaged and his house burned down, with Celia dead or not dead, with Sylvia burned and Marianna burned and Kathleen's husband burned, he had passed that imaginary limit that his lawyer Dan Tabares called the GAS Line. After you've passed the GAS Line, whatever happens, you simply don't Give A Shit.

"Get out of my way, old man," he told Otto.

"Hey! You don't speak to Mr. Mander with such disrespect!" Helmwige interjected, jostling her shoulder forward.

Lloyd tried to be calm, but it was difficult. "Get out of my way, all right?" he insisted. "Because if you don't get out of my way, believe me, I'm not going to call the manager. I'm not going to call a cop. All I'm going to do is beat the living shit out of you, octogenarian or not, and then I'm going to do the same to Miss Cut-Price Leather Couch here."

Otto lifted his chin in controlled fury. His neck rose out of his withered cream shirt-collar like a turtle. "Mr. Denman, you are not a wise man, my dear sir. All of your difficulties would be solved by simply returning the charm—please. Which in any event is not your property. You have no claim to it. I am sure the police will understand that."

"Get out of my way," Lloyd insisted.

There was a long moment in which none of them spoke: in which all of them were trying to outguess each other's reactions. Then, without warning, Lloyd shoved Helmwige back against the nail-polish display, and there was a sudden brittle scattering of pink and red bottles. Then he jabbed his elbow deep into Otto's concave ribs. Otto gave a barking cough, and clutched himself tight.

Lloyd snatched Kathleen's hand and pushed open the drugstore door. They ran together across the sidewalk, colliding with a young skateboarder, tangling themselves with a couple in Bermuda shorts and baseball caps, then climbed into Lloyd's BMW and skittered away from the curb with tires howling and rubber esses snaking all across the street.

Otto threw open the drugstore door, and immediately pressed both hands to his forehead. Helmwige said, *"Otto! Vorsicht! Er hat den Talisman!"* But Otto's fury was locked together jigsaw-tight and nothing could have broken it, not then. A sharp arrow of fire chased across the blacktop after Lloyd's BMW, flaring against the car's rear bumper for an instant. But Lloyd was too quick, and the BMW had roared out of sight before the fire could take hold.

"Scheiss!" Otto cursed. He whirled around and walked stiffly back to his parked Mercedes, wrenching open the passenger door

as if he wanted to tear it off its hinges. Helmwige walked around the car and opened the driver's door.

"What now?" she asked him.

"Go after them, of course!" Otto instructed her. "Come on, quick, quick! Why do you stand there, staring at me like an idiot? Follow them!"

"They could have turned off anywhere," Helmwige retorted.

Otto screeched at her, "Do what I tell you! Follow them!"

The Mercedes bucked and heaved away from the curb. From the back seat, a gray-faced figure bent forward and said, "If you catch him, you won't hurt him, will you?"

"What, you think I'm *verrückt?*" Otto snarled back. "But where will you be, without your talisman? A Salamander, forever! A living fire!"

Lloyd raced northward out of Del Mar, steering choppily and erratically with his gauze-bandaged fingertips. He skidded to a stop whenever they hit traffic signals; revved impatiently, watching behind him; then ripped ahead as soon as the lights turned green.

Kathleen said, "Lloyd! My God! Are they following us?"

Lloyd flicked his eyes to the rearview mirror. "I can't see them yet."

"Maybe they've given up."

"No," said Lloyd. "They need that charm too badly."

"But they're terrible! They're so threatening! Can't we call the police?"

"Sure we can call the police. But what do you think the police are going to do?"

"I don't know. But they set fire to your house, they set fire to your car! Look at your hands! Surely the police can charge them with *something?*"

Lloyd shook his head. "Kathleen, I don't want to call the police. If I call the police, I'll never find out what's going on. They won't let me. Besides, what I am going to say to them? 'My dead fiancée set fire to my house, then this cheesy old man set fire to my steering wheel from fifty feet away'? You think they're going to believe me?"

"But they threatened us; they're chasing us."

Lloyd said, "Just tell me how we get to your house. They haven't caught up with us yet."

"Lloyd, I'm frightened!"

"Me too. But calling the police isn't going to help. In fact, it'll probably make things worse."

Kathleen was quiet for a moment. But then she said, "Do you really think that Celia is still alive?"

"I'm beginning to believe that she is, yes."

"I don't understand this at all," said Kathleen.

Lloyd checked his rearview mirror again. "I don't understand it, either. But Otto promised everybody who came to his group that they were going to live forever. Somehow, it looks like he's managed it. With Celia, anyway. I saw her! She was different, but she was still Celia."

"People can't die and then come alive again."

Lloyd shook his head. "I don't know. Maybe they can, in a different way. Burning seems to have something to do with it. Maybe you live forever, if you burn."

Kathleen said, tightly, distractedly, "You can take a right here."

They turned away from the ocean and started to drive up into the hills. But as they reached the first high crest beyond the interstate, Lloyd became aware that a single pair of headlights was following them, not too close, but close enough not to lose them.

"Look around," he told Kathleen. "Do you think that's them?"

She shaded her eyes. "I can't be sure; but it *looks* like them."

"Hold on tight, then. This is where we shake them off for good."

Lloyd pressed the gas pedal down to the floor, and the BMW surged forward at more than ninety miles an hour. It took them only a few seconds to reach the next intersection, and Lloyd immediately braked hard and swung off to the right, killing his headlights as he did so. Then he swung left, completely off the road, and the car jolted and bounced as he negotiated his way down a dusty slope, through a clump of birds-of-paradise and prickly pear. The BMW's suspension banged unnervingly as they drove over a series of rocky ruts, and the muffler grounded again and again. But then Lloyd wrestled the car around behind a high screen of bushes and brought it to a halt.

"There's no way they're going to find us now," he told Kathleen. "Let's give them ten minutes or so to get tired of looking for us; then we'll go on to your place."

Only a few seconds afterwards, they saw headlights flash past them on the main highway. Then a truck went past, and a procession of much slower cars. Lloyd let out a tight, anxious breath.

"I wonder what they want that charm *for*," said Kathleen.

"I don't know. Maybe it's part of their religious ritual. Otto has the same design on the wall of his house, but much larger."

"They're so *weird*, those people," Kathleen shivered. "I can hardly believe that Mike was mixed up with them."

They waited in silence for five minutes longer. Then Lloyd said, "I've been thinking about your husband's physical. Is there any way we could find out what the results were?"

"Why?"

"Just a guess. Marianna thought she might have had breast cancer, and if your husband had found out that he had something seriously wrong with him . . . maybe that would have made them both a whole lot more receptive to the ideas of somebody like Otto. After all, he *was* promising everlasting life."

"I suppose I could call Dr. Kranz."

Lloyd checked his watch. His hands were still burning dully, but the Tylenol was deadening the worst of the pain. "It's just a shot in the dark. But I've been trying to follow up every possible idea."

"You don't think—" Kathleen began.

Lloyd glanced across at her. He knew what was she was thinking, and what she was going to say. She had listened patiently to his stories about seeing Celia on the *Star of India* and at Tom Ham's lighthouse, and about the break-ins, and the Wagner libretto inside the piano. But he wasn't surprised that he was stretching her credulity by insisting that Celia was somehow still alive.

All the same, he shook his head. "No, I don't think I'm cracking up. I'm not superstitious; I don't even believe in astrology. I don't believe in the supernatural, either. But I saw Celia and she wasn't a mirage or a hallucination or a trick of the light. There's an explanation for all of this. I don't know what it is, but I'm sure as hell going to find out."

He held up the charm. "First of all I'm going to find out what *this* is all about. Then I'm going to take that Wagner libretto to somebody who knows something about music."

"All right, then," Kathleen agreed. "And I'll phone Dr. Kranz, and ask about Mike's physical. But if none of this adds up to anything—well, I don't enjoy being chased around by people like this Otto of yours. It scares me."

Lloyd raised one bandaged hand, and pledged, "If we can't come up with anything that makes any sense, then you're out of it. I promise."

She leaned across the car and unexpectedly kissed his cheek. "You were good, back there in the drugstore. Like *Lethal Weapon.*"

"Flattery will get you anywhere."

"Well, home would be a good start."

Lloyd cautiously steered the BMW out of the trees and back onto the highway. There was no sign of the Mercedes anywhere. He turned right, and rejoined the winding road that would take them through Rancho Santa Fe and eventually out past Lake Hodges to Escondido. The night was exceptionally black, a strange liquid black, as if the world had been silently drowned by a seamless oil spill.

Rancho Santa Fe was lit up, neat as a toy town, its streets unnaturally deserted, as if all of its elderly residents had been taken away by friendly aliens. But once they had driven out into the hills, the blackness covered them yet again. Lake Hodges lay black between its black forested banks, betraying its presence only by an occasional secretive sparkle.

Kathleen tried to tune KOGO on the radio to hear if there were any bulletins about Lloyd's house burning, but all they could pick up were six or seven country-music stations and a long tedious interview about the Navy hospital. She switched the radio off again.

Kathleen said, "What are you going to do if Celia *is* still alive?"

"I've been trying not to think about it," Lloyd replied. "It gives me the shudders."

"You still love her, though, don't you? The way that I still love Mike?"

Lloyd drove in silence for a short while. Then he said, "I loved her the way she was. But the way I saw her tonight—well, she wasn't at all the same. She looked really strange. Her skin was kind of—I don't know—*grayish,* and she didn't seem to have any eyes. She was alive, for sure. At least she was walking and talking, and she recognized me. But she looked like she was dead."

He cleared his throat. "I keep trying not to think about the word *zombie.* It sounds like some dumb teenage video with dead people shuffling through shopping malls."

Kathleen didn't answer, but she gave a small shiver, as if somebody had stepped on her grave.

They turned toward Escondido. Kathleen's house was on the southwestern outskirts, on a secluded road opposite the vineyards of the Altmann Brothers Winery. She touched Lloyd's shoulder as they approached it, and said, "It's best to go slow. It's a real sharp turn into the drive."

The BMW's headlights picked out the *San Diego Tribune* mailbox with the name M. Kerwin painted on it in silver reflective letters. The late M. Kerwin. Lloyd slowed the car down to a crawl, and steered carefully around the tightly curving driveway.

"Lucy and Tom are probably still over at Rancho Bernardo," said Kathleen. "They were visiting my parents this evening. Mom's been so good about everything."

Lloyd saw bushes, flowers, a two-story brick and wood house. Then, to his horror, he saw a silver Mercedes sedan, parked facing him. Beside it stood the unmistakable and menacing figures of Otto and Helmwige. Somebody else, too, standing well back in the shadows behind them. Somebody with a black coat and a black turban and blacked-out sunglasses.

"Oh God, it's them!" Kathleen breathed, her voice high-pitched with fright.

Lloyd slammed the BMW into reverse and twisted around in his seat. The car's tires shrieked in protest as it backed up the driveway at full speed, swaying violently from side to side as Lloyd attempted to steer it straight. With a hideous thumping noise, they collided with a low retaining wall close to the entrance, and Lloyd had to shift back into drive and rev the car forward to unhook his bumper from the bricks.

In the glare of his halogen headlights, Lloyd saw Otto step forward and lift his hands to his forehead. Otto's face was unnaturally white and his eyes were pinpricks of flashing yellow, as dead and as bright as a snake's eyes. Grunting with pain, Lloyd pushed the gearshift into reverse again, and began to steer his way backwards around the curve in the driveway, scraping the wall all the way.

They had almost reached the mailbox when the BMW's tires exploded into flame, all four of them. Kathleen screamed. Lloyd shouted, "Hold on! It's okay! We're almost there!" The car's rear bumper hit the mailbox and knocked it flat. Then Lloyd slewed the car around and they sped off into the darkness, their tires blazing like catherine wheels, or the red-hot wheels of Union Pacific locomotives careening down the High Sierras on nothing but their brakes.

"How did they know where I lived?" Kathleen screamed, almost hysterical, as they roared along the highway with flames flickering all around them. "How did they know where I *lived?*"

Lloyd was tempted to say, "Maybe Mike's still alive, too. Maybe Mike told them." But he decided that Kathleen had been through enough horrors for one night. Besides, his most urgent concern now was to extinguish their tires.

They flashed past an irrigation faucet by the side of the road. Lloyd skidded the BMW to a halt, and backed up until they were parked right beside it. "Out!" he told Kathleen. "Careful! Don't stand too close! And keep an eye open for Otto!"

He climbed out of the car, and wrestled with the faucet. He cried out "*Shit, shit, shit!*" in agony as the knurled knob dug into his bandaged hands, but at last the faucet shuddered and shook, and splattered blood-rusty water onto the ground. Lloyd found a discarded cardboard fruit-box only a few feet away, and filled it up to the top. The box gushed noisily from all its crevices, but it held enough for Lloyd to be able to heave water over the burning tires, one by one, and to douse them in a sizzle of rubbery-smelling steam.

"Okay, let's get out of here!" he called. But as he tossed away the box and opened his door, he heard the rushing noise of a fast-approaching vehicle, and out of the darkness beside the Altmann winery sped the silver Mercedes with the blacked-out windows.

Kathleen ran back to the car, and Lloyd dropped into the driver's seat and twisted the key in the ignition. But before Kathleen could reach the passenger door, the Mercedes cut in front of them and slid to a crunching, emphatic halt. The Mercedes' doors flew open at once, and Otto and Helmwige climbed out. Helmwige circled the BMW toward Kathleen, while Otto remained where he was, desiccated and thin, his hands clasped in front of him, his face darkly shadowed by the brim of his hat.

"No!" cried Kathleen, as Helmwige approached her. Lloyd came around the back of the car and stepped in between them, but Helmwige simply grinned at him.

"Now, with no more nonsense, you're going to give us the charm?" she demanded.

"Not a chance," Lloyd told her, shakily. "Now get the hell

out of here and leave us alone. This time I'm going to call the cops."

"Oh, yes? And what are you going to tell them, these cops?"

"I'm going to suggest that they search your little hideout on Paseo Delicias, for starters. Kidnaping and imprisonment are pretty serious offenses, wouldn't you say?"

"Oh, you've been prying around our house, too?" asked Helmwige, still grinning. "Well, I agree with you. Kidnapping and imprisonment are *very* serious offenses. But there is no law against a man who *wants* to be chained up, now is there? That man would not be at all happy to be free. He is guilty, you see, that he has not lived up to his promise. He is only content when he is being punished."

"You can tell that to the sheriff, I'm sure," Lloyd challenged her.

"By all means. I will also tell him that you have an item of valuable property which belongs to us, and that you refuse to return it."

Lloyd held up the charm between his gauze-wrapped fingers. "You show me who else you've got in that car, and tell me why you want this charm so badly, and then maybe I will."

Otto called out dryly, "What is he saying?"

Helmwige, without relaxing her grin, turned back to him. "He wants to see our passenger."

"Then let him. Perhaps then he'll come to his senses."

A large furry moth flickered into the beam of the Mercedes' headlights, and clung quivering for a moment to the dazzling lens. Otto reached out smoothly and cupped the mesmerized insect in his hand. Lloyd and Kathleen watched him in disgusted fascination as he licked it all over until its wings were stuck down with his saliva, then placed it into his mouth as if it were a piece of fruit. He sucked hard, and then swallowed.

"Celia!" called Helmwige. "Why don't you come out, my dear?"

Although Lloyd had already guessed that it was Celia, he still felt an acid-sharp tingle of fear. He had seen her burned body in the police morgue downtown; he had seen her eyeless and terrible in their blazing bedroom. He didn't know how she could still be walking around, unless she had undergone some extraordinary kind of advanced operation, or unless she was a zombie, or a ghost, or a robot, or her own twin sister, or unless he had gone into shock when he had heard of her death, and this was nothing but a nightmare.

One slim ankle stepped out of the car. Then a long familiar leg. Then a slender woman in a black raincoat, with a scarf tied around her head like a turban, and impenetrable dark glasses. She stood close to the car, slowly buttoning first one black glove and then the other. Her face shone softly gray.

"Hello, Lloyd," she called, and it was Celia's voice, no question at all.

Lloyd was swept by such a surge of emotion, such a turmoil of fear and longing and shock and disbelief, that he could hardly speak.

"Celia," he said. "Celia, what the hell is going on? Are you really alive?"

"I'm saved, Lloyd, that's what's happened."

"Did you really burn yourself?"

But Otto interrupted, "Mr. Denman . . . the less you know about this, the safer you will be. Please . . . you have seen her. You know that she is saved. Give us the charm and the whole matter can be forgotten."

Lloyd slowly and emphatically shook his head. "That's where you're wrong, friend. This matter isn't going to be forgotten. No goddamn *way* is this matter going to be forgotten. You've been burning people to death, you've been terrorizing people, you've burned down my house, you've wrecked my car. Look at my hands, for God's sake! And now you bring Celia out, who's supposed to be dead, and tell me she's saved!"

"Mr. Denman, she *is* saved, believe me."

"I wouldn't believe you if you told me it gets dark at night. I want to know what the hell's going on."

Celia said, "Lloyd, my love, please. Don't argue now. Let them have the charm. Otherwise I can't survive."

"I just want to know what this is all about," Lloyd insisted.

Otto stepped nearer, brushing dust from the sleeves of his suit. "Mr. Denman, your fiancée is in a particular state at this moment which you might call *volatile*. When the year reaches its fullest point, at the summer solstice, in just a few days' time, we will be able to stabilize her condition, and she will become whole. She will have attained a state of perfection that will make her nothing short of immortal. But, it is essential for her to have the talisman which she lost by accident on the day of her burning. Each talisman belongs solely and individually to the devotee who has taken the oath of allegiance to our cause. It is beyond price, and irreplaceable. Without it, your fiancée will become more and more volatile, until one day she will flare up and become nothing more than white ash. Unless you wish that to happen, you will now return it."

"Celia?" asked Lloyd, ignoring Otto as pointedly as he could.

"He's telling you the truth, Lloyd," Celia replied. Her voice sounded like the softest of brushes on silver. "What I said to you was true. . . . The talismans are made from the bowl in which Pontius Pilate washed his hands. They have the quality of releasing your soul completely from the laws of God. The Lord may have given, but once you have made your path on the talisman and burned your earthly body, then He no longer has the power to take away."

"But why?" Lloyd wanted to know. "Why did you try to kill yourself like that? Weren't you happy? Was something wrong? Were you depressed? You didn't *have* to marry me, you know, if you didn't love me!"

"I loved you then and I love you now, and I will *always* love you," Celia replied.

"So why did you burn yourself? What was it supposed to achieve?"

"Exactly what Otto told you. Perfection."

"Don't you understand that as far as I was concerned, you *were* perfect? I wouldn't have changed you in any way for anything!"

Lloyd took a step toward her, and held out his hand. He couldn't stop his eyes from filling up with tears. "Just tell me what's happened to you! Can't you do that? Tell me what's going on!"

Helmwige stepped between him and Celia, and said, firmly, "No nearer, Mr. Denman, or you will regret it. We will *all* regret it. Your interference has caused us enough trouble as it is."

"But she's my fiancée, for Chrissake!" Lloyd yelled at her. "She's the woman I want to marry! *Wanted* to marry! Still want to, if you'll tell me what the hell's going on!"

Otto took off his hat, and wiped around the inside with his folded handkerchief. "Enough of this lovemaking. We can't spare the time. Mr. Denman, my lawyers will contact you regarding any damage that might have been done to your house and your car."

"Your *lawyers?* God damn it, I'm going to the police! I'm going to have you locked up, you goddamn maniac!"

Otto ran his hand through his white feltlike hair, and looked away. "Going to the police would be a grave mistake, Mr. Denman. A wicked mistake. We would have to cut short our procedures, and delay Celia's transformation until the *next* solstice, in a year's time. Who knows what might happen to her in between now and then."

"I don't understand this at all," Lloyd told him.

Otto smiled, and replaced his hat. "No, I don't suppose you do. But then it isn't really necessary for you to understand it. In fact, you're probably not *capable* of understanding it. Like most men who place foreign cars and designer clothes higher on their list of priorities than spiritual strength and absolute achievement, you have an intellect no higher than any of those cockroaches which infest your restaurant."

"Now, you damn well listen to me—" Lloyd began, angrily.

But Celia called, "Please, Lloyd! Please! Just give Helmwige the charm."

Lloyd hesitated, glancing from Celia to Otto and back again. But then Helmwige suddenly seized his wrist, and raised the fist in which he was holding the charm. Lloyd gasped with effort, trying to push his arm down again. But Helmwige was startlingly strong, and he couldn't move a muscle.

At the same time, he began to feel Helmwige's fingers growing gradually warmer and warmer. He frowned at her in effort and disbelief. But it was only a matter of seconds before her fingers were so hot that his skin started to redden, and the edge of his gauze bandages began to singe. The hairs on his wrists shriveled, and wisps of smoke rose from between his fingers.

"Lloyd, please!" Celia begged him.

But Kathleen slapped Helmwige's shoulder and shouted, "Let him go! You're all crazy! You're vicious and you're crazy! Let him go!"

Otto gave her a fleeting, dismissive glance. "Very spirited, Mrs. Kerwin. But it won't help at all."

Lloyd kept his fist closed for as long as he could, but the burning of Helmwige's fingers was more than he could take. Gasping, sweating, shaking with pain, he slowly opened his fingers and exposed the charm. Without a word, Helmwige picked it fastidiously out of his palm, and pressed it to her lips. Metal sizzled against saliva.

"Thank you for your somewhat reluctant cooperation, Mr. Denman," said Otto. He suddenly stooped forward, and caught a hopping cicada by the leg. It struggled and danced, but he pushed it into his mouth until only its head was showing between his lips, its black beady eyes staring. Then he crunched it up between his teeth, and swallowed it. "I like to give them one last look at the world they are leaving," he remarked.

Shuddering with emotion and pain, his burned hand pressed against his chest, Lloyd could do nothing else but watch Celia climb back into the car, followed by Helmwige and Otto. Otto raised one gloved hand in dismissal, and then they drove off into the darkness. Their brake lights glared momentarily as they rejoined the main highway, and then they were gone.

Kathleen came up to Lloyd with tears in her eyes, and put her arms around him. "Oh God, are you all right? That must have hurt so much."

"It's okay," said Lloyd. "I'll get over it. A college friend of mine lost both his legs in Vietnam, and he got over it."

"Was that really Celia?" Kathleen asked.

Lloyd nodded. "It looked like her. It *sounded* like her. I don't know how it could be, though. I think I'm just about ready for the Yoyo Hotel."

"But Lloyd," Kathleen insisted, "I saw her too. So she must be real. Just different, like that awful Otto said. God, he's disgusting! She's in a different state, that's what he said, didn't he? *Volatile.*"

Lloyd said, "Let's see if we can get the car back to the house."

"What are you going to do?" Kathleen asked him. "Are you going to call the police?"

"Not yet . . . not till I know what's going on. If there's a chance that Celia *could* be saved, then the last thing I want to do is blow it."

Kathleen said nothing. There was nothing to be said. They had both been confronted with the evidence that the dead could really walk; that the grave and the crematorium might not be the end at all, but a new and mysterious beginning.

15

He was deeply asleep when the doorbell rang. He opened his eyes and for a long moment he couldn't think where he was, or what had happened to him, or even *who* he was.

He was lying on a chestnut-brown velour couch in a large rustic-style living room. An empty red-wine bottle stood on the glass-topped table close by, with three wine-flecked glasses. On the brick-effect wall above the cabin-style fireplace hung a huge oil painting of Indians riding through a blizzard. It was entitled *Winter in the Sangre de Cristo Mountains*.

The doorbell chimed again. He sat up and tried to rub his eyes, but found that his hands were thickly bound in clean bandages, like a boxer. He was wearing nothing but his shorts. He looked around him, and saw his shirt neatly folded over the back of the chestnut-brown armchair opposite. It was only when he heard Kathleen calling from upstairs, "Lloyd! Could you get the door please?" that he remembered exactly where he was.

He tugged on his pants and held them together with one hand because he couldn't fasten the button with his bandaged fingers. The dark wobbly shape of a man in a blue suit was visible through the hammered glass door. Using his hand like a big white lobster claw, Lloyd opened the door on the chain and said, "Who is it?"

The man turned around. It was Sergeant Houk. A little further away stood Detective Gable, with his hands in his pockets, whistling to himself. In the driveway, parked alongside Lloyd's burned and scraped BMW, stood Sergeant Houk's Buick, and behind it, a blue and white squad car from the San Diego County Sheriff's Department, with a pale-faced young deputy sitting in it.

"Do you mind if we come in, or are we interrupting something?" asked Sergeant Houk.

Lloyd released the chain. "Surprised you knew where to find me."

"We *didn't* know where to find you, as a matter of fact. We put out a county-wide bulletin for your car last night, and that smart young deputy happened to notice it in Mrs. Kerwin's driveway first thing this morning, and called us. There can't be too many white BMWs in Southern California with the license FISHEE."

As he stepped into the house, he looked back at Lloyd's car and commented, "Pretty beat up, too. Hope you're not thinking of driving it on the highway in that condition."

"I had a slight accident," said Lloyd, trying to push the button of his pants through the buttonhole with the heel of his hand.

"You're not kidding. Was that how you hurt your hands?"

"That's right, burned them. It's not too serious. More blisters than anything else."

Sergeant Houk walked into the living room and looked around at the couch with its scrumpled-up cushions and its dragged-aside blanket, the empty bottle of wine, the three glasses. "I didn't know that you and Mrs. Kerwin were old acquaintances," he remarked.

"We're not. We only met yesterday."

"Impolite to ask you how?"

"Of course not. I went out to the Anza-Borrego Desert to look at that burned-out bus, and Mrs. Kerwin was there, tying on a wreath, in memory of her husband."

Sergeant Houk nodded. "Any particular reason you went out to look at that burned-out bus?"

"Celia was a member of the San Diego Opera, so was Marianna Gomes. I guess it struck me as something of a coincidence that both of them had burned to death within two days of each other."

"So you went to look at the burned-out bus?"

"Yes, that's right."

Sergeant Houk stood in the center of the living room with

his arms folded, making a show of thinking. "Can I ask you what you thought you might find, if you went to look at the burned-out bus?"

"I don't know. Some kind of clue why Celia might have committed suicide."

"Oh! And did you?" asked Sergeant Houk.

"Did I what?"

"Did you find any clues why Celia might have committed suicide?"

Lloyd gave a small, uncommunicative shake of his head. "I guess I didn't."

"But you did find Mrs. Kerwin? Just by chance?"

"That's right. We got talking. In the end, I asked her to come back to La Jolla with me for dinner."

"At your own restaurant, I presume?"

"That's right. We ate pretty early, as a matter of fact. But Mrs. Kerwin seemed to be tired, so I suggested that she leave her car in the parking lot and come back to my place for a nightcap."

Sergeant Houk sniffed. "With what intention?"

"I don't follow you."

"What I'm trying to get at, Mr. Denman, is what you had in mind when you invited Mrs. Kerwin back to your house. Was it just for a drink, or did you have something more serious in mind?"

Lloyd stared at him indignantly. "Are you sick in the head, or what? Both of us had just lost people we loved in the most horrible way you can think of. And you're trying to suggest that I asked Mrs. Kerwin back to my house so that I could *seduce* her?"

Sergeant Houk was unfazed. "I'm sorry, Mr. Denman, I was simply trying to assess the degree of your intimacy with Mrs. Kerwin. For all I know, you and Mrs. Kerwin might have been acquaintances *before* these burnings occurred."

"And what's that supposed to mean?"

"I'm asking you."

"You're not suggesting that *I* could have burned that bus?"

Sergeant Houk shrugged as if, well, it was *possible*—sure, now that you mention it. "You see the difficulty we have here is *why* Mr. Kerwin was riding that bus at all. Or why *any* of the passengers were riding it. It was chartered by somebody calling himself Jim Ortal, and it was supposed to be a tour by the El Cajon Astronomical Society to visit Mount Palomar Observatory.

Of course there is no El Cajon Astronomical Society and there is nobody with the name Ortal at the address that was given. The deposit on the bus and one day's rental plus full insurance was paid in advance in cash, so there's no bank account number and no credit card billing address."

At that moment, Kathleen's older sister Lucy came downstairs in her black gingham robe, closely followed by a nine-year-old boy with dark hair and dark circles under his eyes. Lloyd had met Lucy and Tom late last night, when they had returned from visiting Lucy and Kathleen's parents in Rancho Bernardo. Kathleen had said nothing to Lucy about the unwelcome visit from Otto and Helmwige, and Lloyd had explained the devastated condition of his car by telling her that he had misjudged the turning into the driveway, struck the garden wall, and that the car's fuel hose had fractured and started a fire. Lucy seemed to believe him; and Tom had thought that any man who could cause such spectacular damage just by turning into somebody's driveway was practically super-powered. And total a sixty-five-thousand-dollar BMW, too!

Lucy looked very much like Kathleen, only thinner and drier-skinned and more deeply suntanned; and she had acquired a slower Western drawl from all her years in Arizona. "Kathleen'll be down in a minute," she said. "Have these gentlemen come about your accident?"

"That's right, ma'am," grinned Sergeant Houk. "Sorry to disturb you so early."

"Don't concern yourself," Lucy replied. "Would you care for some coffee?"

"Black, please," said Detective Gable.

"We won't, thank you," said Sergeant Houk. "We're kind of pressed for time."

"Lloyd?" asked Lucy.

"Yes, black please, Lucy," Lloyd told her. Sergeant Houk was beginning to make him feel cornered, and he was glad of a momentary interruption. He didn't want to tell Sergeant Houk anything about Otto and Helmwige, not yet, not until he understood what Otto and Helmwige were actually into, and what was going to happen when Celia was "transformed." He could imagine far too vividly the police bursting into the house on Paseo Delicias and arresting everybody in sight, and condemning Celia forever to that strange gray-faced state in which he had seen her last night.

Lloyd's whole night had been haunted by echoing, flaring nightmares. He had glimpsed Celia again and again, behind reflecting shop doors, on the opposite side of the street, on bridges, in the rain, masked by the windows of passing cars. He couldn't logically believe that she was still alive, in any shape, in any form. But he had seen her with his waking eyes and all he could do was to force himself to suspend his disbelief: to open his mind to any possibility, no matter how strange, no matter how grotesque.

It upset him that she was still in the hands of Otto and Helmwige; but in the end he supposed that there was no alternative for her. Even if they had originally been responsible for her burning herself (and by God he would kill them with his bare hands if he found out that they were), Otto and Helmwige had somehow raised her from the dead. He had to trust them to complete their ritual of "Transformation," whatever that was. If that was the only way in which Celia could be whole again, he couldn't interfere.

Sergeant Houk paced across to the fireplace and examined the oil painting of Indians in the snow as closely as if it were a Van Dyck. "Nice picture," he remarked.

"Not exactly my taste," Lloyd told him.

"Oh, yes. I've seen your restaurant. You're more into what d'you-call-'em, Depressionists."

"Impressionists."

"Whatever. They may impress you but they depress the hell out of me."

Lloyd said tautly, "If it sets your mind at rest, I never met Mrs. Kerwin before yesterday; and the only reason I went out to the desert was because I wanted to take a look at the bus. Morbid interest, I guess."

"Well, I'd say that hits the nail on the head," Sergeant Houk replied. "Morbid interest, Mr. Denman, that's what you've got. But a very special variety of morbid interest."

"I don't think I know what you're talking about."

"You don't think you know what I'm talking about?" queried Sergeant Houk. He lifted one hand, and began to count items on his fingers. "Your fiancée burns to death in the parking lot of McDonald's. You meet with Sylvia Cuddy of the San Diego Opera and then she burns to death in her apartment. You talk to Robert Tuggey, a short-order cook at McDonald's, and he dies in an unexplained fire in his automobile, in the same parking lot where your fiancée died. You visit the wreck of a burned-out bus, in which an acquaintance of yours from the San Diego Opera was killed. The same night, your house is seriously damaged by fire; and you and the widow of another victim of the burned-out bus are seen driving away from the scene of the fire with the interior of your car apparently in flames. This morning I arrive to find not only the interior of your car damaged by fire, but the tires burned, too."

Sergeant Houk had only a couple of fingers left to count on. "Mr. Denman," he said, "wouldn't you say that all of those incidents would lead a reasonable person to believe that you had a morbid interest in fire?"

Lloyd opened his mouth, then closed it again. Sergeant Houk had obviously spent all night trying to build a circumstantial case against him, but whatever he said, it would only make matters more difficult.

"You're not going to arrest me, are you?" he asked.

"No, sir, I'm not going to arrest you. I just wanted you to know how things look from our point of view."

"I think I'd better speak to my lawyer," said Lloyd.

"All right," nodded Sergeant Houk. "That's your privilege."

Lloyd said, "Let me tell you this, though. Whatever it looks like from your point of view, you're wrong. You're way off beam. I wasn't responsible for any of those deaths or any of those fires, and by the time this is over, you're going to find that out for yourself, and you're going to knock on my door the same way you did this morning, and you're going to have to say that you're sorry."

"Be my pleasure," grinned Sergeant Houk. "Come on, Detective, I think that's enough for now."

"Yes, sir," said Detective Gable, without taking his eyes off the tray of coffee that Lucy was carrying into the room.

"You're going so soon?" Lucy asked them.

"I think we have everything we need, thank you, ma'am," said Sergeant Houk.

Lloyd showed them to the door, and opened it.

"Oh, by the way," Sergeant Houk said, as if it had only just occurred to him. "Did you by any chance visit a house yesterday morning on Paseo Delicias, in Rancho Santa Fe? When we put out the APB on your car last night, an officer from White Shield Security called in to say that he'd seen a white BMW with the license plate FISHEE out on Paseo Delicias yesterday morning. He'd also seen a man answering your description entering the property in a manner that made him look twice."

Lloyd felt a tightness in his chest. The last thing he wanted was for Sergeant Houk to call at Otto's house. "I'm sorry, I can't help you," he replied.

"You mean you weren't there?"

"I mean the security officer must have been mistaken. I told you where I was yesterday, out in Anza-Borrego."

"Well . . . just asking," Sergeant Houk smiled. "Have you been back to your house yet?"

Lloyd shook his head. "I was planning on calling my neighbor to find out how bad it was damaged."

Sergeant Houk sniffed. "It wasn't as serious as it might have been; that's what the fire chief told me. Apparently the back roof collapsed, and the kitchen's burned out, but the main structure is still safe. You were lucky the fire fighters got there so quick."

He turned to leave, but then he hesitated and said, "You'll stick around, won't you? And you'll let me know where I can get in touch?"

"Is that because I'm a suspect?" asked Lloyd.

"It's because I don't want to have to put out a county-wide APB every time I want to ask you a couple of questions, okay? Is that reasonable?"

Lloyd nodded, and closed the door. As an afterthought, he slid the security chain into place.

Kathleen came down, wearing jeans and a plain white blouse. "What was that all about?" she asked him.

"Just questions," said Lloyd. "He seems to have gotten it into his head that you and I might have planned to burn that bus so that we could collect your husband's insurance and run off to Acapulco together."

"You're not serious!"

Lloyd swallowed coffee. "Almost. But that doesn't worry me. We didn't do it, and he can't produce any evidence that we did. What *does* worry me is that he knows where I went yesterday morning."

"You mean to Otto's house?" Kathleen asked.

"That's right. And he's enough of a keen detective to try checking it out."

"Oh, God. Otto will think that you tipped him off, won't he?"

Lloyd said, "That possibility had occurred to me. And Otto isn't exactly your genial, forgiving type, is he? With any luck, he might allow me one last look at the world, like that cicada."

"What can we do?" asked Kathleen.

Lloyd shrugged. "Nothing. Have breakfast. Hope for the best."

"Piove sul bagnato," said Kathleen. "It never rains but it pours." When she caught Lloyd's quizzical look, she smiled gently and said, "I used to have an Italian boyfriend once. Trouble is, I didn't like the idea of competing with a two-hundred-twenty-five-pound arm-wrestler for the rest of my life."

"He was an arm-wrestler?"

"I'm talking about his mother."

Sergeant Houk drew up underneath the overhanging eucalyptus trees on Paseo Delicias and switched off his engine. "That's the house," he told Detective Gable. "Look at all those goddamn Mercedes. It looks like Hitler's garage."

The deputy's car drew up behind them, and the deputy came up and leaned on the roof of Sergeant Houk's Buick, next to the open window, and flipped his notebook. "The sheriff just came through on the radio. The property is owned by Matt Orwell, the movie producer, and rented through Rand and Stewart, of Rancho Santa Fe. The present renter is the Salamander Corporation, registered in Butte, Montana. The rental documents were signed on behalf of the corporation by Mr. J. Ortal."

"Bingo!" breathed Sergeant Houk. "And what's the betting that Mr. J. Ortal turns out to be Mr. L. Denman?"

"You seriously think that Denman burned that bus?" asked Detective Gable, taking off his sunglasses and hooking them into his shirt. "He don't seem like the type to me."

"*Type*—will you listen to him?" mocked Sergeant Houk. "Did you ever see a single perpetrator who ever ran true to type? Type is for the movies. This guy Denman is a pyromaniac. You know? He loves to see things burn."

"That still doesn't mean that he burned the bus," Detective Gable insisted.

Sergeant Houk sighed. "Let me suggest a scenario, right? Denman meets Mrs. Kerwin at his restaurant one evening, very romantic, they flirt, et cetera, et cetera, they date, eventually they fall in love. Come on, he's a reasonable-looking guy and she's a pretty reasonable-looking woman, and one thing we know about Mr. Michael Kerwin is that he was away most of the week on business. Between the two of them Denman and Mrs. Kerwin work out this plan to off her husband. Denman used to work in insurance, remember; he must know all the wrinkles. Only Denman's fiancée begins to suspect that something's wrong. Maybe she picks up on a telephone call, and hears Denman and Mrs. Kerwin talking, and faces Denman with the awful truth. They decide to off her, too."

"But why did they fry a whole busload of people, just to nail this one guy?" Detective Gable asked him, looking more like Jackie Gleason than ever. His hair was frizzy and wild, and there were clear beads of perspiration on his upper lip.

"It's been heard of before," the young deputy remarked, trying to sound experienced and professional. "You remember that case when a guy bombed an entire airplane, just to collect his mother's insurance? A hundred innocent passengers blown out of the sky, and for what? Just to get rid of one person. Hard case to solve, too: you've got scores of suspects, and as many motives as there are passengers."

"Yes," said Sergeant Houk, caustically, "I saw that movie too."

Detective Gable wiped his forehead with his sleeve. "So what are we going to do? Are we going to go in there, or what?"

"Of course we're going to go in there," Sergeant Houk told him, with exaggerated patience. "You know what my motto is: No Stone Unturned. Maybe Denman *didn't* do it. But maybe he did. Maybe he's Ortal and maybe he isn't. But we're not going to find out by sitting on our rear ends."

He climbed out of the car, and combed his hair. Then he said, "Let's go," and they went.

They negotiated the interlocked maze of closely parked Mercedes, and Sergeant Houk admired each one in turn. "Beautiful, beautiful. Clean them up, and they'd be worth a fortune. You see that one, that tourer? One point five, easy."

"Pretty small engine for a car that size," Detective Gable remarked.

"Engine? Who's talking about engines? One point five *million*, at auction. They sold one at Christie's just like it."

They climbed the broken steps to the veranda. "Don't know how much Orwell charges for this dump, but it's got to be too much," Sergeant Houk remarked. "Have you seen the prices around here? Three quarters of a million for a three-bedroom home, and a view of what?"

They reached the door. The lizard doorknocker hung in front of them heavy and fat and black, more like a flaccid overripe fruit than a doorknocker cast out of bronze. Sergeant Houk took a look along the veranda, at the broken boards, at the grimy windows. "Place looks deserted to me. Deputy—why'nt you scout round the back? See what you can see. But be careful what you do. Don't touch anything, even if it looks like evidence. *Especially* if it looks like evidence. We don't have a warrant."

He took hold of the knocker and clapped it forcefully against the door. It startled a brace of California quail on the roof ridge, and sent them fluttering into the bright morning sky.

"Nobody here, Sergeant," the deputy called back, as he reached the end of the veranda.

Detective Gable looked this way and that, as if he were trying to cross the street. "You know something, Sergeant, this case is totally weird. This is the weirdest damned case I ever handled."

Sergeant Houk shook his head. "This case isn't weird. There's nothing weird about it at all. The perpetrator wants us to believe it's weird, that's all, to throw us off. A woman burns herself to death in a parking lot. A busload of people burn themselves to death in the desert. A woman gets burned in her apartment, a McDonald's chef gets burned in his car. It's not weird, Gable, it's just death; and death is death no matter how it happens. You wouldn't think it was weird if they were shot, or stabbed, or strangled."

"Well, I know. But I still think it's weird."

Sergeant Houk knocked again, but the front door remained adamantly closed. The deputy came back along the veranda, his boot heels making a hollow rocking noise, his thumbs wedged into his belt.

"Okay, Matt Dillon. Go check the back," Sergeant Houk instructed him.

"The name's Roger," the deputy replied, somewhat put out.

"Okay, Roger; sorry, Roger; go check the back, Roger."

The deputy skirted the garage and timidly fought his way through the overgrown weeds, using his gun barrel to push aside the thistles. Sergeant Houk watched him go with the expression of a man who has had to learn patience the hard way.

"All right," he said, at last. "Let's give this doorknocker one last workout." He banged it seven times, grotesquely loudly, and Detective Gable winced every time.

"If they don't answer that, they're either out, or dead," said Sergeant Houk.

They waited and waited. "Nobody in," said Detective Gable.

But as he did so, the front door suddenly unlatched itself and swung open, and there stood Helmwige, tightly swaddled in a bronze silk bathrobe, with a towel tied around her head.

"Yes?" she said, as if she hadn't heard Sergeant Houk beating at the door as if it were the Gate of Hell.

Caught off balance, Sergeant Houk dropped his badge. As he bent down to retrieve it, he saw that Helmwige was wearing heavy silver anklets. "I'm sorry to disturb you. Sergeant Houk, San Diego Police Department. We're investigating a series of homicides in the San Diego area. Can you tell me who you are, please?"

Helmwige blinked at him with spiky wet eyelashes. "Helmwige von Koettlitz," she said, as if she were amazed that he didn't know. And then, before he could ask her anything else, "But what could I possibly know about homicides?"

Sergeant Houk coughed. "I'm not suggesting that you know anything about them directly, ma'am. It's just that you may be able to assist the investigation by clearing up a couple of peripheral queries."

Helmwige said nothing. Sergeant Houk wasn't at all sure that she had understood him.

"For instance," he ventured, "do you happen to be acquainted with a man called Lloyd Denman? He owns a fancy fish restaurant at La Jolla. Tall guy, thin, kind of aquiline nose."

"Beaky," added Detective Gable, when Helmwige still failed to respond.

Helmwige, without taking her eyes off them, called, "Otto! *Kommen Sie hier, bitte!*"

After another lengthy pause, during which Helmwige stared back at Sergeant Houk and Detective Gable without volunteering a single word, Otto appeared from what was obviously the kitchen door at the back. He was wearing a white T-shirt and voluminous gray cotton shorts, which made him look even thinner and paler and more dried-out than ever. He was wiping his hands on a small threadbare towel, over and over and over.

Helmwige said, "These gentlemen are detectives. They want to know if we have heard of anybody named—what was it, Detective?"

"Sergeant," Sergeant Houk corrected her. "And the name of the man I was asking you about is Lloyd Denman."

Otto inspected Sergeant Houk and Detective Gable with cold yellowish-gray eyes. He continued to rub his hands as if he were obsessive about having them completely dry. "Why should you ask us this?" he wanted to know.

"Well, sir," said Sergeant Houk, "we're investigating a number of homicides. . . . You may have heard about them, a whole lot of people in the San Diego area have been burned to death . . . and Mr. Denman happens to be a suspect in this case."

"A suspect?" asked Otto, and then nodded.

"Do you know him?" repeated Detective Gable.

Otto pursed his lips dismissively, and shook his head. *"Nein. Ich könne ihn nicht."*

Sergeant Houk opened his notebook. "He was supposed to have visited these premises yesterday morning, round about eleven o'clock."

"Das ist ganz unmöglich," Otto replied.

"What'd he say?" Sergeant Houk asked Helmwige.

"He said, it is not possible."

"He was seen entering these premises, sir." Then, to Helmwige, "Tell him that Lloyd Denman was seen entering these premises."

"Have you seen this man Denman?" Otto asked him.

"Sure I've seen him," said Sergeant Houk guardedly. "I saw him about a half-hour since. And I'll tell you something else—"

He was interrupted by a splintering of glass from the back of the house, which sounded distinctly like a young deputy sheriff putting his boot heel through a cucumber-frame. Otto's eyes instantly flared wide open, and he hissed at Sergeant Houk, "You have sent somebody around to the back of the house?"

"Well, yes, I'm sorry; but we didn't think there was anybody here and we were just checking to make sure that—"

"You have a warrant?"

"Not specifically as such, but—"

"Who knows you are here? Which of your superiors? Which of your colleagues?"

"Sir—we weren't sent by anybody—this happens to be part of an ongoing investigation, that's all—and if that deputy has damaged anything—"

But Otto turned away from him, opened the kitchen door, and disappeared. Sergeant Houk said to Helmwige, "Listen—I didn't intend to cause any problems here, but—"

Without a word, her face grim, Helmwige slammed the door. Sergeant Houk and Detective Gable were left standing on the veranda.

"Didn't I tell you this case was weird?" said Detective Gable, hitching up his pants.

"If I had a goddamn warrant I'd bust in there like fifteen tons of hot shit," Sergeant Houk snarled. "Goddamned Krauts. Just because we beat the shit out of them during the war, they seem to think we owe them some kind of apology."

"Well, how can they expect that?" said Detective Gable. "We weren't even *born* during the war."

"Oh God give me strength," Sergeant Houk retaliated.

At that moment, they heard an appalling high-pitched scream. It sounded like a bird at first, or a coyote caught in a rabbit trap. But it was quickly followed by another, more like a bellow of pain than a scream, and then a shout of *"Help me! Help me! Aaaahhh! Help me!"*

Sergeant Houk slapped Detective Gable on the shoulder and snapped, "Round the back! Quick! You go that way, I'll go this!"

They both drew their guns. Detective Gable jumped heavily off the veranda and ran around the garage block, battling with the weeds as he went. Sergeant Houk sprinted along the veranda, around the other side of the house, and with a fierce kick broke the latch of the whitewashed wooden gate at the side. He forced the gate wider, pushed himself through, and galloped up a flight of six or seven shallow brick steps to the back corner of the house. He caught his foot in a loosely coiled garden hose; tripped; took three flying, loping, off-balance steps forward, and grazed his hand against the path.

The screaming went on, almost inhuman. As he came around the corner to the small backyard, Sergeant Houk saw the deputy engulfed in roaring flames, flapping at himself in a convulsive attempt to put them out. His arms jerked up and down like a clockwork toy, but all he was doing was fanning the flames even more. His eyes were squeezed shut. Both his ears were burning, shriveling like raddichio leaves on a kitchen burner. Fire poured from the top of his head, sending up a column of black smoke that rose higher than the house. He dropped to the ground with a sound like a heavy sack full of ash, rolling over and over, in the way that all policemen and fire fighters are trained to do, if their clothes catch fire. But this seemed to make the flames burn more furiously than ever, and after a few seconds of fiery thrashing about, he staggered back to his feet, screaming in hopeless agony.

Detective Gable appeared on the other side of the house,

fighting aside the last of the weeds. He stopped and stared at the deputy in open-mouthed horror.

"You coat, Gable, for Chrissake!" yelled Sergeant Houk. "Use your coat!"

He looked desperately around. How the hell do you extinguish a burning man? There was a swimming pool in the yard, but it had obviously long been empty, and was peeling and cracked and silted up with dry eucalyptus leaves. The rest of the yard was mainly concrete, with a few sorry yuccas and a tangled flower border, and a glass vegetable frame hidden among the overgrown crabgrass.

The garden hose!

The deputy was still flapping, still dancing. Detective Gable had twisted himself out of his coat was waving it at him like a matador, trying to get near enough the blazing deputy to smother the flames. Sergeant Houk ran back to the garden hose. The faucet was stiff, but he hit it twice with the butt of his revolver, and it loosened.

Hurry, Christ, hurry, the man's on fire!

All the time he knew that he was far too late; that it was no goddamn use; and that it would probably be kinder to let the deputy die. But he had been trained not to respond to thoughts like that. It was his duty to do what he could to save the deputy's life, human sympathy notwithstanding.

The hose was faded and inflexible from years of lying in the sun, and hideously knotted, but he managed to yank enough of it across the yard to reach the burning man. Water clattered on the dry ground all around him.

The deputy had fallen onto his side now, amongst the grass and the broken glass, and was shuddering and quaking in agony. Detective Gable was on his knees beside him, trying desperately to cover him up with his coat, but every time he moved the coat to suppress the flames that danced around his face, more flames would spring up around his thighs and his groin.

"Oh God!" whimpered Detective Gable, his own hands reddened and blistered. "He's like one of those fucking candles you can't blow out!"

"Roger!" Sergeant Houk shouted. "Roger, you hear me? It's okay! Get ready for a shock! This water's real cold!"

He couldn't tell whether the deputy had understood him or not. The boy's face was blackened like burned beef, his eyes had been poached into blindness, his hair was nothing but crisp black tufts. But somehow he was still alive, still hurting, still burning, still trembling in the very last moments of his life.

Sergeant Houk swung the hose around and drenched him.

Detective Gable heaved himself up, offering his own burned hands to the hosepipe jet, and saying, "Here, Sergeant, for Christ's sake, just one splash."

The second he said that, however, Sergeant Houk saw with horror that the hose hadn't extinguished the deputy at all. In fact, the flames were roaring up even more furiously, as if the water itself were flammable. He was about to say, "*Gable, no—!*" when the arc of water pouring out of the hose-nozzle burst into flame, and Detective Gable was drenched in fire.

Detective Gable screeched, and tried to wave away the fire with his arms, but his arms instantly caught fire. The hose almost immediately became too hot for Sergeant Houk to hold, and he dropped it. It snaked backwards and forwards under the wild pressure of the water, spraying Detective Gable again and again with liquid fire.

He fell to the ground, rolled over, thrashed, but he was burning even more fiercely than the deputy.

"Daddy!" he screamed. "Daddy! For Chrissake, Daddy!"

This time Sergeant Houk knew that the time for the rulebook had passed. He dodged the cascade of fire from the hose, and stepped up to Detective Gable quick and intent, his muscles tense as springs. He was holding his service revolver in both hands.

"God forgive me," he said, and shot Detective Gable once in the head. Blood and brains sprayed outwards, and sizzled sharply in the heat.

Then Sergeant Houk turned around, his gun raised, and saw Otto standing at the kitchen window, his face white, his dry hands raised over his eyes as if he were staring at something very far in the distance. Helmwige stood a little further back in the shadows, but she wasn't even looking at the burning men in her backyard; she was admiring her fingernails.

Sergeant Houk pointed his gun stiffly at Otto and screamed, "*Freeze! Freeze, you bastard! You're under arrest!*"

But instantly he felt a wave of heat roar over him, as if a huge furnace door had been opened right in front of his face. His hands blistered, his sleeves caught fire, his gun fired on its own, smashing the kitchen window. Instinctively, he threw the gun away, a split second before the rest of its rounds exploded in the chamber, blasting fragments of shrapnel in all directions. One of them caught Sergeant Houk deep in his left calf muscle.

You bastard! he thought. *You won't burn me!*

With his clothes on fire with his hair smoking, he ran back around the house, leaping over the hose, thundering along the veranda, vaulting the porch, and hurdling the long guano-spattered hood of Otto's Mercedes tourer.

He didn't notice the pain at first, but when his hair suddenly flared up, he felt a searing sensation on the top of his head that made him yell out. He had to get away! He had to get away!

His pants were blazing, his shirt was almost completely burned off his back. Nylon was fused into skin, manmade fiber into man, until it was impossible ever to separate them again. His shoes fell away from his feet in burning chunks; then the soles of his feet were torn off, with two sharp ripping noises, as his was skin fused to the blacktop.

He heard his breath coming in huge, channel-swimmer's roars. He saw the road ahead of him, juggled in his vision like the view through a hand-held camera. He saw the eucalyptus trees swaying, although he couldn't hear them rustle. He saw his Buick, parked and ready for him, ready to take him away. He smelled fire, and smoke, and some indescribable odor that was *himself*, burning.

You—German—bastard—you—won't—

He reached his car, tugged open the driver's door with fingers that seemed to be dripping flesh.

Won't—burn—me—you—

His coat was gone, his shirt was gone. His torso was a mass of reddened flesh, on which small well-fed flames still licked. But he still had his car keys, embedded in his skin. With fingers that were tipped with nothing but bone, he pried the keys out of the blistered layers, pulling even more skin after them. He screamed in despair more than in pain.

"You won't burn me, you bastard!" he shouted. He rammed the key into the Buick's ignition and the end of the key penetrated the palm of his hand, wedging itself right between his finger bones. Still shouting, still blazing, he turned his hand so that the engine started, yanked the parking brake, and skidded away from the side of the road in a blizzard of eucalyptus leaves and a cloud of dust. A Mexican gardener was raking the lawns of the house on the opposite side of Paseo Delicias. He turned around in horror as Sergeant Houk's Buick slewed past him; tires shrieking like a chorus from *Tannhaüser*, with a man of fire in the driver's seat. The gardener dropped to his knees and crossed himself.

Swerving the Buick around the next bend, Sergeant Houk knew that it was over. His legs were still alight, his scalp was tightening and shriveling like a bathing cap. The pain was already so intense that he didn't know whether he could still feel it or not. It was like being *eaten*, rather than burned.

Ahead of him, up the winding hill of Paseo Delicias, he could see a huge blue and white truck toiling. Genuine GM Auto Parts.

Thank you, God. he thought to himself. *So you have forgiven me, after all.*

Behind the next embankment, he saw the top of the truck approaching. He pressed his foot as far down on the gas pedal as he could, and wildly steered the Buick onto the left-hand side of the road.

He saw lemon trees passing, like trees in a dream. He saw rocks, bushes, fragments of sky, everything floating past him so gently and so normally, with the rocking motion of a carousel. He remembered the carousel at Disneyland, when he was a kid, floating up and down, up and down. But his tires were still singing their merciless chorus, somewhere on the edge of his consciousness. *Fearful and loud thy rage is! Like a storm-wind you come!*

He opened his mouth to say something, but then his entire windshield was filled with the massive chrome radiator grille of the oncoming truck.

The Buick hit the truck at a closing speed of over seventy miles an hour. Its front end dived under the truck's front bumper, and the entire car vanished underneath the truck as if it had never existed. The truck driver didn't have the time to blow his horn.

Only a second afterward, however, the Buick's gas tank detonated with a sound like a huge and distant door slamming. The truck's body was blown apart in the middle, and a lethal hail of automobile parts was sprayed in all directions. A Caprice crankshaft was driven right through the back of the driver's cab, right through the back of his seat, and with a terrible and decisive crunch, right through his lower back. A spare Oldsmobile hubcap sang through the air with the alien certainty of a flying saucer, and sliced the head from the Mexican gardener who had witnessed Sergeant Houk's blazing ride down the hill. He stood headless with his sickle in his hand, as if, headless, he was unable to decide whether to fall over or not.

Then he dropped to the ground and began to irrigate the marigolds with a thick and glutinous stream of blood.

It was almost ten seconds before the last echoes of the explosion came back from the distant mountains, and the last fragments of shattered automobile parts came ringing down from the sky.

Otto turned away from the living-room window, and gave Helmwige a thin smile. "It makes me impatient, you know, to show them who will be the masters next."

"You should take more care," Helmwige replied, in a voice that was meant to show him that she was deeply unimpressed.

"You heard what he said. Nobody knew that he was coming here, neither his superiors nor his colleagues. He came because our friend Herr Denman told him where to come. Herr Denman has an unpleasantly inquisitive turn of mind, you know, and the fact that we are keeping Celia here is obviously not enough to keep him from hounding us."

"So what are you going to do?" asked Helmwige, flatly. "You're not thinking of burning him, are you?"

"Of course not. Our future lies with men like Herr Denman. Good stock! Good fathers! Heaven knows that we are going to need all that we can get. But . . . he is not behaving himself. I am going to be obliged to bring him here, and keep him out of harm's way until *der Umgestaltung*, the Transformation. Then he can burn. But not before. You remember what *der Führer* always said to me. 'Otto,' he always said to me, 'the search for purity will take the lives of many martyrs. But we must seek purity first and last. *Die Reinheit zuerst, die Reinheit letzt. Die Reinheit is alles.*"

Helmwige drew her silk bathrobe even more tightly around her and stalked across to the far side of the living room. The young naked man was still chained there, sitting cross-legged now, his face etched extremely sharp and pale against the Southern California sunlight, every hard well-exercised muscle clearly defined. Helmwige stood over him for a long time, apparently admiring him, yet obviously despising him at the same time.

"The master race," she said, shaking her head. "What a pathetic specimen."

Otto came and stood beside her, his hands in the pockets of his shorts. "I suppose I have to agree. But then it was difficult for so many of those doctors to make such a leap of the mind.

Mengele, what an idiot! And even the best of them, the very finest, Bloss and Hauer and von Harn, they could never understand that the master race was not just a question of genealogy, not just a question of breeding, but a question of the elements, too. The old, unquestioned power of the earth. That is what makes a master race."

Helmwige ran her red-clawed hand through the young man's hair. "Still, you know, I like him."

"You like him!" Otto sneered. "He is nothing more than a failed experiment! A racial dead end! My God, if *der Führer* hadn't made me promise, I would have destroyed him years ago; yes, and his father before him; and his father before him."

"But you *did* promise," Helmwige reminded him.

Otto walked across to the curved 1930s cocktail cabinet, found a bottle of schnapps, and poured himself a drink. "Yes, I did promise," he agreed. "And look at the result. A creature with perfect physique. Perfect body, perfect eyesight, perfect hearing. Pity his IQ is slightly below room temperature."

Helmwige continued to stroke the young man's blond, flat-cropped hair. He didn't lift his eyes to her once, didn't smile, didn't scowl, didn't acknowledge her at all, except when she began to run the very edges of her fingernails down the back of his neck, through those fine tiny almost-invisible hairs. Then his penis gradually swelled and uncurled, not fully erect, but visibly enlarged and thickened.

"Helmwige," Otto admonished her, with a flatness in his voice that betrayed the fact that he was neither jealous nor interested. To him, the young man had less value than a laboratory chimpanzee. He was simply a nuisance, who had to be fed and exercised and accommodated. If Helmwige hadn't adored him so much, he probably would have set him on fire years ago. That big fat prick would have burned like an altar candle.

Helmwige ran her fingernails all the way down the young man's knobbly spine. Then she traced the clearly developed lines of his deltoids, his teres minor and teres major, his latissimus dorsi. His chains clanked slightly as she stroked his shoulders, and his penis swelled even larger, until the foreskin gradually rolled back of its own accord, revealing the bare plumlike glans, with its high distinctive ridge and its deeply cleft opening.

"You should have given him a name," said Helmwige. "How can anybody exist without a name?"

Otto sipped a little schnapps, ran a thin tongue-tip across thinner lips. "He doesn't need a name."

"How can he live, without a name?" Helmwige protested. They had been through this same argument more times than Otto could count.

"All he has to do is to *live*," he retorted. "A name is unnecessary. A dog may understand English, but you don't buy books, even for the cleverest dog."

Helmwige stroked the young man's buttocks, and the sides of his thighs. Then she said to him, quite matter-of-factly, "Turn over; you can be the cleverest dog."

With a scraping and jangling of chains, the young man turned over until he was on all fours. He remained exquisitely handsome. His back beautifully curved, his thigh muscles taut. But he remained silent, too, and willing to obey.

"Now, look at him," grinned Helmwige. "Should I take him for a walk, on the end of a leash?"

"He will probably kill you one day," Otto remarked, draining his schnapps and immediately pouring himself another.

"Oh, he won't kill me. He loves me. He adores me! I am the only one who treats him to what he likes!"

"That's what you think," Otto told her. "You humiliate him. Even a masochist has his pride, you know." He patted his shorts, and said, "Where are my cigarettes?"

"On the table," Helmwige replied.

"Those are Marlboro. You know that I smoke only Ernte 23."

Helmwige laughed, without humor. "You smoke detectives, too, and all kinds of people!"

Otto snapped, "Leave that boy alone! Go and find my cigarettes!"

"Oh, find your own cigarettes," Helmwige replied. "Just look at this."

She spread apart the young man's buttocks with her long red fingernails. Then, with the kind of taunting smile in her eyes that she knew Otto would find infuriating, she licked her index finger, and plunged it without hesitation into the knotted muscular rose of the young man's bottom. He flinched, uttered a low gasp, but accepted her sharp-nailed finger without complaint.

"I suppose you were worse at Ohrdruf," Otto commented.

"Everybody was worse at Ohrdruf. Guards, prisoners, everybody. The prisoners were as much to blame as we were. They brought it upon themselves. Have you ever experienced a race of people with such a death wish! How can a murderer be a murderer without a victim? In every murder, my dear Otto, the victim is an accomplice."

Slowly, she withdrew her finger. Then she cupped the young man's testicles in her hand, and squeezed them and massaged them, over and over, until they bulged between her fingers.

Otto looked away. "You are appalling, my dear. You always were. I suppose your only redeeming feature is your complete disregard for human life, including your own."

"Turn over," Helmwige commanded the young man; and silently, he did so. Helmwige grasped the huge veined shaft of his penis in both hands, and rubbed it up and down, looking intently and questioningly into his eyes as she did so.

"How does *that* feel, then?" she asked him. "Do you like it? Do you hate it? You don't really know, do you? What a vegetable!"

Now the head of his penis was gleaming and slick. Helmwige rubbed him harder and quicker. A faint flush of color appeared on his perfect cheekbones; his stomach muscles tensed; and he closed his eyes. If possible, his penis appeared to grow even larger, and the opening gaped like a huge fish gasping for air.

"Now," ordered Helmwige, with unexpected softness, and bent her head forward. Her mouth enclosed the head of his penis just as he shuddered, and ejaculated. She waited with her braided head bent forward in his lap for almost half a minute; and before she finally sat up, she pulled back the foreskin as far as it would go, and gave his shining skin one last definitive lick.

She stood up, and approached Otto with shining lips. The young man remained where he was, his head still bowed, his penis sinking.

"Don't you know what a tribute I pay you, Otto?" Helmwige teased him. Otto flinched and turned away, his thin fingers tightening on his schnapps glass.

"Otto—you are always the true master. Look what I have done for you! Mengele produced his so-called master race, and I have simply swallowed it!"

Otto refused to look at her. A few moments passed; the road outside was chaotic with sirens. Helmwige said, "What is death, Otto? Where does it begin, where does it end? Supposing your mother had swallowed your father's sperm, on the night when you were due to be conceived? She would have killed you! You would have died, and been digested, and floated out to the Baltic, the tiniest atom in a whole universe of atoms."

"Helmwige," said Otto at last, still averting his face. "If you touch that young man again, I will burn him to death in front of you. And that is my warning."

Helmwige smiled. "Why should I worry, Otto? You can frighten many, many people; but you can't frighten me. In any case, why should I care, when you plan to burn the whole world?"

16

Lloyd was pouring himself another cup of Kathleen's espresso when he saw the Mercedes pull up outside. After a moment, Otto climbed out, closely followed by Helmwige; but by nobody else. They came up to the front door, and rang the bell. Tom said, "It's okay, I'll get it!" but Lloyd called, "No! Leave it! Don't answer it!"

Kathleen was halfway down the stairs. "What's the matter?" she asked. "What's wrong?"

Lloyd strode quickly to the stairs and took her arm. "It's them again. Otto and that woman."

"They've come back? What do you think they want?"

"I don't know; but it might be better if you kept Lucy and Tom well out of the way."

The doorbell rang again. They could see Otto's distorted shape through the window. Otto had already begun to inspire in Lloyd a kind of nagging dread, like waking up in the night with the fear that he might have cancer. Kathleen said, "All right, just to be safe. Tom . . . Auntie Lucy's upstairs; why don't you take her another cup of coffee?"

When Tom had carefully carried the cup upstairs, Lloyd went to the door and opened it. Otto was standing on the step in his old-fashioned gray suit and his wide-brimmed hat, smiling coldly in the sunshine; while Helmwige stood a short distance away, dressed in a black Spandex miniskirt and a leather jacket that looked as if it had once belonged to Judge Dredd.

"What do you want now?" Lloyd asked Otto, tautly.

Otto peered into the house as if he were inspecting it for dry rot. "You don't mind if we come in?"

"Yes, I very much do mind if you come in. What do you want?"

Otto's roaming eyes settled on a crane fly that was trembling on the side of the doorway in the warm morning breeze. "You gave me your word, Mr. Denman, that you would tell nobody about us."

"I've kept it."

"Oh? Then perhaps you can explain a visit we received this morning from three police officers, inquiring if we knew you. A very unpleasant visit, I might add. A visit that ended in a most regrettable tragedy."

"Tragedy?" queried Lloyd. He was aware that his left eyelid was involuntarily fluttering. He was exhausted; he was stressed; and most of all he was terrified of what Otto might take into his head to do to them.

"There was a fire, and an automobile accident," Otto explained, his eyes still fixed on the crane fly. "As I said, most regrettable. But we all know that police work has its risks."

"A fire? You burned Sergeant Houk?"

"Was that his name? You shouldn't have told him where to find us, you know. That was a great mistake."

"I didn't tell him anything."

Otto's eyes sloped toward Lloyd, and he gave him a thin, lazy grin. "Oh, come now, Mr. Denman. Do you take me for a *Dummkopf?*"

"Christ, you're insane," Lloyd breathed at him.

"On the contrary," Otto replied. "In all the world, I am probably the only man who is in a state of complete mental balance."

"What do you want?" Lloyd repeated.

"I want *you,* Mr. Denman, and I want Mrs. Kerwin."

"I don't understand." Lloyd hated him so much at that moment he could have seized him by the neck and throttled him. But as if she could sense the sudden surge in Lloyd's hostility, Helmwige stepped forward and stood close to Otto's shoulder, with an expression of threatening disinterest. Lloyd had seen the same expression on the faces of security guards at rock concerts. They'll break your back or they won't break your back; it's up to you. But they'll do it if necessary.

"Mr. Denman," Otto explained, "the summer solstice is next

Wednesday. Then our Transformation ceremony will be complete. I will no longer have to worry if inquisitive people disrupt our preparations. But until that time, I must ask that you and Mrs. Kerwin stay as my guests, in order not to spread undue alarm about us, amongst people who may not be friendly."

"You expect *anybody* to be friendly to you, the way you're acting?" Lloyd demanded.

"I expect only to be left undisturbed," Otto replied.

"Well, if you think we're going to stay with you, you're crazy."

Otto couldn't resist the crane fly. His hand passed over it, and cupped it, and discreetly he pressed it into his mouth. Lloyd grimaced in disgust.

"You shouldn't rush to judgment, Mr. Denman," Otto told him. "There are other ways of life, apart from *nouvelle cuisine* and the pursuit of custom homes with real brick fireplaces."

"Don't you mock me, Herr Mander," Lloyd cautioned him. "Now get the hell out of here, and don't come back."

Otto raised his hand. "I've come to get you, Mr. Denman, one way or another. If you don't agree to stay with me until the solstice, you and Mrs. Kerwin, then believe me, you will burn, too."

Lloyd said, "You're bluffing. Now get out of here, before I do something I might be sorry for."

Otto stared at him. Almost immediately, Lloyd felt a sharp pain in the middle of his forehead, and heard the snap of burning skin. He shouted out, and lifted his hand to his forehead. Otto had burned a small circular mark on him.

"You see that is *O* for Otto," Otto smiled. "You are branded now, Mr. Denman, like a dumb animal. You belong to me.

"I could have burned you to ashes where you stand, Mr. Denman. But I have something special in mind for you and Mrs. Kerwin . . . and I do not wish to harm you unless you give me no choice . . . not too much, anyway. Although, as the Marquis de Sade once said, agony is only relative."

Lloyd took a cautious step back. His forehead felt as if it were still on fire. "You want us to stay with you? At your house in Rancho Santa Fe?"

"Until next Wednesday, for the sake of my peace of mind. You wouldn't want to disturb my peace of mind, would you, Mr. Denman?"

"I guess I wouldn't," Lloyd replied. Helmwige laughed.

At that moment Kathleen appeared. Otto bowed, and clicked his heels together. "*Guten Morgen, gnädige Frau.*"

"Lloyd?" asked Kathleen. "What's going on? What's the matter with your forehead?"

They were driven to Rancho Santa Fe with the sounds of *Die Walküre* on the Mercedes stereo. Inside the car, it was like a black leather freezer, so cold that Kathleen shivered. Helmwige drove, Otto sat neatly in the passenger seat with his knees together and smoked a cigarette with an amber holder. The music was too loud for sensible conversation.

Kathleen's sister Lucy had been confused and worried by her sudden request to take care of Tom for a week, and she had obviously been suspicious of Otto and Helmwige. But Kathleen had explained that Otto was a grief counselor with the psychiatry faculty at UCSD, and that she needed to spend a few days with him to help her get over Mike.

"He's a good friend, too," she had assured Lucy; as Helmwige had lifted their bags into the trunk.

"You never mentioned him before," Lucy had replied. "And he sure doesn't *look* like any kind of counselor. Let alone anybody that *you'd* like."

"It takes all kinds," Kathleen had told her, and kissed her cheek. "I'll be back Thursday morning. Take care of Tom for me."

"You know I will."

They reached the house on Paseo Delicias and turned into the sloping driveway, parking close to the Mercedes 380SL. Helmwige opened the door and they dutifully climbed out.

"Helmwige will bring in your bags," Otto told them. "Follow me. . . . I will show you where you can stay."

"Where's Celia?" asked Lloyd, looking around. "Is she here someplace?"

Otto turned to him, his face as crumpled as white tissue. "I will explain everything to you in due course, Mr. Denman. And in due course, I will show you your bride-to-be."

"You're sick," Lloyd told him.

"History will be the judge of that, not you," smiled Otto.

"How about that friend of yours?" asked Lloyd. "The guy in the chains?"

"What about him?"

"Is he still here? I'm not sure that he's exactly the kind of sight that Mrs. Kerwin ought to be exposed to."

"He's nothing. He's not even a person."

"What do you mean, 'He's not even a person'? What the hell is he, then—two orders of eggroll to go?"

Otto stopped on the veranda and fixed Lloyd with a look that could have set fire to a lake. "Don't joke with me, Mr. Denman. Don't think that you have that privilege. You have voluntarily and unwisely involved yourself in a matter which is no concern of yours, and now you are paying the price for your inquisitiveness. I could have burned you many times. Be thankful that I didn't; but watch what you say. I can always change my mind."

Lloyd said nothing. He could sense that he had pushed Otto way too far, and just because Otto didn't have a gun, that didn't mean that he wasn't capable of killing him with all the effectiveness of a gun, and a hundred times more painfully. He allowed Otto to lead him into the house, and Kathleen followed a little way behind.

Otto showed them into the living room. Lloyd noticed that the chain rings were still in the floor, although the young man was gone. Inside, the living room looked even more like a period piece from the 1930s than it had from the outside. The wallpaper was dull brown, the furniture was mostly laminated plywood and chrome. On the walls were dozens of sepia photographs of Germany before World War II. Pretty girls in fur stoles, smiling young men, balconies and snowy mountaintops.

An old-fashioned gramophone stood in one corner, with a stack of 78 records beside it. The top record was *Die Wacht Am Rhein*.

Lloyd looked up at the huge drawing of the lizard on the wall. "Our friend the cross-legged gecko," he remarked.

Otto stared at him coldly. "That, my friend, is a salamander. The symbol of our Transformation."

Kathleen came in and looked around. She gave Lloyd a meaningful glance, but both of them guessed that they would be safer if they remained quiet.

Helmwige showed them upstairs to their rooms. Both rooms were small, with sloping dormer ceilings, and in Lloyd's room the bed was no more than a mattress on the floor. He had a restricted view over the treetops, downhill toward the Fairbanks Ranch, but he saw immediately that there was no prospect of escaping out the window. Below the sill, there was a short slope of oak-shingled roof, and then a sheer drop down to the yard. He peered out and saw the young man who had been chained up in the living room, digging in the yard with a shovel. The young man wore baggy shorts and a T-shirt, and the back of his T-shirt was dark with sweat. Lloyd wondered what he was doing gardening on such a blistering hot afternoon. At least he wasn't naked. But when Lloyd looked again, he saw that the young man was still restricted by a long chain around his right ankle. *Very* bizarre.

"You are free to do anything except leave," Helmwige told them. "You will be well taken care of. Otto is many things, but he is always a man of his word."

"Glad to hear it," said Lloyd. "What time's lunch?"

Helmwige said, "He will tell you everything this evening. I know Otto. He talks about secrecy but he is so impatient to show the world what he has achieved. Your Celia is part of that achievement, Mr. Denman. He won't be able to resist the temptation to boast."

"He burns people, and then he boasts?"

Helmwige smiled, almost friendly. "You still don't get it, do you, Mr. Denman? It is right in front of your eyes. You should try perhaps to see things for what they are, instead of what you would like them to be."

She went back downstairs, and left them alone. Kathleen came up to Lloyd and held him close, without saying a word. Lloyd circled his arms around her and said, "Don't worry . . . really, don't worry. Everything's going to be fine. So long as we play it cool and easy, and don't lose our nerve."

"But what are they *doing?*" asked Kathleen. "Are they spies, or what? And if it's all such a big secret that we have to stay here, why does Otto want to boast about it so much?"

"And what is it that's right in front of my eyes, that I don't see?"

Kathleen shook her head. "It's all so strange. I feel like I'm going to wake up any minute and Mike will be lying in bed next to me and none of this will ever have happened."

Lunch didn't materialize, but by six o'clock they began to smell the strong aroma of cabbage throughout the house. Shortly after seven, the young man knocked at their doors, and asked them to come downstairs to eat. He was wearing the same shorts and T-shirt that he had been wearing in the yard, and he smelled of sweat.

Kathleen said to him, "You like gardening, huh? I just love it!"

The young man looked at her without expression.

"We saw you in the yard," Kathleen told him, trying to sound bright. "You were digging, yes? We saw you digging."

Still the young man said nothing.

"Looks like the lights are on, but there's nobody home," Lloyd remarked.

"You do *comprenez anglais?*" Kathleen asked the young man. "I mean, you asked us to come eat. Or was that just something that Otto taught you?"

"You must come down to eat now. That is all I am allowed to say."

"You're not even allowed to say 'How are you, have a nice day'?"

"Come on, Kathleen, forget it," said Lloyd. "Let's just go eat."

The young man led them downstairs, and showed them through to a small dining room furnished in dark oak. Otto was already sitting at the head of the table, Helmwige on his left. Around the walls hung lurid amateurish paintings of Bavaria, purple mountains and black pine trees and lime-green lakes, although pride of place was given to a framed photograph of a stern, rectangular-faced man with acne-scarred cheeks and long bushy side-whiskers.

"Wagner," said Lloyd, immediately. He had seen so many pictures of Wagner in Celia's treatises.

Otto nodded. "Yes, Wagner, to whom we owe so much."

"Isn't—*he*—eating with us?" asked Kathleen, nodding toward the young man.

"No, no," said Otto, quite surprised. "He doesn't eat with us."

Helmwige lifted the lid from a huge blue and white china casserole dish. A strong aroma of pickled cabbage and ham filled the room. "Choucroute," Helmwige announced. "I make it myself. Pickled cabbage with pork belly and liver dumplings."

She heaped three plates high, and handed them to Kathleen, to Lloyd, and to herself. Otto ate nothing but a little dry bread, which he broke into tiny pieces. *Too many bugs in between meals*, thought Lloyd, but decided against saying it out loud. Helmwige's food was fatty and unappetizing enough without thinking about Otto eating insects.

Kathleen lifted up a huge slice of white vibrant pork fat on the end of her fork. "I'm sorry," she said. "I can't eat this. I'm on the F-Plan diet."

Plainly irritated, Helmwige took the fork and shook the fat onto her own plate. She cut it up and ate it with gusto, juice running down her chin. "I've seen people kill each other for such food," she said.

Lloyd put down his fork. "I guess that must have been before the days of *nouvelle cuisine*," he remarked. Actually, if he had been able to eat the kind of heavyweight food that sustains Alsatian farmworkers, he probably would have found Helmwige's cooking very good. He tried a little of the cabbage and it was strong and savory and delicious.

Lloyd and Kathleen picked at their food in silence for a few minutes, while Helmwige noisily devoured fat and meat and potatoes and pickled cabbage. Occasionally Otto fastidiously ate another small piece of bread, or sipped a glass of Alsace Riesling, but most of the time he sat at the head of the table as if he were waiting for something, but didn't know what. He cracked his knuckles one by one, and sighed.

Kathleen said, "Who is that young man?"

Otto turned to stare at her. "Are you speaking to me?"

"Yes. I wanted to know who that young man is. The one who called us down to supper."

"He isn't anybody," Otto replied.

"What do you mean? Everybody's *somebody*."

"Not him. He belongs to a geneaological line which should never have existed. He is—what do you call it?—a freak, a mistake."

"He looks all right to me," said Kathleen.

"Of course!" Otto smiled. "Physically he is flawless. But inside his mind . . . well, who knows what goes on inside his mind? Sometimes I think he is a genius; sometimes I think he is an idiot. When you ask him where he lives, he says he lives inside a black sack. Yet he can lay bricks like a professional bricklayer and do mathematical calculations in his head that make most people's heads spin. Then again, if you take him out at night, he throws stones at the moon, trying to hit it."

"Well, that's terrible," said Kathleen. "He's so good-looking."

"A master race is not made up of looks alone," Otto told her.

It was then that Lloyd raised his eyes from his half-finished meal and saw the symbol of the salamander inside the circle, and understood at last what it was that had been right in front of his eyes, and which he had failed to see. *Master race.* The salamander's head was crooked; its feet were crooked. If he half-closed his eyes, he found that he was looking at nothing less than a swastika.

"Let me explain what we are doing," said Otto. "It won't do any harm, since you will be staying here until the Transformation is over."

Helmwige, with her mouth full, rolled her eyes up at Otto's predictability. She gestured with her fork at Kathleen's plate and said, "Mmm-hm, mmm-hm!"—encouraging her to eat up.

Otto said, "In 1936, as soon as he was appointed chancellor, Hitler commissioned doctors from many different scientific disciplines to explore the possibility of creating a master race, based on the natural supremacy of the Aryan. Immediately these doctors set to work in their laboratories and their hospitals, trying to breed perfect little babies."

He sat back in his seat, and interlaced his fingers. "*Der Führer* also asked me to contribute to this program. I was very young in those days, a philosophy student in Basel, but already I had shown my interest in the National Socialist ideals, and come to the attention of Joseph Goebbels. It was Goebbels who recommended me to Hitler.

"I pursued other ideas, quite different from breeding babies. I was a thinker, not a farmer! Besides, I thought breeding was too slow, too uncontrollable! *Der Führer* wanted to change the racial characteristics of the world in a decade, not wait for the unpredictable results of several centuries!

"How many generations does it take to produce children who are blond and beautiful and possess the required size of brainpan? And what guarantee would you ever have that these perfect creatures would grow up capable as well as beautiful?

"No . . ." he said, smiling as he sipped his wine. "I was searching for a master race that was not only guaranteed to be beautiful and not only guaranteed to be mentally brilliant, but to be ready within a matter of years, perhaps months, perhaps even weeks! That meant selecting people who had already shown themselves to have these desirable characteristics. Not breeding babies, you see, but transforming adults."

He scraped back his chair, and stood up. "I spent years and years at Salzburg University, looking for a way. I searched right back in history and legend, right back to the days of the Vikings, looking for any kind of clue. At last I began to come across references to a Transformation ceremony in northern Jutland, in which the bravest and most intelligent people in several communities were burned alive *in order that they might never die.*

"If the proper ritual was observed, the fire did not destroy them, but transfigured them, immortalized them. In other words, the Danes were burning alive their best people to preserve them forever, and to make them the founding members of a pure and immortal race. They had tried to preserve people before, by pressing them into their peat bogs, but without success. The answer was fire!"

Kathleen looked across the table at Lloyd, but the expression on her face was one of apprehension, not disbelief. They had both seen enough of Otto's abilities to know that at least some of what he was saying must be true.

"In Salzburg I also came across previously unpublished diaries by Paracelsus, the sixteenth-century alchemist, who had proved to his own satisfaction that there is a direct physical and mystic connection between life and fire. Both life and fire fed on other lives; but if they were *combined* they created first a life that was fire, and then, at the moment of complete Transformation, a fire that was life.

"This was my breakthrough! I searched libraries in Leipzig and Dresden and London, too, and time and time again I came across references to the life-giving properties of fire. I discovered that when a living human being is burned, there is a Norse ritual which ensures that the soul and the fire combine, to form a half-being which I call a Salamander, after the legendary lizard which hides itself in the hottest recesses of blacksmith's forges.

"Salamanders are highly volatile. They can be as cool as flesh or as hot as fire, according to their temperament. At times they feel bitterly cold, which is why they mask themselves in scarves and coats and gloves. At other times, they feel unbearably hot. If they become too agitated, they can catch fire spontaneously, and burn like phosphorus. Like Walpurgis Night!"

He paused and cleared his throat. His snake-yellow eyes seemed to be focused not just on something else but on *somewhere* else. Another time, another place: when fires had burned at night, and black and red banners had flapped, and voices had roared like the sea.

Helmwige finished eating and began noisily to clear away the dishes. Otto said, "The Transformation ceremony must take place at the summer solstice, when the forces of the earth are at their strongest. I am not talking about magic here, or mysticism! These forces are gravitational and magnetic and psychokinetic—*measurable* forces, which have controlled the balance of the planet Earth for millions of years.

"The ancient music must be played; and the ancient words must be sung. Then the Salamanders will become flesh. Not just flesh, but immortal flesh! And flesh that still has the power of fire!"

Lloyd nodded toward Helmwige. "Is she . . . ?"

Otto nodded. "Immortal, and blessed with the power of fire. You felt her fingers on your wrist. But she is no use to me, as a propagator of the master race. She was a camp doctor at Ohrdruf during the war, and she caught some filthy Semitic disease which left her barren. It would have killed her, if she hadn't agreed to be burned."

Lloyd swallowed, in an effort to control the revulsion that Otto aroused in him. "So when somebody's burned, with all the appropriate chants, they cheat whatever illness they have, and live forever?"

Otto smiled. "*Ach so,* Mr. Denman. You learn quickly. Because—until it has unequivocally been shown to be true—who could you convince to burn themselves alive but those who know that they are terminally ill?"

"Like Marianna, with her breast cancer?" asked Lloyd.

Otto nodded. "And your husband, Mrs. Kerwin. He was suffering from a brain tumor which would have killed him within six or seven months."

"So *that* was why he was so depressed after his check-up," said Kathleen, shocked.

"Dr. Kranz referred him directly to me," said Otto. "In Southern California, there is a network of doctors of German background who refer their terminal patients directly to me. Because, what choice do these people have? To die a mundane death, having achieved nothing at all? Or to become immortal, and to change the whole course of human history? That is why they agree to burn themselves alive. That is why they agree to become Salamanders."

"But Celia wasn't sick," Lloyd protested. "She never even caught a cold."

Otto laughed. "They always say, don't they, that the husband is the last to find out! Or, in your case, the husband-to-be. Your beloved Celia was very sick, Mr. Denman. The only thing was that she was desperate that you didn't find out. You would have insisted that she go for treatment. She would never have had the opportunity to do what she did. Where could she have found gasoline and matches in a clinic? Or at home, under your watchful eye?"

"What was wrong with her?" asked Lloyd, his mouth as dry as a torn-open kapok mattress.

Otto turned away for a moment, as if he hadn't heard, but then he turned back and said, "Multiple sclerosis. Gradual wasting, gradual loss of muscular control, inevitable early death."

"I don't believe you. You killed her!"

"Do you want to see Dr. Warburg's records? I have them all in my files. You're not a doctor of course, but perhaps you noticed that when you stroked the soles of her feet, her great toe bent upwards, and her toes spread apart? That's the Babinski sign. In normal people, when you stroke the soles of their feet, the toes bend downwards."

Otto couldn't have said anything more telling. Lloyd could clearly remember stroking her feet one night when they were making love, and noticing the way her toes spread out. "How do you *do* that?" he had asked her. "I can't do that!"

She had smiled and kissed him, and said, "I hope you never find out."

Lloyd was shaken. "She had multiple sclerosis? And that was for sure?"

"That was for sure," Otto replied. "She could never have given you the children you wanted; she could never have been anything else but an invalid wife. Your married life together would have been a tragedy."

"So she burned herself? She turned herself into one of these—what do you call them—Salamanders?"

"That is correct. That is what she is now. But when we hold our Transformation ceremony at the summer solstice, she will become flesh; or flesh of a kind. Fire transformed into life. You will have her back, Mr. Denman, never fear—and with the threat of illness erased forever!"

Lloyd said, "All of those people on the bus? Were they sick, too?"

"Every one of them. Some had years to live; some no more than weeks. But they had all decided that the way of the Salamander was the way for them, and they were prepared to suffer the pain of burning in the hope of the life everlasting.

"They had faith, Mr. Denman. They were like Shadrach, Meshach, and Abed-nego, who defied King Nebuchadnezzar and stepped into the burning fiery furnace. In fact, there is historical evidence that the Babylonians in the sixth century before Christ had a ritual which was very similar to the Salamander ritual."

Lloyd asked tautly, "Why did Celia burn herself alone, when everybody else was burned together on the bus?"

"Celia was impulsive, Mr. Denman. You know how impulsive she was. We were driving her back downtown after our last meeting when she suddenly said, 'Now; let's do it now.'

"I argued with her. I asked her if she was sure. But she insisted. She wanted to do it immediately."

"And you let her," Lloyd said, his voice as dull as a '53 nickel.

Otto's hand was spread flat on the table. His fingernails were ridged and chalky. "I had no choice, Mr. Denman. It takes so much for a person to build up the confidence to set fire to themselves. How do you express it? They have to be 'on a high.' At that moment, driving along Rosecrans Street, Celia reached that peak. She had to burn herself then and there, or else she may never have done it. We stopped at the gas station and bought a can and gasoline, and the rest you know."

Lloyd didn't know what to say. Celia had summoned up the courage to burn; Celia had summoned up the courage to change her life; Celia had summoned up the courage to become immortal. But she hadn't confided in him, her husband-to-be. Hadn't said a word. He didn't know who had failed whom. Maybe he had failed Celia, because he hadn't recognized that she was sick. Maybe Celia had failed him, because she hadn't trusted him to help her.

He could have nursed her, he could have taken care of her. But maybe she hadn't wanted nursing. Maybe she hadn't wanted him to take care of her. Maybe she had wanted what she had always wanted. Independence, freedom, and the pursuit of happiness, no matter what.

Helmwige came into the room, bearing a huge cut-glass bowl filled with aggressively pink trifle.

"Wait, wait," Otto told her. "We can have that later. Let me show Mr. Denman the Salamanders who are awaiting the solstice with the same impatience that he is."

"Your pride will be the death of you one day," Helmwige replied.

"And your insolence will see you burn!" Otto rapped back.

Helmwige bared her teeth at him. "Remember which one of us is immortal, Otto. I shan't be laying any flowers on your grave."

Otto pushed his chair back and stood up. "Come with me," he told Lloyd and Kathleen, and led the way out of the dining room. They hesitated for a moment, glancing at Helmwige, but Helmwige was already spooning a vast triangular cliff of bright pink trifle onto her plate, and she didn't seem to be at all interested in what they were doing.

They walked through the kitchen and out to the back of the house. The sun had just set, and the sky was the color of pasqueflowers, high and clear. Kathleen suddenly reached out for Lloyd's hand. Slim fingers, soft warm skin. Lloyd felt something that he hadn't felt for years, not even with Celia. A sense of being responsible. A sense that a woman was depending on him to make things work out right. In high school he had once dated a thin gray-eyed girl called Jane who had made him feel like that. Jane had probably married a real-estate agent or one of those used-car salesmen who scream at you on television.

Otto unlocked the back door of the garage, pushed it open, and switched on the overhead light. "Go ahead! Look! *Hier schläft die Zukunft!*"

Lloyd peered inside. The huge garage had been built with whitewashed cinder-block walls, and a low whitewashed ceiling. In the far corner stood a solid and well-used workbench, with rows of drill bits and wrenches, a professional vise, and an automobile battery charger. But there were no automobiles here, not one. Every available inch of floor space was taken up by gray-faced bodies, lying down, dead or sleeping. Every one of them wore impenetrably dark sunglasses, and every one of them had a heavy gray blanket drawn up to the neck. It looked like a morgue for dead sun-worshipers, rather than a sanctum for people who were desperate enough to want to live forever.

There was a heated smell in the air, like a communal sauna, or singeing wool, and the temperature was way up above normal. Lloyd noticed a small thermostat on the wall, which was registering into the red.

"Salamanders," Otto announced. "Smoke and soul, combined. Eighty of them, so far."

Kathleen, in a voice as pale and as transparent as a glass of water, said, "Oh, God, Lloyd. That's him. That's Michael. That one there, close to the wall. That's Michael, I swear it. Oh, God."

She started forward, but Otto held her arm and restrained

her. "Believe me, Mrs. Kerwin, you will be doing yourself no favors if you wake him up. At the moment, he is not the man you knew. Only when he has undergone the Transformation will you recognize him again, and then you can keep him for ever."

"Can't I even *talk* to him? Let him know that I'm here?"

Otto gave her the tiniest dismissive shake of his head. "He is too volatile. He could be quite calm, when he sees you. But on the other hand, he could explode. He might feel resentful. He might feel angry. You never know. But the point is that he could burn you. He could burn everybody around him, too. I can't risk a fire in this garage, not with all of the Salamanders here. Well, it doesn't bear thinking about, does it, Mr. Denman? There's Celia, too; can you see her? There, by the door."

Kathleen twisted her arm free of his fingers. "I want to look at him, that's all. He's my husband."

"Very well," Otto agreed. "But if you disturb him, and wake him, then do not blame me for what happens. I have worked too many years for this to allow some hysterical *hausfrau* to destroy it."

Kathleen stepped carefully between the gray-blanketed bodies until she reached the far side of the garage. She stood over the wrapped-up body of a white-faced man, her hand clasped over her mouth, her eyes glistening with tears.

"She has no need to cry," Otto told Lloyd. "Michael will live forever, long after she has gone. It is *he* who should be crying for *her*."

Lloyd couldn't keep his eyes off Celia. She looked so gray. She looked so waxy. She looked so dead.

"When they're Transformed . . ." he asked Otto, "what kind of life are they going to be able to lead?"

"Very different, in some ways. Very ordinary, in others."

"What does that mean?"

"It means, Mr. Denman, that what you are looking at here is the beginning of the master race. These people, and many like them, will recreate that ideal world which we tried to establish during the war, but failed. They are all people of pure blood, of great talent, and of high intelligence.

"When they are Transformed, they will be able to do anything they please, because simply by touch they will be able to generate enormous natural power. If they are angered, they will be able to burn anything they please, and anyone they please. They will be invulnerable."

"So Celia could set fire to me, if I annoyed her?"

Otto laughed. "She could burn you to a cinder, my friend! But we don't want her to do that. We want you to be married, and to have children together."

"She'll be able to have children?"

"Oh, yes," Otto nodded. "She certainly will. In fact, we encourage it. The future belongs to the young ones, yes? The special children . . . half-human, half-fire."

Kathleen came back across the garage. Her face was very pale.

"You, too, Mrs. Kerwin," smiled Otto. "All the children you wish!"

17

"By the end of 1943 I was quite sure that I had found what I was looking for," Otto told them, as they sat in the living room with Asbach brandy and cigars. The air was thick with blue flat-smelling smoke. The room was growing cold. With theatrical inappropriateness, Otto was trying to play the genial host, sitting in his huge 1930s armchair with his leg swinging, smoking and drinking relentlessly and telling them all about the heyday of the National Socialist party. "What times we had in Berlin! Unter den Linden, at night, in 1936! We shall never see times like that again!"

Kathleen was exhausted, and sat with her head bowed, saying nothing. Lloyd was tired, too, but he wanted to hear Otto out. He sipped his brandy to keep himself awake, and he glanced from time to time at Helmwige, who was so bored with what Otto was saying that she was finishing the crossword in the *San Diego Tribune*, sniffing and talking to herself.

Otto said, "I had heard of an ancient ritual chant which could change a burning human into a Salamander, but although I searched through thousands of books, I could not find it! At Ohrdruf concentration camp, with Helmwige's assistance, I tried seven hundred different Norse and Hebrew prayers, burning a Jew each time in order to test the prayer's effectiveness, sometimes sixty or seventy Jews a day! Years went by, thousands were burned, but still to no avail. Not one of them survived; not one of them became a Salamander!

"However in March 1943, an old rabbi came to my office and

asked me why I was burning these people. I explained that I was looking for the secret chant which could give a man immortality by fire. He begged me to stop burning people. He said that he would try to find out for me what the chant was, if only I would stop burning people. Well, what kind of an offer was that? I was a German officer and the experiment had been personally ordered by the Führer, and I said no.

"Eventually, however, this same rabbi returned to me. He said that the word had been sent throughout the camps, and that there was a young Jewish music professor at Flossenburg who could tell me everything that I wanted to know.

He offered Lloyd more brandy, but Lloyd held his hand over his glass. He found it disturbing enough having to share a room with Otto, without having to accept his hospitality, too.

Otto said, "The young professor had made a special study of Wagner and the origins of Wagner's music. He had heard that Wagner was supposed to have been interested in basing an opera on the Norse fire-burial chants, but he wasn't convinced that Wagner had ever written it. Apparently, the chants had been lost in the eighth century, during the Viking Migration period. The Book of Salamander, the runic book in which all the chants were contained, was sent by sea from Tollund to England, but it was sunk in a winter storm. However, the wreck must have been washed up on the northern coast of Germany, and the book salvaged. It reappeared in Bavaria, in the seventeenth century.

"By a very circuitous route, and after many dubious transactions, it had come into the possession of the burgomaster of Bamberg, Johann Junius. Junius had long been fascinated by alchemy and by the secrets of eternal life. By remarkable good fortune, he already had in his possession one of the greatest and most mystical artifacts—one essential to eternal life . . . the bowl in which Pontius Pilate washed his hands after the trial of Jesus Christ.

"How Junius acquired the bowl, no one knows. But it is second in its life-giving powers only to the Holy Grail. It was originally fashioned from melted-down Salamander amulets from Tollund; the amulets by which the people of that region had achieved eternal life. From there, it was traded and stolen and bartered, until at last it appeared in A.D. 32 in Judea. A Hebrew elder gave it to the Roman procurator as a gift, and Pilate further increased its powers by using it as the ultimate symbol of abdication.

"Junius translated the Norse runes, and asked a local goldsmith to fashion a section of the bowl into amulets . . . back into what it had originally been. He experimented at first by setting fire to live cats and dogs. The story goes that eventually he succeeded in creating an unkillable cat.

"However, Junius was spied on by his neighbors. He was arrested and taken before the courts, and accused of witchery. He was tortured with thumb screws and leg vises and the strappado, and in the end, of course, he confessed. Anything to escape further pain! He was burned at the stake, and apparently he shrieked and sang while the flames devoured him. Perhaps the good witchfinders of Bamberg managed to kill him; perhaps they didn't. But the story has it that Junius was seen many weeks afterward in various towns in Bavaria, looking pale and strange."

Lloyd said nothing. He found it almost impossible to speak to a man who had calmly confessed that he had burned thousands of innocent people for the sake of a mystical theory, no matter how earth-shattering that mystical theory might be. It hadn't been worth a single one of those lives. Not one. But who remembered those lives today?

Otto said, "The Book of Salamander, the amulets, and the remaining piece of Pilate's bowl, as well as all of Junius's notes, were locked up in the *rathaus* in Bamberg for two hundred years. But somebody found them, we don't know who. It could have been a plague doctor called Gunther Hammer, or an astrologer known only as Stange. Whoever it was, he must have been a fanatical devotee of Richard Wagner, because in November 1882, he sent everything immediately to Wagner with a long unsigned letter pleading that Wagner use it to achieve immortality.

"Richard Wagner had begun to fall ill in the last year of his life. Bad heart, you understand. In the letter, Hammer or Stange wrote to him, 'Play these melodies, O Master, and you will live forever.' Wagner was deeply impressed by the Norse chants. They were so *barbarisch,* so powerful! But he completely misunderstood his well-wisher's intentions. He thought that he was being exhorted to turn the chants into an opera, so that he would achieve everlasting *fame.* It simply didn't occur to him that he could actually live forever.

"He liked the amulets, but thought the bowl was rather dull, and sent it to his friend Franz Lieber in Berlin, as a belated wedding gift."

"At Flossenburg concentration camp, the young Jewish music

professor told me that in his view the existence of the opera *Junius* was only a myth, and that it was quite probable that Wagner had never written it. But now I had a scent to follow! With five historians to assist me, I discovered from the private diaries of Wagner's friends that he had been working on a new opera in the last year of his life which he jokingly referred to as his *Wikingsgesangbuch.* He took it with him to Venice and he was still working on it when he died.

"Unfortunately, when Wagner died, neither the opera nor the Book of Salamander was found amongst his possessions. For a long time, I thought that I had reached a dead end, and that the young music professor was right about the opera being nothing but a story. But in a moment of inspiration, I discovered the name of the doctor and of the priest who had attended Wagner on his deathbed. The priest was Father Xavier Montini, a Jesuit, and a famous scholar on the subject of pagan ritual.

"Now I used my logic, Mr. Denman! My powers of deduction, and also my lifelong suspicion of Jesuits! I deduced that when Father Xavier Montini saw what Wagner had been working on, he became alarmed, and smuggled the Book of Salamander and the unfinished opera out of Wagner's house, and hid them. After all, isn't immortality supposed to be the exclusive territory of God Almighty? His unique selling point? The priest didn't want that challenged by some pre-Christian mumbo-jumbo from Jutland!

"Mussolini's military staff gave us all the cooperation we needed to comb Venice looking for the opera and the book. In the end, after three months, we found them, bricked into the cellar wall of a house that had belonged to one of Father Xavier Montini's friends. We were sad to discover that the cellar had flooded four or five times since the books had been concealed there. Although they had both been carefully wrapped in oilskin, the wrapping around the Book of Salamander had been gnawed by rats, and most of the original runes had been obscured by damp. But the opera was almost as fresh and as bright as the day Wagner had laid down his pen.

"We had in our hands the means to create the master race of which Hitler had always dreamed; a race of pure-blooded immortals who would rule the world with force and wisdom."

"So what stopped you?" asked Lloyd.

Otto's eyes followed a blowfly as it droned across the room, and the tip of his tongue ran across his lips. "Wagner had taken many liberties with the original chants. He hadn't understood their importance, you see, and he had made many changes, for the sake of his opera. It was necessary for musical experts to work through the opera, note by note, in comparison with Wagner's diaries, and with what we had managed to salvage from the Book of Salamander, in order to recreate the original ritual music.

"Otherwise, our dream would have been *totgeboren*, you understand? Born dead."

He stood up. He swayed a little, as if the Asbach brandy had made him drunk. He seemed taller than before, a giant ash-gray stick insect. Thin and tall and long-legged. Lloyd watched him with apprehension. He walked over to the window where the blowfly was furiously bizzling against the glass.

"Our work was still not complete when the Russians entered Berlin. I was in the *Führerbunker* with Hitler and those who remained. Goebbels, Bormann, and the rest. On Hitler's instructions I was still working with Helmwige on the opera. We burned a whole contingent of forty Polish prisoners, but still without success. I theorized that perhaps a Salamander needed to be racially pure to begin with, and so we burned alive two young volunteers from the Hitler Youth. Still we could not manage to achieve what we so desperately sought. They simply died in terrible pain. Then on the night of April 29, with the Russians only hours away from us, my assistant Wernher von Hudde arrived in Berlin from the south, at considerable personal risk to himself.

"He said that he had been studying Johann Junius's papers once again, and had come to believe that the word *schar*, which means a crowd of people, was in fact a badly written version of the word *schale*, which means bowl. So instead of saying 'The crowd is essential,' Junius had said 'The bowl is essential.' Von Hudde had sent four SS officers to Franz Leiber's grandson's house in Berlin, and only a day before the Americans overran the city, they had found the bowl—gathering dust, unbelievably, in the kitchen cupboard.

"Now—*endlich*—we had everything we needed, but time was running short. My brave Helmwige volunteered to be burned, in order to prove that it was safe. Hitler's chauffeur Erich Kempka went to fetch two hundred liters of gasoline, and two SS men dug a sandy pit in the Chancellery garden."

He paused for a second, then scooped the blowfly into his hand. He held it up, and Lloyd could hear it furiously buzzing.

"We chanted the ritual chant, and then we drenched Helmwige with gasoline and she set fire to herself with a lighted rag.

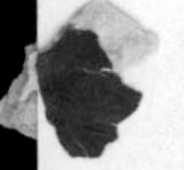

She said nothing. Didn't scream, didn't protest. At last the fire-chants had worked. Her smoke and her soul arose; and although her body remained, her spiritual essence became a Salamander, a creature of fire and spirit. It was amazing to watch. It is *still* amazing to watch. The body burns, the smoke rises. At first the Salamander is so insubstantial that you would mistake it for a shadow, a twist of smoke. But as it descends and cools, it takes on the shape with which in life you were always so familiar. Hitler witnessed it for himself, and he was in tears."

"Helmwige and I escaped from the *Führerbunker* along with Martin Bormann, and we were helped by SS officers to obtain International Red Cross passports, and to make our way to America. We arrived in New Orleans in time for the summer solstice, and we were able to complete the ritual in a room at the Pontchartrain Hotel. Helmwige then became what she is today. A living example of the master race."

Otto held his fist close to his ear, so that he could hear the blowfly's desperate struggles. He smiled in anticipation of the tiny treat that he was going to give himself.

"What about Hitler?" asked Lloyd. "If he saw what happened to Helmwige . . . didn't he want to try it for himself?"

Otto gave a noncommittal shrug. "The Führer, of course, was deeply impressed with what I had achieved. I was immediately put in charge of all genetic and racial experiments, including those of Mengele and von Harn. Not that it counted for much, of course. By that time, the Russians had already reached Potsdamer Platz, and the Reich was obviously at an end.

"Hitler told me to leave Berlin with Helmwige and with a young Aryan boy whom Mengele had bred . . . the father of the young man who acts as our servant now."

"But Hitler didn't take to the idea of setting fire to himself?" Lloyd persisted.

Otto turned and stared at him narrowly, although the curved shadow from the mock-parchment lampshade made it difficult for Lloyd to see his face.

Otto said nothing for a while. Then he looked away. "What happened to the Führer will always remain a secret," he said.

"Did you turn him into a Salamander?"

Otto shook his head. "*Ich weiss nicht.* If the Führer went through the ritual, he did after I left the *Führerbunker*. Helmwige and I and the boy escaped from Berlin in the early hours of April thirtieth. Later that same day, Hitler's body was burned, yes, that is a matter of historical record. But the historical record does not say whether he was alive when he was burned, or whether he was already dead. He was supposed to have shot himself in the mouth, but when they carried his body out of his room, his head was covered with a blanket, so that none of the eyewitnesses could tell for certain."

"But if he *did* go through the ritual—?"

Otto shrugged. "If he *did* go through the ritual, then the probability is that he is still alive. But where . . . who knows?"

He opened his hand, and lifted out the blowfly by one leg. He picked off its wings with the concentration of a man picking the stalk off a raisin. Then he popped it quickly onto his tongue, and held it in his mouth for a moment, so that he could feel it vibrating against his cheeks. He sucked, and swallowed. "Helmwige," he said, "switch on the television." The conversation appeared to have ended.

They watched *21 Jump Street* for a while. Then Otto switched over to the eight o'clock news. Lloyd looked at Kathleen but there was nothing that either of them could do. Otto watched a long item about crack dealing in San Diego schools, frowning and muttering to himself. Then the news turned to the accidental death of San Diego detective Sergeant Houk, and the disappearance of Detective Gable and Deputy Bredero.

"Sergeant Houk and Detective Gable were assisting state police in their investigation of the deaths by burning of thirteen men and women in the Anza-Borrego Desert State Park. . . . While Sergeant Houk's death appears to have been an automobile accident, state and metropolitan police are still unable to account for the complete disappearance of Detective Gable and Deputy Bredero. . . . Deputy Bredero's patrol car was found abandoned at the Five Flags shopping center close to Highway I-5, with no fingerprints on it apart from his own. . . ."

"You're very thorough," Lloyd remarked.

"I had a scientific training," said Otto. "Besides, what we are doing here is too important to allow any margin for mistakes."

"You don't think the police are going to track you down?"

Otto used his thumbnail to pick something black from between his teeth. "You are talking to someone who escaped from Berlin on the very last day of Hitler's Reich," he said. "You are talking to a man who discovered an opera which had been hidden for sixty years, and who was able to revive a mystic ritual which had been lost for eleven centuries. Now . . . I have work to do, letters to write. I would appreciate it if you and Mrs. Kerwin would retire to your rooms. And, please, make no attempts to leave the house. Our young man has been instructed to use physical force if necessary to keep you here, and you have seen for yourself what I can do."

"But you're not one of these Salamander people, are you?" asked Kathleen. "How come you can set things on fire?"

Otto closed his eyes. He remained silent for such a long time that they thought that he wasn't going to answer. But then he opened his eyes again, and said, "I have told you quite enough. Some secrets must remain secrets. On your dying day you will remember that you once knew me, and you will shudder in awe."

Lloyd retorted, "I'll shudder with something, but it damn well won't be awe."

Otto flicked him a look as sharp as a whip-crack. "Don't tempt me, Mr. Denman. It's growing cold, and I'm sure we'd all appreciate a fire."

The young man escorted them wordlessly up to their rooms, opened their doors for them, and then locked them in. Lloyd sat down on his mattress, eased off his shoes, and then lay back, feeling exhausted and grimy and shocked, as if he had just survived a minor but unpleasant automobile accident. His hands were sore, and he thought that it was probably time his bandages were changed, but at the moment there was nothing he could do about it. He watched the nodding fanglike shadows of yucca fronds on the sloping ceiling. There was still so much that he couldn't accept, even though he had heard Otto's cruel and lascivious confessions with his own ears, and seen with his own eyes how remorseless Otto could be.

All those gray-skinned people on the garage floor—how could they really be composed of nothing more than smoke and spirit? How could a ritual chant transform an agonizing death into a fiery rebirth? How could anyone live forever?

He thought of Celia lying there and wondered what she was thinking, if she was thinking anything at all. Out on the road at Escondido, she had said that she still loved him. But could *he* still love *her?* How could you love somebody who had died and come back to life—somebody who wasn't really flesh anymore? Most difficult of all, how could he accept her back into his life when she had so readily embraced a creature like Otto—a man who had burned alive thousands of innocent people for the sake of one insane ideal?

Beneath everything that Otto was doing, Lloyd could feel the terrifying legacy of the Third Reich moving like a black, silently thunderous glacier. Hitler had reawakened something in the human mind that would take more than guns and bombs and forty-five years of economic reconstruction to destroy. When he had claimed that his Reich would last for a thousand years, he had been right. And if Otto were able to transform all of those Salamanders sleeping on his garage floor, it would be even more than a thousand-year Reich. It would be a Reich that dominated mankind forever.

Lloyd had read plenty of books and articles about the war. But until now he had never felt the real fear of war, the fear of living under somebody else's will. It was more disturbing than he had ever imagined possible, and he suddenly began to understand why people were prepared to risk their lives for political freedom. Without political freedom, life was simply not worth living.

He fell asleep, and almost immediately he dreamed of Celia again. He dreamed that he was wading across a glossy-green meadow, through varnished grass and huge wide-awake daisies, under a sky the color of tarnished bronze. Celia was standing naked on a distant levee, beside a gnarled and whiskery planer tree. Her hair was ablaze, and a plume of orange fire was rising from her head. He tried to shout out, but his voice sounded as tiny and ineffective as the blowfly buzzing in Otto's fist. He tried to run, but the grass was too deep.

The key turned in his door. He opened his eyes. For a moment he could hear nothing but the insects in the yard outside, and the soft chattering of his wristwatch. He thought for a moment that he must have dreamed the sound of the key, but then he heard a floorboard creak.

"Who's there?" he demanded, his heart racing—knowing all the time that he couldn't do anything to defend himself, no matter who it was. The nameless young man was obviously powerful enough to break his neck. Helmwige could fry him alive just by touching him. And Otto could turn him into a human incendiary bomb simply by *looking* at him.

The door slowly opened. He lay still, although every tendon in his body was pulled tight. A single second passed as slowly as the world turning on its axis. Then the young man appeared, and stood beside the open door, watching him.

"What do you want?" Lloyd asked him, at last.

"I came to see if you were asleep." The young man's voice was soft.

"I *was* asleep, until you came in."

"I'm sorry. I wanted to ask you something."

Lloyd propped himself up on one elbow. The young man's apologetic tone was in direct contrast to Otto's dry-voiced hectoring. "Does Otto know that you're here?" asked Lloyd.

The young man glanced quickly behind him, as if the mere mention of Otto's name could somehow invoke Otto's presence. "No. Otto is working. He . . ." making a scribbling gesture with his hand ". . . writes, you know? Always writing."

"What did you want to ask?"

The young man closed the door behind him, and knelt down next to Lloyd's mattress. Although he was so muscular, he had the gentlest of airs about him. A boy, rather than a man. Uncertain, anxious, unexpectedly shy.

"They have always hated me, Otto and Helmwige. They have always told me that I am nothing but an animal. They hated Mengele, you see, because up until the very end, Mengele was always the Führer's favorite. They talk about it over and over, as if it happened only yesterday."

Lloyd said nothing, but waited for the young man to carry on.

"I have no name, I have nothing," the young man told him. "I asked Otto what was my name, and he said, 'You're not even a person; you deserve no name. Do I give names to cabbages, or eggs, or chairs?' That's what he said."

Lloyd said, "Otto isn't exactly the most sympathetic person I've ever met."

"I have to do everything for them, everything. I have to clean, I have to do everything. Helmwige expects me to have love with her, any time that she wants to. They told me that to work for them was my punishment, because so many people had died so that I could live. I was made by Josef Mengele; and this is my punishment for having been made."

"Nobody's to blame for their own existence," said Lloyd.

"I am to blame for myself."

"Bullshit; you were born because somebody else wanted you born, for whatever reason. It doesn't matter what the reason was, you had no hand in it. It's not your fault."

The young man raised his head so that the light from the corridor fell across his face, and shone in his eyes. Eyes like crystal-clear marbles, young and hopeful and innocent. "I wanted to ask you if you would like to leave this place, and take me with you."

Lloyd sat up. "You're going to help us to escape?"

"Only if you wish to."

"Only if we wish to? Are you kidding? You think we're here because we felt like an early vacation? We're here because Otto threatened to burn us alive."

The young man nodded. "He has done that many times, to many people. He does not say so, but burning people is Otto's pleasure."

"But you're going to help us get away?"

The young man nodded. "Very early in the morning, when Otto sleeps his deepest. I will come to your room and guide you away. We can take Otto's own car; that will prevent him from following, for a while. None of the other cars is working."

"What about Celia?" asked Lloyd. "He won't do anything to her, will he? He won't harm her in any way?"

The young man shook his head. "Your Celia is most important to him. Celia is the only one who can understand the music. He will never harm Celia."

"You're sure about that?"

The young man nodded. "I heard him talking to Helmwige. He said that Celia was his godsend . . . his savior. When they escaped from Germany, you see, they lost many of their notes, and Celia was the first person they had found who was able to play the music for them."

"Okay, then . . . it's a go," Lloyd told him. "Wake me up whenever you're ready, and I'll be right behind you."

The young man checked his wristwatch. "Three o'clock . . . that will be the best time."

Lloyd said, "You're sure I can trust you?"

The young man lowered his head again.

"Supposing I give you a name?" Lloyd asked him. "Can I trust you then?"

"A name?" the young man asked him, incredulously.

"Sure, a name. Your very own name."

"How can you give me a name?" the young man asked. "You're not my father."

"For Chrissake, I don't have to be your father to give you a name. What do you want me to call you?"

The young man shrugged. "I don't know any names."

"All right, then . . . we'll call you Franklin, after Franklin Roosevelt. How about that? Franklin Free, because you're going to be free."

The young man pressed his hand to his chest. "And that can be me? That name? Franklin Free?"

Lloyd nodded. "That can be you."

Never in his life had Lloyd seen anybody lifted so quickly from his own lack of self-importance as Franklin Free. He quivered with new strength, like a butterfly emerging from a chrysalis; and he breathed more deeply, and knelt up straight. "That can be me? Franklin Free?"

"That *is* you. You're a human being, every human being has a name, and your name is Franklin Free."

Franklin stood up. He didn't seem to know which way to turn. Softly, he repeated the incantation, "My name is Franklin Free; and that can be me. My name is Franklin Free and that can be me."

Lloyd checked his watch. "Listen, Franklin . . . it's way after eleven. Let me try to grab some more zees. If you're planning on breaking out of here at three o'clock in the morning, we all need to be fresh and alert and ready for anything."

"*Franklin,*" Franklin repeated, in awe.

He reached out and grasped Lloyd's hand, and squeezed it with the trembling restraint of someone who would dearly love to have hugged him, but knew that he couldn't.

"Franklin," he said. "That's good."

"Glad you like it," Lloyd told him. He felt genuinely touched, more touched than Franklin could have understood.

Just then, they heard Helmwige calling from downstairs. "Bath! Come on! I want my bath!"

The newly named Franklin gave Lloyd's hand one last squeeze, and then said, "I have to go. Helmwige wants me."

"I'll see you at three," Lloyd replied.

Franklin said, "If it doesn't work out—if we don't get away—"

"We *will* get away," Lloyd assured him. "Don't even think about it."

"But if we don't; if he burns us—"

"He's not going to burn us, all right?"

"But if he *does*—I just want you to know that what you've given me—well, it's worth more than anything that Otto and Helmwige have ever given me. It's worth the world."

"Draw my bath!" Helmwige screamed.

Franklin went to the door. "Three o'clock," he promised. He held up the door key. "And just to show you that I mean what I say . . . I won't lock the door."

He hesitated, bit his lip. "If I do that . . . you won't escape without me?"

"I trust you," said Lloyd. "Don't you think that you can trust me?"

"I don't know," Franklin replied, suddenly hesitant. He obviously wasn't used to making up his own mind about anything.

"Do you have any *choice*, but to trust me?" Lloyd suggested.

Franklin thought about it, and then he said, "No. I guess I don't." He tried to give Lloyd a brave smile; and then he left the room and closed the door behind him. Lloyd waited to hear the key turning in the lock, but it didn't. Franklin had kept his word. One way or another, they were going to be free.

He heard water running like muffled thunder out of the hot-water tank. Then footsteps on the stairs, and creaking boards on the landing, and Helmwige talking as if she were slightly drunk. He lay on his mattress without moving. He had tried to sound confident about escaping, but he wasn't at all sure that Franklin was bright enough to be able to get them out of the house, or that Otto and Helmwige would be sleeping deeply enough to allow them to go. If they could just get out of range of Otto's fire-raising, they would be safe. But he wasn't at all sure how far away that actually was. For all he knew, Otto only had to think hard enough, and he could ignite a fire in the next county; or the next state; or anywhere he liked in the world. His talent for fire-raising was the one secret that Otto had refused to discuss.

Still—Lloyd recalled that when Otto had set fire to his steering wheel, he had taken two or three steps forward, as if to bring himself closer. And when he had chased them out of the twenty-four-hour drugstore in Del Mar, his arrow of fire had been able to pursue them only for thirty or forty feet.

If they could just get clear of the house, he guessed that they would probably be safe. Then all they had to do was to find someplace safe to hide and to wait for the solstice—wait for Otto and Helmwige to perform the ceremony of Transformation—and then rescue Celia and Mike Kerwin, too.

Nothing to worry about. Nothing that the Lone Ranger couldn't have handled; or maybe Dirty Harry. Lloyd would have loved for Otto to make his day.

After a few minutes, he eased himself up off the mattress and went to the door. He turned the handle, and found that Franklin had been telling the truth. He had left it unlocked. Lloyd opened it two or three inches, and listened. At the far end of the landing, the bathroom door was ajar, and he could hear splashing and murmuring, and then Helmwige saying, "Gently, gently, *du bist so plump.*"

He hesitated for a short while, and then he opened the door wider, and crept out into the corridor. It sounded as if Otto was still downstairs, writing. The whirling sounds of "The Ride of the Valkyries" came from the record player in the living room, played at top volume; and Lloyd heard the clinking of Otto's brandy bottle as he poured himself another drink.

Holding his breath, he tiptoed along the corridor until he reached the half-open bathroom door. Cautiously, he put his eye to the crack in the door. The whole room was foggy with rose-smelling steam, and from where he was standing he could see only the edge of a large white enameled bathtub, a bottle of Vidal Sassoon shampoo, and a glistening pink curve which he took to be Helmwige's shoulder. Helmwige was sitting with her back to him, so he took the risk of leaning across the doorway and peering right into the room.

Franklin was kneeling beside the bathtub wearing nothing but white Fruit of the Loom shorts. He was facing the door and he saw Lloyd at once. He frowned, and mouthed the word. "What . . . ?" but Lloyd gave him a quick wave to reassure him that everything was fine, and that he wasn't trying to escape just yet.

There was nothing that Franklin could do, in any case. Helmwige was watching him too intently. He was massaging her shoulders with soap, while she ran her hands up and down his muscular forearms, and kept saying, "*Mmmmmmm*, that's better . . . gently, gently."

Lloyd watched as Franklin rubbed more soap on his hands, and then began to lather Helmwige's enormous breasts. Her wet skin squeaked as he grasped her breasts tightly, and rolled her nipples between finger and thumb. She continued to murmur, and to splash, and to run her hands up and down his arms.

"Harder, you can do that harder. Pinch me! I like to be pinched! Ohhh . . ."

Franklin rinsed her breasts with a huge natural sponge. Then he scooped his arm into the bath, so that his hand was right underneath her bottom, and he raised her hips right out of the water. She had heavy thighs, and a rounded stomach, but she was still in voluptuous shape for a woman who must have been immortalized when she was well into her forties.

"You must make sure that I am *completely* clean," she told Franklin.

"Yes," said Franklin. His voice was flat. He glanced at Lloyd but Lloyd remained where he was, not moving. Downstairs the Valkyries continued to thrash and to tumble, although it sounded as if this part of the record had suffered from years of being played almost every evening.

Helmwige reached down with both hands into her dark blond pubic hair, and opened her vulva as wide as she could, so that Franklin could soap his finger and slip it inside. "Ohhh, *höchst erfreulich,*" she murmured.

Franklin slid his finger in and out of her, and she threw back her head and moaned and warbled like a dove. Then he slid in a second finger, and a third. Helmwige gasped, and splashed, and pulled herself even wider open. At last, panting, his muscular chest glistening with perspiration, Franklin worked his his entire soapy hand up into her, right up to the wrist.

Helmwige made an extraordinary growling deep-breathing noise that reminded Lloyd of a sea lion. She gripped Franklin's wrist fiercely in both hands. Then she suddenly shuddered, and shook, and screamed out loud. The bathwater churned as wildly as if it were full of piranha fish. Fascinated and horrified by what he had seen, but strangely aroused, too, Lloyd turned quickly away. He tiptoed back along the corridor until he reached the door of Kathleen's room. Franklin had left the key in the lock, so all he had to do was quickly to turn it, open the door, and slip inside.

Kathleen was awake and sitting up in bed. When he came in, she switched on the bedside lamp, a cheap clip-on with a broken plastic shade. "Lloyd? What's happening? How did you get out? Somebody's screaming!"

"Don't worry about that—that's Helmwige, having a little bathtime fun. Listen—that boy came into my room a few minutes ago. It seems like he's had it up to here with Otto and Helmwige, and he wants us all to make a break for it."

"You mean escape? Do you think you can trust him?"

"I don't see any reason not to. He's not exactly Albert Einstein, but he seems willing enough. And he doesn't have any *reason* to double-cross us, does he?"

"But what if Otto catches us? He'll burn us alive!"

"I wouldn't be too sure that he's not planning on doing that anyway. He's determined to start where Hitler left off, and, believe me, he's not going to let anybody stand in his way."

Kathleen brushed back her hair with her hand. "He'll never manage it, though, will he? The police are bound to track him down him sooner or later."

Lloyd shrugged. "I'm not so sure. He's got people who can burn you as soon as look at you—people who can live forever. How are you going to stand up against people like that? And how many other people are going to be tempted to join him, once they realize that they really could be immortal? Besides, you've got Otto himself to contend with. You know what he did to Sergeant Houk. He could do that to anybody who tries to stop him. One glance and you're humanburger."

He heard water emptying out of the bathtub, and the sound of voices. "Listen—I'd better get back to my room. The plan is that we sneak out of the house at three o'clock in the morning, when Otto and Helmwige are really out of it. Franklin is going to wake us up, if we're asleep."

"Franklin? I thought he didn't have a name."

"I christened him. He was as pleased as a dog with two tails."

"Lloyd . . . do you really believe that we're going to be able to get away? I mean, safely? If anything should happen to me . . . well, I don't know what Thomas would do."

"Do you want to stay?" Lloyd asked her.

Kathleen shook her head. "I guess it's just that I never felt frightened before. Not like this."

"Franklin told me that Otto wouldn't harm Celia at all, if I escaped. I guess he wouldn't harm your husband, either."

Kathleen said, "That man lying out in the garage, Lloyd—that isn't Mike Kerwin. Leastways, it's not the Mike Kerwin I married. The Mike Kerwin I married was burned to death on that bus in the desert."

Lloyd saw the tears glisten in her eyes. He couldn't help admiring her bravery and her realism. He hadn't yet accepted that he had lost Celia forever. Somehow, with a Disneylike optimism, he had kept on believing that the Celia he had hoped to marry was still there; that she would reappear just as she was before and say, "Fooled you!"

But he knew now that he was going to have face the truth. Celia had been burned; Celia was gone. The creature that had taken her place was a creature of fire and sorcery, a creature that he would never be able to accept back into his life. He could understand why Celia had chosen youthful immortality over a gradually worsening disability and an early death. But the more he learned about Otto and his Salamanders, the more difficult he found it to come to terms with the fact that Celia had embraced his idea of a master race. The Celia that Lloyd had loved would never have accepted a single minute of life that had been bought at the price of thousands of innocent people being deliberately incinerated.

He had lost Celia now, lost her for good. The world had had enough of camps, enough of gas chambers, enough of ovens.

Kathleen must have sensed what he was feeling, because she put her arms around him and laid her head against his chest. Tears slid down his cheeks and dropped into her hair like warm pearls.

"Ssh, it's over," she said.

Lloyd wiped his eyes with the heels of his hands. "Thanks," he said. "I guess I've been the victim of my own bravado."

She kissed his cheek. "I'll see you at three."

Lloyd went to the door, listened, then opened it. He returned to his room, quietly closed the door behind him, and lay back down on his mattress.

He hadn't expected to be able to sleep, so he had recited the lyrics of all the rock songs that he could think of; then all the poems that he could remember ("By the shore of Gitche Gumee, By the shining Big-Sea-Water . . ."); then the address section of his Filofax, with the full telephone numbers and zip codes of all of his friends; then the Padres' batting averages for the past three seasons.

He was aware that it was three o'clock only when he felt

Franklin shaking his shoulder and whispering, "Mr. Denman? Mr. Denman? Wake up, Mr. Denman; it's time to go."

He stared into the darkness. "Is it three o'clock already?" he asked, his mouth thick and woolly. He sat up, and rubbed his eyes. "Jesus. I dreamed I was having dinner at Mr. A's."

"Come on," breathed Franklin, "as quietly as you can. Otto is so deeply asleep that he's practically dead, but Helmwige is very jumpy."

Lloyd cleared his throat. "I'm not surprised, the way she was playing in the tub tonight."

"She will do anything and everything," said Franklin. "What does she care? She's going to live forever. She's a morphine addict; Hermann Goering got her on to morphine during the war. But she takes every kind of drug you can imagine. She has sex with anybody she feels like it. She doesn't have to care about AIDS. She will perform any kind of sex act you can imagine, and some that you can't. I've seen her have sex with two dogs, while Otto watched her and ate flies."

"Let's go," said Lloyd. He didn't particularly want to hear any more. He stood up, and caught his head on the sharply sloping ceiling. He swore more foully than he had sworn for years, not so much because it hurt but because he was tense and tired and frightened. In some ways, Helmwige frightened him more than Otto. At least Otto was mortal; at least Otto could be killed. But how could you fight against somebody who had no regard for her own life whatsoever?

Franklin opened the door, and crept out into the corridor, with Lloyd following closely behind. They crossed to Kathleen's room, and Franklin quietly turned the key. Kathleen must have heard them whispering, because she was waiting for them right behind the door.

"Are they asleep?" she breathed. Lloyd nodded, and took hold of her hand.

Quickly and silently they tiptoed along the corridor, past the half-open bathroom, and then past Helmwige's bedroom, which was wide open. By the light of a flickering black and white television movie, they could see Helmwige sprawled naked on her frilled four-poster bed, her legs wide apart, her mouth open. She was breathing coarsely and irregularly, as if she were having a nightmare. The movie was *The Thin Man,* with William Powell and Myrna Low.

"I read you were shot five times in the tabloid."

"It's not true. He didn't come near my tabloid."

With infinite care, they went downstairs. Franklin was so heavy that the treads squeaked whenever he put his weight on them, and Lloyd winced. But at last they reached the darkened hallway, and the house remained silent.

Franklin beckoned Lloyd and Kathleen to come closer. "All we have to do now is get out of the front door, head for the car, get into it, and go." He held up the car key. "I took these from Helmwige's purse."

"What about the other cars?" asked Lloyd.

"Only the coup works, and I let the air out of the tires."

"Where does Otto sleep?" Lloyd whispered. "Will he hear us leave?"

"Oh, he'll hear us leave all right. He works in the living room every night till one or two o'clock, playing his records and drinking brandy. Then he goes to sleep on the couch, fully dressed. He doesn't even bother to wash."

"Thanks a lot," Lloyd replied. "He's already won the Lloyd Denman Award for the Man Most Likely to Make You Barf on Sight."

"Okay, let's go," Franklin told them. "But let's make it real quick."

He released the security chain, and then silently slid back the bolts. He opened the latch, and the front door swung open with the faintest of creaks. Outside, the night was as black as only a Southern Californian night can be. They could barely distinguish the faint gleam on the roof of Otto's Mercedes sedan.

"Okay, go!" whispered Franklin. Together, they ran across the porch, into the driveway, and quarterbacked their way between the parked Mercedes. Kathleen caught her knee against the rear bumper of the 380SL, and hissed, "Shit!" but they reached the sedan, wrenched open the doors, and threw themselves into the leather-upholstered seats. Franklin pushed the key into the ignition, roared the car into life, and switched on the headlights.

"Oh, God, no!" said Kathleen, in panic.

The headlights had instantly illuminated the thin uncompromising figure of Otto, standing in front of them in a short-sleeved shirt and gray slacks, his arms folded, his withered mouth puckered with anger.

"Run the bastard down!" Lloyd shouted at Franklin. But Franklin sat in the driver's seat staring at Otto in complete paralysis. Franklin had been bred by Otto and raised by Otto. Franklin's will had been subjugated by Otto from the moment he was born.

Otto walked up to the side of the car and held out his hand. "The keys, please," he demanded.

18

"Franklin, *go!*" yelled Lloyd, and yanked the Mercedes' gear-shift into drive.

Franklin stared at him as if he didn't recognize him. "I—what—?"

"Go, Franklin, go for Chrissake!"

Otto snapped, "Don't you dare!"

But at that critical instant, Lloyd had one call on Franklin's loyalty that Otto couldn't match. He had given Franklin a name.

"Go, Franklin, go!" he shouted at him, almost screaming.

Franklin slammed his foot onto the Mercedes' gas pedal, and the huge sedan swerved and snaked, its rear tires blasting out pebbles and dust. Otto made a desperate bid to snatch the keys out of the ignition, but he couldn't quite reach them. However, he seized hold of the steering wheel and wouldn't release his grip, and as the Mercedes roared out of the driveway, and bucked on to the road, he was still clutching it, running at first, then allowing himself to be dragged.

His white face glared into the window of the moving car like a nightmare. They had reached over twenty miles an hour on the curve toward Rancho Santa Fe, and they were still accelerating. "*Du bist ein Verräter!*" he shrieked at Franklin. "*Wo ist deinen Dankbarkeit?*"

Franklin whimpered in terror, but Lloyd continued to shout at him, "Keep going! Keep going! He can't hurt you now!"

"*Verräter!*" cried Otto. "*Schon bist du Tot!*"

Franklin frantically twisted the steering wheel from side to side, trying to dislodge Otto's grip, and the car rolled and dipped from one side of the road to the other, its tires giving out a chorus of continuous howls. But Otto hung on, his shoes dragging and scrabbling on the blacktop, showers of sparks flying from his heels.

They slewed into the brightly lit streets of Rancho Santa Fe, with Otto still holding on. Every now and then a burst of flame came out of the Mercedes' tires, but the swerving and swaying of the car was obviously making it difficult for Otto to concentrate.

"Stop the car, you traitor!" he panted at Franklin. "Stop the car or I'll kill you now!"

But Kathleen, from the back seat, shouted out, "Lloyd! Here!" and passed over one of the car's cigarette lighters. The spiral tip was glowing red-hot.

Without hesitation, Lloyd pressed the cigarette lighter onto the back of Otto's hand. There was a sizzle of puckering skin, and Otto let out a deep, outraged roar. Just as they skidded past the entrance to the Inn at Rancho Santa Fe, he released his hold on the steering wheel, and Lloyd twisted around in his seat to see him flying and tumbling across the triangular green, arms and legs, over and over, a malevolent cartwheel, the long-legged scissorman from *Struwwelpeter*.

"We did it!" Franklin whooped. "We did it! We did it! Hot dog, hot dog!"

Lloyd kept his eyes on Otto as they sped around the next curve and headed toward the coast. A second before the green disappeared from view, Lloyd saw him climbing to his feet. With a sense of dread and disappointment, he realized that Otto obviously hadn't been badly hurt. Kathleen had seen him, too, because she turned to Lloyd and her expression was grim.

"He's not going to forgive us for that," she said.

"Hot dog!" Franklin kept repeating.

"You did good, Franklin," Lloyd praised him.

"The question is, where do we go now?" Kathleen wanted to know. "We may have gotten away, but Otto's going to come after us, for sure."

Lloyd said, "I just want to lie low till Wednesday, till they've completed their Transformation. Then at least we'll have a chance of getting Celia and your husband back. I know they'll have changed. I know we may not even be able to love them anymore. Maybe they won't be able to love *us* anymore. But we have to give them that one chance. They can't stay as Salamanders. You heard what Otto said; they're really volatile. They're as much of a danger to themselves as they are to other people."

"Maybe we should drive up the coast, and find ourselves a quiet hotel," Kathleen suggested.

"I've got a better idea. Let's drive out to that Indian place in Anza-Borrego. They had trailers to rent out there, and that's just about the last place that Otto would think of looking for us. Then as soon as the Transformation's over, we can take that young Indian boy to the police."

"What for?"

"He's our only witness that Otto was chanting when the bus was burning, that's what for. What other witnesses do we have?"

Kathleen shrugged. "I guess you're right."

Franklin said, "I can't believe it. We did it; we got away!"

"It's all thanks to you, buddy," Lloyd told him.

"I never saw Otto so angry," Franklin grinned.

"Oh good, that makes me feel a whole lot better. As if he isn't frightening enough when he *isn't* angry."

Kathleen said, "We could call the police now, you know. They'd find the Salamanders, at least."

Lloyd shook his head. "There'd be a massacre, no doubt about it. And you'd blow any chance of seeing Mike again."

Kathleen stared at her own reflection in the black-tinted window. "I'm not too sure that I want to."

"Well," said Lloyd. He suddenly realized he was still holding the cigarette-lighter, and he handed it back to Kathleen with a wry grin. "It's a damn hard life, so long as you don't weaken."

"Weaken?" she said, and he could see in the window that she was crying. "No, I'm not going to weaken. I'm just a little tired."

"Were things okay between you and Mike?" Lloyd asked her.

She wiped her eyes with her fingers. "Mostly, until he went for his check-up."

"Now you feel guilty because you don't care for him as much as you think you should?"

She nodded. "The trouble is, how can I explain that to Tom? He worshiped Mike, really worshiped him. Half the time I don't know whether I'm really feeling grief-stricken, or whether I'm acting it for Tom's sake. That makes me feel so bad."

Lloyd said, "I guess that everybody feels the same way, when they lose somebody close. I remember when my grandfather died. I was really upset, but at the same time I had this peculiar sense of relief that I didn't have to worry about him anymore. I was almost happy for him. We all get born, we all have to die. I guess there really isn't any reason why we shouldn't be happy at both events."

Franklin said, "Helmwige will never die."

"That's a creepy thought, isn't it?" said Lloyd. "That woman's still going to be forty-something when we're dead and gone."

Kathleen asked,"Will she really never die? Never, ever? Can't anybody kill her? What happens if she's involved in an auto accident, or somebody shoots her, or something like that?"

They were driving down toward Solana Beach, under the interstate. Lloyd said, "Take a left here, onto the freeway. I want to take a flying look at my house, before we head out for the desert, and maybe check with Waldo, if I can."

Franklin swerved onto the entrance ramp with squealing tires. Lloyd glanced behind them. "It's okay, you can slow down now. I don't want to get pulled over by the cops for a traffic violation, not now."

"Sorry," said Franklin. But as they joined the almost-deserted I-5, he said, "They can be killed by Him."

"Who?" asked Lloyd. "Who can be killed by whom?"

"The ones who live forever. Helmwige, any of them. They can be killed by Him."

"Him? Who's He, when He's at home? Did Otto say?"

Franklin shook his head. "But I heard him talking to Helmwige one night. That was when Celia first came. He said, 'She doesn't know about Him, does she? Even you can be killed by Him; and so can all of our master race.' "

Lloyd gave Kathleen a quick, excited look. "Did Otto come out with any clues about who He might be?"

"No," said Franklin. "But the reason I remember what he said was because he kept talking about it, over and over, like he was really worried about it."

Lloyd sat back. Otto had half-suggested that Hitler might have been Transformed, burned, and immortalized. Maybe He was Hitler. Maybe *Der Führer* still held absolute sway over all of his followers, just as he had during World War II.

"Are you thinking what I'm thinking?" he asked Kathleen.

"I don't know. What are you thinking?"

He explained, but he could see that she found it difficult to believe. "I'm sure Hitler's dead," she said. "Didn't they identify him by his dental records?"

"It doesn't matter if they did. His original body's dead, for certain. Just like Celia was dead and Mike was dead. But what happened to the smoke and the soul that rose right out of that body? It's hard to believe that Hitler could have seen Helmwige turn into a Salamander, without wanting to try the same thing for himself."

"It doesn't bear thinking about," said Kathleen.

"No, it doesn't. But it could be true."

It was still two hours before dawn when Franklin drove the Mercedes quietly through North Torrey, so that Lloyd could inspect his house. Lloyd climbed out of the car and walked up the sloping driveway, then circled the house to the back. The kitchen doors and windows had been boarded up, and plastic sheeting had been draped over the kitchen roof. There was a strong noxious reek of smoke, and when he peered in through one of the side windows, Lloyd could tell that apart from rebuilding the kitchen, he was going to have to redecorate almost the entire house. Still—being a one-time insurance salesman, he had made sure that his fire policy was comprehensive and up-to-date. For the money he was going to get, he could have afforded almost to tear down this house and build another one, from scratch. In a way, he found that a very tempting thought. This house reminded him so strongly of Celia, and the life they had been planning to live together. They had even thought of filling in the gravelike conversation pit, in case baby fell into it.

Lloyd rattled the front door to make sure it was locked. The house seemed to be reasonably secure, and around here the neighbors were too nosy to make burglary much of a practical proposition. Jesus, the Kazowskis even noticed when he put out the trash in new pajamas. "Noticed your new pajamas, Lloyd. The Ascot Shop?"

Lloyd left the house and walked back to the car. Kathleen said, "Is there any place we can get some coffee and something to eat? I think I'm just about to pass out. I keep tasting Helmwige's sauerkraut."

"Sure, we can go to the restaurant," said Lloyd. "I can ask Waldo to meet us there."

The sky was beginning to lighten as they drove toward La Jolla. Lloyd was feeling tired, but strangely changed. Stronger, somehow; as if he had at last accepted the burning of his house and the burning of the woman he loved, and was preparing to face what a new day was going to bring him. He looked around at Kathleen and she managed to summon a smile.

Waldo was delighted to see him, but horrified by his appearance.

"You look like you won first prize in a Mickey Rourke lookalike contest," he said, bringing over a large white jug of espresso coffee and a stack of steaming baguettes. "Why don't I call Louis, and have him come over and cook you a proper breakfast?"

"We don't have time for that," Lloyd told him. "Listen—we have to keep our heads down for a few days. We won't be too far away, but I'm not going to tell you where we're going to go, in case you get asked by somebody who won't take no for an answer."

"Mr. Denman, my lips are sealed," Waldo assured him.

"How's business?" Lloyd asked him. He looked around at the restaurant, at the neatly laid tables and the neatly folded napkins and the shining wineglasses, and for some reason he didn't find it enchanting anymore. Instead, it looked prissy and claustrophobic, the kind of place where people were more concerned about *foie gras chaud poêlé aux blancs de poireaux* than they were about life, and the struggle that most of the world went through daily, simply to stay free.

Waldo offered Franklin some more baguettes. "Business is fine. Do you want to see the books? Maybe leveling out a little, but nothing to worry about. People will always demand good fish, cooked good. Do you know what I read yesterday? The reason human beings got such big brains, they always ate fish. People who don't eat fish, they're going backward, like evolution in reverse. You don't eat fish, you're going to wind up like Barney Rubble."

Kathleen smiled tiredly. "You've got yourself a wonderful maître d' here, Lloyd. I never knew any restaurateur who worried about Darwin as much as Paul Bocuse."

"Where'd you read that stuff, Waldo?" Lloyd demanded.

"It's true," Waldo insisted. "Same with birds. They used to be land creatures; but then they started eating shellfish that didn't contain hardly no calcium; their bones got lighter and lighter; and in the end they literally blew away into the air."

"This is true?" asked Franklin, fascinated. Waldo glanced at Lloyd, alarmed by Franklin's loudness.

They talked for almost an hour. Outside, the sun had risen,

and La Jolla Cove shone golden and pale in the early-morning fog. Lloyd went to the men's room for a wash and a shave, while Kathleen called Lucy and asked after Tom, and Franklin unashamedly devoured more baguettes.

"Your friend has an appetite," smiled Waldo, taking hold of Lloyd's hand.

Lloyd smiled, and nodded.

"Listen," said Waldo, "I don't know what you've gotten yourself into here. Maybe you want me to call the cops about it?"

"Not yet," Lloyd told him. "I have to get my revenge first."

"Revenge?" sniffed Waldo. "I don't know. I used to think about revenge. I used to think about going back to Europe, and looking for the people who killed my family. I could have been like those Nazi-hunters, you know? I could have brought them all to trial. But what's it worth, in the end, this wonderful revenge? It doesn't achieve nothing. It doesn't make you feel any better. It ends up makes you worse than the people you're trying to punish."

"Maybe," said Lloyd, and gave Waldo's hand a last affectionate squeeze. This little fat guy, who took so much pride in his work, had so much to give to the world that the world probably didn't have room for it all. "Sometimes you have to think of the future, as well as the past."

They left La Jolla a few minutes before nine o'clock and headed eastward, with the sun in front of them. This time, Lloyd did the driving, wearing Otto's tiny green-lensed sunglasses, which he had discovered in the Mercedes' glove compartment. Kathleen said, "God, you look like that Nazi in *Raiders of the Lost Ark.*" Franklin had made himself comfortable in the back seat, and by the time they started climbing toward Sanba Ysabel, he was already snoring.

"You want me to talk to you?" asked Kathleen, suppressing a yawn.

"Not if you want to sleep."

"I'll just close my eyes for a moment, okay?"

And that's how it was that Lloyd sped across the scrubby outskirts of the Anza-Borrego State Park in a stolen Mercedes sedan with Kathleen lolling in the front seat, her forehead knocking softly against the passenger window with every bump in the road, and Franklin stretched out on the back seat, snoring in two distinct keys. Lloyd wryly wished that Celia were with them: she could have identified the exact key in which Franklin was snoring, and maybe sung along to it, too.

Celia had been brilliant, bright, and always funny. Lloyd tuned the Mercedes radio to KFSD on 94.1, and caught Bruch's *Kol Nidrei*, played by Vladimir Ashkenazy. It was uncanny: the *Kol Nidrei* had always been one of Celia's favorites, and Lloyd felt almost as if Celia were trying to get in touch with him.

Ahead of him, the desert burned bright, a land of hills and mirrors. Behind him, the dust blew high. But Lloyd felt neither lonely nor sad; nor particularly grief-stricken, not now. He had a job to do that nobody else in the world could do, and for which (in all probability) nobody would thank him. He hummed along with Bruch, and watched the miles ticking steadily upward on the Mercedes' odometer.

By early lunchtime, they drove past the place where the bus had burned. The wreck had been towed away now, and there was no reminder of what had happened except for a cross that somebody had fashioned out of two charred aluminum roof-supports, a cross that was hung with dried-out wreaths and withered flowers. Kathleen was still asleep as they drove by, and Lloyd didn't wake her. Some places are worth remembering; other places are best forgotten.

But Kathleen woke as they drew up outside Tony Express's store, and stared at Lloyd for a moment as if she couldn't think who he was.

"You know, I was having the weirdest dream? I dreamed I was swimming off Baja with Mike. The ocean kept rocking me up and down. I guess it must have been the car." But then she frowned, and said, "Mike looked so *strange*, in this dream. He looked like he didn't have any eyes."

"Come on," said Lloyd, and opened the car door. "Let's go see what accommodation we can find for ourselves."

He found Tony Express sitting inside the shadowy darkness of the store, threading beads. Considering he was blind, Tony Express was working with extraordinary speed, his fingers sorting out beads of different color and texture and swiftly impaling them on his threading needle, almost as if he were an insect collector. *Or an eater of flies*, thought Lloyd, obliquely, and it was a thought that seemed to take a long time to go away, like a train disappearing across the flattest of horizons.

"Tony? How're you doing?" he asked.

The blind Indian boy kept on picking out beads, picking out

beads. "Doing fine, thanks. Doing what Indians are best at. Walla-walla-walla, heap good necklace, all that stuff."

"Looks good to me," said Lloyd.

"Ho ho," Tony Express retaliated. "A heap of shit would look good to you, if I painted it red, white, and blue."

"Do you remember me?" Lloyd asked him. Because—God almighty—if he couldn't remember Lloyd's voice, then how could he clearly remember the voice of the man who had called out "Junius! Junius!" to a busload of burning disciples?

"Sure I know you, man," said Tony Express. "What you come back here for? I told you everything; there's nothing else." *I'll tell you everything I can; there's little to relate.*

"I was wondering if we could maybe hang out here for a while."

"You're wearing Hugo Boss aftershave and you want to hang out *here?*"

"I'm looking for a little peace, that's all. A few days' break from the hurly-burly of yuppiedom."

"You're not hiding from the law?"

"Of course not."

Tony Express suddenly lifted his head. "Who's the big guy, man? He wasn't with you before."

Lloyd was taken aback, and turned around to Franklin and shrugged. Maybe Tony Express was only kidding that he was blind.

But Tony Express immediately said, "It's a knack, man. I can only do it in the afternoons, when the sun's shining into the store. I can feel him blot out the warmth."

"I'm sorry," said Franklin, stepping out of the sunshine.

"Don't worry about it, man," said Tony Express. He deftly knotted the necklace he was stringing, and closed the lid on the cigar box full of beads. "There's an empty trailer next to ours. It belongs to an Indian called Zuni Tone. He's no damn Zuni and he sure doesn't have no tone, but there you go. You can rent it for twenty a week."

He led them around the back of the store, where instantly two brindled mongrels launched themselves furiously out of their makeshift packing-case kennel, their eyes bulging, until they were brought to a throttling halt by the chains around their throats. "Don't mind them," said Tony Express. "They only eat lawmen and truancy officers. They've got the Good Housekeeping Seal of Approval."

Kathleen held Lloyd's arm as they skirted around the growling, slavering dogs. "That's one guarantee I wouldn't like to put to the test," she told Tony Express.

Tony Express opened the high wire gate to the compound; waited patiently while they filed in; and led them between the trailers with the nonchalance of somebody who knows exactly where he wants to go. He dodged potholes, clotheslines, upturned Coca-Cola crates. He acknowledged old men sitting on dilapidated armchairs under tattered awnings; he called to women and children and even said, "Hi, Geronimo!" to a cat that was sleeping in the middle of a worn-down tire.

"It's hard for me to believe that this boy is blind," Franklin remarked.

"In his way, he can see more than we can," Lloyd replied. "He's a damned sight more intelligent, too."

Tony Express didn't say anything, didn't turn around, but he lifted one finger in the air to show Lloyd that he had heard.

At last they reached a large, sagging, green-painted trailer with overgrown window boxes and a Charley Noble stovepipe sticking out of the black-tarred roof. Tony Express opened the front door for them and let them take a look inside.

The trailer was gloomy and fiercely hot, but almost the first thing they bumped into was a huge Westinghouse air-conditioner, which looked as if it had previously been used to cool the Astrodome. The rest of the trailer, however, was surprisingly clean and neat. There was a table set with a vase of dried flowers, a hutch with willow-pattern plates arranged along it, an old-fashioned but scrupulously neat kitchenette, and a tiny bathroom with a mahogany-veneered Civil War washstand and a bean-shaped reenameled bath.

Lloyd went to one of the trailer's bookshelves and picked out a paperback at random. "The poems of Sterling Brown?" he queried.

Tony Express laughed and quoted,

> O Ma Rainey
> Li'l and low,
> Sing us 'bout de hard luck
> Roun' our do';
> Sing us 'bout de lonesome road
> We mus' go

He added, with a smile, "Zuni Tone is heavily into the emancipation of oppressed peoples, man."

"Yes, well, I think we are too," Lloyd replied.

Tony Express circled around and around in the middle of the trailer floor, as if he were looking at everything. Maybe he was picking up vibrations; maybe he was picking up smells, or noises; all of those nuances that sighted people are usually too insensitive to notice.

"You like it, man? What do you think?"

"It's better than I could have expected. Cleaner, for sure."

Tony Express stopped circling. "You think that Indians are dirty or something?"

Lloyd felt uncomfortable. "No, no. Of course not. What I meant was—"

Tony Express flapped his hand at him as if to tell him to forget it. "The twenty up front, man. In folding. Our credit machine's broke."

Lloyd produced a twenty, and pressed it into Tony Express's hand. "It's yours," said Tony Express. "Power extra, depending on what you use. There should be clean linen in the closet; Zuni Tone's very particular. Like he always sweeps up the rug after he's been clipping his toenails."

"Glad to know it," said Lloyd.

Tony Express was about to leave the trailer when they heard a car horn honking, out by the front of the store. "Wait up," he said, and swung himself down the steps, and jogged off between the trailers. Lloyd went through to the kitchenette and tested the gas and the water. The gas was working and after a brief, asthmatic pause, the water came coughing out of the faucet.

Kathleen sat down on the bed. "You know, you always picture these trailer parks as being so slummy. But look how neat everything is. I guess it's the discipline of living in such a small space."

They were still talking when Franklin lifted the net curtain and peered out. "The boy's coming back," he said. "He's got two policemen with him."

"Oh, what?" Lloyd demanded. He lifted the other side of the curtain and saw that Franklin was right. Tony Express was weaving his way back between the trailers, closely followed by a fat, ruddy-complexioned Highway Patrol officer, and a thinner, darker officer in designer sunglasses and a sharply pressed shirt.

"What are we going to do?" Kathleen asked, as Lloyd let the curtain fall back.

"Nothing we can do," Lloyd told her. "Tough it out, is all."

They stood waiting in silence while Tony Express and the two Highway Patrol officers approached the trailer. The door opened, and the entire trailer groaned and dipped to one side as Sergeant Jim Griglak climbed aboard, closely followed by Ric Muñoz. Jim Griglak shuffled his way toward the living area, holding his wide-brimmed hat pressed against his chest, as if he were paying a respectful visit to some friends of the family. Ric Muñoz was relentlessly chewing Orbit, and he left his sunglasses on.

"Sergeant Jim Griglak, Highway Patrol," said Jim Griglak, although Lloyd could read that for himself. "We've been asked to stop a Mercedes-Benz sedan answering the description of the vehicle parked by the roadway back there, and detain the occupants. Are you the occupants?"

Lloyd shook his head. "Don't know what you're talking about, Sergeant. I never owned a Mercedes-Benz in my life. Beverly Hills Skodas. I'm a BMW man, myself."

Jim Griglak breathed patiently. "We're not talking ownership here, sir. We're talking grand theft auto."

"Still don't know what you're talking about. If I don't *like* Mercedes-Benzes, why should I steal one?"

Ric Muñoz put in, "Sometimes any vee-hickle is better than no vee-hickle."

Jim Griglak looked around the three of them. "Do you want to tell me your names, and what you're doing here?"

Lloyd said, "We're an ethnic study group from UC San Diego. I'm Professor Holden Caulfield; these are my assistants. We're putting together a social profile of small disaffected Indian communities, such as this trailer park."

Jim Griglak closed his eyes for a moment as if summoning huge internal reserves of patience. At last he said, "I'm arresting all three of you on suspicion of grand theft auto. I've read *The Catcher in the Rye,* too, Professor Caulfield. Pity you couldn't have thought of some much more convincing alias, like Bruce Wayne."

He sniffed, and recited their rights. Then he said, "Let's go. You're going to make me late for my lunch."

Ric Muñoz added, "Sergeant Griglak gets seriously pissed if he's late for his lunch."

There was nothing they could do. Led by Tony Express, they filed out of the trailer, and back through the gate toward the store, where the dogs snarled and yapped and hurled themselves wildly against their chains.

"Thanks a lot, pal," Lloyd told Tony Express, as they walked around the side of the store. "Remind me to do *you* a favor some day."

"I couldn't help it, man," Tony Express replied. "They'd already seen the car, they knew you had to be around someplace."

Lloyd said, "That guy we're trying to catch . . . the one who said 'Junius, Junius' when the bus was burning . . . I want you to know that he's just about most disgusting slime on two legs. So if we *do* manage to get this sorted, and we *do* manage to catch him, I hope you're going to be ready to come forward and identify his voice."

"What if I don't?"

"Then he and his friends are going to do to today's Americans what yesterday's Americans did to the Indians. *Capiche?* He and his friends think they're some kind of master race, do you understand what I mean? They think the world belongs to them, and they're the people to rule it. You ever hear of Adolf Hitler?"

"Sure I heard of Adolf Hitler. I told you I was overeducated for a kid my age."

"Well, what this Junius guy is trying to do is carry on where Adolf Hitler left off."

"Here? In California?"

"Why not? It's one of the richest and most influential countries in the world. What California does today, the rest of the world is going to be doing tomorrow."

"Give your mouth a rest, will you?" Jim Griglak called out. "You chose to remain silent, so frigging well *remain* silent."

Tony Express looked pale and his breathing was oddly shallow. "I couldn't help it, man. They'd already seen the car."

They reached the road. It was grillingly hot, and heat rose from the blacktop like the shallows of a wind-ruffled lake. Jim Griglak opened the rear door of his Highway Patrol car and indicated with a curt nod of his head that Franklin should climb in. Franklin hesitated, and looked dubious.

"Come on, bonehead, we're going for the scenic tour," Jim Griglak rasped.

They climbed into the back of the patrol car and Jim Griglak locked the doors. Then they U-turned and headed back toward the main highway, while Tony Express stood forlornly by the side of the road, listening to them go.

Ric Muñoz picked up the handset and reported back to headquarters that they were bringing in three suspects for the theft of Otto Mander's Mercedes. Jim Griglak sang to himself under his breath as he drove, and occasionally made comments about the passing scenery, or if there was life after retirement, or baseball. He went with tedious detail into an explanation of the Boudreau Shift, which is when a manager counters a slugger who always pulls to the right by shifting all of his fielders to the right of second.

Lloyd and Kathleen and Franklin said nothing. Franklin was bemused: Lloyd and Kathleen were both physically and emotionally exhausted. The jiggling of the car began to send them to sleep.

"I have often walked . . . down this tooty-wooty before . . ." sang Jim Griglak. "And the pavements tooty-woot frooty-woot before. . . . Hey, did I ever tell you that story about Yogi Berra, when they gave him a check that said 'Pay to Bearer'?"

"I'm not sure," Ric replied, manfully. He was beginning to look forward to Jim Griglak's retirement.

Jim Griglak chuckled. "He said, 'Hey, they spelled my name wrong!' "

They had traveled nearly six miles across the dazzling desert landscape before Jim Griglak suddenly began to slow down. The change in speed woke Lloyd almost immediately, and he sat up abruptly and said, "What is it? What's happening?"

But Jim Griglak didn't answer. Instead he drove slower and slower, peering ahead of him as if he couldn't believe what he was seeing.

Kathleen grasped Lloyd's arm and said, "Lloyd, look!"

Lloyd shifted his position and frowned ahead into the sunlight. What he saw gave him a feeling of delight and terror, both at once, as if he had woken up one morning and found that he could fly.

"This can't be so," whispered Jim Griglak.

"It's so, all right," said Ric Muñoz, echoing the moment that they had found that burned bus, and all of its charred and grisly occupants.

Standing beside the road not a hundred feet ahead of them were two figures. One was an elderly Indian, in jeans and a red plaid shirt. The other was the skinny, wind-tattered figure of Tony Express. In his hand he was holding the long stick decorated with rags of skin and rags of fur and squirrel tails and beads, the sun-dance doll that he had shown them back at the store, the first time they had met him.

The sun lanced off the lenses of his sunglasses. He wasn't afraid. He was simply waiting. Jim Griglak slowed the patrol car to a whining crawl, and at last to a halt, still thirty feet shy of the skinny Pechanga blind boy with the ragged stick.

He applied the parking brake with a heave of his foot, and then switched off the engine. It was hot and bright and suddenly silent.

"What's wrong?" Lloyd asked him, at last.

Jim Griglak shifted himself around in the driver's seat and stared at Lloyd balefully. "You're looking at a young blind Indian kid who has just managed to overtake a car traveling at fifty-five miles an hour; on foot; across a desert landscape heated well in excess of one-hundred-ten degrees Fahrenheit. And you're asking me what's wrong?"

"Maybe he has a brother," Kathleen suggested, without much hope. "Maybe he telephoned him, and arranged for him to meet up with us here—you know, pretending to be him."

Jim Griglak slowly and fatly shook his head. "That is the same kid. That is the exact same kid who stood outside his dad's store less than fifteen minutes ago and watched us drive away."

Ric Muñoz gave an unbalanced laugh. "Come on, Sergeant, what are we saying here? We know there's only one kid. Anyway—who's the old guy with him? You're making a mistake; you must be."

But Jim Griglak was adamant."That's the same frigging kid, Muñoz, on my mother's grave."

He turned back to Lloyd and Kathleen and Franklin and said, "Stay put, you got it? Watch my lips. S-t-a-y p-u-t."

Grunting, he heaved himself out of the car. Ric Muñoz hesitated for a moment, then unclipped the pump-gun from its rack in front of the dashboard and followed him, keeping the gun held high. Lloyd watched them walk slowly toward the two Indians; the old Indian in the baggy jeans and the young blind Indian in the headband; and for a moment he found himself unable to speak. It was like watching history.

Kathleen whispered, "Is that really him? It looks like him!"

"It can't be him," Lloyd told her. "How could anybody run six miles in less than ten minutes, and arrive here well ahead of us? He may be precocious, and he may be just a little crazy, but he's human."

"So you think that's his double?"
"It makes a damn sight more sense than it being him!"
"But supposing—"
"Supposing what?"
"I don't know," Kathleen replied, flustered. "It just seems to me that if Otto is capable of burning people and bringing them back to life again, maybe there's more to this world than we usually allow ourselves to see."

19

Jim Griglak approached the old man and the young boy with all the caution that a working lifetime in the Highway Patrol had taught him. Watch the eyes. Watch for the slightest flicker of movement. Watch the hands, too. Apart from good old straightforward honest-to-God handguns, there are plenty of other weapons that can kill and maim. Knives, small-caliber guns that spring out of the sleeve, and all of that ninja crap, like stars and chains.

The boy was standing with his head held slightly higher than a sighted person would have held it, his lips drawn back across his teeth; but with great poise and certainty. The furs and tails that decorated his sun-dance doll swung around and around in the hot afternoon wind. Jim Griglak saw the tiny malevolent face on top of it and decided that he didn't care for it *at all*.

In contrast, the old man appeared to be quite benign, just one of those old coots that you might see at a charity lunch for senior citizens. His face had that distinctive leathery look that only Indians have; his eyes were bloodshot and filmed over, but he was smiling to himself as if everything was just the way he liked it.

Jim Griglak stopped, and sniffed, and wiped his nose with the back of his hand. "How'd you get here?" he asked, bluntly.

"How'd *you* get here?" the boy replied, with a blind smile.

"Listen," said Jim. "Don't you start jerking me around. I want to know how you got here."

The old man said, "Same way that you did, sir. By air, by fire, by wind, and by water."

"What's your name?" Jim Griglak asked him.

"John Dull Knife. What's yours?"

"Mind your own goddamn business."

"Interesting," John Dull Knife nodded. "Don't like it much, though. Your parents atheists?"

"Listen," said Jim Griglak. "I don't know how the hell you managed to get here so quick, less'n you've got yourselves a Ferrari Testarossa hidden behind that dune. But I do know one thing. You're going to get yourselves back where you came from, both of you, and stay well out of stuff that's not your frigging concern."

John Dull Knife said, "My parents always taught me to speak to everybody, even my enemy, with respect. Respect is power, my friend. Contempt is weakness. The greatest power in the universe is the appreciation of one human being for the strengths of another. Only the weak seek out weakness."

"How'd you get here so quick?" Ric Muñoz asked him. "Come on, let's hear it. You know some secret shortcut, or what?"

John Dull Knife turned to the boy and smiled. "We were not quick, my friend. It is you who were slow. Look at the time. Look at the position of the sun. How did it take you six hours to travel no more than six miles?"

Jim Griglak lifted his head and looked around. John Dull Knife was right. All of the shadows had mysteriously swiveled from one side of the compass to the other. High up above them, the sky was already beginning to show signs of darkening. He checked his wristwatch and it was almost five. They had been driving at the legal limit all the way from Tony Express's store, and yet they couldn't have chalked up more than one mile an hour. At that speed, John Dull Knife and Tony Express could have strolled past them with their hands in their pockets.

"Ric," said Jim Griglak, between tightened teeth, "what time do you have, please?"

"Almost five, Sergeant."

"That's what I have, too. And look around you. It's definitely five o'clock, no mistake about it. But you know and I know that it takes less than seven minutes to travel six miles at fifty-five, and you know me, I always hit fifty-five right on the nose. So what the hell's going on, I'd like to know?"

The blind Indian boy shook the sun-dance doll. "We don't

have your firepower, man. We never want to, and we never will. But this land is ours, and always will be. So if we want you to go slow, then all we have to do is to ask the land to carry you slow. You don't even understand 'traveling,' do you? Why 'traveling' is so important? When you travel, it's not just you moving over the ground; it's the ground moving underneath you. Time and distance, they're elastic, don't you understand that? After all that Einstein taught you? It's not fantasy, it's not magic, it's *true*."

"How old are you?" Jim Griglak asked him.

"Thirteen come February."

"Jesus," said Jim Griglak. "When I was thirteen, my parents thought I was a genius because I could recite 'Casey at the Bat.' "

Ric Muñoz took distastefully out of his mouth the gum that he must have been chewing for over six hours. "*Thought* the goddamn flavor'd all gone out of it."

"Listen," Jim Griglak told Tony Express and John Dull Knife. "I don't know what the hell kind of a stunt you've pulled here, but it amounts to interference with officers of the law in the execution of their duty. I don't have room for you in my vehicle right now, but I'm warning you that you face possible arrest, and that as soon as I've delivered these two suspects to San Diego, I'm coming back for you."

"That could take you many hours," smiled John Dull Knife.

"I don't care how frigging long it takes," Jim Griglak retorted. "I don't care if it takes me past my frigging retirement. You've been frigging around with me, injun, and nobody frigs around with me and gets away with it, never."

"*Never* is a white man's idea," John Dull Knife answered him. "My people only say 'ever.' "

"Well get this," Jim Griglak snapped back. "Nobody never frigs around with me, ever. Understandee?"

He jerked his head to Ric Muñoz and said, "Come on, Muñoz. I'm getting hungry."

He turned around, but to his astonishment, their patrol car had disappeared. As far as the eye could see, there was nothing but empty road.

He turned furiously back to Tony Express and John Dull Knife, but they had disappeared, too, and the road was just as empty ahead as it was behind. He turned and stared at Ric Muñoz but all Ric Muñoz could do was stare back at him.

"Where'd they go?" he demanded. "Did you see them go?"

Ric Muñoz shook his head. "I didn't see nothing."

Jim Griglak stood in the middle of the Anza-Borrego Desert, and for the first time in his career he let out a long bellow of frustration and rage.

To Lloyd and Kathleen and Franklin, who had been sitting in the back of the hot patrol car waiting, it had seemed that Tony Express and John Dull Knife had simply walked around the two Highway Patrol officers, leaving them standing by the side of the road.

John Dull Knife leaned into the open driver's window with a smile. "Do you think you can drive this vehicle back to the trailer park?" he asked Lloyd. "Then you can take your own car and be on your way."

Lloyd frowned at Jim Griglak and Ric Muñoz. "What about those two? They're not exactly going to stand and wave while we take off in their patrol car, are they?" John Dull Knife continued to smile, unconcerned. "For the next hour, those two will be living at a different pace from the rest of us. By the time they regain their normal perception, we will have long been gone."

"How do you *do* that?" asked Kathleen, amazed.

"You must have heard of the Yaqui, and their ability to change perception. What I have done to our friends from the Highway Patrol is a very similar procedure, not at all unusual or difficult to achieve."

Lloyd gave Jim Griglak and Ric Muñoz a long uncertain stare, and then opened the patrol car door and stepped out. The two officers remained where they were, not even turning their heads around. "That's incredible," Lloyd told John Dull Knife. "That's the weirdest thing I ever saw."

"How do you think Crazy Horse managed to outflank General Custer at the Little Bighorn?" asked John Dull Knife. "So many eyewitnesses said that first the Sioux were there, and then they were not there. But of course they were there. It was simply that Custer couldn't see them."

Lloyd climbed into the driver's seat. "Do you want a ride?" he asked John Dull Knife, "or will you get back the same way you came?"

"I'll have a ride, thank you," John Dull Knife told him. "We may have appeared to you to have arrived here quickly, but we still had to walk six miles in hot sun."

Tony Express sat next to Lloyd, and John Dull Knife climbed

stiffly in beside him. "Hey man, can we switch on the sireen?" asked Tony Express, as Lloyd started the engine and turned the patrol car around.

"Don't talk like a child," John Dull Knife told him.

Kathleen leaned over from the back seat. "What are we going to do now?" she asked Lloyd. "Once those two patrolmen wake up, they're going to come directly to the trailer park looking for us, aren't they?"

"My lawyer has a small beach house at Del Mar," Lloyd told her. "I'll see if we can use it for a few days. I don't think Celia would think of looking for me there."

John Dull Knife said, "You should take Tony with you. He has told me of your struggle. He knows the magic, and he knows how to use the sun-dance doll."

"Why don't you come along?" Lloyd asked him.

John Dull Knife shook his head. "I am too old, my friend. My days of adventure are long gone."

"Tony?" asked Lloyd. He was more than a little dubious of taking responsibility for a twelve-year-old blind boy, particularly when they were being pursued by somebody as dangerous as Otto Mander.

"Sure, man, I'll come," Tony agreed. "Franklin can be my bodyguard, hey, Franklin?"

Franklin grinned and nodded, although he was still plainly bemused by what had been happening to them. "I'll be your eyes, too. You can do all the thinking. I can do all the looking."

"Hm," said Tony, as if he wasn't completely convinced by this arrangement.

They drove back to Tony's store, where Otto's Mercedes was still parked. John Dull Knife shook them by the hand and wished them well. "If I had been many years younger, I would have gladly come with you," he said. "But all I can say to you is what Chief Speckled Snake said to his Creek warriors when the white people began to invade their territory."

"What was that?" asked Kathleen.

"You would not understand the Creek, but the words exactly mean, 'Go out there and kick the crap out of them.' "

Lloyd used the store telephone to call his lawyer Dan Tabares. But the phone rang and rang and nobody picked it up. He hesitated for a moment, and then he called Waldo at the restaurant.

"Waldo, it's me."

"You're okay, Mr. Denman?"

"I'm fine. But I have to change my plans a little. I'm thinking of using Dan Tabares' beach house at Del Mar for a few days. The only trouble is, he's not at home right now. I wonder if you could call him in about an hour and ask him to leave the beach house keys under the step, same place as he did when Celia and me—well, the same place as he did before."

"Okay, Mr. Denman, sure thing."

After Lloyd had hung up, Kathleen used the phone to call her sister and talk to Tom. Lloyd stood outside the store in the long shadows of the setting sun and watched her. There was no mistaking the light in Kathleen's eyes when she eventually got through. Lloyd looked away, and thought about Celia, and about the children that *they* would never have.

Tony Express came up, carrying an Adidas sports bag crammed with jeans and T-shirts and grayish-looking undershorts, which John Dull Knife had packed for him. A spare pair of sneakers were knotted around his neck, and he was swinging the shaggy, stringy-looking sun-dance doll. His eyes were invisible behind his dark glasses.

"We ready to roll, man?" he wanted to know.

Lloyd nodded. "I guess so. But you listen. If this looks like it's going to get at all dangerous, then you're right back here on the next available bus."

"I can take care of myself, man," Tony Express pouted. " 'Sides, I got my bodyguard now, don't I?'

Franklin grinned at him, and said, "You bet," and Lloyd rolled his eyes up, wondering what the hell he had gotten himself into.

20

Waldo waited until he had closed the door behind Angie, the last waitress to leave, and seen her safely across the sidewalk to her boyfriend's Corvette. Then he turned the key in the door, and shot the bolts, and turned around the American Express placard that said Closed. He walked back across the darkened restaurant, between the tables set with fresh napkins and softly gleaming cutlery, and opened the sliding door that led out to the deck.

All around him, the lights of La Jolla glittered in the warm night wind, and the sea fussed and phosphoresced on the rocks of the cove. He had rescued a third of a bottle of Barossa Valley Cabernet Sauvignon from a party of elderly ladies who had gotten too giggly to finish it all, and he poured himself a glass and leaned on the wooden rail and took a deep breath of ocean air.

Although he wouldn't have presumed to usurp Lloyd's authority, he was beginning to enjoy the responsibility and the rewards of running the Original Fish Depot on his own. He had managed to keep the place busy and lively, and he had allowed Louis a free hand to try dozens of new fish dishes, including a spectacularly successful brill with oysters.

He had also become much more cheerful and sociable, and as his confidence had increased, his French accent had become less and less exaggerated—until, as Louis had remarked, he was practically speaking English.

He sipped the cabernet and rolled it around his tongue. It

wasn't quite cold enough but that didn't matter. He was enjoying the night too much.

He had been out on the deck for only a few minutes when he became aware that the seagulls were crying. He had never heard them cry in the dark before. He sensed a disturbance in the wind, an anxiety in the seething of the surf. He stood up straight and listened, and he was sure that he could hear somebody calling his name.

Waldo, don't run too far; don't run too fast; Grandpa is coming, Waldo; Grandpa is coming!

"Grandpa?" he said, out loud. Then he shook his head, and smiled at his own stupidity. He must be really tired to imagine that he had heard his grandpa. "Finish your wine and lock up for the night, and get yourself some sleep," he told himself, trying to sound the way his grandpa used to sound.

He turned, and shouted out loud in shock. Standing in the shadows at the end of the deck was a black figure with a pale face and dark glasses. A figure that stood and watched him and said nothing at all.

"Who are you?" Waldo cried out, his throat tight. "This is private property. Private restaurant. Nobody is allowed here."

The figure stepped forward, into the dim light that shone through the restaurant from the half-open kitchen door.

"Not even the owner's fiancée?" she said, with a gray-lipped smile.

Waldo shuddered, and made an odd noise through his nose that sounded like *hnyuh!* The figure stepped closer still, so that Waldo could see himself reflected in her glasses, and the air was strong with the aroma of heated metal.

"I'm looking for Lloyd," she said, very quietly.

Waldo breathed with terrified heaviness, and he could feel his heart racing and plunging like a surfer trying to paddle out beyond the incoming waves.

"I am having a nightmare about you," he told her. "I am asleep, and you have come out of my dream. You must go away."

"Waldo," Celia insisted, "I'm looking for Lloyd. I have to find him, before it's too late."

She came a fraction closer, and Waldo screamed and lifted his arm to protect himself. "You must go away! You are absolutely dead!" He stumbled back against one of the chairs and had to snatch at the wooden rail to stop himself from falling. "Go away! Go away!"

"How can I be dead, Waldo, when I'm right here in front of your eyes?"

Waldo had retreated right to the end of the deck, and his back was pressed against the rail. He glanced quickly behind him, and it was a long drop down to the concrete footpath below. "Oh God help me, oh God help me," he muttered.

Celia pushed aside the chair that Waldo had toppled over and came after him. The smell of heated metal seemed even more pungent, and Waldo coughed.

"What do you want?" he asked her. "What do you want? You're a dead person; what do you want?"

"Waldo, I'm not dead. This is me. This is Celia."

"But you're hot! I can feel it! You're hot!"

"Waldo, my earthly body burned but my soul survived. You mustn't be frightened of my *soul!* It's still *me*, it's still the same Celia!"

"Don't touch me!" shouted Waldo.

"I'm not going to touch you."

"Then what do you want?"

Celia took off her dark glasses. In the shadows of the deck, her eyes appeared to Waldo to be extraordinarily dark. More like pits than eyes. More like holes. He felt that he could see right inside the blackness of her head.

"Waldo—I have to know where Lloyd is, that's all."

"He's not at home?" Waldo quaked.

"Don't take me for a fool, Waldo. We both know that the house burned down."

"Well, I don't know," said Waldo. "He doesn't tell me nothing."

"You're running the restaurant. You're in charge of his pride and joy. You must know where he is."

"Ms. Williams—I swear—I don't have no idea."

Celia unbuttoned her glove, and rolled it up. She tucked it into her raincoat pocket. Then, without warning, she snatched hold of Waldo's hand, and squeezed it tightly. Waldo shouted out, "Hey!" and shook his arm violently, to break free of her. But Celia clung on, and her fingers weren't only tenacious but burning hot.

"Hey, you're hot, you're hot, you're burning my hand!" Waldo shouted out. "Get off me, go away!"

"Where's Lloyd, Waldo? I have to know!"

"I don't know where he is. I swear it! He went away and he

didn't tell me where he was going! He did it on purpose, in case somebody should find out. I didn't know it was *you!*"

"Waldo—I don't believe a word of it. Lloyd is one of those careful, careful men who never leaves anything to chance. He doesn't leave his restaurant to chance, he doesn't leave his house to chance, he doesn't leave his *life* to chance. But here's some unpredictability, Waldo. Here's a bit of improvisation. If you don't tell me where he is, I'm going to set fire to you."

Gasping, Waldo tried to pull his hand away from Celia's, but suddenly her fingers flared so hot that she burned through skin and muscle and tendons, and fused their hands together. Waldo shrieked in pain, and dropped to his knees on to the deck; but still he was unable to pull himself free. *God, if I pull myself free, I'll pull my whole hand off!*

"Don't! Don't! Don't!" he cried; but then Celia tugged open her raincoat with her free hand, and revealed herself naked and gray-skinned, and smelling of molten zinc. A curl of metallic smoke rose out of her coattails.

"Tell me where he is, Waldo," Celia insisted. "I have to know!"

"I don't know, I don't know. I swear to God I don't know!"

But then Celia tugged off her left-hand glove with her teeth, and placed her bare hand on top of Waldo's balding head. There was a furious sizzling noise, and his scalp puckered up red and blistered. Smoke poured out from between Celia's fingers, and Waldo opened his mouth wide and let out a white scream of agony and fear.

Celia abruptly stopped that. With her fingers burned deep into the flesh on top of his head, so that Waldo couldn't have wrenched himself away without being scalped, she pressed his face flat against her bare stomach. His scream was muffled for two or three seconds. Then smoke billowed up between Celia's breasts; the smoke of Waldo's face burning; and she breathed it in with lubricious satisfaction.

"Haven't you wanted to do that to me ever since you first saw me?" she taunted him. Then she rubbed his face up and down her stomach, and between her thighs, and he shuddered and shook in overwhelming agony. It was like having his face rubbed against an electric hotplate. With each rub, more strips of burned skin were dragged from his face. He felt the flesh seared from the side of his nose. His cheeks almost seemed to *melt*, like wax. But Celia kept on rubbing his face against her until his nose bone was being clicked up and down against her like a skeletal trigger.

He could scarcely speak. His face was raw and blistered, and nobody would have recognized him now, nor would again. His eyes bulged from reddened sockets, his nose was nothing more than a twist of fried gristle, with two huge gaping nostrils, and his lips had swollen three times their normal size. He was trembling in shock; but still Celia wouldn't let him go.

"Listen to me, Waldo! I have to know where he is!"

She began to pull his face toward her again, but Waldo lifted a hand to stop her. His fingers crackled against the ferocious heat of her thighs, but he was too far gone to scream any more.

"Be—beach house. Dan Tabares's beach house. Up at Del Mar."

"Thank you, Waldo," said Celia. "Why didn't you tell me that in the first place? You could have saved yourself such pain!"

Waldo tried to climb to his feet, but he was shuddering too much. Celia stood watching him, her coat flapping softly against her naked body, her skin subtly fuming like a metal baking sheet. "You know what your trouble is, Waldo?" Celia asked him, although he probably failed to hear her. "You were always too loyal! A man like Lloyd needs people to question him. He needs people to needle him; people to upset him. You shouldn't give a man like Lloyd too much of an easy life. He'll take advantage of you, and forget to pay you for it, too."

Dumbly, with the head-dipping motion of a wounded hippopotamus, Waldo shuffled on his knees toward her. She stepped back once, then twice; then stepped back again.

"I'll *kill* you," Waldo blubbered, through grotesquely inflated lips. "I swear to God that I'll *kill* you!"

He threw aside one of the chairs, then tipped over the table.

"Whatever you are, I'm going to *kill* you!"

He tried to pick himself up, stumbled, and fell heavily on top of her. She jarred backwards onto the deck, and where her hand clawed against the planking, she burned black bitter-smelling fingerprints into the wood. "*Kill* you—!" Waldo repeated, and lifted both fists high above his head, ready to smash them down onto her face, the way that he had once seen his father kill a berserk dog.

But Celia clung onto him, arms and thighs, and said wildly, "Come on, Waldo! Maybe you and I were always meant to make love together! A special kind of love, yes? Really hot!"

She pressed his blistered face against her bare breasts; and then she ignited him, like a bonfire. He shrieked and twisted and clawed for anything to help him get away. His shoes drummed against the planking of the deck. "Help me! Somebody help me!" But the flames consumed him as fiercely as if he had been molded out of paraffin wax.

Somehow the pain became so intolerable that he managed to drag himself up onto his knees again, and then onto his feet. He was blazing from head to foot. His shoes crackled and spat as the polish burned.

He stood by the rail with the ocean wind fanning his flames until they roared. The pain, at first excruciating, seemed to burn out and fade, and soon he felt that it was possible to stand here ablaze and not to die. The seagulls were crying. It was dark but the seagulls were crying. He was sure he could hear his grandpa as they walked along the seashore. *Don't worry, young Waldo. Never fear. Now you can fly, too.*

He climbed burning onto the wooden rail around the deck, and balanced for a moment with flames flying out behind him like a monstrous cloak. He opened his mouth to call to his grandpa and fire burst out from between his teeth. He felt as if he were on fire both inside and out.

You can fly, Waldo. You can fly.

So, he flew. Over and over in the darkness, forty blazing feet, until he landed with a thunder of flame and a smack of steam into a bubbling hot tub on the deck below. The tub was occupied by a hairy-chested orthodontist and a redheaded woman who wasn't his wife. They were blissfully and obliviously listening to the water bubble and Beethoven's Sixth on the stereo, and Waldo's fiery arrival in the orthodontist's hot tub marked the moment when his marriage, his affair, his practice, and his sanity instantaneously and simultaneously vanished.

On the deck above them, Celia listened to them screaming and gibbering in horror. Then she buttoned her gloves, walked through the restaurant, and let herself out. A Mercedes 380SL was waiting by the curb, its engine running, its hood dull with bird droppings and grime. Otto was sitting behind the wheel, his mouth pursed, his cheeks oddly puffed out.

"Del Mar," said Celia. "They're hiding in his lawyer's beach house. I'll direct you."

Otto nodded, without saying a word.

"Are you all right?" Celia asked him.

Otto nodded again, and then opened his mouth. His tongue was crowded with twenty or thirty glistening green and black blowflies, all alive, all struggling, but stuck to his tongue with saliva. Otto closed his mouth again, then sucked, then crunched, then swallowed.

Celia said very little on the way to Del Mar, except "Right here," or "Slow," or "Watch this intersection." She was beginning to feel that perhaps her burning had changed her more than she had realized . . . more than Otto had promised her. She knew that she had liked Waldo—loved him, almost. Yet she had felt no remorse when she had burned his face. She had felt no regret when he had plunged blazing off the deck. In fact, she had felt something disturbing and dangerous—a pleasure that was almost sexual—in witnessing the agonized death throes of another human being.

She slipped her hand into her raincoat, and cupped herself between her legs. Moisture and fire. Death and delight. She could hardly wait to find Lloyd again. She could hardly wait to hold him. She trembled at the thought of what they would be doing on the night of the solstice, when the year turned, and the fires burned, and the master race would be reborn.

Otto glanced at her out of the corner of his eye. "*Was machst du*, Celia?" he asked her.

"I'm thinking, that's all."

"Did you burn Slonimsky?"

She whispered, "Yes."

Otto wiped stray fly wings from his lips with the back of his withered hand. "So for all Jews," he remarked. "They escaped once; we won't fail a second time."

Lloyd managed to adjust the antenna of the worn-out Zenith television so that they could watch the late-night news. For most of the program, the Chinese anchorwoman's face was livid blue, with a thin wavering green mustache, but intelligible sound was all that they needed.

"—Highway Patrol officers were forced to walk five-and-a-half miles across the Anza-Borrego Desert State Park this evening when their patrol car was borrowed by two men and a woman whom they had arrested on suspicion of grand theft auto. The suspects commandeered the Highway Patrol vehicle when the officers temporarily vacated it to interview two hitchhikers, and used it to return to the Mercedes sedan which they were originally suspected of having stolen—"

"Hitchhikers!" exclaimed Tony Express, scornfully. "Even the cops can't tell the truth these days!"

"What did you expect them to say?" asked Lloyd. " 'We stopped to talk to these two Pechanga Indians, one thirteen and one seventy, because they overtook us on foot when we were traveling at fifty-five miles an hour in a car'? Give the poor guys a break."

They had made themselves as comfortable as they could in Dan Tabares's beach house. It was one of a row of twenty or thirty shabby oceanfront properties, reached by a derelict back street behind restaurants and stores and automobile bodyshops. Most of the beach houses were owned by inland hotels who liked to boast that they had somewhere for guests to enjoy the ocean, or by downtown San Diego businessmen like Dan Tabares who brought noisy gangs of middle-aged men out for a weekend of fishing and Miller drinking and leering at the local nubility.

The large damp-smelling living room was furnished with white-painted cane sofas with bamboo-patterned foam cushions, and it was appallingly lit from above, so that they all looked much more tired than they really were. The kitchen was decorated in brown and orange, and boasted a filthy microwave, an electric can opener encrusted with age-blackened tomato sauce, and an old Betty Furness–style refrigerator containing two bottles of flat soda water and something khaki and effervescent that, in another life, had probably been a quarter pound of liverwurst.

After they had arrived, Lloyd and Kathleen drove to the nearest late-night market for bread, bacon, fresh vegetables, peaches, doughnuts, Cheerios, coffee, 7-Up, chocolate bars, Smirnoff vodka, Wild Turkey whiskey, and all the other essentials of a civilized existence.

There was nothing in the beach house that didn't look as if it had been rejected from Dan Tabares's main house, right down to the Goodyear ashtray and the tattered real-estate poster for Rancho Jamul Estates, "Your place . . . in the country (actual view)." Two of the bedrooms were smallish and mean, with folding beds. The main bedroom had been painted in garish purple, with a tasteless reproduction oil painting above the bed of a girl in a wide-brimmed hat standing on the seashore with her skirt billowing up, so that her bare bottom was revealed.

Kathleen went out to the boardwalk in front of the beach house. From there, a half-dozen wooden steps led down to the sand. She stood for a while listening to the sound of the surf. Once he had listened to the rest of the news, Lloyd came to join her.

"Hope those Highway Patrol officers didn't get into too much trouble," he said.

"I don't care if they did," Kathleen replied. The wind blew her hair across her face. "The fat one was obnoxious and the young one was just plain stupid."

"Freshen your drink?" Lloyd asked her.

She shook her head. "I'm going inside in a moment. The ocean always scares me at nighttime. It sounds like hungry bears."

"Maybe you should get some sleep," Lloyd suggested. "I've straightened the bed for you."

"So where were you thinking of sleeping?"

"I'll take one of the couches."

She shook her head. "Those couches are disgusting. They stink of beer. I'm sure that you and I can manage to sleep together without doing anything immoral."

Lloyd smiled, and swallowed whiskey. "Depends what you mean by immoral."

"Just try me."

They stood outside a while longer, finishing their drinks, and then they went back inside. Tony Express had showered and brushed his teeth and was already in bed, his dark glasses folded neatly on his bedside table. His milk-white eyes stared at the ceiling; his hands were clasped across his chest.

Lloyd sat on the side of his bed. "Do you ever pray before you go to sleep?" he asked him.

"Unh-unh," said Tony Express. "Praying's for the birds, man."

"You'd be surprised how often it helps, even if you don't believe in it."

"Well, I'm desperate, man, but I'm not *that* desperate."

"Didn't your grandfather ever read to you?"

"John Dull Knife? He can't read, man. But he knew some pretty good stories about the old days, before the paleface honky long-knives stole our land and took all our women and turned our sacred lodges into Safeways."

Lloyd smiled. "And what does he say to you, before he turns out the light?"

"He always says, 'I don't know why the hell I'm doing this; you can't see it anyway.' "

Lloyd reached out and took hold of Tony Express's hand. "You're something special, you know that?"

"Yeah, man, I know it."

Switching off the cheap bedside lamp, Lloyd left Tony Express and went to see Franklin, who was lying on his bed fully dressed, looking tense.

"Everything all right?" Lloyd wanted to know.

"I guess so. I feel funny, that's all. Edgy. I'm not used to being free."

"You'll get used to it quick enough. You sure don't want to go back to Otto and Helmwige, do you?"

"I don't know. I still don't feel right."

"What do you want me to do, chain you to the bed?"

Franklin glanced up at him, and then said hoarsely, "No. No more of that. That was when I didn't have a name, and they made me feel like everything bad that happened in the world was my father's fault, because my father had been bred by Josef Mengele, and because it was all my father's fault, it was *my* fault, too.

He paused for a moment, and then he said, "It's still hard for me to think that it isn't."

"What made you change your mind about it? What made you decide to run away?"

"It was something I overheard you say to Otto, when you first came to the house. He told you that I wasn't even a person, and through the window I heard you say so angry, 'What the hell is he, then, two orders of eggroll to go?' "

Lloyd couldn't help laughing; but Franklin was quite serious. There were tears in his eyes. "That was the first time that anybody had said that I was a person, and was angry with Otto because he tried to say that I wasn't."

Lloyd said, "All right, eggroll. Time to get some sleep."

"You know something?" said Franklin. "I never knew my father, although Helmwige showed me some pictures they took in New Orleans when they came to America after the war. I never knew my mother either. Otto had to choose somebody. I don't know who, or how."

"Your father wasn't around when you were young?"

Franklin shook his head. "Nor my mother neither. I never even saw a picture of my mother."

There was nothing that Lloyd could say. He was already aware that Otto was completely cold-blooded, and that he would do anything to anyone in order to achieve the birth of his master race; but somehow the way in which he had arranged for Franklin's conception and upbringing—not because *he* had wanted to, but because the Führer had decreed it—was beyond the edge of any kind of human cruelty that Lloyd could think of. It was almost unbearable for him to think of Franklin's childhood years—nameless, unloved, beaten, and sexually abused. The fact that he had somehow managed to survive with his sanity intact was a miracle deserving of anybody's prayers, even Tony Express's.

Franklin said, "You know what I used to pretend? You won't laugh, will you?"

"Of course not. Tell me."

"I used to pretend that the mom and dad in *Flicka* were my real parents. Whenever they came on TV, I used to turn down the sound and talk to them."

Lloyd laid his hand on Franklin's shoulder. "A whole lot of kids do the same kind of thing, Franklin. A whole lot of adults, too." He was suddenly taken back to his own childhood, lying on his stomach on the worn-out brown rug in front of the black and white television watching Duncan Renaldo cantering across the screen. *Adios, amigos, see you soon!*

He closed Franklin's door and returned to the living room. Some old late-night movie was playing, and he switched it off. Kathleen was already in the bedroom: the door was ajar and the light was on. There was a smell of Badedas shower gel, too. He went to the bedroom door and knocked.

"You want a nightcap?" he asked her.

"Sure. You can come on in, if you want to."

Hesitantly he edged open the door, and then stepped inside. The bedcovers were folded back, the pillows plumped up. Kathleen was standing in front of the bathroom basin, washing her pantyhose. She was wearing a man's striped shirt that she had found in Dan Tabares's closet.

Lloyd said, "This reminds me of an old Clark Gable movie. You're sure you don't mind if we sleep together?"

She hung up her pantyhose on a wire coathanger and came into the bedroom. "That's very gentlemanly of you. But aren't you being a little arrogant?"

"What do you mean?"

"Aren't you being a little arrogant in assuming that I might even *think* of doing anything but sleeping?"

Lloyd sat down on the end of the bed and pried off his shoes. "I'm sorry. I didn't mean it to come out that way. I guess I'm just exhausted."

He went through to the tiny bathroom and stepped into the pink-tiled shower stall. He turned on the faucet and stood for a long time letting the water gush straight into his face. He hoped to God that he had the strength to carry this thing through, and that he would understand how to deal with Otto and Helmwige when the time came.

Even more than that, he hoped that he would understand how to deal with Celia.

He dried himself and dressed in voluminous white shorts and a T-shirt that said Mothers and Fathers Italian Association. By the time he came back into the bedroom with his mouth tasting of Crest, Kathleen was already in bed, reading an ancient copy of *Reader's Digest*. He climbed in beside her. She felt warm and he was surprised how good it was to lie next to a woman again.

"Anything good?" he asked her, nodding toward the magazine.

She shook her head. "The usual. How the pilot of a crashed plane crawled nine miles with his leg torn off."

He rested his head on the pillow and looked at her closely. "Are you a tough lady or is that just the impression you're trying to give me?"

She closed the *Digest* and dropped it onto the floor. "I lived for twelve years with a man I wasn't sure I loved, and then I lost him. I've cried about it, for sure, although I'm not sure why. Maybe I've been crying for me, rather than him. All those years that could have been better, and weren't. Maybe it took Mike's death to wake me up."

Lloyd said, "You've got Tom."

Kathleen nodded. "Yes, you're right, and I wouldn't give up Tom for anything. But if I'd never met Mike, Tom would never have been born. I would have had some other child, by somebody else."

"I don't know whether you can think like that," Lloyd replied.

"Well, maybe not," she said, her finger tracing invisible patterns on the quilt. "But everybody's entitled to some 'might-have-beens,' don't you think so?"

"I guess."

Lloyd tugged the light-cord, and the bedroom was swallowed in darkness. Kathleen leaned over him and kissed his cheek and said, "Sleep well." He was very conscious of the weight and warmth of her breast inside the shirt she was wearing, but he didn't want to think about getting involved with her. Not now, not with this crisis on his hands.

"Good night," he told her, and turned over.

He lay awake for a long time, listening to Kathleen breathing next to him and the nearby churning of the surf. He kept thinking of that rhyme that Tony Express had repeated,

> O Ma Rainey
> Li'l and low,
> Sing us 'bout de hard luck
> Roun' our do';
> Sing us 'bout de lonesome road
> We mus' go.

He slept. He dreamed that Celia was standing watching him, with fire pouring from her eyes and mouth. He dreamed that Celia was sliding closer. He dreamed that she was bending over him. He dreamed that she was kissing his cheek.

He opened his eyes and found that she was.

"Lloyd?" she whispered.

He lay absolutely still, sweat-soaked, stiff with terror.

"Lloyd, it's me, Celia."

Still he found himself unable to move, unable to speak. His mind was clamped tight like a vise that wouldn't unlock; his teeth were immovably clenched.

"You have to come back with us, Lloyd. This is much too important. It's only one more day now till the solstice . . . things mustn't go wrong."

Kathleen murmured and shifted in her sleep. Celia glanced at her behind her impenetrable dark glasses, and said, "Unfaithful so soon?"

Lloyd lifted himself up on one elbow, and whispered back at her, "Back off, all right? Stand away from me. Let's talk about this next door."

He climbed out of bed as carefully as he could, and then quietly opened the bedroom door and went through to the living room, with Celia following close behind him. He could smell that hot metallic smell, and it frightened him. He closed the bedroom door so that Kathleen wouldn't be disturbed.

"*Guten Abend,*" said a dry voice, as he switched on the overhead light. Otto was sitting in one of the bamboo armchairs, with his legs crossed, his face shadowed by his hat. "*Sein T-shirt ist sehr amüsant.*"

"How did you find us?" Lloyd asked him. "Why the hell can't you leave us alone?"

"Some fellow called Slominsky told us where you were," Otto remarked, picking with his fingernails at the fraying raffia that held his chair together. "He was *most* cooperative."

"Waldo? *Waldo* told you where we were? I can't believe that!"

Otto shrugged. "It took a little persuasion. But—as I say—he was most cooperative."

"Jesus Christ, if you've hurt Waldo—I'll see you in hell!"

"My dear Mr. Denman, you will probably see me in hell in any event."

"Celia," asked Lloyd. "Is Waldo okay?"

Celia nodded. "Waldo's fine, darling. Just fine."

"Are they all here?" Otto wanted to know. "Mrs. Kerwin? Mengele's creature?"

"You're taking us back to Rancho Santa Fe?"

"I have no choice, Mr. Denman. Tomorrow evening we are holding the grand Transformation at Civic Theater. You cannot be allowed to jeopardize my greatest moment—the moment for which I have prepared for so many years."

Lloyd said, "What time do you have?"

"Three minutes after three," Otto replied. "Why do you ask?"

"It's just that—okay, we'll come back to Rancho Santa Fe. We don't really have any alternative, do we? It's either that or having ourselves burned alive."

"You're beginning to grasp the situation rather well," Otto smiled.

"Just let these people have a few hours' sleep," pleaded Lloyd. "They've been under all kinds of stress. Why don't you have a drink? I'll make some coffee if you like. We'll leave promptly at eight o'clock, how's that? But don't get them up now, especially the kid."

Otto thought about that, and then said, "Very well. I have no particular objection. I could use a little sleep myself. Perhaps you and your bride-to-be can use the time to become reacquainted. After all, the future will soon be yours, *nicht wahr?*"

He reached down and unlaced his large black welted shoes. Then he propped both of his stockinged feet onto the coffee table. His socks were made of thin gray wool, covered with pills. They looked as if he had been hand-washing them in hotel basins since the war. He interlaced his fingers, and closed his eyes.

Lloyd looked at Celia, in her black turban and her dark glasses and her black raincoat. "Is that it?" he asked her. "He's asleep?"

"He'll sleep till seven now," she told him. "He goes to sleep almost instantly, and he sleeps very deeply. No dreams. He says it's something to do with what happened to him during the war."

"Let's go through to the kitchen," Lloyd suggested. Celia walked in front of him, but he made sure that he kept his distance. He couldn't bear the strange grayness of her skin.

"Do you want a drink?" he asked her. "*Can* you drink?"

She took a glass from the drainer beside the sink and poured herself a glass of water. She swallowed a mouthful, and left her mouth open, watching him with what looked like a mocking expression. He heard the water boil sharply, inside her stomach. Steam rose out of her mouth and nose.

Lloyd's hand was shaking as he splashed out a large glassful of whiskey. "I wish you'd told me what you were going to do," he told her. "Maybe I could have coped with it better. Maybe I could have understood it."

"I'm sorry, Lloyd," she said. "I truly am. But I was never the kind of woman who could give up without a fight. And when Otto promised me that I would live forever . . . never sick, never growing old . . . well, I'd already begun to feel the effects of multiple sclerosis. I'd seen what happened to Jacqueline DuPré. I didn't want the same thing to happen to me."

"And you think this is better, being a Salamander? You think this is really *you?*"

"It's my soul, Lloyd. It's my spirit. I'm still Celia. I still love you. Inside of me, I'm just the same as I always was."

Lloyd vigorously shook his head. "The Celia that I knew wasn't interested in immortality or master races or shriveled old Germans who eat bugs."

"Lloyd—it's not like that! You should have heard Otto, the first time he talked to me! I was terrified of what was happening to me, and he gave me such hope! All of a sudden, I had a future;

and not just one future, but a thousand futures, and a thousand futures that I could share with you!"

Lloyd swallowed whiskey. "Celia—*I'm* not going to live forever. I don't even *want* to live forever. I want to get married and run a successful restaurant and have a couple of kids and grow old gracefully. . . . That's what I want to do. I don't want to burn myself alive so that I turn into some kind of Nazi nightmare."

"You don't have to live forever, if you don't want to," said Celia. "But you can still have a child. On the night of the Transformation, when all the songs are sung and all the rituals have been recited, I'll be flesh again, like Helmwige. There's no reason why you and I can't live together just the way we always planned it."

Lloyd let out a sarcastic grunt. "Oh, yes, for sure . . . with me growing steadily older and you staying young. With you capable of burning the living shit out of me every time I make you angry. I can see it now!"

"Lloyd, darling . . . it wouldn't have to be like that at all."

"So what *would* it be like? And apart from anything else, what would our children be like? Half immortal and half mortal? And if so, which half?"

"Ah . . . that's the whole point," said Celia. "The true master race will eventually be made up of the children of people like me—people who have been burned and Transformed—and their human lovers. Those children will have all the properties of immortality and humanity, combined. Don't you see, that's why Otto didn't want to let you go before the solstice. . . . He wants us to have a child. . . . *I* want us to have a child . . . one of the first of the new everlasting order. Ancient magic, modern flesh. The combination will be irresistible, Lloyd."

"Well, heil Hitler," Lloyd told her.

"Lloyd—you don't understand. A child of ours could be almost holy! A beautiful magical creature who could rule the whole world!"

"Like the Hitler Youth were beautiful magical creatures who were going to rule the whole world? What the hell did Otto do to you, Celia?"

"He showed me the future!" Celia retorted. "He showed me this rotten, diseased, crime-ridden, fear-ridden world for what it is, and he showed me the future!"

"Oh, did he?" Lloyd countered. "Well, there's one thing he

predicted wrong, and that was that you and I would ever have a child. Because if you think I'm going to touch you ever again, you're very mistaken, my lady. I wouldn't touch you again if you were the last woman left on the whole goddamn planet!"

Celia was quiet for a moment. She lowered her head, as if she were thinking, but of course she had no eyes to give her away.

"I was hoping I could persuade you," she said, at last, with a catch in her throat that made her sound much more like the Celia he had known before.

Lloyd said, "It's nothing personal, believe me. It's just that I don't happen to believe in master races. And I don't believe that people should live forever, either. What value can your life possibly have, if you're never at risk of losing it?"

"Maybe, when the Transformation's done, you'll think differently."

"I doubt it."

"You'll come, though, won't you?"

"Do I have any choice?"

"We're holding it at Civic Theater. One thousand and one specially invited guests. Music by the San Diego Opera Company."

Lloyd frowned at her. "You have a thousand guests and music by the opera company? How the hell did you arrange that? The opera company's convinced that you're dead and gone."

"It wasn't difficult," said Celia. "About six months ago I asked Don Abrams the production supervisor to let me mount an evening of Wagnerian-style opera—operas written by other composers as a tribute to Wagner. I played him some of the music from *Junius*, and of course he agreed. It's magnificent, one of Wagner's most dramatic operas ever—his masterpiece! And even more persuasive, I was even able to fix up a Gramma Fisher Foundation grant to fund it.

"But of course the opera company is still completely unaware that they're going to be singing an actual lost opera by Wagner himself. The only people who *will* be aware of it will be Otto and Helmwige and all of us Salamanders, who will come on stage at the climax of the opera, when the company sings the Transformation chant.

"At the climactic note of that chant, we will all be transformed into flesh, and the master race will at last be born. Think of it!"

"And what will your thousand and one invited guests do then? Stand up and sing the Horst Wessel song?"

"Lloyd, my darling," Celia pleaded. "This isn't Nazi Germany in the 1930s. This is California, today. Otto knows that. He's not trying to recreate the Third Reich, nothing like that. He just wants to see the world put into the hands of people who have the strength and the ability to run it as it should be run. He wants to see an end to suffering and cruelty and drug addiction and poverty."

Lloyd poured himself another drink. "God almighty. If only Wagner had known what he was doing."

"But Wagner did know."

Lloyd dragged over a bar stool, and sat down. "Otto was sure that he *didn't*."

Celia shook her head. "He didn't know at first. But he found out. When he was in Venice, he played the Fire Ritual from *Junius* to a young music student called Guido Castelnuovo who was helping him to write the libretto. Two days later Castelnuovo set fire to his own clothes and killed himself. Wagner assumed that Castelnuovo was dead, and of course he was very upset. But about a week later, the student reappeared at dawn in St. Mark's Square, when Wagner was out walking. He was a Salamander, just like me. He had stolen one of Wagner's amulets before he set fire to himself. He begged Wagner to play the Transformation music for him, in order to turn him into immortal flesh."

"And did Wagner oblige?"

Celia said, "Of course—and it worked. But Wagner was so horrified by what had happened that he threw away all the remaining amulets and he sought out a famous Jesuit priest called Father Xavier Montini, who was an expert on pagan rituals, and told him all about it. Father Montini told Wagner that the only way in which he could put Guido Castelnuovo to rest was to write a Hymn of Atonement.

"This hymn had to include Wagner's own prayer for forgiveness, as well as the famous runic chant which the Pope had sent to St. Augustine in Britain in A.D. 597. St. Augustine had needed it to destroy the immortal followers of a bloodthirsty pagan called Ethelfrid.

"So that's what Wagner did—he wrote a Hymn of Atonement. Then he invited Guido Castelnuovo to his apartments in Venice, and played it to him. Nobody will ever know what happened that night, but at the end of it, one room was found fiercely burned, and Wagner was found dead of a heart attack."

"How do you know all this?" Lloyd asked Celia, searchingly.

Celia gave a thin, gray-lipped smile. "It was all in Father Montini's diaries and notebooks, in the Boston University library, of all places. They were sent there with a whole heap of other nineteenth-century Jesuit literature in 1924."

"Nineteen twenty-four? So when Otto was searching for *Junius* during the war, he could never have found them?"

"Of course not."

Lloyd narrowed his eyes. "So Otto doesn't *know* about this Hymn of Atonement?"

"Oh, he knows about it, all right," said Celia, "but he doesn't realize I have it. It was all there, where Father Montini had hidden it, mixed in with all the rest of the opera."

Celia glanced quickly toward the living-room door, but they both knew that Otto would still be deeply asleep, dreaming of nothing at all.

"Why didn't you tell him about it?" asked Lloyd; and for one instant he thought he sensed a flash of the old Celia—the Celia he had once loved. Headstrong, clever, and determined.

"I didn't tell him because I knew what he would do. He would take it as a threat to the master race, and he would burn it. But I worship Wagner. To me, you know, it would be absolutely inexcusable to burn the only copy of a Wagner hymn, written in the master's own hand. That would be like burning the Mona Lisa."

"So you hid it at home in your piano?" said Lloyd. "And that's what you came looking for, the night you set fire to yourself?"

Celia said, "No . . . originally I came looking for my salamander talisman. I'd lost it; I didn't know where. Otto insisted that I had to have it for the Transformation ceremony. I thought I might have dropped the talisman inside the piano when I was hiding the manuscript there."

Lloyd was silent for a long time.

"What's wrong?" asked Celia.

"For Chrissake, tell me what's *right*."

"The world is going to be a better place to live in, Lloyd. Believe me."

"Did you burn Sylvia?" he asked her.

Celia looked away. "No, I didn't burn Sylvia."

"Sylvia had the hymn. You wanted it back. Who else could have burned her?"

"I went to get it and she gave it to me. I don't know what happened to her afterwards!"

But Lloyd wouldn't let her get away with that. "You burned her, Celia," he repeated. "You personally cremated her. Maybe Otto was responsible for the others, but if Otto still doesn't know that you have the hymn, then Sylvia's burning must have been down to you."

Celia was oddly flustered. She spoke in a quick, sideways manner, like Joan Crawford denying that she had ever punished her children. "Lloyd, I swear—things haven't been easy. Burning yourself, it isn't easy. Coming out of your body as nothing but smoke and soul, do you have any idea what that's *like?* I felt as if I were walking into a blast furnace. Pain, panic, terrible self-doubt. Thinking to myself, Why did I do it? Why?"

"Celia," said Lloyd, "when this Transformation ceremony is over, and just as soon as Otto will let me, I'm walking. I don't want to hear any more about your master race; I don't want to hear any more about your immortality. As far as I'm concerned, we were finished the moment you struck that match and set fire to yourself. In fact, we were finished the first day you went to Otto for help, and not to me. Talk about trust—Jesus! Talk about truthfulness!"

"Could you have cured me of multiple sclerosis?"

"Of course I damn well couldn't."

Celia removed her dark glasses and revealed eye sockets as black as memories, as black as the insides of cameras. "You could join me, you know. It would be wonderful if you could join me."

"I've told you, Celia. I don't want to live forever. I'm not that goddamn proud. I'm not that goddamn *important.* You know, to the general Scheme of Things."

"Many hundreds of people will."

"Not your invited audience?"

"Of course."

"You're going to persuade a thousand people to set fire to themselves? Jesus, Celia, I thought this was all pretty farfetched, but now you're talking like a cloud-jockey."

"We don't expect them to set fire to themselves," said Celia. "Recruiting so many Salamanders would take far too long. But we can make the decision for them. We shall have the music, and of course we shall have the bowl, which will act as a collective talisman, and we will burn them—whether they choose to burn or not."

"You're going to burn a thousand people? A *thousand?* Just like Auschwitz? Just like Belsen?"

Celia shook her head. "No, not Belsen. It's the golden age, at last. That's what it is."

"And all of these people are going to be Salamanders, just like you?"

"In a way. Not in *quite* the same way. Because we'll be burning them all together, as a crowd, and because they will be sharing just one talisman between them, they will have no independent will. They will be our army, our servants; our drones. The Salamanders who fight for us, the Salamanders who serve us. Every race has to have its servants, Lloyd; even the greatest and the fairest."

"I don't believe what I'm hearing," said Lloyd. "And I don't believe that I'm hearing you say it. Christ almighty."

"Lloyd—we chose the audience very carefully. If they had been given a choice, believe me, most of them would have chosen to become Salamanders. Otto chose them personally, you know. It took him years. Each one had to be checked and cross-filed. It took so long that some of them had died before we could send out the invitations."

"So who's coming?"

Celia made a face. "The faithful, I guess. The old Germans; the new young rich. The right-wing intellectuals. The scientists. Half of UC San Diego. Some from the Scripps Institute. Anybody intelligent and good-looking and progressive."

"Any Jews?"

"Lloyd!" smiled Celia, in disbelief. "We won't have enough room for *everybody!*"

Lloyd finished his drink, and set down his glass on the drainer with exaggerated care. "I think that's what they said the last time they tried to create a master race."

They were still talking when the kitchen door opened and Franklin appeared, tucking his shirttails into his jeans, and blinking in the light. "What's going on?" he asked. "I heard voices."

Celia stepped out from behind the refrigerator with a smile

on her face. "Hello, you've woken up? That's a good boy. We're all going back to Rancho Santa Fe in just a while."

"His name's Franklin," said Lloyd.

Celia frowned at him. "What?"

"His name's Franklin. That's what we've named him. Franklin Free."

"Well . . . not free just yet, I'm afraid," Celia told him. "Not until Otto decides it."

Franklin's face fell. "Lloyd, I don't want to go back. Please don't make me go back, Lloyd."

Lloyd said, "Listen, Franklin, it's all right. Everything's going to work out fine. Why don't you go get your little doll? You understand me? Go get your little doll, and then we can all think about leaving."

Franklin didn't appear to understand at first, but then he left the kitchen and went back toward the bedrooms, closing the door behind him.

"Poor mutt," Celia remarked. "I guess he *means* well."

"Yes, I guess he does," Lloyd agreed, trying not to sound too sharp.

They waited for a minute or two, and then they heard soft shuffling footsteps coming back toward the kitchen. They stopped right outside the door, and for a long moment there was silence. Celia stepped back in uncertainty. "Why doesn't he just come in?" she asked.

"Maybe he wants to make a dramatic entrance," said Lloyd.

But the door eased open very slowly, very quietly. Franklin stepped back into the kitchen, and this time he was carrying Tony Express on his back, white of eye and grinning with sleep, brandishing the "little doll"—the shaggy, bead-decorated sun-dance doll, with its tiny cross face and its tattered fur hangings.

Celia stared at Franklin and Tony Express for what seemed like endless seconds. Then, button by button, she opened her raincoat; she paused, and let it slide to the floor, so that she was confronting the two of them completely nude, her grayish skin already beginning to darken and to rise in temperature. Smoke rose flatly from her shoulders.

"For God's sake, be careful," Lloyd warned Franklin. "Don't let her touch you!"

The kitchen was filled with the nostril-burning smell of intense metallic heat. Celia stalked toward Franklin and Tony Express, trailing one hand along the kitchen counter, and where she trailed it, she left a deeply burned furrow, and the acrid smoke of plastic laminate and chipboard.

Tony Express raised the sun-dance doll; but Lloyd said, "Back off, Franklin. Back off. She'll cremate you alive!"

Celia whipped her head around and stared at him, grinning. She plucked off her dark glasses and then he saw her for what she really was: a creature of smoke and fire. Both open eye sockets flared with orange flame, like blowtorches, and her grin seethed with sparks.

21

But Tony Express, out of all of them, was unafraid. Tony Express couldn't see Celia, although he could hear her, and feel her heat, and smell the smoke of melting Formica. He sat piggy-back on Franklin's broad shoulders, and lifted his sun-dance doll higher still, and softly shook it.

"*Weksa-dek!*" he breathed. Quietly, insistently, as if he were coaxing a child. "*Weksa-dek!*" Again he shook the doll, and it rattled and rattled, bones and beads.

Celia began to move toward him, her arm half-raised, but then she hesitated. Flames still funneled out of her eyes, and rainbows of coppery heat still crawled across her bare back, but much more slowly now.

Tony Express shook his doll yet again and began to build up a strange soft rhythm, so quiet that Lloyd could scarcely hear it. It reminded him of the panting breath of an animal, a dog or a wolf, something that comes hurrying after you in the night. "*Weksit-patesk! Weksit-patesk! Na! Na! Weksit-patesk!*"

At last Celia stood completely still, and even from three or four feet away, Lloyd could feel that she was cooling. Tony Express slid down from Franklin's back and approached her, and laid his hand on her bare breast.

"See, she's cold now. Easy."

"What the hell did you do? Some kind of Pechanga magic?"

"Algonquin, as a matter of fact. Their stuff is older, much more in tune with the Norse magic, know what I mean? Like the

Norse people lived in America years before Christ. You know '*Weksa-dek*' is Algonquin for 'It's getting hotter'—and the Norse for 'It's getting hotter' is '*Vaeckser hedt.*' You know, like, 'It's waxing hot.' Everybody in the whole damn Western world speaks the same language."

Lloyd walked around Celia slowly, touched her shoulder. She was quite cool, and she didn't seem to react at all.

"Did you hypnotize her, too?"

Tony Express groped for Franklin's hand. "I did the same to her as I did to those cops. Lowered her vital what's-their-names, so that's she living at about a hundredth of the normal speed. As far as she's concerned, we're moving around this kitchen so fast now that she can't even see us."

"What about Otto?" asked Lloyd.

"Who's Otto?"

"Otto's the Junius man. The one who burned the bus. He's sitting in the next room asleep. Least, I *hope* he's asleep."

"Is he hot, like this one?"

"No," said Lloyd. "He's mortal. But he can start fires, just by thinking about them. He's pretty damn dangerous. Look what he did to my hands."

"He can set fire to things just by *thinking* about them?"

"That's right."

"Then maybe we can make him think about something else, man, apart from us."

"I'm not too sure what you mean."

Tony Express squeezed Franklin's hand and said, "Go see if Otto's still asleep, would you, Franklin?"

Franklin looked anxiously across at Lloyd, as if to say, *What's going to happen if Otto's awake, and he orders me to stay where I am, and I can't disobey him?* But Lloyd nodded and said, "Go ahead, Franklin, you'll be okay. You're Franklin, right?"

"Sure, I'm Franklin."

He circled around Celia, glancing at her from time to time as he did so, obviously afraid that she was going to spring back to life, and set fire to him. As a matter of fact, Lloyd could actually see Celia moving, as gradually as the hour hand on a clock, but her movement was so long-drawn-out that it would have taken her the rest of the day to cross the kitchen floor.

Franklin pushed the door open a little way so that he could see into the living room. "He's there," he reported back hoarsely. "He's still asleep."

"Men with no mothers sleep like the dead," Tony Express remarked. When Lloyd raised an eyebrow in response, he said, "Old Pechanga saying, man. Don't ask *me* what it means."

Lloyd said, "We're going to have to get out of here, now that Otto's found us. They're holding the Transformation ceremony at Civic Theater tomorrow evening. It sounds like Otto's got a whole lot of arranging to do, so it should be pretty easy to stay out of his way. First of all I need to get back to Escondido."

"Escondido?" asked Tony Express. "Why d'you have to get back to Escondido?"

Lloyd looked at Celia. Her metabolic rate may have been reduced to that of a turtle, but he still preferred not to say anything about Wagner's Hymn of Atonement right in front of her. "I'll tell you later," he answered. "Meanwhile, let's get our stuff together and get the hell out of here."

He took hold of Franklin's arm and indicated to him in pantomime that he should go pack up his clothes, and Tony Express's clothes, too. Then he stepped quietly into the living room and crossed the rug on tiptoe, right past the sleeping Otto.

Otto's eyes were deeply sunken, his mouth was slightly open, and he was breathing so quietly that he might just as well have been dead. Only the slightest tic in the muscle of his left hand indicated that he was still alive. Lloyd passed within six inches of him, grimacing with the effort of keeping so quiet.

He went into the bedroom. In spite of all the noise they had been making in the kitchen, Kathleen was still asleep. She must have been totally exhausted by everything that had happened to her. Lloyd sat on the bed beside her and shook her shoulder.

"Kathleen? Kathleen? Wake up; we have to get out of here."

She stirred, then tangled her fingers into her hair, and turned over.

"Kathleen, come on, we have to go."

At last she sat up. "What time is it?" she asked, blurrily.

"Nearly dawn. Otto's found us; he's here; we have to leave."

"He's here?"

"He's asleep, but I don't know for how long."

Kathleen climbed out of bed, and while Lloyd kept an eye on the door, she dressed. "I didn't hear a thing," she admitted. "I must have been completely out of it. I was dreaming about Mike again."

"Quick as you can," Lloyd urged her.

As soon as she was ready, they crept out of the bedroom and

back across the living room. Otto remained where he was, silently breathing. It was only when they had reached the kitchen door that he opened his eyes and said in that husk-dry voice of his, "You're not leaving, Mr. Denman?"

Lloyd gritted his teeth. *Shit,* he thought. *Nearly made it, and now the bastard's woken up.* He pushed Kathleen ahead of him into the kitchen and indicated wildly that she should call Tony Express.

He heard Kathleen say *"Ah!"* as she encountered Celia in the kitchen, but then there was silence.

Lloyd turned back to Otto, chafing his hands together, and said, "We were getting ourselves packed and ready to go back to Rancho Santa Fe, that's all."

"And are you ready now?"

"Yes, well, pretty much."

Otto gave himself an almost imperceptible stretch, and Lloyd heard the cracking of vertebrae. Then Otto stood up, and replaced his hat, and stood looking at Lloyd with an expression that Lloyd found impossible to interpret. It was partly amusement, partly cruelty, partly the tiredness of the postwar years. After the fall of Berlin, the rest of the twentieth century, for Otto at least, had been one long anticlimax. Only tomorrow's Transformation could possibly redeem it. Only the re-establishment of the master race.

He said, distractedly, "We'd better think of leaving, then. Do you have any food here? You'd better take that, too."

Lloyd said, "Celia told me what you plan to do tomorrow . . . all about the Transformation."

"Oh, yes? And what was your reaction to *that,* Mr. Denman?"

"I, uh—well, you know how I felt at first. But I think I begin to see the logic of it now. You know, the master race, all of that. I didn't think too much of it to begin with. I guess I thought you were trying to bring back Nazi Germany. But Celia explained that you weren't." He hesitated, and shrugged. "And, uh—she told me that we could still have a child. Still live together, just like we planned. It sounds . . . well, it sounds attractive. Magical, almost."

Otto listened to this fastidiously. Then he said, "You're trying to tell me, then, that you have changed your mind? That you will be helpful, rather than obstructive?"

"I guess that's the size of it, yes." He looked quickly over his shoulder. *Where the hell are you, Tony? We have to get out of here!*

Otto tugged his fingers so that his knuckles popped. "It will be the greatest occasion in modern history. The very creation of a new race of demigods! Men and women at whose feet you will be glad to fall."

"Oh, sure thing," said Lloyd; and at that moment the kitchen door opened and Tony Express stepped in, a slight misstep to the left, holding up his sun-dance doll, and shaking it.

"*Na! Na!*" Tony Express screamed out.

"This is the boy?" asked Otto, calmly.

"Er, yes," said Lloyd. "He's kind of—ebullient, I'd guess you'd call it."

"He's blind."

"Yes, he's blind. He's also an Indian. His parents called him Child-Who-Looked-at-the-Sun. He's okay. Very well-meaning."

Tony Express came slowly forward on the softest of soles. He held the sun-dance doll up to Otto's face and shook it very, very gently, so that it sounded flat and threatening like a rattlesnake under a rock.

"You're the one, man," he declared.

"I'm *which* one?" Otto asked Lloyd. He seemed to be unable to address himself to Tony Express directly, as if his blindness made him deaf and mentally defective, too. "What is he talking about?"

"You were the one who torched the bus, man, out in Anza-Borrego."

"How does he think he knows such a thing?" asked Otto, with a smile. "He has no eyes."

"I can recognize voices, man," Tony Express told him. "And I can recognize yours. '*Junius!*' That's what you said! '*Junius!*' "

"Well . . . I hope you think this will do you some good," Otto replied.

"Good testimony, in a court of law, man," Tony Express suggested.

"I don't think so," said Otto. He was growing irritable now. "Let's get out of this place, now we've all had our sleep, and get back to Paseo Delicias."

Tony Express shook his sun-dance doll. "No, Otto," he said, and his voice sounded peculiarly sweet and high, almost feminine. "*We're* going, but *you're* staying."

"Enough of this nonsense!" Otto snapped at him. "You will all get into the sedan, now, and drive to Rancho Santa Fe. Celia and I will follow in the sports car."

"Otto . . . not a second time," Tony Express told him, in that clear girlish voice. He shook his sun-dance doll once, twice, three times.

Right in front of Otto, the air began to curdle and eddy, as if it were water. Then gradually a figure began to take shape: dim and shadowy at first, but gradually clearer. Lloyd stared at it and a thrill of fright scuttled right up the back of his neck. It was a young girl, no more than fifteen or sixteen, with long shining blond hair. She was standing between Otto and Tony Express with her head bowed. She wore a dark pinafore dress with a white smock over it, and short white socks, and black lace-up boots.

"Don't leave me again, Otto," Tony Express repeated, and this time it sounded as if he were talking in stereo, two voices overlapping.

Otto stared at the apparition of the girl in fascination and shock. He took off his hat and leaned forward, so that he could see her better.

"Gretchen?" he trembled. "Is that really Gretchen?"

"Don't leave me again, Otto," the girl pleaded, although she still wouldn't lift her head so that Otto could see her face. "You hurt me so much the last time . . . but the worst hurt was when you left me."

Otto stroked her hair, over and over, and even though it was almost invisible, it built up static electricity, and rose softly crackling into the palm of his hand. "Gretchen, I had to leave you. . . . How could I have taken you with me, when you were dead?"

"I hated that ditch," Gretchen whined. "It was so cold, and wet, and dark; and I was all tied up with wire. Why did you leave me, Otto?"

Tony Express took one step back, then another, and then nudged Lloyd's elbow. Lloyd was so enthralled by the apparition that Tony Express had conjured up that he was reluctant to leave, but Tony Express hissed at him, *"Go! Go! This won't last much longer!"*

"Oh, Otto, why did you hurt me so much?" Gretchen kept on whining.

"Little one . . . you were so beautiful," Otto told her, his voice cracking with dryness. "I had to have you; I had to take everything that you had to offer. Even in that ditch when you were dead, white skin smeared with black mud—even in that ditch you were beautiful. I knelt in that ditch and I didn't care about my clothes and I took you one last time."

"I honored you, Otto," Gretchen replied, as Lloyd and Tony Express slipped out into the kitchen and softly closed the door behind them. "I respected you, and worshiped you. To me you were more like a knight from the days of old than a real man."

Otto bent forward and kissed her hand. "You were always so sweet, my little Gretchen. You could not have died better."

"Creep," said Gretchen.

Otto thought he had misheard her. He lifted his head and said, "What? What did you say?"

"I said creep rat fink A-hole, that's what I said."

Gretchen lifted her one stiffened middle finger at him, and then raised her face so that he could see it. Her silky blond hair fell back and there was the blind black grinning expression of Tony Express.

Otto stood very still and rigid. So! *Die Zauberei!* He had never realized that America was a land of sorcerers, too! And what kind of magic was this—that the girl on whom he had inflicted the cruelest acts of his entire life could be materialized in front of his eyes—could *speak* to him, accuse him directly of everything that he had done? He had left Gretchen in that ditch near Wuppertal in the winter of 1943, and nobody else had known about it except him.

"*Got you worried, man?*" Gretchen asked him, in Tony Express's voice.

Otto snarled, his thin lips dragging themselves back across his teeth. He lifted both hands to his head, and stared at this mocking apparition of Gretchen in rising fury. "Nobody does this to me! *Nobody!* Ever!"

There was a deafening burst of incandescent flame, and the apparition exploded in front of Otto's eyes. But instantly he screamed, and slammed the heels of his hands against his temples, and dropped to the rug in agony. The sun-dance doll had drawn the ghost of Gretchen out of his own memory, and all that he had succeeded in burning was his own memory cells. In fact, he had cauterized his recollection of her altogether, so that he would never be able to remember her again.

He lay on the floor, folded up like a storm-broken umbrella, shaking. *Gott in Himmel,* what had happened to him? He knew that it was something huge and dramatic, but he couldn't think for a moment what it was. Somebody had laughed at him. Somebody had mocked him.

"Celia!" he called out. He climbed onto his knees. "Celia, *wo bist du,* Celia?"

He called again and again, but there was no reply. Eventually he managed to drag himself to his feet and shuffle toward the kitchen, holding onto the furniture for support. He felt as if he had been hit in the head with the back end of an ax; and the light of dawn straining through the venetian blinds in the kitchen made his eyes water.

Celia was standing only a quarter-inch further from the spot where Tony Express had first suspended her metabolism. Otto walked up to her, and stared directly into her face, and said, "Celia, *was ist los?* What have they done to you? Why don't you move? Why don't you speak?"

But Celia remained practically motionless, her empty eye sockets wide in surprise, one arm lifted; a cold gray statue of a woman in a shabby oceanside kitchen.

Die Zauberei, Otto repeated to himself, in disgust. Indian tricks, hocus-pocus; men who were there and then they weren't there; shamans who turned themselves into eagles; tricks, mirrors. Sand that poured upwards, clouds that refused to rain. He had heard about it but he had never taken it seriously. He didn't take it seriously now. The day of the Transformation was almost here, and *then* the magicians of every culture would see who ruled the realms of the dead, as well as the realms of the living.

He was still standing in the middle of the kitchen with angrily clenched fists when he heard the tires of his Mercedes sedan squealing on the road outside. He ripped apart the slats of the venetian blinds in time to see Lloyd wildly U-turning, and driving back toward the main Pacific highway. He also saw that they had let the air out of the tires of his 380SL.

Angrily, he scooped handfuls of dead blowflies and moths from the windowsill, and crammed them into his mouth, swallowing most of them without chewing. He coughed on one large mouthful, and as he did so, Celia suddenly phased out of her slowed-down metabolic state and turned to stare at him.

Tony Express and his sun-dance doll must have driven away too far to influence her any longer.

"Otto?" she asked, bewildered. "Otto—what's wrong?"

Otto spat out flies so that they clung quivering with trails of saliva to his chin. Then he slapped Celia so hard across the face that he bruised his ring finger, and shouted out, *"Scheiss! Scheiss!"*

"Otto—" Celia quavered, picking up her fallen raincoat, and wrapping it around her.

"The first thing we do after the Transformation is that we hunt down every Indian in every reservation and we finish with them! *Versteh'?* We *finish* them!"

22

"Here," said Lloyd, with relief, lifting the envelope out of the door pocket of his BMW. "Wagner's Hymn of Atonement, courtesy the Rosecrans Street Copie Shoppe."

Kathleen took the pages and leafed through them carefully. "Do you really believe this can stop them?"

"Celia seemed to think so. And remember what Franklin overheard Otto saying to Helmwige . . . 'They can only be destroyed by Him.' I think Franklin probably misheard. Otto wasn't talking about *Him,* he meant the *Hymn.*"

"Well, I suppose if they can be *created* by a ritual chant, they can be destroyed by one," said Kathleen, although she sounded dubious.

"Of course the problem is having this properly scored and played," said Lloyd, as they walked back to the house. "Not only that, but having it played at exactly the right moment, after the Transformation."

"You must know some of the musicians at the opera," Kathleen suggested.

"For sure . . . but I don't know how many of them are members of Otto's jolly little study group . . . or which of them might give us away without realizing it." He checked his watch, and looked around Kathleen's house. "We won't be able to stay here too long, either . . . not without Otto or the cops catching up with us. We're not exactly the least conspicuous quartet of people I've ever seen. I mean we don't have that capability of melting into a crowd, do we?"

Kathleen opened the front door, and let them in. "Lucy!" she called. "Tom! We're back!"

There was no reply. Kathleen ran upstairs and checked the bedrooms, and then came down again. "They're not here. They must have gone over to my parents." She picked up the phone and punched out the number. Lloyd asked her, "You want some coffee?"

"I'd kill for some coffee."

"Franklin? Tony? How about some orange juice?"

"I'd sell my grandpa for a root beer," said Tony Express. "You don't realize how much you miss it till you don't have it."

Lloyd was scooping espresso into the coffee machine when Kathleen came into the kitchen looking anxious. "I've called my parents' house and there's no reply."

"Hey, don't let it worry you," Lloyd told her. "They probably went to the market, or out to the zoo."

"Weird day for the zoo."

Lloyd touched her shoulder. "We're living in weird times."

All the same, he started to feel a small sharp anxiety of his own when he called the Original Fish Depot and there was no reply from Waldo. It was a little too early, maybe; but when he called Waldo's home number, Waldo wasn't there, either. Oh, well. Maybe he was on his way to La Jolla, stuck in the rush-hour traffic on I-5; or maybe he was down at the Embarcadero, buying snapper.

They risked staying at Kathleen's house long enough to have a good breakfast of eggs and corned beef hash, although Tony Express wasn't too keen on corned beef hash because he said it reminded him of adobe.

Kathleen kept trying to call her parents, but still nobody answered.

"You don't think that anything's happened to them?" she asked.

"What could have happened? Your parents are old enough to go out without telling you, aren't they?"

But Kathleen remained worried and there was nothing he could do about it. And *he* remained worried because Waldo still didn't pick up the phone at the Original Fish Depot. He prayed that Celia and Otto hadn't taken their questioning too far.

"We'll take the BMW," Lloyd decided. "But I'll switch plates with your Camaro, Kathleen. FISHEE's a little too conspicuous. Franklin—do you want to do that for me?"

"There's a whole set of wrenches in the garage," said Kathleen. "Mike always kept his tools so tidy. Totally tidy guy, on the whole."

Although it was only twenty of eleven, Lloyd poured himself a medicinal whiskey. Then he went back to the phone and tried the restaurant again. This time, the phone was instantly picked up.

"Waldo?" he asked.

"Who is this?" a flat voice demanded.

"Lloyd Denman. I own the Fish Depot. I'm trying to get in touch with Waldo Slonimsky. Who are you? What's going on?"

"My name's Officer Tarrant, sir. I'm afraid Mr. Slonimsky was killed last night, burned in a fire."

Lloyd opened his mouth and then closed it again. So Celia had been lying when she had told him that she hadn't hurt Waldo. And she had probably been lying when she had sworn that she hadn't burned Sylvia Cuddy.

But Waldo, God damn it. He couldn't bear the thought of losing Waldo. Waldo had been so much more than a friend; he had been the last surviving member of a family who had sent him desperately and optimistically to America in the hope that he would carry on their name, long after *they* had all been burned and forgotten.

His eyes filled with tears. Even though officer Tarrant kept repeating, "Sir? Sir? Can you hear me, sir?" he couldn't speak anymore, and he put down the phone. He was going to kill Otto now. He was going to kill Helmwige. His feeling of revenge, already strong because of what Otto had done to Celia, now surged up inside him like a huge black tidal wave.

In the den, with his feet up on the magazine table while he listened to *The Real Ghostbusters* on television, Tony Express suddenly lifted his head. He had heard something, the softest of rattles. It was the sun-dance doll, which he had left propped up in the hall. The sun-dance doll, which was especially sensitive to men's revenge—*ask what revenge you want, and it will give it to you.*

Now why should the doll suddenly rattle? thought Tony Express. It only rattled if somebody came close to it who was so hungry for revenge that they could scarcely wait.

He stood up and groped his way to the den doorway. He heard footsteps.

"Who's that?" he asked.

"It's me, Lloyd," a choked-up voice replied.

Without hesitation, Tony Express said, "Waldo's dead."

"How'd you know that?"

"The doll can feel your revenge, man. And from the way you've been talking, there's only one person you care about enough to want to kill for."

He paused, and then he added, "I'm really sorry, man. I know he meant a lot to you."

"Well, yeah," said Lloyd, scarcely able to catch his breath.

But hardly had Lloyd told Kathleen what had happened, when Franklin came in from the garage, and Tony Express could tell from his quick, harsh breathing that he was seriously upset.

"Lloyd," he said, "can I talk to you?"

"If it's about the license plates, Franklin, don't bother. I've just this minute heard that Waldo died last night."

Franklin was confused. "Oh, no, that's terrible. Was it Otto, do you think?"

"Otto or Celia, one of the two. I don't know. Who cares? They're both as mad and as dangerous as each other."

"Lloyd—" Franklin began. He glanced with uncertainty at Kathleen.

"What is it? Come on, can't it wait until later?"

Franklin dumbly shook his head. "You'd better come see for yourself."

They went outside to the garage. Franklin had closed the automatic doors, but as they approached, he said, "You're sure you're ready for this?"

"Just open up, for Chrissake," said Lloyd.

He didn't know what he had expected, but he certainly hadn't expected a corpse. A black charred figure was sitting upright in the middle of the concrete floor. The figure was so comprehensively burned that it was impossible to tell whether it was a man or a woman; or even if it was an adult or a child. It was sickening, but what made it slightly less shocking was that it had no identity.

It could have been an artist's wooden figure, which somebody had perversely decided to char all over with a cigarette lighter.

Lloyd approached the body slowly, and then stood quite still in front of it.

"Who do you think it is?" Franklin asked him. "Look at this garage—there's black smoke all over everything."

Lloyd circled around the burned body and ran his finger across the roof of Kathleen's Camaro. Its elk-grain padded vinyl was sticky with black powdery ashes and human grease.

At that moment, Kathleen appeared around the corner. Lloyd had asked Tony Express to keep her away, but there wasn't much that a twelve-year-old blind boy could do to control a determined middle-aged mother who was worried about her only son.

"Kathleen—" Lloyd began, and tried to step in front of her.

"Oh my God," she said, her face as white as wax. "It isn't—?"

Lloyd took hold of her arms, but she quickly twisted herself free. "*Who* is it?" she said, in a breathless scream. "*Lloyd, who is it?*"

It was then that the draft through the garage toppled the figure's precarious sitting position, and it fell to the floor with a soft crunching sound. One charred arm broke free, revealing a thin discolored gold ring, set with diamonds.

Soundlessly, Kathleen pressed her hand to her face. She stood shaking for a moment, and then she almost collapsed, and between them Lloyd and Franklin had to help her back to the house.

"Lucy, oh my God, Lucy," she said, over and over again in a high-pitched hysterical voice. "Oh my God, Lucy."

In the hallway, the sun-dance doll rattled ominously as she passed it by.

Lloyd gave Kathleen a dose of the Valium that her doctor had prescribed after Mike had died, and put her to bed. She came downstairs three or four times, trembling and quivering, but in the end Franklin went upstairs with her, and sat beside her, and talked to her and stroked her forehead until she relaxed.

Lloyd poured himself another drink, and another root beer for Tony Express. Then he stood and stared out of the window for a long time, while Tony Express sat beside him, humming to himself.

"It must have been Helmwige," said Lloyd, at last.

"Sure," Tony Express agreed. "Celia and Otto went thataway to look for us; Helmwige came thisaway."

"God, that poor woman," said Lloyd. "None of this was anything to do with her. Nor was it anything to do with Waldo. God knows what's happened to Tom."

"As a matter of record, man, it wasn't actually nothing to do with *me*, neither," said Tony Express. "Not wishing to sound ungrateful or nothing."

"I'm sorry," said Lloyd. "I seem to have gotten all of these innocent people caught up in my own crusade."

"Don't worry about it, man," Tony Express told him. "My horoscope said that I was going to do something useful this month, for a change."

"John Dull Knife tells horoscopes?"

"No, man, the *San Diego Tribune.*"

Lloyd thought for a while, and then he said, "I don't know what the hell we're going to do. You were pretty damn good at holding off Otto and Celia this morning, but could you do the same at the opera tomorrow night? I mean, what's the extent of your strength?"

"Let's put it this way," said Tony Express. "I can't fight any Little Bighorn for you. The sun-dance doll can help you take personal revenge on somebody you hate real bad . . . like the way it slowed Celia down because she was threatening Franklin, and the way it used a spirit out of Otto's own mind—a spirit who really hated Otto—just to hold him off for a while.

"But I don't think I've got the power to *kill* anybody with a sun-dance doll. And I sure couldn't hold off a thousand people; maybe not even ten. The old Indian sorcery's gone, man. It came out of the ground and it came out of the sky and it came out of the water. Now the ground's all built on and the sky's all chopped up into pieces by airplanes and you sure wouldn't want to drink the water."

Lloyd picked up the Wagner libretto. "So what you're saying is . . . this is our only hope?"

"Wagner raised these Salamanders up, man. Only Wagner can send 'em back again."

"So how am I going to get it played? The only person I know who could have done it is dead."

"Who?"

"Sylvia Cuddy. She worked for the opera company with Celia.

She was almost as much of an expert on Wagner as Celia was. In fact in some ways she was better."

"You were telling me about her. You reckon that it was Celia who burned her?"

Lloyd nodded. "I could sure use her now."

"Well, man," sniffed Tony Express. "Maybe you can."

"What are you talking about?"

"If Sylvia Cuddy is suffering in hell because Celia burned her, then she's going to be feeling pretty damn vengeful, right? And revenge is what we're tapping into here. Anybody who gets unjustly sent to hell can get themselves released by taking revenge on whoever it was who unjustly sent them there. Come on, man, *everybody* knows that. What do you think ghosts are? Why do you think they moan and they groan? They're spirits who think they shouldn't be suffering in hell, searching for the bastards who put them there."

Lloyd said gently, "Am I beginning to understand you correctly? Because if I am—God help me!"

"Pass me the doll, man," said Tony Express, lifting himself off the sofa and sitting cross-legged on the rug. "I'm going to show you something now you won't forget."

Lloyd reluctantly picked up the sun-dance doll and gave it to Tony Express. It felt almost *alive* in his hand, throbbing, swollen, and pliable, like a man's erection felt through a woman's fox-fur coat.

"Sylvia Cuddy you say?" asked Tony Express.

"That's right," Lloyd agreed.

"Okay, then . . . what I want you to do is to think hard about Sylvia Cuddy. Try to remember what she looked like . . . where she lived. Her belongings. The sound of her voice. Imagine a real small Sylvia Cuddy standing inside of your head. Do you think you can do that?"

"I can sure as hell *try.*"

He closed his eyes. Tony Express said, "Come on, man, keep your eyes open. How'm I going to be able to see her, unless you keep your eyes open?"

"How did you know I had my eyes closed?"

"It's a characteristic of white people. They can't think and look at the same time. It confuses them."

"All right, I'll do my best."

They sat facing each other on the rug, while the morning sunlight fell like a golden fog between them. Tony Express hummed very softly to himself, occasionally articulating words that Lloyd couldn't quite understand, but which sounded as if they meant something. "*Nequet . . . mmm . . . nadtow-wompu . . . mmm . . . wejoo-suk . . .*"

At the same time, he gently rattled his sun-dance doll, and the malevolent little face on top of it hopped and bobbed in front of Lloyd's eyes like a taunting puppet show.

"*Wejoo-suk . . . mmm . . . wejoo-suk . . . mmm . . .*"

Lloyd did his best to think of Sylvia. He thought of her backbrushed hair and her pink lips and her huge designer eyeglasses. Then he thought of her neck, with the first sign of middle-aged wrinkles, and a heavy gold necklace. He thought of her hands; of her jungle-patterned blouse. He thought of her tiny apartment, and he could almost hear her voice saying, "I'm so tired of living in Lilliput. It's so damn small here I can do swan dives off the ironing board, straight down the toilet."

"Think of her," Tony Express was urging him. "Think of her clearly, man, think of her hard."

"I can see her," said Lloyd, and he could. She was standing inside his head like that tiny holographic image of Princess Leia in *Star Wars*. She was standing inside his head and she was sharp and she was clear and she was *real*.

Tony Express said, "Look at me." Or perhaps Lloyd only imagined that he said it. But all the same, he turned to him and stared at him directly, with the tiny image of Sylvia still bright and sharp behind his eyes.

Tony Express took off his dark glasses. Lloyd saw his sightless milky-white eyes. But in that instant, he felt as if something bright had been sucked right out of his own eyes; a brilliant image that had left him dazzled.

Although he was dazzled, however, he was able to see that Tony Express's eyes were dully glowing like forty-watt bulbs. Then Tony turned his head and stared toward the far corner of the living room.

Lloyd had already seen today the materialization of the girl called Gretchen, whom Otto had tortured and killed. Gretchen had been the faintest picture from a long-dead past. But he still shuddered when the sunlit air in the far corner of the room began to flow and coagulate, and gradually the shimmering outline of a woman began to form. Not just any woman, either. As the image grew more distinct and more colorful, he could see that it was unmistakably Sylvia Cuddy.

She took on no more substance than a translucent image in the air. An overexposed transparency, its colors so thin—ivories and roses and pale jade greens—that Lloyd could barely see what they were. But it was Sylvia, all the same, and she moved, and turned her head, and her eyes looked at Lloyd with a sadness that made him feel impossibly guilty. After all, if he hadn't been rash enough to lend her the *Junius* libretto, she might still be alive.

"Sylvia?" he called her.

". . . Lloyd, what's . . ." her voice strengthened and faded, as if they were hearing on the very edge of a shortwave radio frequency.

Lloyd stood up and approached her. "Sylvia, I'm sorry. I'm so sorry for what happened."

". . . n't your fault, she . . ."

"Sylvia . . . are you suffering at all? Sylvia, listen to me! Are you suffering at all?"

". . . always the day . . . every day . . ."

"What day, Sylvia?" He was so close to her now, yet she was so transparent that he felt he could have stirred her image around like sheets of colored gelatin dissolving in warm water.

". . . day my father died . . . every day . . . so much grief . . ."

Tony Express was standing close beside Lloyd's elbow. "In hell, you suffer the worst thing that ever happened to you when you were alive, over and over, every day. Didn't you know that? That's what hell is. You white people don't know nothing."

Lloyd hesitated, and then he said, "Sylvia . . . that libretto I gave you to look at . . . the Wagner libretto . . . could you score that for me? Could you sing it for me, so that I know what it's supposed to sound like?"

". . . n't understa . . ."

"Score it for me, teach me how to sing it! It's desperately important! It's a hymn, written by Wagner, to destroy all of the fire people . . . to make atonement for all of the Salamanders!"

At last, Sylvia began to nod, as if she had grasped what it was that he wanted her to do. Lloyd went over to Kathleen's upright piano, opened the lid, and set the manuscript pages on the music stand. Then he turned back to the glassy, flowing image of Sylvia, standing in the sunlight, and there were tears in his eyes.

"Try, Sylvia, please."

For the next two hours, they were treated to an eerie but enchanting scene. Sylvia's image sat at the piano, carefully scoring

Wagner's music with a pencil that almost seemed to jiggle in midair by itself. Every now and then, she would play a short phrase from the hymn on the piano, and the room would resonate as if the notes were being played on every frequency in the known universe.

At last, Sylvia announced that she had finished, that she was ready: that her scoring and arrangement of Wagner's Hymn of Atonement was as close to Wagner's original as she could manage.

Tony Express elbowed Lloyd's ribs. "Tape recorder," he reminded him.

"Oh, sure," said Lloyd; and switched Kathleen's Sony to record.

The Hymn was strong and primitive, a pagan hymn rather than a Christian hymn. But it had a soft wild beauty that stirred a feeling in Lloyd that he hadn't felt for years.

> Forgive the beacons we have lit,
> Forgive our wrath; our ire
> Forgive the souls that dared to burn
> Within th'immortal fire.

Sylvia sang the words high and clear: so high and clear that Franklin suddenly appeared in the doorway and stood staring at the piano mesmerized.

The hymn died away. Sylvia turned to Lloyd and raised both hands to her lips. Her eyes were filled with affection and regret. But at least she had a chance now to live an afterlife that was free of suffering and agonizing grief.

". . . bye, Lloyd . . . remember I . . ."

She was gone. The pages of the libretto were ruffled by a sudden breeze, and blew one by one to the floor. Lloyd knelt down and collected them up.

"Who was playing the piano?" asked Franklin, stupefied.

"Didn't you see anybody?" Lloyd replied.

Franklin came closer, and peered around the piano. He lifted the drapes and looked behind them, too. Then he stared at Lloyd in complete bewilderment.

"Were you playing that piano?"

"No," said Lloyd. "Didn't you see her—the woman in the floral blouse?"

Very slowly, Franklin shook his head. "I didn't see anybody. There was nobody here."

Lloyd looked across at Tony Express, but Tony Express was still sitting cross-legged on the floor, his head thrown back a little like Stevie Wonder, rocking on his haunches and humming to himself. Lloyd had read about the doors of perception, and the extraordinary levels of different reality into which Indian shamans had always been capable of removing themselves, but this was the first time he had experienced it so intensely and so emotionally for himself. He wondered who was experiencing whom; and if Tony Express should ever gain sight, whether the rest of the world would instantly become blind.

23

"I have to come with you," Kathleen insisted. "If they've got Tom, then I simply have to."

"You realize how dangerous it could be," said Lloyd, although he had known all along that he wouldn't be able to persuade her to stay at home.

"It's no less dangerous here," Kathleen argued. "Look what they did to Lucy."

"All right," Lloyd agreed. There was no arguing with that. They had decided yesterday not to try hiding anywhere else, because they had all been tired and Kathleen had still been suffering from shock. But they had taken turns to keep watch all night, in case Otto or Helmwige or any of the Salamanders came after them.

It had been difficult for Lloyd to persuade Kathleen not to call the police. After all, Lucy had been killed and Tom was missing, and there was no guarantee that their hymn would have any effect on the Salamanders at all. Lloyd only had Celia's word for it—that, and a half-heard conversation that Franklin had reported. It was quite possible that Celia had been lying, the way she had lied about almost everything else, and that Franklin had simply misunderstood what Otto had been talking about.

Nevertheless, they were carrying two duplicate cassettes with Wagner's hymn on them—in case one of them should get lost or caught—and their plan was simply to play it over the Civic Theater loudspeaker system at the end of the opera.

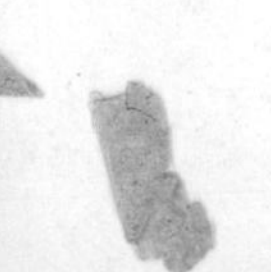

"Simple, man," remarked Tony Express. "All we have to do is gate-crash an invitation-only opera, hide, stop ourselves from being burned alive, mess with the Salamanders' hi-fi, duck their subsequent wrath, rescue Kathleen's kid, call the cops, make the cops believe that we're not totally out to lunch, and bingo."

"You make it sound so easy," Lloyd remarked.

By calling the Civic Theater, they had discovered that night's opera evening started at nine o'clock, and finished at midnight. "But, I'm sorry, sir, it's strictly by invitation only, and there are no more seats available."

They spent the day resting and pacing about and nervously watching television. Lloyd would have done anything for a drink, but he resisted it. He sat in the kitchen watching Kathleen make sandwiches for everybody, and drank Perrier with a wedge of lime and salt round the rim, a teetotaler's tequila.

Kathleen seemed to have lost a lot of her defensiveness since they had discovered her sister burned in the garage. She was still practical; still disinclined to show her feelings; but as he watched her against the afternoon light he could see her femininity shining through. Those graceful movements; those soft and appealing expressions.

He had never had a woman solely as a friend before—as an ally, rather than a lover. He had never appreciated a woman for being just what she was. It was a strange and new experience, and in a curious way it made him think less of Celia, and the feelings that he had once had for her.

Lloyd and Kathleen were bonded in the same way that men who went hunting together were bonded. They both hated Otto and Helmwige and their "master race"; and they both nurtured the same need for revenge. They both needed revenge so much that it physically hurt them, like the need for crack.

"Do you think Tom's safe?" Kathleen asked, as she cut the last of the sandwiches.

Lloyd nodded. "Almost certain of it. Otto can't catch us, but he's going to keep Tom as his insurance policy, in case we start trouble."

"What happens when we *do* make trouble?"

"Then I'll do everything I can to make sure that Tom gets out of there safely."

Kathleen was silent for a moment, as if she were making her mind up about something. Then she said, "Okay, thank you. I guess that's the most that anybody could promise."

* * *

They drove south toward San Diego on I-5, so nervous that they could scarcely speak to each other. Lloyd switched on the radio for a moment, but it was Chris Rea singing "The Road to Hell," and so he switched it off again. He would have done anything for a drink, a cigarette, an excuse to take the next turnoff and head back to La Jolla. But it was too late now. He had many more lives to think about than his own. Even Celia's. Perhaps Celia's more than any of the others, because he had failed her.

And what would happen when Otto's master race emerged, and began to impose its will on a nation whose moral certainties were already foundering? *God,* thought Lloyd, *I've been afraid before, but never like this. I've never been afraid that I'm going to wake up tomorrow, and America's going to have changed forever.*

They passed the Seaworld turnoff, and the glittering lights of downtown San Diego began to rise up in front of them. Tony Express crossed himself.

"I didn't know you were a Catholic," Kathleen remarked.

"I'm not," he said. "But, you know man, you might as well give yourself all the protection you can."

It was a hot, windless night. There was no smell of ocean, only burned gasoline and stale air-conditioning and cigarette smoke. The sky reflected the lights of the city so that it was almost purple. Lloyd took the Civic Center turnoff, and then bore left until he reached the Civic Theater garage entrance at 2nd and A.

It was 8:35. Already the theater garage was busy with lines of glistening Cadillacs and Mercedes and Porsches, and crowds of people in evening dress were taking the elevators down to the street. There was a smell of imported cigarettes and pot and Giorgio perfume.

"All right?" asked Lloyd, as they parked. "Anybody want to back out?"

"Come on, Lloyd," said Franklin, laying his hand on Lloyd's shoulder. "Let's just go. Don't let's think about backing out."

They climbed out of the car. They had raided Mike Kerwin's closets to make themselves look as presentable as possible. Lloyd was a little taller than Mike, so the pants of his dinner suit flapped around his ankles, but the dress-shirt fitted quite well. Franklin had managed to wedge himself into a blue Yves St. Laurent blazer and a pair of slacks that made his muscular legs look as if they had been sprayed with dull gray paint; while Tony Express had found a black jacket of Kathleen's that fitted him. He had gelled his hair and combed it like Robert DeNiro's.

Kathleen wore a black velvet evening gown, low-cut, with a large diamond pin on her left breast. She was tired, and her cheeks were colorless; but then she was just beginning to feel the full effects of Tom's disappearance, and of her sister's ugly cremation in the garage. All the same, Lloyd thought she looked exceptionally alluring, and he was proud to have her on his arm.

As they walked across the parking level, Lloyd noticed two black minibuses with mirror windows parked close together in the far corner. Balboa Hi-Way Bus Rental was lettered on the side panels of each of them. And what was the betting they, too, had been rented by Mr. Ortal? Mr. Imm-Ortal—big joke, Otto.

They took the elevator down to street-level and then turned left to the Civic Theater entrance. It was bright and crowded, although there were uniformed security guards at every door checking invitations, and the sidewalk was roped off to prevent anybody from straying into the theater entrance by accident.

"How on earth are we going to get in?" Kathleen asked, behind her black-gloved hand, as they approached the doors. A man behind her was laughing loudly, and saying, "She came for rhinoplasty and went away with new lips, new ears, new breasts, and twelve thousand dollars' worth of liposuction."

"Well, Kurt, you're a good salesman, I'll admit that," his companion was saying. "You probably couldn't remodel an outhouse, but you sure can sell."

They both laughed loudly. Then Tony Express and Lloyd reached the door, closely followed by Franklin and Kathleen. The security guard was a big-bellied black man with a glossy peaked cap pulled down low over his eyes.

"Check your invitations, please?" he asked, suspiciously.

Tony Express lifted his sun-dance doll and shook it twice. "*Na, na'lwiwi!*" he said, sharply. The security guard frowned at him, and said, "What you doin' that fo'?" so he shook it again. "*Na! Na! Na'lwiwi!*"

Lloyd was sure that the security guard was going to turn them away, but then an extraordinary thing happened. The air in front of the security guard's face seemed to *bend*, like a distorting mirror at a funhouse, and no matter how much he turned his head from side to side, he appeared to be unable to see past it.

In the end he turned to the two cosmetic surgeons right

behind them and said, "Okay, gentlemen. How about *your* invitations?"

"But you didn't check—" one of the surgeons began, pointing at Lloyd and Franklin and Kathleen and Tony Express.

The security guard looked back at them, but the air was still flexing, and it was obvious to Lloyd that he simply couldn't see them. Tony Express had somehow summoned his powers of light and air to distort the man's vision.

"Come on, man," Tony Express urged him. "That's nothing but a trick and it don't last more'n a minute." Together, they shove-shuffled their way through the crowded lobby and up the stairs, and through the open doors into the main auditorium.

The Civic Theater could take nearly twice as many people as Otto had invited, and so there were plenty of spare seats. Lloyd and Kathleen found themselves orchestra seats close to the left-hand exit, while Franklin and Tony Express went to sit on the opposite side. The stage curtains were still closed, but already some sections of the orchestra were beginning to tune up. Their persistent off-key scraping and whining did nothing for Lloyd's already-tightened nerves.

He looked around him at the gradually filling theater. If he hadn't known that each of them had been personally selected by Otto for their racial characteristics, their politics, and their intelligence, it would have taken him a long time to realize that there were no blacks here. There were several light-skinned Hispanics, and some Asians, but none of them looked like anything but wealthy and well-domesticated Southern Californians.

Under the sparkling chandeliers sat a thousand and one of Southern California's finest and most successful: doctors, lawyers, dentists, accountants, politicians. Although they didn't yet know it, they were the master-race-to-be.

"Where do you think Tom is?" asked Kathleen, looking anxiously around.

"If Otto's got him, he'll be here," Lloyd reassured her. "He's Otto's hostage, remember, in case we try to mess things up for him." In spite of his confident tone, however, he wasn't at all sure that Otto would have brought Tom here—nor even that Tom was still alive.

"Oh God protect him," Kathleen whispered.

Franklin gave Lloyd the thumbs-up from the far side of the theater. They had planned to sit through the first part of the opera, until the second intermission, and then Franklin and Tony Express would make their way backstage to see if they could find Tom and locate the theater's audio equipment. As the opera drew to its climax, toward midnight, Lloyd and Kathleen would join them. They would play the hymn, if they could, and with luck, make their getaway.

It wasn't much of a plan, and they would probably have to decide what to do as they went along, but then Lloyd's vice president at San Diego Marine Trust had always said, "When you haven't got a fucking clue, extemporize."

It was that advice that had led Lloyd to quit the insurance business and open the Original Fish Depot. He hoped it would hold out tonight, on the night of the summer solstice, on the night of Otto's sorcerous Transformation.

Kathleen took hold of his hand and squeezed it. "Come on, Lloyd," she whispered. "We've got God on our side."

Lloyd gave her a tightly drawn smile, and tried to look as if he believed it.

As nine o'clock drew near, the doors of the auditorium were closed, and Lloyd noticed that a security guard stood by each. Maybe the invited audience thought they had been posted there to keep out gate-crashers, but Lloyd was pretty damn sure that they were intended to keep the invited audience from getting out.

Gradually the lights were dimmed, and the hubbub of conversation died down. There was a breathless moment when nearly a thousand people sat in complete silence, and then the drapes parted and Otto stepped out, in white tie and tailcoat, fussily tugging at his shirt cuffs. *Like a mortician*, Lloyd thought. *Like the angel of death.*

He lifted his hand for quiet, and waited until long after it was quiet. Then he said, "Good evening, ladies and gentlemen. You have all received a personal invitation to this gala evening of Wagernian opera selections. You were selected because all of you are staunch supporters of the San Diego Opera—both by your regular attendance and your financial contributions—and that makes you a very special audience indeed.

"As it was explained in the covering letter that came with your invitations, this evening is your reward—when the opera says 'Thank you' for being so supportive.

"I am hoping that tonight we will form amongst ourselves an

exclusive and special society of those who are devoted to the operatic works of Richard Wagner and the fundamental principles which inspired his music. Not just for ourselves, you understand, but in memory of the late Celia Williams, who worked so hard over the past six months to make this evening a reality."

There was a short burst of applause, but it quickly died away when Otto raised his hand again.

"I am now going to say that you have all been invited here under false pretenses."

More hubbub; an occasional laugh.

Otto almost managed to smile. "What I am going to say is that you thought you were coming here tonight to witness a collection of works by various composers, paying tribute to Richard Wagner. But—what you have come to witness is a complete and previously unknown opera by Richard Wagner, his last."

A low roaring of excitement and surprise went through the audience, like a long roller breaking on the beach. Even the orchestra turned to each other in amazement, and began furiously to leaf through their scores. Celia must have given them music which appeared to be several unconnected pieces; but which in fact made up the entire opera, cunningly disassembled.

Willard Bright, the conductor, stood up and said something to Otto, which Lloyd couldn't hear. But Otto turned to the orchestra and said brightly, "You have rehearsed it, *ja*? You know how to play it? You will be magnificent!"

The conductor consulted with his orchestra for a few minutes, but none of them appeared to have any objections. In fact most of them looked eager to start playing.

"Here then," said Otto, "is Richard Wagner's lost masterpiece *Junius*. It has been arranged and developed by our late friend Ms. Celia Williams, and it is in her memory that it is performed this evening. It was I who discovered this opera in Germany, but it is Ms. Williams who made this first performance a reality."

There was more applause. Lloyd noticed a reporter in a tuxedo leaving the press seats, and heading toward the exit. But the reporter was turned back by one of the security guards, and shushed when he tried to protest.

Otto said, "It is appropriate that *Junius* should be played for Ms. Williams, because it has as its central theme *immortality*, and tonight will make Ms. Williams immortal. It tells the story of a

Bavarian burgomaster who made a pact with the powers of darkness in exchange for eternal life . . . how he was misunderstood by his fellow citizens and sacrificed . . . but how he triumphed over death, and how glory and brilliance came out of that darkness, and forged an empire the like of which had never been seen before, but which will rise again!"

He paused for a long moment, and then he said, "You will perhaps ask who I am, to have found such an opera, and to be presenting it to you tonight. You will perhaps ask how such a thing could have happened, without publicity, without sensation.

"I am a simple music lover of independent means, devoted to the works of Richard Wagner. I wanted to share this unique discovery not with those who would seek to sensationalize it, but with those who had an ear for music . . . those who had already shown that they cared about opera.

"Before tonight, very few knew of *Junius*. Only historians and specialists. But tonight will see *Junius* launched in a blaze; and you will be part of that blaze; and your names will be remembered forever."

Otto stepped back. There was a ripple of applause; but not for long. Otto had excited his audience, but also bewildered them.

Now Willard Bright stood up, and tapped his baton. The theater gradually quietened, apart from sporadic coughs. There was a moment of silence on which the whole world seemed to hinge.

Then—like a thunderstorm breaking—the orchestra broke into the overture. It was wilder and more powerful than any Wagner that Lloyd had heard before. Despite himself, his scalp tightened and prickled, and he could feel his heart pumping. The music was primitive, sweeping, unbridled, a hurricane blowing through the theater. Already overwhelmed by Otto's compliments, and by the fact that they were going to hear the first-ever public performance of a long-lost opera, the audience sat enthralled.

For most of the overture, the auditorium was plunged into darkness; but suddenly the curtains were drawn back, and at the same time the timpani set up a rolling, reverberating, primitive rhythm.

Onto the stage filed a hundred-strong chorus, cloaked entirely in black, with their heads covered, monkish and strangely threatening. They carried lighted torches, and sung a deep, dirgelike, repetitive chant.

Who has been trading with his Satanic Majesty?
Who has been offering his very soul for sale?
Who has turned his back on the Lord his God?

The chorus shuffled around the stage in a never-ending figure eight, faceless, black, their robes whispering on the dusty wooden boards. Their torches flickered as they walked, and cast huge and complicated shadows on the backdrop and across the faces of the audience.

In spite of his fear, in spite of his hatred of Otto and everything that Otto was trying to do, Lloyd found the opera hugely moving and disturbing. It had all the elements of a Nazi rally: darkness, torches, flags, symbols . . . and monotonous chants of triumph that swelled like the ocean at night.

Who has found the life everlasting?
Who has conquered death?
Who has conquered death—death—death—death?

Turning around, Lloyd could see that the audience was transfixed by it—by the music, the chanting, the torches, the thundering drums. It had drummed up their deepest terrors, it had stirred up all of their anxieties and their prejudice. It was war music, battle music, intolerant and fierce. It had given their hatreds a musical voice.

Junius appeared, a white-faced man cloaked entirely in scarlet, with a scarlet-feathered hat. He sang a long tenor solo about his search for immortality.

Why should men be born
If only to die?
What is the purpose of learning so many secrets
If only to take them to your grave?

Now the music became tedious and drawn-out but strangely eerie, too. It was like listening to the sea at night, or somebody whispering something indistinct, over and over again. The mood in the theater began subtly to change, and some of the audience turned around in their seats, as if they were afraid of who or *what* was sitting behind them.

Lloyd began to feel the same feeling. He had never felt it in a theater before. But—after all—as you sit in the darkness, facing the stage, who can tell what is right behind? He tried to resist the temptation to turn around, but in the end he had to, and caught the pale staring face of a matron in a gold lamé evening gown.

"*Ssh!*" she scolded him, even though he hadn't said a word.

As the first act of *Junius* came to a close, a gray-sheeted figure appeared on a balcony in the background, with a huge leather-bound book under its arm. Junius himself fell to his knees and begged the figure to give him the book, with all of its magical secrets and mysteries.

In a high, penetrating alto, the gray-sheeted figure told Junius,

> This book contains the secrets of fire and life
> This book contains the secrets of man's darkest desire
> But when you open this book, and read its text
> Beware! Because the price of eternal life is eternal pain.

Gradually, the background was illuminated by one spotlight after another, until Lloyd could see that it was designed like a complicated Bavarian castle, with spires and flying buttresses and overhanging balconies. Although they were only painted, there was something sinister about the shuttered windows on every balcony and every wall. Lloyd had a feeling that he would prefer them to stay shuttered, in case there was something inside that he would be too terrified to see.

In fact, as the sets became brighter and brighter, they became increasingly alarming—not only because they looked so fortified and shut-up, but because they began to take on an eerie reality. Lloyd turned to Kathleen and he could see that she was equally mesmerized, her hands gripped tight, her face brightly illuminated by the lights from the stage.

"Kathleen," he said, and she reached across and took hold of his hand, but didn't take her eyes away from the opera.

"Have you noticed?" she whispered. "You can't see their faces. None of the chorus, none of the other characters. Only Junius."

The music grew louder and more insistent, like huge feet dragging across an unknown desert. It became more and more difficult for Lloyd to distinguish which was real—the audience and the auditorium, or the towers and castles of Wagner's Bavaria. He felt that he had been living in this fortified town all his life:

hiding behind its shuttered windows, climbing its steep painted staircases, gazing mesmerized from its turrets and towers at the painted clouds that forever sailed by, and never sailed by.

And all the time, the deep voices of the chorus roared the theme of "*Glory! Purity! Power and strength!*"

Lloyd felt as if the world were opening up; as if the ceiling were opening up; as if everything in which he had ever believed was being spilled into the darkness, like the tumbling penitents in some medieval vision of hell.

"*Glory! Glory! Purity! Purity! Power and strength!*"

At the end of the first act, the orchestra finished with a deafening finale of horns and drums, through which the chorus chanted the insistent theme, "*Glory! Purity! Power and strength!*" over and over and over again, until Lloyd could hear some of the audience chanting it with them.

"*Glory! Purity! Power and strength!*"

God, he thought. *How easy it was to start it all over again.*

By the close of the first act, the audience was in a frenzy of excitement. They rose from their seats and gave the opera company a standing ovation that roared on and on and seemed to rise rather than diminish. The second act started with a long, quiet passage set in the twilit mountains of Bavaria. The scenery was dimly blue and luminous, and the voice of the leading soprano Eloïs Steiger seemed to slide through it with a coldness that Lloyd could feel in his bones.

> I have seen with my own eyes
> Dead men walking in the streets
> Dead men tapping at the children's windows
> Not speaking, not calling
> But waiting for me at every corner.

Gradually the aria became another chant; a low throbbing chant that put Lloyd in mind of a galley drum, or the beat to which a Viking longboat might have been rowed. He had the unsettling feeling that this was the prelude to the Fire Ritual, the magical chant that prepared a would-be Salamander for the flames.

He was right. The mountains of Bavaria moved away to reveal a barbarians' encampment, and in the center of the encampment a monstrous bonfire blazed. The effect had been achieved with flickering lights and shreds of flying tissue paper, but the stage technicians had achieved the right degree of lurid, mesmerizing light. The chorus appeared, and began a chant which underlay everything sung by Eloïs Steiger, and by Robert Kupka, the baritone who was playing the sorcerous burgomaster Johann Junius.

Lloyd looked along the chorus. They wore gray monklike habits, and their faces were partially concealed in shadow. But he was sure that he recognized Celia, fourth from the left, and he nudged Kathleen and whispered, "Can you see Mike there? Somewhere in the chorus."

Kathleen picked up the opera glasses from the seat in front of her, and carefully scrutinized the stage. "There—" she said at last. "I think that's him . . . the tall one just behind the fire."

They both watched the remainder of the second act in dread and curiosity. Lloyd checked his watch and there were only forty minutes remaining until midnight. Forty minutes to complete the last act of Wagner's opera, and the first act of the master race.

As the fire scene came to a drumming, low-key ending, Lloyd leaned across and signaled to Franklin that it was time for him to go. Franklin nodded, and as the audience rose for the last intermission, he and Tony Express disappeared into the crowds.

Although the audience was allowed through to the Civic Theater bars for champagne cocktails, Lloyd noticed that all the street exits were closed and guarded. He and Kathleen stood in a corner saying nothing to each other, but listening to the chatter all around them.

"—says something you could never say in print without somebody branding you a bigot—"

"—it's loud, for sure; and very Germanic. But what music! Do you realize what a privilege it is, to hear that music for the very first time—"

"—makes me feel strange—like I've heard it before, but I can't think where—"

Lloyd took Kathleen's hand and together they walked back to the auditorium and sat down.

"Did you *hear* them?" said Kathleen. "It's happening already."

"I know," Lloyd agreed. "The Third Reich, all over again. And *here*, in Southern California."

"I'm afraid," Kathleen told him.

He leaned across and kissed her. "Do you want to know something?" he told her. "Me too."

* * *

There was feverish excitement as the audience returned to the theater for the final act. Somehow a rumor had circulated that the last aria was magnificent beyond belief; that tonight was going to be legendary in world opera for decades to come. "The night that *Junius* was performed in public for the first time." "The night that Eloïs Steiger reached a fortissimo A-natural above high C that had the audience screaming in denial that such a sound could exist."

Lloyd recognized the rumor for what it was: propaganda. A way of stirring up more excitement in an audience that was already tired and excited and ready for almost anything.

The drapes came back, revealing a megalithic Aryan city, under a threatening sky. Lightning flickered and thunder crashed. Horns bayed in unison. Then the chorus marched diagonally right and left across the stage, wearing breastplates and heavy helmets, and carrying spears.

> We march toward the future . . .
> We will make war on decadence and sloth
> Like a black wind we will storm through the world.

The music grew louder and louder, the chorus shrilled and roared. Lloyd peered at his watch and saw that there were only a few minutes to go before midnight, the critical moment of Transformation. The chorus was gathering in a semicircle, holding hands, and chanting "*Storm! Storm! Storm! Storm!*"

Eloïs Steiger moved center-stage, wearing a huge black cape and a black horned helmet. Several of the audience stood up in awe, and nobody attempted to make them sit down again. Drums rolled, thunder shook the auditorium.

"*Now is the moment of our Transformation!*" she sang, in a voice as powerful as a gale. "*Now is the moment when men become gods!*"

"*Storm! Storm! Storm! Storm!*" chanted the chorus, raising their joined hands with every chant.

Women were shrieking in the audience. Some of the men were stamping their feet in time to the chant of the chorus; others stood with their mouths open in disbelief as Eloïs Steiger reached the final measures of the opera. The orchestra swept them all along like survivors clinging to a life raft.

"Now is the moment of our triumph! Now is the moment when all will fall before us!"

Eloïs hung for a moment on the penultimate E-flat. The orchestra was suddenly silent; the audience hushed. Lightning danced in the painted sky, and there was a suppressed buzzing of electrical contacts, but that was all. Kathleen clutched Lloyd's hand, although neither of them were really sure what they were expecting.

It was then that they heard a sound that didn't sound like a human voice at all. It sounded like some uninvented, unimaginable instrument. A shiver of dread ran through the audience that they would only hear this once in their lives, and this was the moment.

The sound broadened and widened and swelled and rose. Eloïs Steiger flung wide her arms and threw back her head, and in that rippling black cloak she uttered an A-natural that filled the theater like an atomic explosion, dazzling and deafening, wider and wider and louder and louder until Lloyd felt that the whole auditorium would collapse on top of them.

But there was more to come. At the instant the note died—in that stunned hiatus before an audience usually roars its approval—the chorus threw back their cloaks and revealed themselves naked, gleaming with the gray metallic skin of Salamanders. They raised their joined hands, and shouted together, "Glory! Purity! Power!"

The entire theater shook. Pieces of plaster dropped from the ceiling, and a battery of spotlights fell onto the stage and smashed. Somebody screamed, "Earthquake!" and a moan of terror went through the audience. But then they immediately saw that it wasn't an earthquake. It was the power that was rippling through the chorus; a sullen crimson light that throbbed from one to the other, through the arms, through their hands, until all of them were glowing the color of red-hot coals.

The audience stood and stared at them in bewilderment, but Lloyd and Kathleen knew what was happening. Their volatile bodies of smoke and spirit were being transformed by the most ancient of pagan powers into something that resembled human flesh—the flesh of the gods. These were going to be the parents of the master race.

Gradually, the light died and the smoke drifted away. The audience was left in stupefied silence. Some of them were sobbing.

They didn't understand that the enormous emotions stirred up by the opera hadn't been for their benefit, but for the benefit of Otto's Salamanders. They were left aroused, excited, but completely disoriented, unable to understand what they had witnessed.

"Now," Lloyd muttered. "Now, Franklin—the hymn, for God's sake! The hymn!"

But no hymn came. Instead, the drapes slowly and silently descended, and Otto reappeared on the stage. He was carrying in his upraised hands a small dull golden owl, which he presented first to one side of the auditorium, like a conjurer about to perform a new and complicated trick, and then to the other.

"Sit, please, sit," he said, and the audience gradually sat. He waited until they were completely quiet, and then he said, "You will not know what it is that you have seen; not yet. It was a Transformation, of fire into flesh, of insubstantial souls into immortal beings who can walk this earth as gods.

"You too can be gods like they are. In fact, that is why I chose you. All of you here can take part in the ritual of fire, and become leaders of men such as the world has never known."

Nobody spoke. Nobody challenged him. Nobody knew what to say.

"You are not aware of it," Otto continued, "but the ritual chant in the first act prepared all of you for what is going to happen now. You will survive it, as the men and women of my chorus survived it; to be transformed, when the time is right, into glorious creatures such as they."

Otto raised the bowl again; and now the faintest flicker of convulsive light appeared inside it. "This is the bowl in which Pontius Pilate washed his hands, and gave responsibility for Jesus to the Jews," said Otto. "This is the talisman which represents all of those who refuse to accept the burden of their duties; and all of those who betray the great and the good."

"My God," Lloyd whispered to Kathleen. "We have to get out of here! Do you see what he's going to do?"

"What? What is it?" asked Kathleen, still bemused by the climax of the opera.

"Salamanders!" Lloyd hissed at her. "He's chosen this audience to be Salamanders! This is his master race! He's going to burn the whole goddamn theater!"

At the instant he spoke, there was a shrill scream of surprise from the back row of the stalls. Lloyd turned, and saw that a man's head had caught alight, and was furiously burning. The woman next to him was trying to flap at the flames with her fur stole, but then she burst into flame, too. One by one, with alarming speed, like a lighted taper running along a row of candles, the whole row of people were ignited, and then the next row, and then the next.

"*Out!*" Lloyd yelled at Kathleen, and pushed her along to the end of the row to the exit. A security guard was standing in the way, but he looked as shocked by the fires as they were, and Lloyd shouldered him to one side and kicked open the exit before he had time to stop them. He twisted around, and shouted, "Hey!" but then the front rows detonated into flame, and he was caught in a roaring fireball of superheated air which took off his face as if it were a plastic Halloween mask.

Lloyd and Kathleen ran along the corridor, until they reached a door marked Offices: Private. The door was locked, but Lloyd gave it three violent kicks, and it fell flat into the drab carpet-tiled office beyond. On the opposite side of the office was a door that obviously led backstage.

"Come on," Lloyd urged Kathleen. "We have to play that hymn!"

They ran along another long corridor, up a flight of stairs, and then they pushed open a swing door and found themselves in the gloom at the back of the stage, among flats and props and cardboard trees and gold-painted thrones and coils of rope. There was nobody around, so they stepped cautiously behind the scenery, looking for the hi-fi console.

"Listen," said Kathleen, holding his hand. "You can hear the fire alarms."

Lloyd paused, and listened. "Sure. But no screaming. Have you noticed that? Nobody's screaming. They're not even fighting to get out."

They could smell smoke and heat and the unmistakable barbecue stench of charred human flesh; but apart from the distant alarms the quiet was uncanny. They crept forward behind the Bavarian mountains, and suddenly found themselves front stage, only partially concealed by what were supposed to be alder trees.

Onstage, the chorus now stood in a circle, still naked, but no longer grayish skinned, the way they had been before. They had eyes, too, like Helmwige's; pale and glistening and unnaturally calm, the eyes of people who will never have to fear for their lives. Otto stood outside the circle, still facing the auditorium.

The theater was the most grisly sight that Lloyd had ever seen. Through a dense veil of human smoke, he could see that all the thousand guests had burned, and that they were lolling in their seats, still smoking. Raw grins stretched over burned teeth. Jewels had melted into charred necks. Everywhere Lloyd looked, bodies sat stiff and blackened. Here and there, a toupee still burned with a guttering flame, or a patent purse flared.

Lloyd had never understood how a Salamander was formed, but now he saw it for himself, over and over again. It was silent, and it was quite uncanny. He had seen many supernatural occurrences over the past week, but nothing as strange as this.

A thick-set man lay slumped in his seat in the front row. The smoke rose from his burned body, and seemed to twist and thicken above his head. As it drifted higher and higher toward the ceiling, it gradually took on a human shape, and reached a point where it started to sink again, until it had reached the floor. The ritual chant had mixed smoke with the rising soul, so that the soul couldn't leave the earth's gravity, so that it was denied its place in heaven.

At the back of the smoky auditorium, more and more Salamanders fell soft as quilts from the air, and gathered together in silence, mute witnesses to their own burned bodies.

Otto turned back to his chorus in triumph, his yellow eyes wide.

"It has begun!" he cried. "It has begun! Now for the greatest transformation of all!"

The chorus parted to allow him into the center of their circle. Otto stood there for a moment, admiring them. "You, my immortals! My master race! Parents of the gods!"

Then he walked around the circle, touching each of them on the arm by turn. "You have an army now, an army of Salamanders . . . servants, comrades . . . and those who serve you well can be Transformed like you at the next solstice, if you so choose. They are your SA; your handpicked regiment of storm troopers, and they will obey you because they all want immortality. You need fear no resistance . . . you cannot be killed, you cannot die. You are the greatest of all living creatures."

He continued walking around and around. "All of you have mortal partners with whom you can breed one child . . . those children will be the foundation of our future, the demigods."

He stopped when he reached Celia and Mike Kerwin, and laid his hand on their shoulders. "You, unfortunately, have a partner who let suspicion overcome love . . . Mike, so did you. But for you, I have two special partners. Partners with whom it is more than an honor to breed."

He looked around once more, and took a long, dry breath. "Now . . ." he said, "the talismans, please."

The chorus held up their salamander charms, fourteen of them in all. Otto took Celia's and placed it on his tongue, and Celia stepped back out of the circle. The other thirteen held theirs up, and began to chant.

"What's happening now?" asked Kathleen. She had her handkerchief pressed to her mouth to stop herself from choking. "What's he *doing?*"

As the chanting grew louder and more strident, Otto appeared, oddly, to grow taller. Lloyd wiped the smoke from his eyes and looked again. But it was true. Otto was growing taller and taller, until he was nearly eight feet tall, thin and attenuated and insectlike. He was grinning down at the stage, his yellow eyes bright, triumphant, fierce.

Suddenly, the top of his scalp parted, and his skin peeled away from his skull like a rubber glove. Underneath Lloyd saw black glistening bone, and yellow slanting eyes that were as dead and as a calculating as any gargoyle's.

Now the skin split down Otto's back, and a forest of shining black spines rose up. The chorus of Salamanders, far from being alarmed, raised their arms and chanted even louder.

"I have done what I was summoned to do," he said, in a croaking rasp that was scarcely human. *"I have recreated the master race. Now I can return."*

Kathleen gripped Lloyd's arm. "Lloyd—he's not even a—*Lloyd!* He's some sort of a—! Oh my God! *What is it, Lloyd? What is it?*"

Lloyd stepped back. "Whatever it is, we have to play that hymn. . . . Once this is over, all of those people are going to go their different ways, and then we'll *never* stop them!"

They backed away from the stage, and around the back of the scenery again. On the far side of the stage was a short flight of steps and a door marked RECORDING: QUIET PLEASE. A small lighted window overlooked the stage itself.

"That's it," said Lloyd. "Follow me, but for God's sake keep a lookout behind you."

They climbed the steps as quietly as they could. The treads

creaked, but the chanting of the chorus was so loud now that nobody could have heard them. In the center of the circle, the reptilian monstrosity into which Otto was slowly being transformed was swaying and clicking and uttering harsh breathing noises. Lloyd glanced at it quickly and then decided not to look at it again. Black claws were tearing their way out of the skin of Otto's fingers.

He cautiously turned the knob of the sound room, and opened the door. Inside he could smell heated electrical equipment. He took the cassette out of his pocket, and stepped inside, nodding to Kathleen to follow him.

"All I have to do is find the tape player," he said, inspecting the rows of switches and lights on the console. "Why the hell don't they have a Walkman, like everybody else?"

He found the tape player, and was trying to slot in the tape when the door burst open again. In blundered Franklin, holding hands with Tony Express. Right behind them came Helmwige, looking darkly angry, with Tom. She was dressed in a skintight black leather leotard, cut impossibly high at the thigh, and black thigh-length boots. She was tugging Tom after her on a steel neck-collar. His neck was raw and his eyes were blotchy from crying.

"Tom!" said Kathleen. "You bitch, let him go!"

"Let him go? I'm going to flay him alive and eat him for my breakfast if you don't shut up! You! Denman! Take out that tape and give it to me!"

Lloyd looked around at Franklin and Tony Express. Franklin said, "We tried, Lloyd. We tried real hard. But she said she was going to kill him if we didn't give her the tape."

"Tony?" asked Lloyd carefully, meaning "What about your sun-dance doll?"

"I didn't dare. . . . I could slow her down, but she could burn him quicker'n I could stop her. I'm sorry."

Helmwige said, "The tape, Denman, or else I burn the boy to a cinder, right in front of your eyes, like I burned his aunt."

"Lloyd . . ." said Kathleen, anxiously.

"Guess I don't have any choice," said Lloyd. He glanced out of the window of the sound booth, and he could see something black and gleaming swaying in the center of the stage. Otto, sloughing his human appearance, and returning to what he really was. The chant of the chorus was muffled in here, but Lloyd could hear that it was reaching a high pitch of hysteria.

He held out the cassette to Helmwige, just two or three inches out of her reach. "What *is* that thing?" he asked her. "*That,*" nodding toward Otto.

Helmwige smiled. "Otto? He used to be a student in Salzburg, before the war. But you see, he discovered a way to make himself not just a scholar but a genius. He made a trade with something dark, I don't know what. He allowed that thing to live inside his body until he had made his mark in history. Now, he has made his mark, and the thing is leaving; back to where it came from."

Lloyd shuddered. Then, without warning, he swung his right arm and punched Helmwige straight in the face. Helmwige staggered back, lost her balance, and hit her side against the sound console. But immediately she was back again, and she slapped Lloyd open-handed across the head so hard that he was thrown against the opposite wall.

"Fool!" she spat at him. He tried to get up, but she kicked him in the ribs, and then in the stomach.

At that moment, however, Franklin grabbed hold of her, and gripped her in a bear hug. At the same time, he yanked Tom's chain out of her hand, and threw it aside.

"Lloyd!" he yelled. "Put on the hymn! Kathleen! Tom! Tony! *Go!*"

"You cretin!" spat Helmwige. "You know what I can do to you!"

"Lloyd!" Franklin bellowed. "The tape!"

Dazed, coughing, bleeding, Lloyd climbed to his feet. He picked up the cassette and jabbed it into the tape player.

Kathleen hesitated at the door, but Franklin shouted, "Go! Go! Go!"

"Mengele's *dummling!*" Helmwige screeched. But Franklin kept her tight in his bear hug, her arms by her sides, her face scarlet with fury and exertion.

Quickly, she began to increase her body heat. Franklin gasped, but he took a huge breath and continued to hold her. Lloyd pressed the start button on the tape player, and after a second or two, he heard the crackling rush of the tape.

Helmwige was now burning hotter and hotter. Her leather costume began to smolder and stretch, but she kept on increasing her temperature. Sweat streamed down Franklin's face, and he gritted his teeth. But still he clung on to Helmwige, even when smoke began to rise from his scorched shirt, and the skin on his chest and his thighs began to blister.

"*Aaaaahhhh!!*" screamed Franklin, as Helmwige's body began to burn into his nerve-endings.

"You fool! You pitiful fool!" Helmwige hissed at him. "You're nothing! You're nobody! You never were!"

The first notes of Wagner's Hymn of Atonement suddenly broke out of the theater's public-address system. Down on the stage, the spindly black creature swayed and turned, and threw back its head. The chanting chorus obviously didn't hear the hymn at first, but then one or two of them began to look around and frown.

"You're nothing!" Helmwige raged. "You're a nameless nothing!"

"Oh, God!" Franklin cried out. "Oh God, help me! I'm Franklin! I'm Franklin Free! I'm Franklin Free!"

Steady and calm and strong, the piano-playing of the dead Sylvia Cuddy filled the auditorium of the Civic Theater. For one heart-stopping moment, Lloyd thought that the hymn wasn't going to work and that they were all going to die. But Helmwige suddenly incandesced, as bright as magnesium flaring, and both she and Franklin screamed at each other in mutual agony.

There was an ear-shattering explosion inside the sound booth, and Helmwige collapsed into gray bones and silvery ash. Franklin dropped to the floor, trembling violently at first, then still.

Lloyd wrenched open the sound booth door and stood on the top step. One by one, the chorus members were incandescing, blazing bright as flares, and leaving nothing on the stage but drifts of ash. Lloyd glimpsed Celia for a moment, her hands pressed against her ears, but then he lost sight of her behind Mike Kerwin, who flared up as brightly as a fallen comet.

In the center of the stage, the black glistening creature had dropped to the boards, and lay quivering malevolently. Its yellow eyes glared at Lloyd with such cold hatred that he had to turn away.

"*You have assured my return,*" the creature croaked at him. "*Until I can capture the soul of a mortal who can change the course of human history, I shall always return.*"

Lloyd turned around and faced it and there were tears running down his cheeks. There was nothing he could say to evil like this.

With a hideous clattering sound, the creature slid between the cracks of two single floorboards, spines and claws and tail, and vanished from sight. Lloyd went to the side of the stage and retched, but all he could bring up was warm saliva.

He looked toward the auditorium. The burned bodies of a thousand of Southern California's most successful suburbanites sat charred beyond recognition. Of the Salamanders, there was no sign at all. They were always volatile, that's what Otto had said, when Otto was Otto, and not some black thing out of hell. He walked up the aisle and saw the deep scorch marks on the carpet where each of them had stood.

From the stage, Kathleen came walking up the aisle. She was shocked, distraught: but she was carrying the bowl—the bowl in which Pontius Pilate had washed his hands to rid himself of the responsibility for Christ's crucifixion, the bowl the Salamanders had used in their attempt to attain immortality. The bowl was tarnished and battered, almost a third of it was missing.

"Here," she said.

Lloyd took it, turned it over, and then shrugged. "I guess the only thing to do with this is take it down to La Jolla Bay, and throw it in the ocean."

Kathleen said, "Thank you for everything. That's all I can say."

"I know," Lloyd told her, and squeezed her hand.

He had almost reached the exit when the first fire fighter came hacking and splintering his way through the locked doors with his ax. The fire fighter took one look at the auditorium, one look at Lloyd, and said, "Jesus."

In a suite at the El Cajon Hotel downtown, a fiftyish man in a tan-colored shirt sat in front of his television set, round-shouldered, silent. Across the room sat a dark-haired woman, watching him anxiously.

"So he failed," said the man, at last.

"We don't yet know why, or how," the woman replied.

The man stood up and went to the window. He drew back the grimy net drapes and stared down into the street. "It doesn't matter why. It doesn't matter how. They always fail. They always betray me. 'You can father a child,' he said. 'I have just the woman for you. And just the man for Eva.' "

"What are you going to do now?" the woman asked.

"Do?" he said. "I shall start again, *natürlich*. I have all the time in the world."

Lloyd was playing cards with John Dull Knife in Zuni Tone's trailer when the telephone rang.

"Heads you answer it, tails we let it ring," suggested Lloyd.

Without even looking at it, John Dull Knife flicked a quarter with his thumbnail. He slapped it onto the back of his withered, liver-spotted hand, and it was tails. He grunted with amusement, and then tossed the coin into the old metal bowl that Lloyd had brought with him to the trailer.

"I should have learned not to gamble with you," Lloyd complained, and struggled up off the couchette to pick up the phone.

"You shouldn't gamble with anybody," replied John Dull Knife. "You gamble like a woman."

"Screw you, too," Lloyd told him, just as a girl's voice said, "Hello?"

"Oh, hi, yes, I'm sorry."

"Is this Mr. Denman? I phoned your fish restaurant but they told me you sold up and moved away."

"Well, that's right. I'm out in the desert at the moment, taking a sabbatical. It's what's called getting your head together. How can I help you?"

"You probably don't remember me, but my name's Lawreign. I work at the souvenir counter in the *Star of India*."

"Hey, I remember you. You're the pretty one."

"Thanks! But actually I called you because you asked me to watch out for a woman in a black raincoat and a yellow headscarf and dark glasses."

"Well, that's right, sure, but—"

"She came in, day before yesterday."

A soft feeling of dread crept down Lloyd's back, like a cold-furred cat. "Say again."

"She came in, day before yesterday and bought a piece of scrimshaw. Quite an expensive piece, too. She said she was going to send it to somebody as a gift, so we wrapped it and everything."

"How did she pay? With a credit card? Check? Did she give her name?"

"No, she paid in cash. But it was a beautiful piece. It was engraved with dolphins and mermaids, and the words said 'I'll Love You For All Eternity.' "

"Those exact words?"

"That's right."

"Lawreign, I owe you one," said Lloyd, and before she could say any more, he hung up. He stood for a long time with his hand thoughtfully covering his mouth, and then he said to John Dull Knife, "Did you check the mailbox lately?"

John Dull Knife looked up at him with rheumy eyes. "Sorry, keep forgetting. Ever since Tony went to live with that Kathleen woman of yours . . . well, he always used to do it."

"Won't be a minute," said Lloyd. He left the trailer, climbed down the steps, and walked across the trailer park. Although it was well past seven o'clock, the evening was still dry and hot, and there was a smell of mesquite in the air.

He walked slowly at first, but as he neared the mailbox he began to hurry. He hadn't even opened the wire fence before he could see that the flag was raised.